DR. ROYAL COE had his own reasons for living in the turbulent Florida peninsula of 1840. And not the least was Mary Grant. The most beautiful woman in the isolated wilderness, she was pledged to Coe's best friend. But before Roy wooed or won any lady, the fierce battle of the cypress bays had to be fought in a bloody struggle of white man against red for the prize of a rich land.

"A vividly narrated and absorbingly interesting portrayal of rugged romance on a long vanished American frontier."
—*Chicago Sunday Tribune*

"Like all Slaughter heroes, Dr. Coe wields a pretty special scalpel. The author has lost none of his gift for dramatizing surgery."
—*The New York Times*

FORT EVERGLADES
was originally published by Doubleday & Company, Inc.

Books by Frank G. Slaughter

Air Surgeon
Battle Surgeon
Buccaneer Surgeon
Constantine
Countdown
The Curse of Jezebel
Darien Venture
David: Warrior and King
Daybreak
The Deadly Lady of Madagascar
Devil's Harvest
Divine Mistress
Doctor's Wives
East Side General
Epidemic!
Flight from Natchez
Fort Everglades
God's Warrior
The Golden Isle
The Golden Ones
The Healer
In a Dark Garden
The Land and the Promise
Lorena
Pilgrims in Paradise
The Purple Quest
A Savage Place
The Scarlet Cord
Spencer Brade, M.D.
Storm Haven
Surgeon, U.S.A.
Sword & Scalpel
That None Should Die
Tomorrow's Miracle
A Touch of Glory

Published by POCKET BOOKS

Frank G. Slaughter

•

FORT EVERGLADES

PUBLISHED BY POCKET BOOKS NEW YORK

FORT EVERGLADES

Doubleday edition published March, 1951

POCKET BOOK edition published April, 1952
11th printing.......January, 1972

Standard Book Number: 671-77495-6.

CONTENTS

I: FLAMINGO KEY 1

II: INDIAN MOUND 120

III: FAKAHATCHEE HAMMOCK 181

IV: BIG SULPHUR 229

I FLAMINGO KEY

i

HERE IN THE SAW-GRASS HOLLOW THE HEAT WAS MERCILESS, though the dugout was nested deep. It seemed as immobile as a dozing 'gator in that wilderness of green spears. Its occupant seemed to doze as well, his long brown legs extended, an Army sombrero all but obscuring his face. No one would have guessed that his repose was only skin-deep, his ear cocked for the slightest sound.

He had rested here for all of ten minutes without venturing deeper into the water maze, though the chocolate-dark slough just beyond his bow was an inviting avenue as it twisted south like a sprawling, indolent snake. Behind him the lake was as vast as a sea—a milky-blue ocean, plumped down without reason in this sun-bitten vastness, wavering into heat mirages at the horizon's rim. Cypress-girdled, sown thickly with saw-grass islands, and empty under a brazen sky, the whole lake might have been an illusion—like its color, which was blue only in the round. . . . The watcher knew the lake was dark as the bogs that circled it—dark and desolate and teeming with dangers all its own. For the hundredth time he wondered why he should be risking death on its shores today.

That, of course, was only part of a question he had put off answering long ago. He raised on one elbow, lifting his sun-faded sombrero from his eyes while he studied the milky surface of the lake the Seminoles had once called Mayami—and cartographers in Washington were beginning to label Okeechobee. Death, he saw, was still muffled in the mist that

1

shrouded the western horizon. Still, it was no time to debate
imponderables. Why, for example, with a surgeon's skill at
his fingertips, he continued to dwell in the Floridas. Why he
took more pleasure in Indian trading than the career that
awaited him in the North. Why, in short, a man with degrees
from London and the Hôtel Dieu should linger here (in the
bustling year of our Lord 1840), preferring the swamper's
life to the gentleman's.

Knowing those answers in advance (and knowing, just as
surely, that any debate on the issues would end in a hung
jury), he settled deeper in his saw-grass nest. It was enough
to know he would never be happier than today—with a
month's sketches in his portfolio, a grubstake in otter skins
aboard, and death still leaning hard on his paddle, far out in
the heat haze of Okeechobee.

ii

All that morning death had been a very real pursuer—a
chunk of paddles in the dawn (when he had glided from his
last scrap of cover on Sandy Bay) a sharp profile against the
sunrise (when he had dared to cross that same bay and dig
for the shelter of the mangroves along its southern shore).
From sunrise to noon he had driven toward the escape corridor of this slough, knowing that his ruse had succeeded, that
his nemesis was still in deep water, searching him among the
cypress islands that divided the bay from the open lake
beyond.

When they had picked up his trail again he had been safe
among the saw-grass tufts—or at least as safe as any man
could be in a doubtful hide-out, where the slightest rustle was
a betrayal. Now, waiting for the snout of Chittamicco's war
canoe to thrust out of the heat haze, he knew that he had enjoyed every moment of that crazy hide-and-seek. He would
enjoy the climax even more. Even if it meant stripping to the
buff and going overside to face Chittamicco with no weapon
but a cane knife.

The challenge had not been offered last night, when he had
sat across the fire from Chittamicco, one with the circle of
subchiefs and sense-bearers, smoking a farewell pipe with
Chekika before paddling east to meet the rising moon. He
had heard hate rumble a dozen times—in more than one

throat. It had all but burst forth when Chekika had turned his back on his younger brother, to wade knee-deep in the shallows and escort the intruder's dugout into the path of moonlight. He had felt Chittamicco's eyes at his back like twin daggers. And he had picked up his paddle proudly, knowing it was fatal to betray the slightest fear.

Chekika had said, "You will come soon, Salofkachee?"

"Whenever the chief finds me welcome."

"You are always welcome, *amigo mio.* No matter what scheme your white brothers are hatching."

"Can you say as much at your council fire?"

Chekika had smiled. His handclasp had been as firm as ever there in the bath of moonlight.

"My council fire burns at my order."

"Go with God, Father of Seminoles."

"Go with God. Salofkachee."

They had spoken reasonably pure Spanish, which even the subchiefs understood well enough. (The Floridas, after all, had only become part of America within the memory of each listener.) Only Chittamicco had obstinately refused to learn any language but his own, even when Florida still took orders from Madrid. He had stood apart from the others, a copper colossus with folded arms. But his voice had boomed like a war drum long before the white interloper's paddle could find open water. . . .

Now, crouched in his saw-grass haven at the mouth of Ten-Mile Slough, that same interloper could afford to smile at his own folly. Hearing the throb of paddle in the heart of Okeechobee, he could remind himself soberly enough that an era was ending.

Long before he had risked this trip into the Glades he had guessed it was the last he would dare to make alone. No white man in the Floridas would have risked as much. Two weeks ago (with time heavy on his hands, with no plans beyond tomorrow) it had seemed a rare lark to provision his dugout at the fort, to strike west on the Miami, and plunge into a watery wilderness that no man had mapped but he. The gamble had paid dividends. When he had found Chekika at long last (and he had never bored deeper in his search for the Seminole encampment) his friends of yesterday had been glad to trade otter pelts for salt and hominy. But the tensions had been there from the first handclasp. They had persisted up to that taut moment of farewell. They had followed him, in the throb of war drums, as he had dug for his life across the moonlit vastness of Okeechobee.

Salofkachee. The Healing Knife. His title had been well earned: his scalpel had been famous in the Glades even before the war had moved into its finale. Now that the Glades were no more than a synonym for the Seminole's hunting ground—and now that Chekika had taken the mantle of Osceola and Coacoochee—a white medicine man needed more than courage to venture beyond the falls of the Miami.

Courage, he thought (watching the snout of the canoe take visible form to the west) is an abstract noun. If he had tried to explain his motive for this journey even to his closest friend, he could hardly blame that friend for howling with laughter. Andy Winter would never have understood. Nor would Dr. Barker or that sullen martinet, Colonel Merrick. No more would Chekika himself. . . . When a man turns his back on his father's inheritance and his father's career to plunge headfirst into the wilderness, he has no right to expect pity. When that same man turns his back on life to paint spoonbills and herons and collect specimens for a naturalist even the War Department considered slightly mad, he has no right to raise more than a cynical eyebrow if his world accepts him at face value.

The canoe was in full view now, leveling out of the mirage along the horizon's rim. Even at that distance he could count a dozen braves at the paddles—in addition to the helmsman at the transom sweep, and Chittamicco himself, larger than life in his egret bonnet. For a moment he was disappointed that his enemy had been able to muster no more than one canoe. Somehow, he had expected a full-dress pursuit, complete with medicine drums and a squaw or two, howling for his liver. Of course, he thought instantly, refusing to panic even now, Chittamicco is only Chekika's brother—a screaming voice at the council fire. He could not prevent this visit of a Washington emissary—if that visit was unofficial. He could not insist, at the moment, that the visitor be dispatched forthwith or held as hostage. The most he could do was separate a dozen firebrands like himself from that same council fire and dig away on the visitor's trail with murder in his heart.

Murder, thought the visitor, is the precise word—but it's a white man's label, after all. The Seminole law of hospitality

would not permit his extermination while he slept in the
chief's house and dipped his fingers in the chief's own bowl.
As the chief's heir, Chittamicco still had the right to challenge him once he had stepped outside the circle—to track
him as one tracks a deer, and throw down the gauge.

He could see the sweat-gleam on copper shoulders now.
All night long, he knew, they had leaned on those paddles,
trusting on their combined strength to cut down his head.
They had hoped to pick up his trail at dawn—and he smiled
in his hideaway as he saw that Chittamicco's handsome face
was creased in a bewildered grimace. Chekika's heir had relied on the white man's stupidity and his own prowess as a
hunter. He had expected to find his quarry in the open lake,
where it would have been a simple matter to run him down.
Once they had locked gunwales, he could not have refused
the Seminole's challenge. Naked as primeval Adams, they
would have tumbled overside together, with cane knives in
their teeth, swum clear of the canoes, and fought until one
was dead. . . . Murder's still the word, reflected the quarry,
watching the canoe spin in the mouth of the slough. Even if
I'd come out the victor, they'd have challenged me in turn—
paying a dozen lives, if need be, to tire me for the final
thrust. A ritual killing not even Chekika could censure. A
combat older than Homer, obeying its own laws. The end all
enemies of the nation must suffer if they dared venture on
the Seminole hunting ground.

The dawn mist saved my life, he thought—and the heat
haze that followed it. They could hear my paddle just ahead;
they could not be sure which way I'd turn, once I reached
Ten-Mile Slough. He watched Chittamicco rise to his full
height in the bow of the canoe to study the long serpentine of
the slough—and blessed the impulse that had made him take
shelter here, at the very mouth. His enemies could see at a
glance that he had avoided the obvious escape route to the
Miami River and the white man's country. Would they guess
that he had burrowed deep in the saw grass, a scant biscuit-
toss away? For a long moment he listened to their voices and
did not dare to breathe.

Realizing that their quarry might be close at hand, the Seminoles spoke quietly. But he could hear every word clearly
across the narrow strip of slough. Their language, after all,
had grown almost as familiar as his own.

"He is a greater fool than we thought," said Chittamicco. "He follows the shore of Okeechobee—to the east."

"There is no sign."

"The mist hides him still."

"What if he hides along the slough?"

"It is a risk he would not take. He hopes to avoid us in the swamp." Chittamicco bent forward across the prow of the canoe as the helmsman leaned hard on his sweep. For an instant the gunwale brushed the saw grass, and the watcher could see the knife scars on his enemy's chest, count each feather in his garish bonnet. Since he was hunting human game, Chittamicco did not wear his ceremonial buckskins or the half-moons of hammered silver that advertised his rank. Only the great fan of egret feathers at his temples and the slashes of vermilion at each cheekbone proclaimed his status. Like the others, he stank of rancid fish oil, the ointment the braves used before battle. The massed odor, sweeping over the watcher like a visible wave, left his senses reeling. A savage odor, old as man himself, it reminded the white quarry of things he had never known. Once again he thought of the gulf that must always separate the Indian and his conqueror, the washed and the unwashed.

"The mist is rising fast," said Chittamicco. "He cannot hide in the swamp. See where he has broken the vine when he forced path through the cypress?"

The watcher smiled. The Seminole was an expert tracker, but he had met his match today. He had forgotten that it was a simple thing to tear a patch of wild grapevine where the swamp came down to meet the lake, and circle on one's own trail. Thanks to the rains, there were four feet of water between those cypress knees. The canoe had skimmed in and out again without a trace.

"We will skirt the lake awhile," said Chittamicco. "When the mist is gone he must show himself. Forward!"

The sweep, turning the enemy canoe in a wide arc, sent a wave crashing into the saw grass. The quarry rose with the surge and for one taut instant seemed about to glide into the slough, in full view. Then he chuckled quietly at his panic. The Seminoles, straining as one man at their paddles, had already put the slough behind them. Even before his heart could resume its normal beat a solid wall of cypress and saw grass had blotted them from view.

For a while longer his ear caught the rhythmic chunk of their paddles. It was an oddly soothing sound, now that their threat was behind him. Then even that far-off disturbance was swallowed into the heat-drugged afternoon. Once more (though it was the last time now) the wilderness of Okeechobee and its Glades was his special domain, unshared by others. His to revel in, as a man might revel in an untamed mistress whose delights are never-ending.

For this high, wild moment he was one with nature—untouched by time or human hand.

He smiled at his crazy heartbeat, for this, too, was the sort of joy he could never share with another. Andy Winter would only gape if he tried to put his communion into words. Even Dr. Barker (that strange man of science who understood most things) would shake his head in wonder.

He sat for a long time in his nest of saw grass, letting the solitude envelop his spirit in its own peculiar balm. How could he explain that the peace of the wilderness, for all its savage peril, was the only haven he had ever known? How, when the opportunities that civilization offered were so various, could he insist that this same wilderness held far greater rewards?

The afternoon shadows were heavy on the slough when he stirred at last and picked up his paddle. Thanks to this delay, he would have to travel until dawn to reach the falls of the Miami. Fort Everglades was a good day's journey beyond. Andy, he knew, would be more anxious than usual for his report. . . . He could not regret the pause on the shore of Okeechobee—or the risk he had taken at Chekika's council fire. He was in no hurry to shed the garb of Salofkachee. He was even more reluctant to take on the speech and manner of Dr. Royal Coe, whilom surgeon of the United States Army and scout extraordinary to the commanding general in St. Augustine.

There was no life to his heart as he turned his face toward civilization again—or the reasonable facsimile thereof he would find at the fort. Perhaps in compensation (or perhaps only because he was still under thirty, and lonely after his fashion) he raised his voice in song. A plaintive minor chant from the Lancashire moorland where his ancestors had been sired. A strange chant indeed to pace the paddle strokes of a dugout canoe deep in the Florida Everglades:

"Black is the color of my true love's hair
Her lips are something wondrous fair . . ."

iii

Two days later he rested easily at his sweep, with both legs spread on the transom of his canoe, letting the sluggish current bear him seaward on the widening estuary of the Miami. He was singing the same tune in celebration of the same mythical lady—a strange chant for a man who had put love and all its trappings behind him long ago.

"I love my love, and well she knows
I love the grass whereon she goes . . ."

He let the last notes boom away in the mangroves, and laughed aloud as a great wading crane spiraled into long-legged flight from the mud flat ahead and gave him a raucous answer. The Glades were behind him now. There, at the next bend of the river, was the lightning-blasted tree that had always served as his anchor while he prepared himself to face civilization again. For a moment more he jammed his sweep hard against the river mud for a last look at the silent land he was quitting.

Far to the west the saw grass was only a yellow ghost, with a few cabbage palms here and there, like feather dusters, against the copper sky. On both sides of the river the muck spread its black carpet to the horizon's rim; not even the Nile, he thought, could boast richer farmland than this—even though no farmer had dared break the soil this close to Chekika's hunting grounds. The river was low here where the tidal thrust from Biscayne Bay had begun its backward pull toward the sea; he could almost count the layers of rich mother earth, mute evidence of the generations of plant life that had flourished lustily in this sun-bright land and had gone back to enrich the teeming soil that nourished them . . . Nature's bounty, in this instance, had not been allowed to seep into the still-distant Atlantic. Even here the thrust of his sweep in the river mud disclosed the white marl that was the true bed of the Miami. Below this, he knew, was the solid bed-

rock of coral limestone that had shaped and held the Florida peninsula since the beginning of time.

Every foot of this land cried out for the hand of the hus-
bandman—and yet, even before the long uncertainty of the
Indian wars, it had been but thinly settled. The Spaniard, in
his centuries of occupation, had hardly scratched the richness
of the Floridas. The young American Republic, still an un-
easy conqueror, had muddled its way through the conflict
with the Seminole with no clear plan for the future. Here on
the doorstep of the Glades, though the fort itself was a scant
ten miles to the east, there was as yet no sign of human habi-
tation. The first cabin, he recalled, would be Jakob Wagner's
combined farm and trading post, and that was a good five
miles beyond. The few settlers along the coast, where farming
was poorer, or in the tidal estuaries that fringed the sweep of
Biscayne Bay, could be counted on to seek the stockade at
the first throb of a war drum.

Dr. Royal Coe sighed over the familiar problem and
stepped ashore under the splintered live oak. The ground was
firm here—one of those high islands in the muckland that
were known as hammocks in the South. Humming lightly, he
began the task of transforming Salofkachee into a respectable
Army courier. The brazier under his forward thwart had
been bubbling for the last half-hour; he poured boiling water
into a cedar bowl and sat cross-legged on the bank to shave,
holding the cracked mirror in his hand and puzzling, just a
little, at the unfamiliar face that emerged under the razor
strokes.

Even when he was clean-shaven and ready to return to the
canoe he continued to scowl at his mahogany-dark image. He
knew that his whole body was as deep-tanned as the craggy
countenance that stared back from the glass like a faintly
mocking stranger. I could pass for Chittamicco's brother
even now, he thought. The hair that fell almost to his
shoulders was as blue-black as any Seminole's. All I need, he
thought, is a lovelock at my temple and a cane's feather
thrust above. Of course a string of scalps on a willow wand
might round out the picture. And yet, despite those matching
scowls, he did not resent the comparison. To understand a
people (especially a nation like the Seminoles, with a tradition that went back before the Spaniards), it was necessary to

be one of them. How else could he have brought back so clear a report from Chekika's council fire?

Moving back to the canoe to stow his gear, he noted the battered instrument case tucked neatly under the lattice of the transom, cheek by jowl with his bulging sketchbook. The tarnished brass name plate winked in the sunlight—a reminder that its owner had once graduated with honor from Harvard College in Boston. . . . Medicine, at least, was a ground where the warring personalities of Salofkachee and Roy Coe might meet and merge. Over the years it had been a bridge that had carried him safely over disputed ground, when white man and red cried out alike for the healing knife at the end of a battle. He lifted the mahogany box between his palms, hefting it gently. Somehow, the cool feel of the wood against his flesh brought back his sense of oneness. Was it too late even now to prove that Indian and white could meet as friends?

iv

'Gators slept in thick clusters on the next mud flat, their eyes slitted against the glare; high in the blue, a buzzard planed in lazy circles—a sooty speck that was the only flaw on the afternoon sky. Already the silt of the Miami was laced with cloudy green as the tide continued to tug Roy's canoe toward the bay. The breeze that always came at four (as clocklike as the drenching showers of the rainy season) was pleasantly cool against his skin as he spun the canoe in midstream.

The mucklands were behind him now for the most part, though the sloughs still gleamed here and there under the westering sun. Thick stands of pine had begun to shoulder the cabbage palms from the landscape. The palmetto scrub was everywhere, its dusty-green fans making a metallic whisper as the sea breeze freshened. Jakob Wagner's cabin was almost in sight now, and Dr. Coe leaned on his sweep in a sudden burst of effort as that breeze brought an unmistakable message from the riverbank. A sick aroma as palpable as smoke in the clean air. The smell of death, lonely and spine-curling.

When he had passed this way two weeks ago on his journey upriver, Jakob Wagner's clearing had been as neat as Ja-

kob's own front yard in Frankfort—the palmetto cabin
shored up on freshly whitewashed blocks, the window boxes
bright with geranium and morning-glory. Jakob's wife had
seen to that, just as she had kept Jakob honest in his trading
with the Indians and prohibited the sale of rum. Today the
cabin was only a blackened shell. The clearing's only tenants
were a score or more of vultures foraging with hideous
efficiency among the fire-gutted foundations of the storehouse
and the small dock at the water's edge.

Dr. Royal Coe, coming ashore on the run (and sending
the carrion birds into swift-waddling flight with a prodigious
war whoop), saw at a glance that he could no longer help
Jakob Wagner. The trader's body swung beside his wife's
from an impromptu gibbet at the clearing's edge; both
corpses were stripped of clothing and violated according to
Seminole ritual. The vultures had been at work about the gibbet, ripping flesh and entrails into a shredded horror. They
had worked as thoroughly on the bodies of three Indian
braves, tumbled on the ground before the cabin door—evidence that Jakob had been able to defend himself, after a
fashion, before the spreading flames had forced him into the
open. At close quarters the stench was overpowering. Dr.
Coe needed all his will power to force his exploration to its
inevitable end, though he was certain, even before he turned
the nearest Indian on his back, that this could be only Chekika's work.

There was no mistaking the war paint or the braiding of
feathers on the arrows that still remained in the Indian's quiver. Fire arrows, he noted grimly, drawing a pair of tar-
soaked shafts from their container and tossing them into his
dugout as evidence. The raid, it seemed, had been planned to
the last detail. The arrows had been ready to ignite Jakob's
palm-thatch roof—probably at midnight, while he slept. The
blunt-nosed carbine in the Seminole's fist had done its part to
cut the trader down as he staggered into the moonlight.

The picture was clear enough now, but the visitor prowled
a while longer in the ruins, pausing at intervals to shout away
the flapping of the scavengers' wings. On the clearing's edge
one detail caught his eye—a square of cloth impaled on the
saw-tooth stalk of a palmetto. Evidently it had been ripped
from one of the invader's bodies during or after the attack.
But this was no Indian garb, he thought; this red-and-blue

design, with its zany zigzag, belonged to the wardrobe of
Thespis, never to Chekika.

He grimaced at the conceit as his mind took a crazy som-
ersault. Back to a college theatrical troupe, where he had
trod the boards with windmill abandon, declaiming the verses
of the Bard. His tights, he recalled, had been patterned in this
same red-and-blue zigzag. What would Shakespeare be doing
on the bank of the Miami River in 1840? He shrugged off the
bizarre question. The carbine in that dead Indian's fist had
come from a Sheffield mill, via a trader in Havana—the same
ghouls who had made a fortune out of the prolonged Seminole war and the chance it offered to trade guns for booty.
Probably that bit of harlequin calico had been shipped from
the same Cuban warehouse.

He dropped the gaily patterned cloth into his canoe and
stepped aboard again. This time he put all his strength into
the last lap of his down-river journey. There was no fear in
that driving pace, no real anger. Chekika had meant this hit-
and-run raid as a solemn warning to Fort Everglades—no
more. A ghastly signature to the message his visitor was now
bearing toward that same fort. . . . Chekika's words at the
council fire came back with added emphasis.

The Seminole had yielded the peninsula to the American
nation—the Seminole would never surrender Okeechobee or
the swamps that ringed it. The swamps, in Chekika's book,
included the rich muckland that fanned out on three sides of
the saw grass, the shores of Biscayne Bay itself, and the
myriad islands of the Florida keys. The chief had been precise in his geography over that last pipe at the council fire. It
was quite in character that he should have tossed his blood-
stained warning on the Army's very doorstep days before.

"Believe me, Father of Seminoles, no white man will invade your hunting grounds."

"I believe *you* are sincere, Salofkachee. I cannot say as
much of Poinsett."

"Our Secretary of War wishes you abundance and peace.
Has he not signed a treaty to guarantee your boundaries forever?"

"Salofkachee forgets that I can read English. Surely you
have seen the Paper-That-Speaks in Washington——"

Even now he could see the chief's eyes—and how they had
glittered above the mockery of the peace pipe he continued

to puff for a long, silent moment. "I have spoken, Salofkachee. I have traced the limits of my nation. Limits that no white man may cross in future."

"Not even a friend?"

"Chekika has no friends save you. In time you, too, must go the way of your brothers. Then the Seminole will stand alone."

The Seminole will stand alone. Roy repeated the words, if only to taste their bitter wisdom. The Indian of the American East would always stand alone now that the young American giant was rising from his swaddling clothes and testing the strength of his youth. Like the Creek and the Cherokee, like the hundreds of his own tribesmen who had suffered deportation in recent years, Chekika and his braves would have the eventual choice of resettlement in the Far West or slow starvation in the heart of Big Cypress.

Remembering the years of warfare that had gone before, the barbarities that had been practiced on both sides, he could understand the calm fatalism of the Indian. He would fight for his land; he would die on it, if need be; but he would never move away. He could hardly blame Chittamicco for hunting him in the saw grass—with the same cold fury that he himself would hunt a mad dog. Or censure the impulse that had sent the raiders to burn Jakob Wagner's outpost farm and butcher its owners.

Joel Poinsett, a secretary of war more noted for social conquests than political wisdom, epitomized the young man's century that Chekika could never hope to understand. The "Paper-That-Speaks" was the Seminole's name for a Washington journal that had recently carried Poinsett's boast that the Floridas would be completely settled within a generation, from the St. Marys to Cape Sable—a repudiation, in a treaty maker's own words, of his solemn agreement with the Seminoles. The fact that Chekika had read that journal (after his fashion) almost as soon as the commanding general in St. Augustine was its own commentary on the times. The same hand that kept the Seminoles in gunpowder and rifles had wrapped the newspaper around the last shipment of ammunition.

Perhaps Chekika was the ultimate realist after all—and Salofkachee, the go-between, a dreamer born too late. Perhaps Osceola's scalping knife was the only signature a white man would respect when peace treaties were on the table.

The go-between looked up from his musings as the canoe swept round the last bend in the Miami and slipped easily into the full wash of the outgoing tide. Dead ahead, the river opened into the clean blue vastness of Biscayne Bay, whipped into gay whitecaps under the breeze from the Atlantic. Wide salt marshes fanned into the bay on both sides of the river's mouth—bright green deltas swarming with wild fowl. Here and there were the palm-thatch roofs of settlers' cabins, though no smoke curled above the roof-trees today.

Closer still, a few rough corrals stood empty in the late sunlight beside a group of traders' stores and a rough wharf of palmetto logs. All these buildings seemed to cluster, like frightened chicks, under the brooding wing of the fort itself. This imposing pile, foursquare against the eastern sky, stood on the high north bank of the river, its main gate insolently wide on the dusty parade ground. Its flag (with the twenty-six stars of Union) whipped smartly from the commandant's lookout on the terreplein. The emissary from the Glades could count the cannon at each western gun port, the sky-blue magnificence of the sentries patrolling the ramparts.

Dr. Royal Coe permitted himself a small grin as he counted the shakos on that westward-facing rampart. Colonel Merrick would never have wasted so many uniforms on sentry go. He could hope, with reason, that his friend Captain Winter was in charge at the fort during the colonel's absence. That Andy had ordered this display along the upper deck in honor of his return from the Glades.

The current purred briskly between high marl banks here at the meeting place of river and bay. The canoe, with only the lightest of guidance, seemed to find its own path to deep water in the shadow of the live oaks that fringed the bank and the army road that swept up from the scrub to the gate of the outer stockade. Chekika's go-between took this channel from old habit, permitting the dugout to ghost into the landing stage without attempting to hail a sentry.

The canoe nuzzled the stringpiece of the landing stage. Dr. Royal Coe looped his painter on the nearest cleat and stepped ashore. He scarcely paused to glance back at his gear; Sergeant Ranson could collect it later—if the sergeant was on duty and sober. Then, obeying an impulse he could not name, he turned back to the dugout, thrust the two fire arrows in his gun belt, and picked up his scrap of harlequin cloth. Walking into the full sunlight of the landing stage, he was a perfect target. But he could trust Andy Winter to post no one but veterans on the ramparts this afternoon; even the youngest private in the First Dragoons knew him by sight, in or out of uniform.

His moccasins made no sound on the rough planks of the landing. About to turn toward the gate of the stockade, he pulled up sharp as he saw he was not alone on the riverbank. Just below the stringpiece—where the stout palmetto pilings of the dock thrust deep into the marl of the river bed—an umbrella was tilted against the afternoon sun. A campstool stood open at the water's edge, with a wide bell of muslin spread across the seat. The muslin, he noted, was part of a lady's dress—and the lady herself half sat, half crouched in the green shade of the parasol. She was working busily at an improvised easel which she had placed at the very edge of the river, so close that the rushing tide threatened to dislodge it. From his vantage point he saw that she was sketching a tall blue heron, planted in the marsh grass across the tidal estuary, as though he had promised to pose on order until the sketch was finished.

The artist was bareheaded, and her hair, parted demurely and gathered in a high chignon, was as *black* as his own; her profile (he was noting details absently as he moved closer) was as sharp as an Italian cameo and just as creamy-white. The eyes were faintly slanted and as gray-green as the water swirling at her feet. For no reason at all he remembered a painting he had admired in Paris years ago—a Watteau shepherdess, complete with *embonpoint* and high-piled pompadour. The present subject was shapely enough, even in muslin, but there was nothing of the shepherdess about her. Even in this moment of discovery he could guess that this was no refugee from a nearby farm.

He wondered who she could be. An officer's doxy, perhaps, up from the Key West base, or down from St. Augustine. Surely she could not be the commandant's daughter. . . . He was directly above her now, careful to keep his shadow from her canvas as he examined the painting in detail. At least she was an artist—and a good one. Though she worked with a loose brush, her composition was alive and glowing—

and accurate to the last detail. She's better than I, he thought grudgingly—and canvases with his signature hung in a Boston gallery beside the work of Audubon.

"You have great tale it, *señorita mía*."

He had put his admiration into words without conscious thought, and since he had spoken only Seminole and Spanish for the past fortnight, the language of the dons came easily to his tongue. He watched her freeze to the campstool, then turn to him, wide-eyed; he had forgotten his bizarre garb, the blue-black hair clubbed Indian-fashion at his shoulders.

Before he could speak again, she was on her feet, a scream choked in her throat; the sudden motion dislodged the canvas, sending it into the water. Leaping to the bank beside her, he swooped down to retrieve the painting. Before he could straighten he felt a stunning blow against his nape—and realized that the girl had lifted the easel, using it as a weapon with telling effect. Numbed by the blow, he felt his knees buckle; in another second he was in the river, rolling like a log in the drag of the tide, the canvas still in his hand.

The sting of the cold salt water cleared his head instantly. He managed to toss the painting to the dock, though he knew it was now ruined beyond repair. Weighted as he   by his buckskin and bullet pouch, he could not quite hold his own against the tide. On the stringpiece above him the girl had already lifted the sweep from his canoe and now stood guard, slapping the strip of water between them with the flat of the blade. Despite his rage, he could not help noticing the clean overhand grace of her swing—a Watteau in muslin, translated in a twinkling to a competent Amazon. She seemed to enjoy her work thoroughly, though her lips were still parted on that soundless scream.

Breathless still he managed to shout after a fashion, "Did you—take me for an Indian?"

"You *are* an Indian. Don't deny it!" The sweep flailed the water, a scant inch from his thrashing arm.

"Look again, please. Did you ever see a blue-eyed Seminole?"

He saw that she was staring in earnest, as though she were seeing him for the first time. Putting out all his strength, he fought his way toward the dock and ripped at the thongs that held his buckskin tunic. He realized his mistake, once he had discarded the garment. His entire body, tanned as it was after that near-naked fortnight in the Glades, was more Indian-like than ever as he rolled in the green Miami.

"Keep your distance—or I'll call the guard."

The sweep made contact with his skull—a glancing blow that exploded a red light in his brain. Instinctively he locked both fists on the blade and tugged with all his strength. As he had hoped, the girl kept her own grip on the pole—a second too late. There was a frothy swirl of petticoats, a startling glimpse of silk-clad legs as she tumbled into the water, swooping above him like a white-winged bird and plummeting into the river a good te feet beyond.

Knowing that her belled skirt would float her for a moment, he was in no hurry to rescue her. Instead he circled lazily about the small whirlpool she was creating with her thrashings, and hoped she would swallow enough water to teach her humility.

The current had swept them well away from the landing stage. He watched the salt marsh coast by, watched the estuary of the Miami widen into Biscayne Bay—and still there were no screams from the white whirlpool, no sign that his assistance was needed. Incredulously he saw that the whirlpool was widening, a circle of petticoats and other unmentionables bobbing gaily in the blue wash of the tide. Apparently the girl was undressing under water—and, as she disrobed, swimming almost as strongly as he.

He shouted a warning that went unheeded, and dug on her trail in earnest. For a moment his flailing arms snarled in a petticoat. He flung it aside in time to see her legs, bare of stockings now, feather the surface of Biscayne Bay; a pair of white arms, Amazonian still for all their shapeliness, flashed in the late sunlight. Already she was a good fifteen feet ahead, and the strip of water between them was widening with each lusty stroke.

"For God's sake, wait!" he roared. "D'you want to be dragged out to sea?"

Even as the words escaped him he realized the futility of the warning. If she could hold her present pace (and she showed no sign of tiring) the girl was quite capable of reaching the distant shore of Key Biscayne, a low-lying island of marsh and humpback dunes that separated bay and open sea. The tidal inlet, creaming with breakers at the bar, was no threat to this kind of swimmer. Even in this panting moment he could see that she was quartering the current expertly, letting it help her reach her goal, avoiding the menace of the tide rips in the channel proper.

He began to put his back into each stroke; it was ridiculous that a woman should outswim him for long, even a woman crazed by fear. For a good hundred yards the space between them was unchanged. Then he began to gain on her, foot by foot. He saw her glance back just once, to measure his nearness, watched her put forth a heart-bursting spring in a last effort to shake him off. Then he buried his face and poured the last ounce of vitality into his effort to overtake her before they should swim too far from the mainland to return.

He heard her scream, muffled by the water. Lifting his head, he saw her shy violently then churn in a wide arc, until she was returning in the direction she had come. Apparently the red nemesis on her trail was matched by a greater peril ahead. He saw the shadow in the bay, heard the leonine snort—and laughed aloud as he cut across her path to put his body between her and this brand-new threat. He could understand her terror, after all. The hairy behemoth that wallowed toward them, sporting in the whitecaps like a brown nightmare made visible. would have struck terror to any heart—even if a half dozen of his fellows had not wallowed in the waves behind him.

"Stay where you are!" he called. "It's only a manatee."

The dark sea cow was almost upon him now. Treading water and veering sharply to avoid a head-on collision, he struck the creature a stinging blow across its whiskered snout. The manatee, bellowing like an outraged calf, seemed to rear out of the bay as it changed its course. Blinking its piglike eyes stupidly, it led the school in its wake, to sport in the first of the tide rips breaking for the channel.

The girl had screamed again as he slapped the creature aside; there had been no time to explain that a manatee, if handled properly, was as harmless as the porpoise it vaguely resembled. He saw that her body had gone limp in the water, and sprinted to her side just as she vanished below the surface. Plunging in her wake, he locked a hand under each of her arms, treading water mightily to bring them both up to fresh air. She had had no time to swallow water, he saw.

Though she was in a dead faint still, she had begun to breathe in great, straining gasps.

"A near thing," said Dr. Royal Coe to no one in particular. "Next time I hope you'll take orders."

For all the strength she had just displayed in that marathon across the bay, she was astoundingly light in his arms. Through what seemed a single thickness of silk he could feel her heart beating steadily against his own—and, without knowing why, he moved quickly away, cradling her in his outstretched arms. It had been a long time since he had touched a woman, informally or otherwise.

Holding her thus, and swimming as best he could, he forced his way toward the shore, working steadily toward the slack water between the marsh and the palm-studded beach of the mainland. Little by little he felt the tug of the tide slacken about his thrashing legs. The eastern rampart of the fort was a comforting nearness now, a sharp mass against the blaze of the western sky; he saw that each gun port was black with heads. He let out a sigh of relief when he heard the creak of oarlocks behind the screen of marsh grass, and the head of Sergeant Ranson (round as a cannon ball, and almost as innocent of hair) bobbed above that bright emerald screen.

In another moment the whaleboat sprang into view, with a brace of seamen at the oars. Ranson, as befitted his station, sat in the stern sheets with one competent leg about the tiller, squinting against the glare of the bay, ignoring the shouted directions from the ramparts. The sergeant's eyes, peering out shrewdly from under eyebrows that were as shaggy as his head was bald, had already located Roy and his burden in the deep water offshore. The sergeant's saddle-brown paw snapped to one ear in a crisp salute, then whipped over the heads of the two oarsmen to direct their course.

At that precise moment Dr. Royal Coe, treading water with the concentration of the damned, felt his burden stir slightly. For a full instant he stared into sea-green eyes that met his own steadily, with no hint of fear. For that moment, at least, floating gently together in this great bay on the edge of a wilderness, they might have been friends forever. . . .

"I was wrong," she said. "Will you forgive me?"

"There's nothing to forgive," he said solemnly. "I enjoyed

every moment." That, he told himself, is the most thumping lie of my career.

"It was a terrible mistake," she said quietly. "I suppose it was the long hair that fooled me. And that scrap of harlequin cloth in your fist."

"Here comes the sergeant," he said. "We can talk later."

"You have blue eyes after all," she said. "It's more than I can bear." Her own eyes closed gently as she spoke. For a moment he thought she had fainted again. But she spoke once more, with her eyes shut tight—so softly that he drew her closer, by instinct, to catch her words.

"That beast in the bay—what was its name?"

"A manatee. A kind of sea cow."

"I don't believe a word. you know," she murmured, and fainted in earnest in the suddenly tightened circle of his arms.

Strangely unwilling to re! qu!sh his burden, he let the tide carry him for a space. The tug of the past, more dangerous than the outgoing tide, had carried him to another world. Across the Atlantic to a champagne-bright city beside the Seine. He was sitting again with Irene in a candlelit ballroom, hearing the muted agony of violins across a shadowed courtyard—too deep in wine to think of tomorrows, too sure of all his tomorrows to doubt that his wild, singing rapture would endure. . . . Irene had been corn-blond, as different from this girl as darkness from dawn. And yet the thud of her heart against him as they had fought their way to air and sunshine there in the green depths of Biscayne had brought back Irene and all her splendors. Irene, who had once been a synonym for the life he had put behind him.

"Hand her up, sir, if you don't mind," said Ranson. "Easy does it, now."

He stared up at the claret-red face of the sergeant looming from the stern of the whaleboat. Ranson held an Army greatcoat open between them, ready to receive its burden; Ranson's eyes, lifted discreetly to the sky, twinkled with a familiar light. As always, the sergeant's averted gaze seemed to say wordlessly that they shared a pleasant secret.

"Is she decent, sir?"

"You'll find her clothed, Sergeant," he said, and rolled the girl's inert body from water to gunwale. where the greatcoat enveloped it instantly. But he had a brief glimpse of alabaster thighs, more revealed than hidden by nankeen drawers, of a

high, proud breast that just missed escaping from a vest prodigal with Irish lace. Once again he closed his eyes and cursed
in a monotone.

"Up you come, sir. Just lock your wrist with mine—you'll
make it."

He settled wetly on the stern sheets and frowned away the
sergeant's arm. "I'm quite all right, Ranson. Manage that tiller, please; *I'll* take the lady. Did you ever see her before?"

"Lord bless you, Doctor, it's Miss Grant. Miss Mary
Grant. Captain Winter's promised bride."

"Say that again, slowly."

The sergeant chuckled. "I'd forgotten how long you've
been away, sir. The engagement's still news at the post."

"When did she arrive?"

"Last week, with the traveling players."

"Are you making sense, Ranson?"

"I think so, sir. But it's the captain's story. I wouldn't care
to spoil it."

"Quite right, Sergeant. I'll see the captain directly, I
hope?"

"You will indeed, Doctor. He's expecting you in his quarters now."

Dr. Royal Coe fell silent and let the cursing flow on in his
brain, unchecked. He felt sure that the girl had just stirred
within the greatcoat. Just as surely he guessed that she had
heard every word, from the moment he swarmed aboard the
whaleboat. But he made no move to verify his suspicion. It
was simpler to sit coldly at her side, with one arm clamped at
her waist. Far simpler to let his silent cursing flow on—and
know it was not Mary Grant he damned or the memory of
Irene.

It was himself he cursed. Himself, and the wasted years,
and the pain of desire this meeting had wakened—so violently that he felt sure it would never die again.

v

Captain Andrew Winter of the First Dragoons had listened
to his report in benign silence—an Olympian detachment that
was matched by Captain Winter's staff. Once again Dr. Coe
let his eyes rove around the circle of intent faces. Thunderbolts of Jove, he thought, to the last man. Graduates of the

Point, with a thirst for combat as bright as their varnished boots and the eight bullet buttons on their sky-blue tunics. He risked a grin in the direction of the commandant's chair, and refused to give ground when Andy matched it with an ice-cold stare. Andy Winter, he knew, was not a man to slight the virtues of protocol. Especially when the absence of Colonel Merrick had placed the mantle of command on his competent shoulders.

He had finished his formal report some time ago: the words were already inscribed in Sergeant Ranson's adequate shorthand. The debate that had boiled round the table was not for the record; Dr. Coe was not surprised when Andy flapped a hand for silence and waved the sergeant from the room. Andy is wearing his mantle like a veteran, he thought. Andy was never handsomer—a red-and-white soldier, from his flaming topknot to the snow-white perfection of his massive revers, starred with every combat decoration from the Withlacoochee to Taylor's Creek. Once again Roy wished that he had paused to change from buckskins and water-soaked moccasins.

"Understand me again, gentlemen"—Andy could bark when the occasion demanded—"we can decide nothing until Colonel Merrick's return. Dr. Coe's report is on the record. Whatever we say is entirely informal. It must not go beyond this room——"

"Then why is Dr. Coe present?"

Andy and the doctor himself swiveled as one man to glare the speaker down. For a moment the doctor found himself fumbling for his name. Then he smiled, ruefully enough: the cockerel was none other than Second Lieutenant Prescott, fresh from the Point, with a polish to match his newly acquired rank. Andy spoke quietly, pulling his friend to his side with the words.

"Will you call this bantam out, Roy—or shall I?"

Prescott spoke quietly, and his Adam's apple just missed collision with his high-buttoned collar. "Believe me, Doctor, I meant no offense. But I understood this was a military meeting——"

"Dr. Coe is still on the Army rolls——"

"As a scout, sir. He has never been an officer."

"Perhaps he never wanted to be," said Andy. "I value his opinion, nonetheless. Will you speak first, Roy?"

Roy spread his hands on the map table and stared hard at the Army's version of the Glades. Bays and islands along the coastal strip were charted accurately enough. Even the long half-moon of keys and broken reefs that swept down from the mainland to Key West had been pricked out with soundings and, for the most part, accurately sketched. The Miami River was well mapped as far as the falls. From that point the map was a virtual blank, save for a few discreetly penciled trails across the pine barrens. Okeechobee itself was only sketchily drawn—a logical omission, after all, since the great lake changed its boundaries each spring and fall, depending on the rainfall and the direction of the West Indian hurricanes which swept the peninsula in those seasons. The first positive line of communication, Roy noted, was the wagon road from Fort King to Tampa Bay—and the Army blockhouses along the Kissimmee River, which emptied into Okeechobee from the north.

Roy lifted his eyes and looked into each face in turn as the officers of Colonel Merrick's staff bent over the map. Lieutenant Prescott met his gaze steadily enough; the boy's no coward, Roy thought, despite his bluster. He found the same gleam of anticipation in the eyes of Lieutenant Hutchens, a dragoon who had fought at Andy's side from the beginning. Captain Stevens of ordnance (serving also as quartermaster here at Fort Everglades) kept his usual mask of boredom, but Stevens could be counted on in the pinches too. Roy spoke steadily, weighing his words.

"The colonel's determined on this raid?"

Andy spoke, patiently enough. "We've been ready for weeks, as you well know. All we've wanted is a reason. Chekika gave us that when he burned Jakob's cabin—with Jakob still inside. I can jump off tomorrow, if need be——"

"You're sure the colonel will return tonight?"

"Tonight or tomorrow—depending on what happened at headquarters." Andy smiled. "Stevens is still hurt that he wasn't invited to sail up to Augustine for that meeting. Of course *I* couldn't be spared. Someone had to command in Merrick's absence."

"We could all do with a change of scene," said the captain of ordnance.

Even Andy echoed the sigh that went round the table. Penned as they were in the fort (with strict orders to leave the Seminoles in peace), they had found the last months heavy on their hands. Roy could understand his friend's eager response, when his commanding officer had suggested that he recruit a special, highly mobile force among the enlisted men and train this company for special detail in the Glades.

The training had been secret; much of it had taken place among the keys to the south, or in the mangrove screen on Biscayne Bay itself. During his last stay at the fort Roy had inspected the specially built dugouts (they had come from a shipyard in Charleston), the waterproof ammunition boxes, the ponchos that could serve as individual tents if need be. Even at that time he had laughed with Andy over such luxuries. Most of the men in his friend's command had been ready for action when their training began. Years of Indian fighting, much of it in waist-deep gumbo, had toughened their spirits along with their skin.

"I gather you welcome this opportunity, gentlemen?"

Hutchen's voice was as thin as a knife blade and quite as cold. "It's our trade, Roy. No man likes to get rusty."

"Have you estimated your chances?"

"I'd say they were excellent—with you to guide us."

"Let me make sure I understand you." Roy turned to Andy with the slight bow that protocol demanded. "You propose to invade the Glades with three hundred men—and bring Chekika back. You honestly believe that he'll stand and fight. Permit me to differ with that pious hope."

Andy returned the bow just as gravely. "It's your privilege, Roy."

"Chekika has never fought a stand-up battle since he took Coacoochee's bonnet. He's wily as a wolf and twice as dangerous. There's just one way to pin him down—drain the Glades. So long as those swamps exist, they'll be a Seminole hunting ground."

"Surely you aren't serious."

"I'll tell you more. The Glades will never be drained west of the falls. That saw grass is really a river, flowing from Okeechobee to the Gulf. I knew as much the first time I crossed it. In the meantime you could lose an army there. Or hide one—if you had half Chekika's brains."

Andy Winter stiffened in his chair. "Are you telling me this raid is hopeless?"

"By no means. I'm only asking you gentlemen to look at this map with a realistic eye."

"There is no map, Roy," said Andy. *"You're* our map."

"I'm not the only white man who has crossed the Glades."

"I know, Roy. We've Sam Slade in our company now. And that Minorcan from Augustine, Tony Genovar. But both Sam and Tony are trappers, nothing more. And they both high-tailed it out of the country years ago to save their hair. They'll help you, of course. But you're still the man who must find Chekika." Again Andy's fist banged the map. "And don't tell me again it's impossible."

"Have you consulted Dr. Jonathan Barker on this move?"

"I'm sailing down to Flamingo Key tonight, the moment the colonel arrives. What's more, you're coming along—and so is Mary. She's enroute to Key West, you know."

It was Andy's first reference to his fiancée since the meeting began. Feeling the officers' stares (and knowing that all of them had witnessed his struggle in the bay), Roy felt his cheeks redden. He plunged into the business at hand; Mary Grant was another topic he could discuss at leisure, when he faced Andy across this same table alone.

"I'm sure Dr. Barker will endorse my judgment. If this raid succeeds, it'll be one of the minor miracles of history."

Lieutenant Prescott rumbled into speech as brashly as ever: "Forgive my stupidity, Doctor—but weren't you seated at Chekika's council fire two days ago?"

"I was indeed. He was camped on high ground on the southern shore of Okeechobee. To be exact, between the Mound and Sandy Bay."

"Sure you can lead us to that site again?"

Roy just escaped laughing aloud. "So could Captain Winter, blindfolded. You won't find so much as ashes to mark the spot."

"I'm afraid I don't follow."

"The Seminole is like most Indians nowadays. In Spanish times he lived side by side with white men in the Florida back country. Most of the chiefs owned slaves of their own; all of them farmed as much as they hunted. Ever since we took over the peninsula they've been crowded south. Today they must live off coontie root and palmetto hearts instead of corn. They buy their powder and lead from Cuban rene-gades, because we won't supply them with guns—and they

must have guns to live. Yes, and move with the game to keep
their children from starving——"

Roy broke off abruptly; he had not meant to launch a
tirade. "The bass were running in Sandy Bay," he said.
"Every man jack of the tribe was fishing when I arrived; so
were most of the squaws. They'll salt down that meat against
the winter—and then move on——"

"The whole village?"

"Why not? Wood's cheap in the Glades; palm thatch is even
cheaper. I've seen a family run up a house, complete with
stilts and dogs, in an afternoon. I've seen them cover fifty
miles from dawn to dark. At this very moment the whole nation may be moving into the Cypress. Or down the west
coast, to hunt in the Thousand Islands. Think how much faster they'd move if they knew we were hunting them."

Prescott folded gloved hands on his sword hilt; despite the
oven-damp heat of the day, he seemed as neat as a bandbox
soldier. Only the turkey-red flush that had crept under his
luxuriant sideburns betrayed his anger.

"Do you defend this savage way of life?"

"Not at all, Lieutenant. I merely point out that our policy
in Washington makes it inevitable."

"Then why won't they surrender—become wards of the
government? Many of these Indians have come to Tampa
Bay for deportation."

Roy closed his eyes on that picture. He had been at Tampa
Bay more than once on Army business when groups of Seminoles had gone aboard the transports for resettlement west
of the Mississippi. They had come to the coast by families—
often by whole clans. Sometimes the pitiful groups were too
hungry to do more than stagger to their last bivouac on
Florida soil. Others had come in defiantly, with pride lifting
their chins high. Proud or cowed, they had knelt as one man,
to scoop up a basket of native earth before boarding the ships
that would take them to exile.

Being a government ward, he thought, can turn into a
dreary business. Especially when you have been a king on the
land where you were born. He did not put his feelings into
words. I'll save my breath for Andy, he thought, knowing in
advance that Andy could be twice as hard as these ramrod-
stiff gentlemen from the Point. Aloud he said only, "Is this
your first Indian war, Lieutenant?"

"My very first," said the well-razored profile. It was still granite-firm and a trifle larger than life, as though Lieutenant Prescott had already settled to pose for a portrait in bronze.

"Then I should point out that the Seminole is a strange breed of enemy."

"Amen," said Andy Winter.

"He fights by his own rules—when he chooses to fight. Usually he hits and runs—as Jakob Wagner will bear witness, along with a hundred farmers from Augustine to the Kissimmee. We've lured the flower of the nation aboard our transport at Tampa—but it's still capable of terrorizing a whole peninsula. Andy's quite right, of course: hanging's the only solution for the breed, if we insist on taking the land that gives him life—down to the last acre——"

"D'you feel he has the right to this land—when we're willing to settle him elsewhere?"

I won't answer that question, thought Roy. *I can't waste breath explaining the meaning of democracy to this sort of mind. Your job, Lieutenant Prescott, is beautifully simple: you'll make this corner of the Republic safe for white settlement until the end of time. Then you'll go West and do the same job in Sam Houston country, in the name of a potent young eagle—a crazy eagle whose pinfeathers have begun to cast their shadow athwart a whole rich continent. . . .* He remembered his place in time and spoke simply.

"There's no quarter with Chekika. You must kill him where he stands—or admit that the swamps are his forever."

No one spoke in the hot, shuttered room; and Dr. Royal Coe, forcing himself to relax after his second outburst, had an odd conviction that the veterans, at least, were on his side. Lieutenant Prescott, taking his cue faithfully, spoke into the silence.

"Every inch of the Floridas is American—by treaty with Spain. America must master them. After all, we've yet to lose a war."

You lost this one before it started, thought Roy. *So far, the death rolls of the United States Army have charged off five thousand names to this Indian rebellion. It's true that only a small percentage are battle casualties—if we discount Dade's Massacre (I have said a quiet prayer beside that pyramid of graying coquina in the military cemetery at Augustine), and the flyblown bodies at Taylor's Creek, and the hairless skulls* still moldering along the Withlacoochee. Most of the deaths are charged to dengue, or the Spanish bends (a fancy name for diarrhea). Or, even more simply, to "fever of undetermined origin." *Your* ticket may be up even now for a death no more glorious. But his voice was mild enough when he spoke at last.

"I assume you've read the records to date?"

Andy cut in just as mildly: "Stop insulting the boy, Doctor —or I'll give him leave to call *you* out."

Prescott, surprisingly enough, held up a detaining palm. "Perhaps I deserve this, Captain. Let Dr. Coe continue."

"Thank you, Lieutenant," said Roy. "If the casualty list has slipped your memory, let me remind you that it's slightly greater than the whole Seminole nation when this war began. And the war's far from over. Chekika still strikes at will, right up to these gates. What's your solution? A treaty he respects? Or extermination?"

"I have my orders, Doctor," said Prescott. "I have no need of choice."

"Spoken like a soldier," murmured Andy. "And stop pretending you aren't on our side, Roy. We all know better."

Roy yielded, not too gracefully. "I've gone to Chekika with a last-minute plea—and I've failed. Like Lieutenant Prescott, I'm on your side—I've no choice."

Andy glared the circle into silence. "D'you think our preparations are—inadequate?"

"I've mentioned the only sane course—drain a swamp that'll never be drained. Make Chekika come begging at that stockade gate. Since that's impractical, I'd suggest you move your force into the Glades. A day's journey beyond the Miami falls—no more. I'd suggest that you and I go scouting from that base camp. Even that's risky enough—with Chekika in his present mood. And the chances are one in twenty that we could map his hiding place in time. There's still no other way."

Andy rocked awhile in the commandant's chair, his eyes on the ceiling. The silence in the staff room was absolute. Roy, rocking in turn and waiting to match his friend, glare for glare, could hear the argument of a mule and a blacksmith in the forge across the parade ground. The chunk of an ax within the palisade as some homeless farmer prepared the meal that refugees have eaten at day's end since war began.

"Perhaps you'll be more helpful if we discuss this *à deux*," said Andy at last.

"When did you take up French, *mon capitaine?*"

It was their private joke, and they enjoyed it together, feeling no need to share it with outsiders. It was no one's business but theirs that they had first met in Paris—over a bottle in a café called the Chat-qui-remue, with a blond siren named Irene to supply the introduction.

Andy Winter rose courteously to answer the other officers' salutes. Roy stayed where he was—flat on his spine in the unheard-of luxury of a cane-bottomed chair. Moccasins would have been mute in the clash of those varnished boot heels.

"The colonel will expect an informal report from us all," said Andy.

"If you'll excuse me, Captain, I'll prepare mine now," said Prescott.

"Guerre à outrance, I trust," said Andy.

"War to the death," said Prescott. He saluted Andy crisply, hesitated a fraction as he faced Dr. Royal Coe, then returned an identical courtesy.

Captain Stevens contented himself with a dig in Roy's ribs before he followed Prescott's dress-parade back through the door. Hutchens lingered long enough to rob the colonel's cellaret of an outsize cheroot. The eye he fastened on Roy was jaundiced as only a dragoon's can be, when that dragoon has served as a foot soldier in a war without surcease or glory.

"You might have been gentler with our young comrade in arms, Roy."

"On the contrary," said Andy. "I'm still hoping the colonel will make Prescott his adjutant when we're in the field. He's much too brave to fight Seminoles—if you follow me."

"I follow you perfectly," said Hutchens, and shambled from the room with his lazy cavalryman's walk, his head wreathed in a cloud of superlative Havana. Andy Winter swung his booted legs up to the map table and grinned at Roy without quite meeting his eyes. For the first time in his swashbuckling life, thought Roy, he's just a little shy with me.

Andy, he reflected, had the medallion quality so common to this young man's century. Yet there was no real bombast about Andrew Jackson Winter; like the American hero for whom he was named, he had a hard core of strength. His explosive ego was as natural as his good humor, his refusal to admit defeat. They had been friends since Roy's own student days abroad, though it was true that friendship with Andy Winter was at times as haphazard as a ride on an untamed mustang, without saddle or bridle. Like all men of destiny (Captain Winter had insisted from birth that he was meant for great things), he accepted friendship as his due.

Roy had known from the start that Andy's stint in uniform was part of a grand design: Andy made no secret of the fact that he would lay aside that uniform when the Indian war was over, to seek greater rewards in Washington. Like his brief bout with the law at Harvard, his extravagant pretense of rounding out his education in London and Paris, this sojourn in the Floridas was only a colorful interlude while he chose his eventual career. With a senator in his family, a banker or two, and a thousand Tennessee acres sure to come to him by inheritance, Andy could afford to weigh his chances—and enjoy his hero's role in the meantime.

Andy, thought Roy with a twinge of envy, is the epitome of his time; he'll ride the crest of the wave to abiding fame. Almost any wave will do. Somehow he had not pictured a wife in Andy's scheme of things—not, at any rate, in its early stages. . . . He put his surprise into words, breaking their silence.

"You might have told me sooner, Andy."

"Come, Roy. You knew we were planning this raid for a long time."

"Never mind the raid for now. I know it's a tour of duty we can't escape. We'll see it through together and try to come out alive. I'm referring to the lady who almost drowned me in the Miami."

Andy kept his aplomb. "Believe me, Roy, I was more surprised than you when she walked through that stockade gate."

"Don't tell me she's a farm girl. I know better."

"She arrived at the fort with a theatrical group—the Avon Players—out of New York and bound for Key West and Havana."

"Then you knew the lady before her arrival here?"

"Of course I did. Marriage is a serious step, my friend. No

man should promise to wed without considering every angle of that promise."

Roy sighed; he had known from the start that Andy Winter would explain this mystery in his own way. "Don't tell me she followed you here?"

"That's precisely what she did. All the way from New York City, where we met a year ago. Remember when I went up on the packet to buy stores? Though I say it as shouldn't, Roy, it was a love match from the start."

"I should congratulate you. But I'm waiting to learn more."

"There's nothing to learn. Why did you fall in love with Irene Boucher? Why have you buried yourself in this wilderness and eaten out your heart ever since she died?"

Dr. Royal Coe stared at a blind spot on the wall without replying. Only Andy could put things so bluntly. He wondered why the old wound no longer ached when he heard Irene's name. Time is said to heal all wounds, he thought. Perhaps I'm over that agony at long last.

"The point is, I *am* in love," said Andy. "For the first time —and, I trust, the last. You should understand me, Roy—as well as any man."

"So you fell in love last year in New York. When did you become engaged?"

"A month ago."

"You just said it was a love match—from the start."

"On my side, yes. Mary required a little persuading." Andy banged his gleaming boots on the rough pine floor and took a turn of the room, pausing to smooth his flaming topknot at the commandant's cheval glass. "Not that she had anything against *me*, you understand——"

Roy could not help smiling at his friend's long-legged strut, even as he admitted that Andy's self-respect was, in a measure, justified. Viewed from any angle, Captain Winter was a fine figure of a soldier. It was inconceivable (to Captain Winter, at least) that any woman could resist him for long.

"Was it the life you led?" he asked.

"So I gathered, at the time. Of course I explained that I'd be a civilian within the year—with a house in Washington and anything she might desire. She still refused to commit herself."

"You've been wooing her in the interval, then?"

"By letter, mostly."

"Why have I never heard of the lady?"

"A man of my temperament," said Andy, "does not discuss his unsuccessful campaigns. When her letter of acceptance reached me you had already gone for your rendezvous with Chekika."

Roy nodded soberly, remembering his own mad passion in Paris. Madness (he had known this, long ago) was the only name for the affection he had lavished on Irene Boucher. The end of that affair had been fated from its beginning, no matter if Irene had lived or died. He could sympathize with Andy's own soul-searching—and see why his friend had conducted that search alone.

"She accepted you by letter—then followed you here?"

Andy shook his head in perplexity. "I've told you her arrival was unexpected. D'you think I'd permit a prospective bride to set foot in the territory while those red devils are on the warpath?"

"But she arrived nonetheless—with the Avon Players?"

"For love of me," said Andy. "To see how I was faring in the wilderness. Or so she insists. Personally, I think her motive for coming here was more complex. I say this in confidence, of course——"

"Of course. Do I gather she made the journey a kind of adventure?"

"You might as well know it all, Roy. She's wanted to act ever since she was ten. Naturally, her father forbade it. She's an only child. Her mother is dead; she was raised by a governess. So far as I can gather, she'd not had a chance to put her head outside the parental door—until I came along."

"May I ask the father's name?"

"Livingston Grant. One of the finest families in the North."

"I've heard the name."

"He made a fortune in shipping and another in land deals in the Western Reserve," said Andy. "There's a great deal to be said for our union—on both sides."

"A light dawns," said Roy.

"Call me a fortune hunter if you like," said Andy. "I won't refuse the label. When I was first introduced to Miss Grant I made up my mind to marry her—for obvious reasons. It wasn't her fault or mine that we fell in love. Her father was determined that the match be made. He wants me as a son-in-law— quite as much as I want his daughter."

"So much so that he permits her to visit you here?"

"At the moment," said Andy calmly, "he has agents searching for Mary all down the Eastern seaboard. He knows now that she's well and safe—and acting with a group of strolling players. Ingénue roles, I'm told—and acting them quite well, if I may believe her colleagues. Ophelia, Ariel, Bianca—and suchlike." Andy sat down again with a little sigh. "Now you have the story, Roy. Do you find it romantic —or merely amusing?"

"At least she was sure of finding you here—if you were still alive. You might say there was method in her madness."

Andy nodded soberly. "She met the players in New York through a school friend. She knew that they would be barnstorming through the South. After Charleston and Savannah they planned to sail to Augustine. Originally, she meant to meet me there—or wait for my first leave—and marry me on the spot. As it happened, I was on Army business at Key West when they reached Florida. She didn't dare reveal her name. There was always her father——"

"So even then you had no idea she was in the territory?"

"None whatever. The Augustine engagement was a great success. The players were offered halls in Tallahassee and Pensacola if they'd risk a trip by coach. On the King's Highway."

"Don't tell me they took the dare?"

They scowled together, remembering the ragged corduroy road that passed for El Camino Real west of Augustine. Designed by the engineers of His Most Catholic Majesty as a direct link between St. Augustine and California, the royal highway had fallen into sad disrepair since the peninsula had passed to American hands. Coaches were supposed to move regularly between the Eastern seaboard and Pensacola, with a stopover at Tallahassee, the capital of the territory. Both of them knew the perils of that journey—even when Chekika was content to hunt in the saw grass.

"They took the dare," said Andy. "The coach foundered between Augustine and Picolata. There was an ambush just beyond; I gather the Indians were quite unhappy when their quarry didn't arrive on schedule. Fortunately, they were after white medicine, not scalps."

Roy nodded; the picture was complete. The top-heavy stage lumbering into a pothole on a dusk-dimmed road. The frantic scramble to lift the axle from the gumbo. The first war whoop, as spine-curling as death itself. The swarm of breechclouted savages from palmetto and dog fennel. Fortunately, the stage had left St. Augustine without a military escort. Chekika's raiders had merely invaded the coach and the passengers' valises—and vanished as quickly as they had come. Roy chuckled and moved to the cellaret to filch a cheroot.

"I'm beginning to understand your fiancée's reaction when I came upon her unawares."

Andy shrugged. "Apparently there's nothing an actor values more than his costume. Of course that's what the raiders were after. They gutted that coach right down to the cushions." Andy chuckled in turn. "Remember how they used to strip our dead—to make white medicine? There's a full set of Shakespeare in Chekika's war chest now—wherever that may be."

Hamlet—Othello—Lear. Caesar and Mercutio and star-crossed Romeo. Jakob Wagner had obviously been murdered by one of Chekika's braves masquerading as a minion of the Bard of Avon.

"I'm beginning to understand Miss Grant's panic. Apparently she mistook me for Caliban. Or was it Mercutio?"

Andy stared for a while at the scrap of harlequin cloth his friend had just tossed on the desk between them.

"I'd say Mercutio, not Caliban."

"Thanks for that small mercy!"

"Apparently you had quite a visit there in Biscayne Bay."

"Were you an observer?"

"An attentive observer. From this window."

"You might have helped me."

"Why? You were in no danger, either of you. Mary's a strong swimmer. I learned that much when I visited her father's estate on the Hudson. It pleased me to watch you get acquainted. Incidentally, do you endorse my choice?"

"Completely," said Roy through clenched teeth, and prayed that Andy had not noted the sudden tension in his tone.

"You'll stand up for me at our wedding?"

"If you like."

"It's too soon to plan, of course, but we might be married in Key West. Or even in Havana—if the colonel can spare me."

"Wouldn't it be wiser to wait—until after the raid?"

"Much wiser—if it weren't for Mary's father. How can I ship her North if she isn't Mrs. Winter?"

"You've written him, then?"

"Chapter and verse," said Andy cheerfully. "Let's hope he forgives us both."

"Shouldn't you wait till he's put that forgiveness in writing?"

"Come off it, Roy," said Andy, and his voice was hard now. "What do you take me for?"

"At the moment, I'm not quite sure. Naturally, I can't blame you for what's happened——"

"You must see that I've a responsibility. Granted, I wasn't really to blame for Mary's presence here. I explained that carefully. She yielded to an impulse that neither her father nor I could control. She wanted to see how the Army lived— in the Army's own world. Yes, and have one last fling on the boards before she became Mrs. Winter. Surely you can understand and forgive that impulse?"

"Gladly. What about her father?"

"He'll believe me if I say she's unharmed. And I think he'll forgive us both if we marry under the American flag in Key West day after tomorrow."

"Are you sure the colonel will give you leave?"

"I told you I've a mission at Flamingo Key. It's more than a visit to Dr. Barker. I'm to make a contract with Dan Evans to provision our raid."

Roy frowned in earnest. Evans, a Britisher whose forebears had clung to their trading post on Flamingo Key when the Floridas shifted from Spanish to English rule—and back again to Spain when the American Revolution ended—had served the pioneers on this coast for more than thirty years. Just as naturally, he had been sutler for the present fort, when the American flag had been lifted at Biscayne Bay. Firmly established at Flamingo Key, where the mad naturalist, Jonathan Barker, had recently put down his myriad roots, Evans had kept the garrison in English whiskey and Jamaica rum since the first officers' mess had opened its doors. A pleasant day's sail from the Miami, he had opened a hotel of

sorts, to accommodate officers (and officers' wives and doxies) on the long, sun-blistered run from Fort Everglades to
Key West. It was understood in advance that any unusual
provision for the quartermaster's stores (whether it was extra
salt pork in bad weather or extra greens from Dan's abun-
dant truck garden on the key) could be lightered north by
Dan's slaves in record time. Roy had always suspected that
Dan served more than one master. But Roy had lived a long
time in southern Florida, where most men began their ca-
reers as renegades. He knew that he would speak no word
against Dan Evans without proof.

Now he said only, "It seems you've several reasons for
going south."

"And so have you. Dan will drive a hard bargain, as usual.
I want you beside me when we sign the papers."

"And what of your fiancée? Does she sail with us?"

"Naturally."

"Isn't that a bit irregular?"

"Not at all. The Avon Players went south *in toto* last night
aboard the packet. All but their wardrobe mistress—a Mrs.
Simmons, who is herself an actress of sorts. I believe she's
called the second woman by the company. Hamlet's mother,
and the nurse in *Romeo and Juliet*. She'll be an adequate
duenna—all two hundred pounds of her."

Roy found he was smiling at the image. He ignored the
strange tug at his heart when he pictured the impending sail
down the coast. Mary Grant had reminded him that life was
worth living—that there were other women in the world who
could stir his pulse over and beyond his memory of a dead
Frenchwoman with corn-silk hair and eyes like tapers in paradise. . . . He walked to the balcony of the staff room and
stared down at the parade ground without seeing it at all. For
a long moment he focused his mind on Irene Boucher—on
all their long, shared rapture. And his heart bounded in earnest when he found that he could recall those images with no
emotion save regret. The ache had vanished, as though it had
never been. Irene was dead, finally and forever.

His vision cleared, and he examined the parade ground as
though he were seeing it for the first time. From the stockade
walls to the central mass of the palmetto blockhouse, the entire area was jammed with tents and improvised lean-tos, cluttered with upended oxcarts, steaming with a score of cook

fires that winked back at him like cats' eyes in the dusk. Children shrieked among the tents in the half-hour of play before the supper call. Mothers bustled over the fires with the intent air of mothers everywhere, as though they had been rooted to this dusty ground from the beginning. There were few men in evidence: Roy knew that most of them were still foraging within gunshot of the stockade, hunting or fishing in the last night, or bringing tomorrow's firewood to their canvas bivouac.

It was an all too familiar sight, he thought, as this Indian war dragged into its bloody and inevitable finale. At least it was better to scramble for rations under the Army's gun ports than to suffer the fate of Jakob Wagner.

He spoke without turning. "Where have you put your fiancée?"

"In my own quarters, of course—with Mrs. Simmons properly bedded at her side. I've been using your room in your absence. Will you give me a shakedown tonight?" Andy rose from the desk and joined Roy on the balcony. "If not, I'll go aboard the sloop and spread my bedroll there."

"Stay where you are, please. *I'll* go aboard the sloop."

Still without turning. Roy felt his friend's hand on his arm. "What's up now, Doctor? Have I said something to offend you?"

"On the contrary."

"Shall we pay our respects to Miss Grant, now you're adjusted to her presence here?"

"If you don't mind, I'll turn in early."

Andy followed him into the staff room, his hand still earnest on Roy's arm. "You're angry because I'm marrying. You think it'll spoil our friendship."

"I think nothing of the kind. From what you've said, this marriage should be the making of you." Roy forced himself to face Andy at last. "But I still can't believe that your Miss Grant is real. I can't help feeling that she'll regret this journey——"

"All the more reason, then, for shipping her home with the least delay. If I weren't under orders I'd take her to Flamingo Key tonight, colonel or no colonel."

"If I'm not mistaken, the colonel is downstairs now."

Andy moved to the door and nodded agreement. Roy's hearing, tuned to the slightest sound, had picked up the unmistakable bellow from the orderly room below. That full-throated baritone (raised, at the moment, in ribald song) could belong to no one but Colonel Elias Merrick, commandant of Fort Everglades, returned from St. Augustine with more rum under his belt than even a dragoon could carry. Andy and Roy exchanged grins as the former snapped to attention.

"He'll be sober by morning," said Andy. "He always is. We can go south with the tide."

"Perhaps I should leave by the back door."

"Perhaps you should. Our esteemed commander won't enjoy you in his present mood."

Again they smiled at one another, their camaraderie restored. There was no love lost between Roy and the colonel. The aging martinet, soured by an unrewarding career, had always suspected that his chief scout was on the enemy's side. He'll like me even less, thought Roy, when he hears my opinion of this raid.

"Join me in a half-hour," said Andy. "We'll dine with Mary in my quarters."

"Thank you, no. I must get ready for our voyage. Who are we taking besides Stevens and the sergeant?"

"I'm putting a pair of riflemen in the bow. D'you think we'll need more?"

"It's well to be safe, with females aboard."

"We can discuss that at dinner, Roy. Say you'll come. They're broiling a brace of canvasbacks for us—and I've some Marques de Riscal, direct from Madrid."

"Sorry, Captain. It's useless to tempt me. Good luck with the colonel."

"Mary won't eat you, Roy."

"Don't be too sure of that," he said, and whisked down the back stairs as Colonel Merrick's boots crashed into the hall. Andy was his best friend, after all. Could he tell his friend that he envied him with all his heart?

vi

Roy eased off on the tiller. The sloop, obeying his touch as gaily as a lady in a minuet, took the wind on her quarter and scudded across the mouth of the Miami with her mainsail belled in a straining arc. Once again he checked the disposi-

tion of passengers and crew and noted that they were arranged as neatly as their gear.

Mozo, the black boatman who would take them through
the keys today, had seen to that; a Cuban-born freedman
who had served the Army since boyhood, the Negro had
made this run a hundred times with heavier passenger lists.
Mozo was spread-eagled in the forepeak now with a sounding
line between his palms. As Roy held the tiller firm the Negro
turned to nod his approval, a signal that they had avoided the
coral outcrop beyond the river's mouth and were riding in
clear water.

Andy had ordered four riflemen aboard under Sergeant
Ranson's command; they lay at ease on the foredeck now,
babying their long-barreled weapons and looking oddly out
of place in the clear-washed morning. Andy sat beside his
fiancée in the roomy cockpit, just forward of the mast. Roy
could see only his head and his high-peaked officer's cap, set
at its usual jaunty angle; the rest of Andy was hidden by a
boat cloak, which he shared with Mary Grant. Roy could
catch only a glimpse of that sleek, dark head in the circle of
Andy's arm; somehow he was glad he could not see more.

Mrs. Simmons, he noted, was still in the tiny cockpit
cabin, volubly prepared to be seasick at a moment's notice.
He had liked Mrs. Simmons from the start, though she resembled nothing more than an unwieldy heap of ballast,
thanks to the shawls she had brought to protect her from the
sun. Captain Stevens (a poor sailor at best) sat beside her,
trying to divert her mind from the long, easy roll of the sloop
as her bow caught the first roller from the Biscayne bar. If
anything, the captain was a shade greener than the lady herself. . . . It was, reflected Roy, a beautiful day for a sail—
even with seasick passengers aboard. Even with this strange
ache in his heart, when he dared let his eyes stray back to
Mary Grant.

"*Qué tal, hombre?*"

"*Bueno, señor médico!*"

Mozo came down the gunwale with all the ease of a cat in
a gutter; at his signal the two coal-black crewmen who handled the sheets broke out the flying jib. It caught the wind in
turn, pulling them toward the Atlantic at a spanking pace.

"Will we dock at Flamingo Key by sunset?"

"With ease, Doctor. You could sail her in yourself with no help from me."

"Does that mean I keep the tiller awhile?"

"As long as you like, *señor médico.*" Mozo glanced down into the cockpit. "Now I will go to save a lady's life. A little brandy is all she needs, I think."

Roy smiled his thanks and shouted an order to come about —a shift the crewmen had already anticipated, as the bowsprit seemed ready to rake the marsh grass on the western shore of Key Biscayne. Once she had settled in her course, the sloop seemed to lift at her beam-ends, as though she longed to fly, like the white sea gull she resembled. Roy kept his eyes hard on the sandbanks on the port bow. Deep water was close inshore at this point. It was a tribute to his skill that Mozo permitted him to take them across the bar.

"May I sit beside you, Doctor?"

The tiller spun crazily under his hand; he righted the sloop just in time, though a great whorl of sand boiled in their wake as they lurched from shoal to deep water. Mary Grant, her hair in a gypsy bandanna, lifted her hand from his shoulder and settled in the stern sheets, with the tiller between them.

"Did I startle you? That makes us even."

He saw that Andy had gone forward and was deep in talk with the sergeant. You've no right to stir me so deeply, he told her—quite without words. As their eyes met and held, he felt sure that Mary Grant had read his mind to the last syllable. Just as surely he could sense that she was enjoying her advantage keenly. . . . It had been a slip to refuse Andy's dinner invitation at the fort. Even more fatal to keep free of the sloop this morning until the last bit of gear was stowed, the last passenger settled.

She thinks I'm afraid, he thought—and she's right as rain. She imagines me a backwoods red-neck with ten thumbs and a stumbling tongue to match. Perhaps it'd be simpler for us both if I let her go on thinking just that—and no more. But even as his mind formed this pious resolve he found himself answering her question as naturally as though they had known each other always.

"I think you'll always startle me a little, Miss Grant."

"Call me Mary," she said. "You're Andy's oldest friend. You'll have to be mine too."

"I'll try," he said. "It won't come easy for a while, I'm afraid. Last night I told Andy that you weren't quite real. It's still true." He did not repeat the rest of his statement—that her presence here would bring trouble to them all. To herself, most of all, he thought swiftly, and pinned his eyes on the course ahead.

"What's unreal about me, Roy?"

He felt himself go hot under his tan as she spoke his name for the first time. His heart could not have thudded faster had she leaned across the tiller and kissed his last scruple away.

"It's hard to explain," he said, choosing his words with care, and hoping they would conceal his real thoughts. "All of us have lived on the edge of this wilderness a long time. Most of us have gone too long without leave. Finding you in our midst without warning was a real shock. I still can't escape the conviction that you're visiting us from another planet."

"Some of the officers have wives. Andy has told me that much."

"Doxies, you mean," he said quickly.

"Be honest. Did you take me for a—a doxy, when you saw me at the wharf?"

"I took you for a lady."

"Even when I pushed you into the river?"

"That merely confirmed my suspicion."

"A lady from another world," she said. "I'll never play that part with distinction."

"You're playing it now," he said, and dared to look at her directly. For the first time he let his eyes take in her costume. She was wearing white again today—a heavily pleated skirt starred with small gold fleur-de-lis, a kind of openwork pelisse that permitted her shoulders to blush through here and there. Under the loose knot of the bandanna, a pertly tilted straw bonnet shaded her laughing eyes. She's found me out, he thought in panic, sensing the twinkle that dwelt in that green glance.

"It's a long time since I've seen a lady," he said.

"I know that, Roy."

"It bears repeating. And you must try to understand if my—my emotions run away with my tongue."

"So far you've been a model of reticence. Can't you tell

me what's really in your mind? Andy's a soldier—he has that excuse. Sometimes I think that even our wooing was a military secret, so far as *he* was concerned." When she smiled, he saw, a tiny dimple formed in one cheek. He bent a little closer, wondering what would happen if he pressed a kiss in that precise spot. . . .

"Did you hear what I said, Roy?"

"Of course," he murmured, and his voice seemed to come from far away. "You accused me of holding back."

"You think I'm a doxy after all," she said. "How can I blame you, now that Andy's told you my life history? Or at least the recent chapters?"

"You're in love with him," he said. "Why shouldn't you follow him here?"

"Andy blames me—bitterly. He's afraid my father will disown us both. It's quite possible he's right."

"Do you regret coming here?"

Mary Grant lifted her face to the wind and breathed deep. "Not for a moment. I've been a prisoner all my life. It was worth the effort—even if I must go back behind bars."

"With your father as the jailer?"

"He's jailed me for my good, of course. It's a way men have always had with ladies—since ladies were invented."

"Woman's virtue—man's greatest invention?"

She dimpled in earnest. "So you read Balzac too, Doctor. Somehow, I didn't think he'd be in your library."

"Only a Frenchman would have dared to state a basic truth so simply."

"Then you understand my revolt—even if you don't approve?"

"I both understand and approve, Mary." Once he had spoken her name aloud, he felt a great sense of relief, as though he had broken another invisible barrier between them. "Every human being yearns for freedom. Why should ladies be an exception?"

"Of course you can say that with safety. You know I'll be going home day after tomorrow."

This time he met her smile halfway. "May I do my part to make your stay in the Floridas—memorable?"

"You've done that now. Where else could I meet an Indian in buckskins and find he's a doctor with a Harvard degree?" She spread her arms wide, embracing earth and sky—and suggesting, without a word, that he was included in that exuberant gesture. "Where else could I find a morning like this?"

The harbor bar was dead ahead. Here, where bay and ocean met, the air was a white medley of gulls quarreling over a school of mullet that had dared to break surface just inside the last sandpit. To the left, the dunes of Key Biscayne stood out in sharp relief against the Atlantic—an endless file of sand and wind-harried palmettos marching beyond the northern horizon. To the south he could already pick out the mangrove thickets that bordered Black Caesar Key, a solid landfall against the blazing cobalt of the sea. Behind them was the solid mass of Fort Everglades, four-square and vaguely forbidding on the edge of the yellow palmetto prairie. On the flagstaff above the commandant's lookout, the flag of the United States made a brave, wind-whipped silhouette, its twenty-six stars an augury for tomorrow.

Watching that candy-striped banner dance in the breeze, Roy took time to wonder if the colonel had slept off the headache he had brought down from St. Augustine. It was well to remember that both he and Andy would be placing their lives in the palm of that same unhappy martinet within the week. Mary, at least, would be out of harm's way—northbound on the first packet from Key West or Havana. Come what may, he thought piously, she'll be a respectable married woman by then—and ready to brave her father's anger. . . . The sloop bounced angrily in a tide rip, then took the thrust of the wind on her port quarter and raced down the narrow channel. He locked both knees at the tiller and faced back to Mary, with his careful mask in place. He could sail this leg of their journey without shifting a muscle. In a way, he regretted the necessity to keep a wary eye on their course. The situation at the tiller was downright dangerous.

"I'm glad you're enjoying your visit," he said warily.

"I've told you what brought me here," she said. "What's *your* story?"

"That's easy. Andy was already in the Army. We'd lived abroad together. In Paris and London. I had a brand-new degree and no place to practice—until I succeeded my father in Boston. Andy suggested I come to the territory as an Army surgeon. I took his advice and fell in love with the land." Roy spread his hands Indian-fashion to signify that his story had ended. "You can understand, I hope."

"I understand perfectly. But you've still told me nothing of yourself. Andy said you went to study medicine abroad after you took your Harvard degree——"

"In those days I meant to be the finest surgeon in New England. I studied at Edinburgh and London. Then I went on to Paris——"

He bit the sentence short, conscious of his too eager tongue. It had been a long time since he had bared his past. With the tiller still between his knees, he rose to bawl a needless order at Mozo. Standing high in the stern sheets, he could see that the regulars in the bow were dozing over their rifles. Andy and the sergeant were still deep in talk, with a map spread on a salt-wet deck between them. In the cockpit cabin Mrs. Simmons had permitted her head to rest on Captain Stevens' doeskin knee. The captain, fanning the lady's gray-green face with a palmetto, seemed on the point of collapsing across her mountainous bosom. . . . Roy snatched at the first conversational straw lest he yield to the urge to tell his whole story in a single rush of words.

"See that row of pelicans in the ground swell ahead? And the way the sea shades off from blue to lemon-yellow just beyond? There's brain coral underneath; we'll sail over it at our peril."

"I'm not afraid. Are you?"

I'm in mortal terror, he thought. You're promised to Andy —and I want you, even now. At this moment I'd give my right arm to pour out my past to you and let you judge my future. That's my penalty for letting you draw me back to life again. For holding you in my arms, however briefly, and finding that life was worth the effort. . . . He went on blindly, speaking the first words that entered his head, hoping that his voice did not betray his inner turmoil.

"We'll make it; I sailed this way to show you Florida Key. Over there, to the left. Andy has already put his name down for a homestead on that point. If Washington is properly grateful, he should have a clear title to the whole island— right down to that light buoy at its tip."

"Why do you stay on here, Roy? You must have a reason."

"An excellent reason. When we've settled this Indian war, I mean to go down to Flamingo Key as Dr. Barker's full-time assistant. Believe me, that's a career for any man who loves the wilds."

To his relief, she seemed to accept this explanation. "You might tell me more about Dr. Barker—since I'm to be his guest tonight."

He leaned on the tiller without answering at once, letting the sloop run away from the lonely sandspit that marked the terminus of Florida Key. Now that they were really free of the land, they seemed to gain speed, as though the vessel, endowed with a life of its own, had decided to seek out bluer pastures.

"Another long tack," he said, "and we'll go behind the reefs again at Monkey Key. If you'll look just ahead, to the starboard, you'll see the spot I mean."

His hand outlined an apparently endless hammock, prodigally tufted with palms and live oak, that rose like a tropical park from the water's edge, to sweep majestically westward. "That is only the beginning of Dr. Barker's grant," he said. "Prime bottom land after that coastal strip. He's already christened it Cocoanut Grove; Eden might be a better name. Once we've settled our quarrel with Chekika, we mean to go in there as partners and justify both titles."

"Couldn't we land there now?"

Roy smiled grimly. "You were introduced to the Seminole through the window of a stagecoach. Would you like to meet him again in his native habitat?"

"You mean there are Indians on that prairie now?"

"My guess is that this sloop is being scouted from the palmetto scrub. You might ask Sergeant Ranson—he can smell out Indian sign at two thousand yards."

"But it's all so peaceful—and so lovely——"

"So it was before Ponce and Menéndez—when it was the Indians' own. Twice a year the squaws come down to that prairie to dig coontie root—it's their only substitute for corn, now that the Army forces them to live like nomads. While they're pounding their winter bread the braves go hunting in the back country. So you see, it wouldn't be safe to explore Eden today."

He felt her shiver beside him, though her eyes had not left the golden perfection of the shore line. "I'm beginning to understand why Dr. Barker lives on an island."

"Even Flamingo Key wouldn't be safe—if the Navy

weren't just across the channel. It's much too near the mainland."

"Andy tried to describe it to me," she said, "but I can't imagine it too clearly."

"Call it Eden in miniature," he said. "And don't try to picture it in advance. You must see to believe."

"Is Dr. Barker really a wizard with growing things? Some people say he's a little mad————"

"Most dreamers are called mad by the people who refuse to dream."

"Do you endorse his dream, then?"

"For the most part, yes. Cocoanut Grove will be only a start. When this war is over, he hopes to open all Florida to settlers. He insists there'll be a great city someday at the mouth of the Miami Plantations all along this coast, rich beyond belief. A viaduct across the islands, linking Key West with the mainland. He even hopes to drain the Glades, right down to Cape Sable, and raise enough food to feed the whole Eastern seaboard. In another generation he thinks that steamboats can put into Biscayne Bay, with ice for ballast, and take back strawberries in January."

"It's a dream that might come true."

"The best part, yet. The territory can become a state in ten years if we settle the Indian question. Who knows what will grow here better than Jonathan Barker? After all, he's made sample plantings all over the Glades."

"You just said it wasn't safe in the Glades."

"Chekika doesn't harm his friends, Mary. We've both been his friend—as long as he kept within bounds."

"And now that he's declared war?"

He looked at her sharply. "Who told you that?"

"Andy. He says he's leading a company into the Everglades to crush him—and that you're serving as guide." He noted that there was no strain in her voice. Evidently Andy had described their prospective raid in the most optimistic light. The Army (an invincible power) would simply bear down on an Indian village, crushing it utterly under a sheer weight of metal and brawn—with Andy himself (an immaculate commander in full-dress uniform, with every medal gleaming) directing the victory from a safe command post.

"Has he told you he might not return?" Somehow, he could not regret the question, crude though it was. This was not the first time that he had rebelled against the dragoon captain's first belief in his immortality.

"He said the danger was negligible—with *you* as guide."

So I'm to bear the onus of failure, thought Roy, if and when we return empty-handed. If I don't deliver Andy on her doorstep, whole on the hoof, she'll never speak to me again. He fought down an impulse to give her a true picture of the ordeal they were facing, and devoted himself to the task of holding their course.

"Don't you accept the compliment, Roy?"

"It's something I'd rather not discuss."

"You think there's danger then?"

"There's danger in any trade. Soldiering is no exception."

"Andy said you could lead his men straight to Chekika's hiding place. He said it'd be a simple matter to surround him——"

"Fair enough. Who am I to contradict Captain Andrew Jackson Winter?"

"Of course Andy feels it's only sensible that we should marry now—as a protection to me. Even though he does expect to join me in New York by spring."

"Do you concur in that decision?"

Mary Grant smiled and let her eyes stray forward. Andy had just risen from his long conference with Sergeant Ranson. Standing at his full height on the wind-swept deck, in his blue and white uniform, he could have stepped into a gallery of heroes and occupied any picture frame.

"Of course I concur," said Mary Grant. "Can you blame me?"

"Not at all. I've already promised to stand up at the wedding."

"Give him his head, Roy," she murmured, and her hair brushed his face as she spoke, as though they were sharing a secret. "He'll finish your Indian war—in record time."

"If anyone can."

"Then you can plant your Eden in peace. And when we're settled across the bay, I'll come and help."

He stared at her with wide-open eyes, letting his feeling come through unashamed. "Do you think that would be wise?"

Andy braced both feet against the bounce of the bowsprit

and cupped his hands to shout into the wind. "Stop distract-
ing the helmsman, Mary! Talk to *me* awhile."

Roy sighed inwardly, knowing the interruption had saved
him after all. Mary's eyes were sparkling as she turned from
answering Andy's shout. If she had caught the hunger in his
glance, she gave no sign.

"Of course it's wise, Roy," she said, laughing. "What
would Eden be without an Eve?"

Then she had gone to join Andy, leaving him alone at the
wind-harried tiller.

vii

He stirred in his dream and wakened with late sunlight in
his eyes; inured as he was to resting thus whenever the opportunity offered, he could usually snap from sleep to complete alertness without a pause. This time he stared about him
in wonder, with no real idea where he was.

At first glance he seemed boxed in a tall brown-black
room, with banshees sighing from every wall. Mozo's voice
called an order from far away, and he heard the slap of bare
feet on planking as the two crewmen ran to obey. He was
conscious of the purr of water nearby, the creak of a block
as the boom came about, blotting the sun from his eyes. For
a crazy instant he was positive that the sloop, by some magic
all its own, had returned to the palmetto sanctuary of Fort
Everglades. Then, as he sat upright, he saw that the brown
wall enclosing him was a mangrove jungle. The trees had
matted into a solid wall on both sides of the creek where the
sloop was ghosting forward, so gently that she hardly seemed
to move at all. The banshee murmur was a dying squall,
thrusting in vain against that stout wall of vegetation.

He remembered the whole sun-weary day now in detail.
Mozo had relieved him at the wheel just before the crewmen
passed the impromptu basket lunch along the gunwales. Mrs.
Simmons (whose recovery, after a third tot of brandy, had
been little short of miraculous) had regaled them with a song
from the London music halls while they discussed the two
wild turkeys—served cold, with a monumental Florida salad
and the last of Andy's Marques de Riscal. He remembered
Mary's banter and his friend's counterpoint—all how surprisingly easy he had found it to join in, after all. . . . Perhaps it

was the wine and sun, or the aftermath of his long sojourn in
the Glades, but he had been glad to take shelter from the
heat in the stern sheets as soon as the ladies had gone down
to the cockpit cabin for their own siesta. Apparently he had
slept through the rain squall and Mozo's run to their present
shelter. With no surprise he saw that the rubber poncho that
covered him was still glistening from the downpour as he
tossed it aside and sat down beside the helmsman.

The others were sleeping still— -lulled by the gentle rhythm
of the sails, the cradlelike motion of the sloop herself as she
glided down this tidal estuary. Only Ranson and his marksmen were astir on either side of the bowsprit. Even from
where he sat he could hear Captain Stevens' deep-bass snoring under the forward coaming—a sound that was matched
by Andy Winter's own contented surrender to Morpheus.
Without knowing why, he was vaguely pleased that he had
wakened ahead of Andy. Just in time he forced himself to
settle beside Mozo at the tiller rather than move forward to
see if Mary was stirring in the cabin.

"Is it safe to go on?"

"Quite safe, *señor médico*. There has been no real delay.
As you see, we are in Angel Creek. You might say it is a
short cut to Flamingo Key."

Roy nodded in appreciation of the sailing master's skill.
His brain had cleared of sleep now; he could pick out landmarks along their narrow course. He, too, had come this way
to Dr. Barker's when he was returning alone from a visit to
the Glades. He remembered now that the creek, which was
really a two-way channel between the massed jungle of Matecumbe Key and the coral maze to the south, was really a natural corridor from the inner passage they had followed during the long, sunburned day to the open sea beyond. It was
quite like Mozo to run for cover when a sudden rain squall
threatened—and use his shelter as a short cut.

"It's a tight fit for a sloop this size, Mozo."

"Tight but not impossible. Already the channel deepens
ahead." The Negro put his helm over, avoiding a snag by
inches. "We will anchor a while until the sea calms. It would
not do to disturb the ladies' sleep."

The jib belled and filled without sound, drawing them gently forward. As the wall of mangrove thinned to the south,
Roy could glimpse the sea again, still roiled with whitecaps,

though the squall had moved far to the north, a visible black wall of rain that all but blotted out the mainland. Here at the edge of the jungle the sunlight blazed full-strength, drawing a green steam from the ramparts of vegetation, merging trees and water in wavery heat mirages. Again Roy applauded the Negro's wisdom in casting anchor until the breeze that always followed these violent storms could sweep the horizon clean and permit them to set a course again.

He stepped out of his boots and walked barefoot along the rainwet deck to stand in the bowsprit shrouds. The sea dead ahead was clearing as he watched. There, just inshore, was the chrome-yellow trace of brain coral, a deadly menace to the sloop if Mozo's hand should falter. He could just discern the dog-leg course of the channel the creek had worn in the coral in its endless tidal push for open water. Farther out, the water shaded from green to cobalt, from the white spume of scarcely hidden reefs to the shining aquamarine of the Atlantic itself.

To the west, the keys curved in a long arc, palm-tufted, wave-harried, and forlorn. Each moment while he watched, a new island seemed to swim into being, a hazy, green-white mirage that translated into a half-moon of sand, a bit of higher ground where the coco palms tossed their fronds like languid dancers. Some of these islands were of considerable extent, with the remnants of a wrecker's shack, blasted into splinters by some long-forgotten hurricane, showing above the water's edge. Most of them were mere dots in the immensity of the sea. Ponce de Leon, the star-crossed conquistador who had discovered them, had once called these islands the Martyrs, because the palms that fringed their beaches, never at rest even on quiet days, reminded him of an endless file of victims twisting at an inquisitor's stake. Today, as the wild, bright horizon opened wide, Roy could endorse the Spaniard's poetry. There was something tragic about these broken fragments of the mainland, as though the keys, scattered haphazardly on the ocean's face, had been forgotten even by time. Yet he loved this amphibian world quite as much as the Glades. A man could find peace in this solitude. Wise in the ways of hurricanes, he could choose his homesite with care and build a house of marl and coquina to outlast any storm.

He came back to what Mozo was saying. "Get under way, by all means. I'll con you through this channel."

The sea was flat under the steady northeast wind when they skirted the last of the brain coral and set their course for a blue tongue of ocean that seemed to curl, like the brush stroke of some celestial painter, around the southern end of Matecumbe Key. Accustomed as he was to sailing this last leg of their journey, Roy could not quite keep down the gasp of admiration that rose to his lips when they glided into deep water at last and ran toward their destination under a full suit of canvas.

The mangroves, etched like midnight against the incredible blue of the sky, made a fitting backdrop for Flamingo Key, which seemed at this distance, to nest within the embrace of the larger island, like a jewel in an ebony setting. Dr. Barker's experimental gardens rioted with color, as always, though the first impression was one of blazing red (that, Roy knew, would be the lusty poinsettias, newly imported from Yucatan and named in honor of the Secretary of War). It was only later that the enchanted visitor noted the tall stand of century plants, the massed greens of orange and lemon trees, the tiers of hibiscus and poinciana, the acre of grapefruit grafts where the clusters of fruit seemed to glow like pale yellow suns. Later still, the visitor would note Dr. Barker's own dwelling —a square marl house with Bahama-type galleries, muffled to the eaves in the mulberry plantation that surrounded it. At that distance the neat little house seemed oddly out of place. Even now Roy could not quite believe that this flowering paradise had ever known the touch of man.

He took a glass from Mozo and focused his eye on the island, taking in a hundred well-remembered details. There, in the shelter of a breakwater, were the covered docks that housed the botanist's sailboats and the low-roofed workshop where he unloaded his specimens after a voyage. Between the boat sheds—and thrust boldly toward blue water—was the covered dock that served as a turtle crawl. Roy felt his mouth water in anticipation of the soup that would originate in that same pen, when John, who combined the functions of major-domo and cook in his bachelor owner's domain, bustled to honor their arrival.

As always, he was obscurely glad that the tall windbreak of casuarina trees behind the house masked Dan Evans's hotel and the untidy, always-busy wharf that served Dan's warehouse. He reminded himself once again that the Englishman was Dr. Barker's friend, that he had served the Army well, both as counselor and provision merchant. The conviction that Dan Evans was a traitor who had no loyalty but self-interest had never downed, though he had always preserved the amenities in the trader's presence.

And yet, if only to set his mind at ease, he let his telescope side along the horizon until it picked up the outline of Tea Table Key—a squat island in the full glare of the open sea, just inside the barrier reef that marked the line of demarcation between the light blue shallows of the coastal waters and the indigo line of the Gulf Stream. The naval station (it was really a kind of outpost protecting Key West) had been anchored there some years ago, when the Indian war first rumbled into ominous motion on the mainland. Anchored, thought Roy, was the precise verb to describe that block of barracks. The small fleet of Navy sloops, each with its howitzer under canvas on the forepeak, was ample insurance that Dr. Jonathan Barker could pursue his researches undisturbed. By the same token, Dan's raffish hotel was guaranteed a tidy profit each year—a logical stopover for coastal vessels that had enjoyed the hospitality of Fort Everglades the night before and could count on an easy run to Key West in another day's time.

The bell buoy at the end of the breakwater was almost under their bowsprit now; the whole compact little island opened for inspection, with no need of a spyglass to pick out the houses from the trees. Despite his good resolves, Roy found that he was staring with distaste at Evans's Inn, proclaimed as such on a garish black-and-gold signboard at the end of his wharf—a legend repeated in yard-high letters on the white roof of the hotel itself. Since this was the hour of the traditional sundowner, he could hear Dan's accordion wheezing briskly behind the latticed windows of the taproom; he could all but catch the swish of the swizzle sticks as Dan's barmen mixed Bermuda punch for the lustily singing guests. Counting the craft moored at Evans's buoys inside the harbor mole and the flags whipping at the masts, he surmised that most of these visitors were Cubans by nationality, with a sprinkling of Bahama spongers and a utility barge from Tea Table Key, here to bring back the officers' rum ration.

Whatever their nationality, he thought dourly, they'll be rascals by trade—not excluding the shellbacks in naval uniform. The keys were no breeding place for saints no matter what their original calling. Almost all of Dan Evans's guests had been wreckers in their time—or smugglers, or both. Most of them ended their evenings in a pitched battle on the stretch of beach between Dan's dock and the breakwater that marked the beginning of Dr. Barker's land. Oddly enough, none of these brawls had spilled over into the botanist's gardens. For all his easygoing ways, Dan could handle his guests with an iron hand. Dan never forgot that Dr. Jonathan Barker had friends in high places—that no less a personage than the American Secretary of War had honored the key with a visit less than six months ago.

The bowsprit nuzzled against the stout palmetto halves that enclosed the turtle crawl. Staring through the cracks in the planking, which permitted the tide to flow freely for the health of the denizens within, Roy felt his heart miss a beat as his eyes met a pair of slitted yellow orbs burning with a fire that might have advertised a soul in hell. For an instant he wondered if Dr. Barker had captured a moray eel from the barrier reef, or perhaps the turtle crawl had been converted into an aquarium for barracuda in his absence. Then he looked close and saw that his vis-à-vis was only one of the less lethargic of the turtles, roused from a contemplative nap by the sound of their arrival and resenting the disturbance with a reptilian hiss and a prodigious beating of flippers.

The sound had not wakened the sleepers, he noted, but Ranson was overside, a step ahead of the crewmen, to help warp the sloop into her mooring. The riflemen, with a caution born of long campaigning, stayed at their posts in the forward gunwales until Ranson ordered them to the dock. Roy was ashore long ago, without a backward glance. He was still obscurely pleased that he had not been forced to share this moment with Mary Grant. Somehow, it was fitting that Mary's prospective bridegroom, and none other, should be the first to hand her into his multicolored Eden.

Dr. Barker himself emerged from the shadow of the bougainvillaea that all but drowned his veranda. This in itself was unusual, for the aged botanist, despite his long friendship with Roy, had always lingered indoors heretofore, to receive his co-worker in his specimen room or among the books in his library. Today, Roy noted, the doctor was in his shirt sleeves, his hair an untidy white blizzard in the breeze. Perhaps it was just as well, he thought, that Mary didn't see him at this moment. Like so many dedicated scientists, Dr. Jonathan Barker seemed more tramp than gentleman at first glance.

Evidently he had just come from one of the plantations. Roy noted the mud that clung to his trousers, almost to the knees, and the smudge that his mentor had not paused to remove from one cheek. For all these minor stains, Dr. Barker was completely alive—and chipper as a sparrow in May. The hand that clasped Roy's was strong with the wisdom of the earth; the snapping brown eyes were as young as his own—and many times as knowing.

"I sent for you at the fort only this morning, Roy. Are you a mind reader?"

"Were you that anxious to see me again, sir?"

"You'll never know how anxious. John is on the table in my surgery now, ready and willing to lose his right leg. Naturally, I'd have done my best to take it off properly. But I was hoping my message would find you in time."

"John—your butler?"

Roy bit down hard on the words. For the moment he could see nothing but the gentle, gray-haired Negro slave who had caught his bowline so competently when he had sailed into this same pier another time; who had served his rum with such fluent grace, to say nothing of the ambrosial meals that Dr. Barker, like all lovers of life, took for granted, no matter where he might set his table. Turtle steaks fit for Olympus, served with a dry white Montrachet that no one but a Boston Brahmin gone native could have produced on the Florida keys. Chilled to the precise temperature in Dr. Barker's deepest artesian well, the wine had been a perfect overture to the *caneton aux oranges* that John had whisked from a silver bell glass, along with new potatoes fresh from the earth, and a wild rice that the botanist had cross-bred in the marsh of Matecumbe Key.

There had been a deep-boiled burgundy with the duck. Later John had served pineapple *au kirsch* with the same loving hand, along with a magnum of champagne that Louis Philippe might have envied. Later still there had been oversize Havanas, black coffee, and enough Fundador brandy to keep the arguments alive till dawn. . . . Now, thought Roy, John is awaiting the healing knife. The whole surrounding area, thinly settled though it was, had come to rely on Dr. Barker, who had been a brilliant surgeon in his day, before an inheritance had permitted him to forsake medicine in favor of his first and only love. He could understand the old man's reluctance to risk a major amputation now.

His fingers had already closed on Dr. Barker's elbow, drawing him down the oystershell path to the house, well out of earshot of the dock and the booming voice of Andy Winter, who had wakened in earnest from his doze.

"John's on the table now?"

"As you see, I was preparing to operate when your sail was sighted. Will you take over?"

"Gladly—if you'll see to your guests." Roy permitted himself a smile of sorts. "You've given me orders before I've set foot on your land. Surely you can take a guest or two—if they're endorsed by Andy Winter."

"Go straight into the surgery, my boy. I'll welcome my company gladly. Are they many?"

"Andy, Captain Stevens, and myself. Andy's fiancée and her duenna—both bound for Key West and Havana. Ranson and his men will sleep at Evans's, as usual."

Dr. Barker's eyes opened a trifle wider. "I'll greet them now and join you in a moment. As you'll see, time is of the essence."

Once again Roy went up the path without a backward glance. In a way he was glad that an emergency had shut off the necessity for thought. Now, at least, he was a man of science, working with the tools at his command. Mary Grant, and the problem her presence raised, could be solved at leisure.

viii

Dr. Barker's surgery stood apart from the main house. Drowned in whitewash like most buildings on the key, its roof weighed heavily with squares of marl to keep it in place in hurricane weather, it seemed innocent enough at first glance—one with the far larger building just beyond that housed the botanist's living specimens, the glass-roofed hothouse where orchids raised imperial heads in the sunset. Roy

smiled once again as he saw that profusion of color. He
could pause to wonder if the good doctor (in his way, the
most humane of men) had preserved a sense of balance,
when he assigned a solid acre to rodents and reptiles and a
few jungle blooms—and a small whitewashed shed to the battle with death that all men must fight, regardless of clime.

His smile faded as he stepped inside and surveyed his patient. John lay on the operating table, his limbs already
strapped to the sweat-stained boards. Mosquito netting covered his body; a pint-sized Negress in a calico apron, her
eyeballs rolling with terror, waved a sketchy palm-leaf fan
above him in a vain effort to keep the flies from swarming on
the wound. John (and Roy made his calculation by rule of
thumb) was hard on fifty now; his chance of surviving the
surgeon's saw was slight indeed. Yet the Negro managed a
grin of sorts as his fever-bright eyes focused on the new face
above the bed.

"Evening, Doctor. It good of you to come so fast."

"We'll make you well, John. Just rest easy."

His hand was already at the Negro's pulse. John was deep
in opiates, as ready for the knife as he could ever be. While
he counted the thudding heartbeat Roy noted that his skin
tone was hot and dry. Not that he needed a tactile sense to
diagnose his case. The stench that pervaded the whole surgery—as dark brown as despair and as sick as death itself
—told its own story. It was a smell common to every battlefield, even the catch-as-catch-can encounters of the Indian
war. He had breathed it too often now—in improvised hospi-
tals on the lip of a swamp, in cabins deep in palmetto scrub
where he had fought to save a life, letting the scalpel slash
and slash again until the last scrap of rotted flesh was sheared
away.

Gangrene, he thought, made its own picture in advance.
And yet he could not keep his flesh from crawling when he
folded back the quilt that covered John's injured leg and
studied the wound itself. The break, he saw, had occurred in
the femur, the long bone of the thigh, beginning just above
the knee. Bone had thrust upward through the long, jagged
wound. It showed now, a dull ivory splinter, lying in a welter
of muscle and skin that seemed to bubble faintly with a separate life—gray-green like cheese in a sunless cave. Below the
knee the skin had already lost its velvet sheen. The entire

limb had swollen to twice its normal size, though a well-marked line still separated the dying and the living flesh, midway between knee joint and thigh.

"It happened on the barrier reef, Roy. Two days ago. He was brought in only this morning."

Roy looked up to find Dr. Barker already at his elbow. Their eyes met above the patient. At the moment no words were needed. Already their hands were moving automatically at the instrument table, where the botanist had ranged his own armamentarium of scalpels, clamps, and surgical saws. Matthew, who was the doctor's second house slave and John's second-in-command, came into the surgery on fearful tiptoe, dropped Roy's own instrument case on the table, and fled at top speed.

"We'll need someone to hold him."

"Ranson is coming with two regulars."

"How did it happen?"

"He was hunting lobsters on the reef with a grains," said Dr. Barker. "Several of the Negroes were out, working with torches. But John was the only one who lost his footing. Unfortunately I was at Key West when it happened. Apparently he was stunned by the fall—and lay there, in and out of the tide, until the next day."

Stripping to the waist while the older doctor set out the sponges and the probes, Roy nodded his understanding of the picture. He, too, had hunted lobsters on the barrier reef by torchlight. He knew how easily a man could lose his footing in a crevasse—and how simply a bone could snap, there in the waist-high surges where coral and ocean met. He could picture John, alone on the reef as the tide fell, dragging his broken leg to the nearest sand bar while he waited in broiling sun for the help that was so long in coming. Filthy as it was with bird droppings and the leavings of the tide, an open sand bar was a poor bed for a compound fracture.

"Had gangrene developed when you saw him first?"

"I'm afraid so, Roy. As you see, I was screwing up my courage to go to work on him at once."

Sergeant Ranson came into the room with two riflemen behind him. Like Roy, they were stripped to the belt for the ordeal ahead; like the surgeon, they had assisted too often at this task to need instructions. At a nod from Roy, Ranson stepped to the head of the table, ready to hammerlock the

patient's neck and shoulders. The riflemen took their stations
at the end of the table. When the scalpel made its first stroke,
they would anchor John's thrashing limbs just as firmly.

"We'll give him a moment to go under," said Dr. Barker.
"The opiate has just begun to take effect in earnest. Perhaps I
should go make my guests comfortable." He skipped to the
door with his odd, jerky gait, for all the world like a white
heron about to take flight. Roy could not help smiling at the
botanist's exit; he, too, could have done with a breath of air
before beginning the operation.

While the Negro's snoring breaths grew deeper Roy
washed his hands and forearms thoroughly at the basin in the
corner of the surgery. He noted with approval that the water
was scalding hot; the thick, strong soap used everywhere on
the keys (it was made by leaching lye from wood ashes and
treating it with hog fat) burned his skin even more than the
water itself. He rinsed methodically, then went to the instrument table to check the bright array of steel. Even when he
had combined his own case with Dr. Barker's there was barely enough for a high-thigh amputation. He counted the scalpels, honed razor-sharp and wrapped in cotton wadding to
preserve the blade. The half dozen forceps would have to
suffice when the time came to grasp for bleeders. He tested
the edge of the bone saw—the inevitable item in a surgeon's
battery, when amputations and a little lancing were his stock
in trade.

Dr. Barker was at his side again, pale but contained. "We
can start at your orders, Roy." The old botanist's voice was
steady enough; he would see the task through.

"Did you—warn your guests?"

"It wasn't necessary. Andy insisted on taking Miss Grant
for a tour of the plantation. Captain Stevens has taken the
other lady to Evans's hotel for a restorative. I shouldn't be
surprised if they dined there."

"You may stand by, Sergeant." Roy picked up a scalpel
and outlined the operative area in a long, crisp stroke. "Fortunately there's a line of demarcation between healthy and
gangrenous tissue. We'll still go in at the upper thigh."

"I have the tourniquets ready." Dr. Barker twisted a strip
of cloth into a tight roll and pressed it hard against John's
groin, until it all but vanished in the fossa where the major

vessels emerged from leg to trunk. "This will control the bleeding, for a starter."

Ranson had already come forward with the first tourniquet, which he placed directly above the linen roll. The broad leather belt tightened cruelly in the sergeant's hands; he pulled it still tighter by placing one knee against the slave's upper leg. A second tourniquet was placed above the first as a reserve, in case of an unlooked-for hemorrhage.

"Steady, all!"

Brawny arms clamped down at the table's edge; together with the straps that had already been notched down above the Negro's inert body, they would control the shrinking flesh as firmly as though John had been held in a vise. Dr. Barker was lighting the lamps along the side wall—three whale-oil reflectors in hurricane chimneys—and a larger lamp above the table itself. The overhead light swayed in the last sighing breath of wind outside; at a sign from Roy the botanist dropped the lattices at each window, shutting out the ambiguous glow of sunset.

The scalpel glittered palely in the gathered flame. Watching it wink there in his palm, Roy knew that it was John's one chance for life. It could be his own death warrant, too, if he made the slightest error. Too often he had watched brother physicians at the operating table, seen the fatal spurt of blood when the steel had nicked their own flesh while their hands were deep in an infected wound. Sometimes another scalpel had saved them, laying open the threatened area in one lightning slash, crippling hand and arm to save the flesh above.

"Will you begin, Doctor?"

He glanced quickly at Dr. Barker, who stood ready across the table with a forceps and a linen pad; perhaps the older man had read his thoughts. Without permitting those thoughts to rise above the surface he forced the steel to inscribe a long arc on the swollen leg. This would be the rough pattern of his incision. Two flaps, the longer in front, so that the thick muscles there could be brought over the end of the bone to cushion the skin—when and if John was able to use a wooden peg for a limb.

The scalpel was moving now, almost independently of his brain, biting through the skin in earnest, severing the yielding layers of fat beneath. Deep though he was in the languor of morphia, John opened his mouth wide in a heart-stopping scream. The pitiful wailing continued as the steel went remorselessly about its work, parting the muscles beneath in a V-shaped trough. Dark blood bubbled thickly from the cut vessels. Dr. Barker wiped the wound clean and clamped the larger bleeders, one by one; while Roy, looping the whipcord sutures above the forceps' jaws, controlled the gush of blood, reducing it to a mere ooze. John, he noted, was quieter now, save for an occasional spasmodic twitch of the injured leg. The sensation deep in the wound was never so acute—not until it was time to sever the great nerve trunk itself.

The scalpel separated muscle fibers at a steady tempo, tending always upward from the opening incision. In another moment, Roy knew, it would reach the femoral artery. He turned the steel in his palm, using the handle to separate fibers, letting his left index finger precede it—until it had found, and anchored, the vital artery which carried most of the blood to the leg. The handle of the scalpel followed his exploring digit, lifting the vessel high in the wound. Dr. Barker's clamps were already there, biting firmly above and below the bridge he had made. The knife blade severed the artery in a single stroke. Whipcord sutures followed the needle, which penetrated the tough arterial wall with difficulty. In another moment a similar maneuver lifted and severed the fat blue vein that pulsed in the same muscle groove.

"If you will lift the leg, Doctor, I'll see what we can do at the back."

His voice was calm now, and as steady as though they were mounting a specimen in Dr. Barker's workroom. He stepped back for a second or two while the botanist elevated the gangrene-furrowed leg, then breathed deep and made his first incision from that angle. Another V-shaped trough opened rapidly; the last of the forceps went into the wound, anchoring the last major bleeder. He saw with relief that there were just enough clamps to insure a complete tie-off, with no danger of hemorrhage later.

The whole fleshy structure of the leg was now severed, as neatly as any joint on a carver's side table. Only the bone itself remained—a column perhaps an inch in diameter, and with it a shining white trunk, as big as a man's little finger, enclosing the nerves. Roy touched it lightly with the knife; the leg muscles jerked wildly above and below.

"Steady, all—it's nearly over."

He slipped his finger beneath the nerve and set the scalpel against it firmly. Muscles knotted all around the table as the knife bit home—a vital precaution, for John's body seemed to bound up under the straps, as though it would burst through every bond. This time his scream pierced the walls of the surgery. Roy was sure that this last fearful wail could be heard in every corner of the island.

The leg hung now only by the white column of the femur, the great bone of the thigh. The saw came into his hand from the instrument table, its tempered blade sparkling in the lamplight. Roy set the teeth against the femur and began to saw gently, pushing the muscles upward as he worked, so that he could cut in well above the level of flesh formed by the actual incision. Once the cutting edge was engaged, he began to saw in earnest. The teeth skidded a little at first; then, as the sharp edge bit deeper, bone dust began to spill from the wound. The thin keening of the steel changed as it moved from bone to marrow. Ten strokes more, and the now lifeless leg dropped from table to floor. Sergeant Ranson bent down calmly and tossed it into the waiting bucket.

"A clean job, Doctor—from start to finish."

"I think you saved him, Roy," said Dr. Barker.

Roy nodded an endorsement of that hope. "There was no sign of inflammation above the wound. Shall we check for further bleeding?"

The tourniquet came off smoothly, and he held his breath, as always, though he was sure that Dr. Barker's expert fingers, aided by his own, had tied off all important vessels as they were severed. The ooze, such as it was, could be controlled easily with a few extra sutures. He closed the flap firmly, leaving the final strands of whipcord free, so that possible gangrene might not be bottled beneath the skin. Fluffed pads of linen covered the area, bound with a wide cap that blanketed most of the thigh that remained. When this was secured in turn, Roy stepped back from the table, blinking a little in the strong light, letting the external world invade his senses again.

"The ketch is berthed at the dock," said Dr. Barker. "I'll put him aboard, with Rachel to nurse him. He'll be safe enough if we anchor just inside the reef."

"Quite safe." Roy stared down at John with blank eyes.

Life, he reflected, could invade a man's brain too fast for comfort. Especially a man who had lived too long alone—and had the double misfortune to fall in love, completely and unreasonably, with his best friend's bride-to-be. . . .

"Your pardon, Dr. Barker. What were you saying?"

"Don't you agree that wounds of this sort heal faster if the patient's at sea?"

"Much faster. Especially if we use wet sea-water compresses. I'll see that he's put aboard at once."

"Leave that to me, my boy. Is something troubling you?"

"Nothing at all, really. But it's been a long day. If you don't mind, I'll have a bit of air."

"Matthew is preparing dinner now for our guests. You'll join us around eight?"

"Not tonight, thank you. I'm not in the mood for company."

He walked out of the surgery quickly, before Dr. Barker could speak again. He realized that he had shocked his old friend more than a little—accustomed as the doctor was to his need for solitude. Yet he knew that he must walk in the night awhile—alone with his dilemma—or cry out his anguish for all the world to know.

Somehow the battle he had just waged with death had sharpened his own perceptions. His brain insisted that he must use every ruse at his command to keep clear of Mary Grant tonight, even as his heart cried out for more of her sweetness.

ix

Stepping from the surgery to the mat of Bermuda grass outside was like plunging from a firelit cave into a bath of quicksilver. He had forgotten that there would be a full moon tonight—or that the apron of lawn before Dr. Barker's house would be almost as bright as day. He pulled back sharply into the shadow of an oleander thicket and waited with a thick pulse at his throat as he heard a crunch of boots behind the windbreak to the north and a laugh that could only be Andy Winter's.

He had sought his ambush just in time; when he looked again, Andy was handing Mary Grant across the stile that separated Dr. Barker's formal gardens from the oyster road—a precaution to keep the razorback hogs that roamed at will on

Dan Evans's side of the key from invading the botanist's domain. Captain Stevens followed with a similar flourish, bringing Mrs. Simmons to a safe landing on the lawn. They've ended their stroll at the inn, thought Roy; the gentlemen, at least, have had a glass too many. . . . He waited, deep in the aromatic shadow of the leaves, while Andy bowed his lady into the tall, moon-shot gallery of the house proper, a procedure that the captain and Mrs. Simmons paralleled, like a grotesque variety team. The kiss that Andy pressed on Mary's hand would not have disgraced a dancing master; Andy's ramrod-stiff salute was part of the pantomime. Captain Stevens saluted, too, his tall horsehair shako bobbing in the wash of quicksilver light.

Mary's laugh went with that magic. The watcher, still burrowed in the oleanders, knew that he would treasure it to his dying day—to say nothing of the way her chin lifted at Andy's homage, the gleam of possession that surrounded her like an all but visible aura.

"Be sure you find Dr. Coe promptly. *This* night he can't avoid dining with me."

"We've a bit of business to discuss with Evans first, my dear," said Andy. "Captain Stevens can handle the details, I hope. I'll do my best to rejoin you by eight."

"With Roy beside you—don't forget, now."

Mary was gone with the words. Mrs. Simmons, a model duenna even now, settled her bonnet vigorously and lumbered in the girl's wake. Roy kept to his cover until the two officers had swaggered over the stile and vanished behind the windbreak. Then, risking a hail from the house, he crossed the lawn in the opposite direction. Following the slope of the rough sea wall that protected Dr. Barker's gardens to the east, he gained his original objective—the long strip of beach that curved north toward Matecumbe Key.

I'll walk for a half-hour, he promised himself. Time enough for Andy and Dan Evans to stop swearing at one another. They'll seal their bargain over a demijohn of Jamaica. If Andy is drunk enough he may forget Mary's orders entirely. If not, I can always say I must go out to the reef and visit my patient aboard the ketch. . . . The sand underfoot, only recently exposed by the falling tide, was deliciously cool. He kicked off his boots, rolled his nankeen Army trousers to the hip, and waded deep into the lazy wash. Walking north, moving as quietly as a prowling cat, he tried not to think at all, though his senses had never been more alert.

The fragrance of orange blossoms, mingled with the salt breath from the Atlantic, assailed his senses as he skirted the last of Dr. Barker's plantations. Flowers for a bride, he thought—and wondered if Andy and his betrothed had paused in the shadow of those dark green trees for a legitimate kiss or two. Give me tonight alone, he prayed, and I'll face her quite calmly, with no more danger of betrayal. Even though she half guesses my feelings. Those feelings will hardly matter, once they are in control. With heaven's help, he added piously, I'll stand up at the altar when Andy takes her as his bride. Chekika can wait awhile longer in the Glades. As for Colonel Merrick, he can sleep off his saturnalia in St. Augustine and fume at leisure. First I must put her beyond temptation and aboard a northbound vessel.

Perhaps it'll be simpler, he thought, if I resign from the Army now. Let Andy and the colonel finish this war between them. Dr. Barker can really use me here; I can become a first-rate beachcomber with very little urging.

He studied the phosphorous wake his feet had stirred in the shallows, and waited patiently while an ungainly land crab bungled through the exposed roots of a coco palm and scuttled away into the lazy waves in search of food. The moonlight picked out the creature's shadow as it ghosted along the stippled bottom and vanished in deeper water. He could even follow the course of a giant conch along the sand, and paused to turn the great whorled shell with his foot. The valve snapped shut instantly as the conch turned on its side, secure against all invaders save man. For an instant he lifted the heavy shell in both hands, estimating the size of that muscular arm that had just withdrawn into its carapace. More than once he had eaten conch meat in his canoe trips among the keys. Roasted over a bed of coals and drowned in a paprika-and-okra sauce, it could be as tender as prime sirloin, with a flavor no words could paint.

Life would be good on the keys. Here, where Gulf and ocean met, he could find his food with ease. Palm thatch and a few driftwood timbers would make a house as snug as any mansion in the cold north. His front porch would be a beach like this. His garden, untouched by human hand, would be rich with fruit and vegetables ready for the taking—papaya and wild orange, the rich milk of the coconut, the succulent palmetto heart he had learned to favor on his long sojourns among the Indians. He need never lack meat, so long as the plump swamp rabbits paddled through the beach grass, turtles crawled ashore to lay their eggs by moonlight, the fish leaped in profusion within the reefs, awaiting only the thrust of a grains to join his day's bag in the skillet.

A little doctoring to keep his surgeon's hands in trim, a little hard work at Dr. Barker's experiment station, and he would have more than enough cash to satisfy his simple wants. . . . Yet it would still be an Eden without Eve.

For an instant he let his fancy roam at will, banishing Andy Winter to limbo, taking Andy's place at an altar in Key West or Havana. Somehow, he felt sure that Mary would agree that the keys were an ideal spot for a honeymoon. An enchanted time that would last forever, in the warm glow of the ever-present sun, in the warmer bath of moonlight. They would live together as innocently and as passionately as the two first tenants of the Garden before the snake of wisdom came. Naked and unashamed, they would fish and hunt by day, swim whenever the fancy took them, sleep when they were weary—in the siesta hush of afternoon or in the deep blue midnight. . . . The insane word picture built and died— and he was alone again on the shore of Flamingo Key. Alone with mother earth and her myriad riches—and lonelier than he had ever been.

His reverie had taken him far around the northern curve of the beach; the last of the straggling shanties that lined this part of the shore was far behind him now. Here the channel that separated the tumbled dunes of Flamingo Key from the high wall of mangroves on Matecumbe was no more than a half mile in width. He was startled at first to note a torch moving among the trees on the larger island—a lightwood knot, to judge by its sputter. He watched it idly for a while, sure that it was moving there with purpose. A spearhead of the invasion that had often threatened the keys, from the days when the Caloosas, the so-called Spanish Indians, were all-powerful on the mainland? Of course it was absurd to imagine that Chekika was lurking somewhere in those shadows, ready to pounce on Flamingo Key and the riches in Dan Evans' warehouse. More likely than not it was a solitary

bird hunter looking for egret nests—or hoping to capture a
brooding spoonbill.

For a while he followed the beach on the Gulf side, tending always toward Evans's hotel and the glass of rum that
might clear his head of fancies. The pound of surf on the
barrier reef was fainter now; the only sound that broke the
peace of the night was the skirl of the accordion in the hotel
taproom, a frontier sound that blended oddly with the darkness. He was almost at the back door of the warehouse now,
and waded deeper in the sea to dodge under the plankings of
the dock itself, cluttered as always with small craft and fishermen's gear.

Again he pulled up short when he just missed barking a
shin on the nose of a canoe—a cypress dugout such as the
Glades Indians used, complete with transom and push pole.
The short, triangular sail had been stepped down and folded
neatly under the thwarts. The push pole, he saw, was still
wet; at the crossbar near the butt (a device which prevented
the pole from sinking too deeply into the mud) the rough
bark surface was covered with a telltale slick of marl.

Had he noticed the canoe on the open beach, Roy would
hardly have given it a second glance. Many fishermen along
the keys still used the Indian canoes—a useful craft in these
waters, since their shallow draft let them float anywhere. This
canoe had been hidden deliberately by a visitor on a clandes-
tine errand. Indian sign was heavy within the thwarts as he
bent to investigate, like a pointer on the scent. A reek of copper flesh, savage as the breath of the Glades themselves . . .
He remembered a breathless moment when he had saved his
life by crouching in a saw-grass hummock while another
canoe, much like this, had all but grazed his hiding place.

Still barefoot, he took the path to the warehouse on the
run. The squat, tin-roofed building seemed enormous by
moonlight; the shadow cast by the eaves spread out to the
edge of the beach itself, dark as a smudge of ink. He saw at
once that the back door of the building was slightly ajar,
though he could hear no stir of life within; he took a step
closer, uncertain of his next move. The visitor, who had obviously entered the storeroom from the rear, might be only
one of Dan's go-betweens after all. Certainly the trader was
far too wise in the ways of his neighbors along the keys to
leave a door unpadlocked after dark.

Roy had half turned toward the path that led through the dunes to the hotel, with the intention of warning Evans of the pilferer, when the warehouse door swung wide and a man strode boldly out, under the shadow of the eaves. Evidently he had expected the beach to be deserted, for he pulled up sharply as he caught sight of Roy at a spot where the shadows were deepest. At that distance Roy could not be sure if he were white or Indian.

"Stay where you are," he snapped. "Who are you?"

The intruder did not speak, though his next move was answer enough. Roy saw a brown arm dart backward into the space behind the open warehouse door. When it emerged there was a long pole in the fist—a grains, with gleaming tines at the end. With this weapon the unknown visitor moved forward step by step, evidently with the intention of reaching the still deeper shadow of the dock and the waiting canoe.

Roy gave ground instantly, knowing the nature of the weapon in the intruder's hands. Those three spear points, sharp as needles and delicate as a triad of stilettos, could skewer a tarpon—or a man—in a single thrust. Just in time he remembered the push pole in the canoe and darted to cut off his enemy's retreat. The pole, he saw, was a crude weapon indeed, but it was fully as long as the grains and, used as a fencing stick, it could ward off the thrust of those steel prongs. Cypress clashed instantly with steel as the deadly game of quarterstaff began—a thrust-and-parry that churned the shallows beneath the dock and sent the splinters flying. Still unable to see his opponent's face, Roy could feel himself outpointed from the first. The man was much taller than he and as strong as a bull; obviously he had handled the weapon in his hand since childhood. Twice Roy just escaped stumbling as he held the tines from his throat; once the man seemed to falter, and Roy pressed home this unlooked-for advantage—only to have his opponent wheel like a stalking tiger and, using the spear as a javelin, drive straight for his heart.

Half expecting the ruse, Roy had not dropped his guard. The push pole absorbed the impact of the spear, deflecting it to the right, where it drove deep in the spongy surface of a palmetto piling. He flung the push pole at his assailant, and followed it with both fists flailing. Even now he felt that a great many questions might be answered tonight if he could capture the man, unharmed. But it was the enemy's turn to give ground, now that he was empty-handed. For an instant they feinted desperately among the rowboats, without a decisive blow on either side. Then the dark form eluded him in a nest of pilings, vanished for a time, and reappeared, as though by magic, at the gunwale of the canoe.

Roy saw the push pole go aboard and knew that his man was about to escape him after all, without trading a single punch. Belatedly he remembered to shout for help before he vaulted the nearest skiff in a last attempt to cut the canoe off. Even as his toes splayed into the sandy bottom he saw the flash of moonlight on steel, and knew why his antagonist had been so eager to reach the dugout. The Indian ax, thrown with uncanny accuracy, just missed his head as he spread-eagled into the shallows; he could hear it sing through the air beyond and lose itself in the shoulder of a dune as he scrambled to hands and knees and made one last, despairing dive at the stern of the vanishing canoe.

Once under way, an Indian dugout can move at a dizzy speed. He saw the futility of pursuit before he could scramble to his feet again. Even if he could have found a pair of oars, the skiffs beneath the dock were hardly built for this kind of race. The push pole, stirring great whorls of phosphorus, had already sent the canoe far beyond the dock's end; thanks to the witchery of the night, it seemed to soar in that mirage of moonlight like a bird that has spurned sea for air. Waist-deep in the Gulf, Roy shouted in vain, in one last effort to delay the invader. While he watched, the triangular brown sail opened wide, pulling the dugout around the point.

Sergeant Ranson had waded out beside him before he had quite stopped cursing. The veteran's hand was steady at his elbow, easing him from the shallows to beach, and up the path to the hotel, where raucous voices were still raised in song.

"I heard you call, sir—being outside at the time. Most of 'em were too blind to notice."

"You saw what happened, then?"

"Enough, Doctor. Including our visitor's calling card." Ranson stooped to pick up the tomahawk from the slope of a dune. "If you ask me, sir, you ducked just in time."

"Did you see his face?"

"The light was too bad." Ranson hacked viciously at a
clump of Spanish bayonet that stood just outside the taproom
door. "Did he make off with much?"

"That's the odd thing—his arms were empty."

"Dan's inside—drunk as a billy goat. Maybe I should go
back with a lantern. Make sure there aren't others."

"Let's talk to Dan, anyway. I'd say this was a solitary
thief. If he *was* a thief—and not a friend of Dan's."

The sergeant growled his approval of this last remark; he
had been Roy's confidant before, when the rascalities of Dan
Evans had been up for discussion. Side by side they shouldered into the thick tobacco haze of the taproom—a rough
pine-board addition to the main building, with cane-bottomed
chairs scattered haphazardly around the bar proper. This imposing structure, built to represent a foundered schooner,
with the rail as serving table and pyramids of straw-covered
decanters at each splintered mast, poured rum from every
scupper tonight; Dan's Shipwreck Bar (which had justified its
name on many occasions) was famous on both coasts of the
Floridas. Most of the drinkers were deep in their cups by
now. The babel of voices, with the sibilant Cuban-Spanish
predominant, continued unabated after Ranson's entrance. A
tomahawk in a man's fist was no novelty on the keys.

Dan Evans, whose accordion had sighed so merrily in the
early evening, sat at a corner table now with his head cradled
in his arms. His snores continued as Ranson lifted one boot
and shook his chair. But he sat up with a cavernous yawn
when the sergeant sent the Indian ax crashing into the table
top, blade down, with enough force to split the yellow-pine
planking.

"Wake up, Dan. D'you recognize this calling card?"

The Britisher stared at them from pale blue eyes. Drunk or
sober, his round moonface was always deceptively mild. The
twist of his mouth, when he offered his brokenhearted grin,
could be as deceptive as a child's—until you noticed the
snaggled teeth behind those pouting lips, the broken nose
above. Scarred though he was by the world, Dan Evans had
always kept his good nature intact. His friends insisted that
he was the richest landowner in the Floridas—and the most
reliable. His enemies (and Dan, like many self-made men,
had stepped on a number of faces in his climb to wealth) en-

dorsed his bank account, bitterly enough, and added that Dan was slightly less trustworthy than a barracuda.

Dan's voice was mild enough tonight. "You're one of my oldest friends, Sergeant. I'd forgive no one else for wakening me so rudely."

"Fair enough," said Ranson. "You might answer our question."

Dan Evans yawned again and pried the tomahawk from his bar table. He weighed it in his hand with obvious distaste, as though he hesitated to give it a name.

"We've all seen these before, Sergeant. Where did you find it?"

"Tell him, Doctor," said Ranson. His eyes had not left Dan's face since he entered the taproom.

Roy told the story as simply as he could, with due allowance for Dan's present state. And yet long before he finished his recital he could not help wondering if the trader's intoxication was more apparent than real. Dan shook his head vigorously as the story neared its end, and seemed to grow slightly larger with each shake. He's reminding himself that I've trespassed on his domain, thought Roy. In another moment he'll tell me that I should stay on Dr. Barker's side of the key and leave the thieves to his discipline.

"So the back door of my warehouse was open, Doctor." The trader still weighed the tomahawk in his palms. "And you were attacked for—investigating." Once again Roy noted that Evans's tongue was oddly fluent for a man deep in liquor. "Could it have been one of my watchmen—mistaking you for a trespasser?"

"Hardly. I asked his name—and I've described his answer."

"Then it was obviously a thief. He chose an odd corner for his—thievery. Must I explain that the south warehouse contains nothing but salt—in hundred-pound tuns?"

Roy shrugged, and let the sneer go by unchallenged. "Why should he attack me—if he was innocent?"

"Let's say it was an Indian—as you infer. Let's assume he was taking a short cut to his canoe. Wouldn't you have been startled—in his place? Wouldn't you have reacted—as any savage would?"

"Then you *do* receive Indians here?"

"Frequently, Dr. Coe. And why not? I'm the Indian's

friend as well as yours. All during the war I've traded salt for otter skins—precisely as you've done within the Glades. Both of us have done our poor bit to keep those wretched Seminoles alive—until Chekika makes up his mind to bury the hatchet. I respect your viewpoint. Why don't you respect mine?"

I don't believe a word of this, thought Roy. It's like you to attack with my weapons. Actually, I'm quite sure you've never shed a tear for any man alive, save yourself. Or the half-breed wench you call your wife. He let his eyes rove around the taproom and wondered if White Heron, the honey-colored *cubana* who called herself Dan Evans's wife, had taken part in the conference with the intruder he had just surprised.

He spoke quietly enough, keeping his voice as mild as Dan's. "Aren't you troubled when a thief enters your warehouse?"

"Are you sure it was a Seminole?"

"Not at all," said Roy, and chalked up a small advantage. He had been careful to refrain from describing his assailant too exactly; Dan's query was an admission of sorts. "Salt or no salt," he said, "I'd suggest you make sure this was a lone wolf on the prowl."

Dan Evans shrugged in turn and shouted at a barman. "I've been robbed before, and survived," he said. "I might add that I've kept my license. I'll go further, Dr. Coe. It might be simpler all around if you stayed on Dr. Barker's side of the island when you go strolling. Not that you aren't welcome here—if you come by the usual path."

I've expected that rebuke from the start, thought Roy. Aloud, he said only, "You'll admit your side of the border isn't too well policed?"

"Not at all. As I just remarked, your recent adversary may well have been a relative by marriage."

Or an envoy from Chekika, thought Roy. *Chittamicco himself—or one of his warlocks.* It's strange indeed that an inferior sense (reserved for the lower vertebrae) should insist that his vanished enemy was Chekika's heir, and none other . . . He pushed the suspicion aside. After all, the keys were swarming with thieves of every stripe. As Dan had just remarked, they had confined their thievery to his side of the island so far.

"It's quite all right, Dan," he said. "Hereafter I'll know my place."

The trader got heavily to his feet. "That's all I want to hear, Doctor," he said thickly. "That will do nicely, in fact. Take my word for it, the fellow will be punished—if I can track him down. Even if he *is* White Heron's cousin once removed."

He let the rest go, and lurched toward the stair that gave to his private quarters. Roy turned as the whole taproom fell silent. No one stirred as Dan fumbled his way toward the honey-colored girl who waited in the doorway above. A girl whose black hair and flashing jet-black eyes betrayed her race. Just in time Roy remembered to get to his feet for a bow that came from the heart. Much as he disliked Dan, he could pity the gentle Cuban mestizo who shared the trader's lot.

Dan paused in the doorway to shake a roguish finger at the Army. "Thanks once again, gentlemen—for your zeal in my behalf. Order what you like. Your money's no good tonight." He was gone with the words, surrendering himself to the girl's arm as naturally as a wayward son might return to his mother's embrace.

Roy stared at the closed door, resentment still boiling within. "Was he bribing us, by any chance?"

"Quite likely, sir," said Ranson. "Are you in the mood to refuse bribes?"

"Certainly not—if I keep my hands clean."

They clinked glasses in unison after one of Dan's slaves shuffled up and poured the blackstrap rum. "Here's to a thoroughgoing rascal," said Ranson. "May he hang in peace before this tour of duty's over."

"By the way, are Winter and Stevens returning?"

"Not to my knowledge, sir. They've ladies to care for at the doctor's. If you refer to their business with Dan, they settled *that* a good hour ago. Signed and sealed. It seems that Dan and the colonel had already agreed on the details. Part of the stores are on their way to the fort this minute—by special lighter. The rest go out with the dawn."

"I should have been present—but I was operating. Between us, we might have saved the Army money."

"The price was agreed on too; Dan was firm about that. At

least we won't go hungry in the Glades, Doctor. He's sold us enough jerked beef to feed a regiment———"

"Cuban, I'll wager—and tough."

"Quite, sir. But we'll be glad it's aboard, once we're in the saw grass." The sergeant refilled Roy's glass. "Shall we drink to the raid—or don't you endorse it?"

"It's as good a toast as any, Sergeant."

Again they downed the fiery dark liquor at a toss. Roy could feel the fumes mount to his brain. I should be back at Dr. Barker's, he thought, even though they've finished dinner long ago. Let's hope she missed me just a little, he added, and lifted the demijohn to pour a third round.

"What do *you* think of the raid, Ranson?"

"I can answer by the book, sir. It'll be the worst tour we've ever soldiered."

"Worse than the Withlacoochee?"

"That was a basket picnic, Doctor. We had a riverbank to fight from—even if it was mostly gumbo. *And* howitzers to keep those devils in their place. This time we'll be fighting in a terrain that's never been surveyed. From boats, with no more base than a water snake. If you ask me, sir, a foot soldier's at his best on dry land."

"And you still want to toast the raid?"

Ranson raised his glass. "Soldiering's my trade, Doctor."

"It isn't mine. Why do I stay with the Army?"

"I couldn't answer that. I can only say we're glad to have you."

"Maybe I've wanted to die all my life. Maybe I won't admit it." Roy stared hard at his glass, then poured and drank again. This demijohn, he thought, is a short cut to dying. At this moment it's the sort of medicine I don't mind at all.

"Drink up, Sergeant. We'll both live forever, you know." It's the fate of most men who want to die, he added silently. To grow old and empty and more bitter with the years. To live by the cynic's book, refusing to envy the happiness of others. . . .

"Will you put me to bed tonight, Ranson?"

"If you like, sir. May I ask what we're celebrating?"

"My freedom. The fact I'm alive and whole and fancy free. How many bachelors can say as much at thirty?"

x

He had expected to waken with a splitting head. And yet long before he opened his eyes he knew that his body, tuned to concert pitch after those long weeks in the Glades, had turned away the rum without losing a heartbeat. He stirred contentedly in his cocoon of blankets, and held the thought of Mary at arm's length while his brain spun back to wakefulness. Never had he felt more rested, more renewed; somewhere in Dan's Shipwreck Bar he had cast his slough of despond.

"Wake up, Roy. You can't stay under those blankets forever."

He sat upright and stared at Andy Winter, who was straddling a chair across the room, his back to the sun-blistered lattice. He saw at a glance that he was in his usual room at Dr. Barker's. Sergeant Ranson had folded his clothes neatly in the armoire and had tucked him into the wide four-poster with his usual skill. He noted with surprise that Andy wore his fatigue uniform today and that his friend's forehead was creased in a scowl.

"I've just three minutes to say good-by, Roy. Are you sure your head is clear?"

"I'm wide awake. Why aren't you in full dress? I thought you were getting married today. Or was it day after tomorrow?" Stepping from bed to floor, he felt a familiar stab of pain behind his eyeballs and shook his head to clear the mist away. "What's this about good-by?"

"Orders," said Andy briefly. "They came in with the tide— by special sloop. Apparently they were chasing us all of yesterday."

"From the colonel?"

"Who else gives me orders?" said Andy crossly. He kicked his chair aside and began to pace the room. With his hands knotted behind his back he might have passed for an outsize Napoleon. Or a child, pouting in uniform.

"The colonel sent you here, Andy."

"And the colonel calls me back to the fort. Council of war, meeting tonight. Now that we've made our deal with Evans, he says, we've no further business here. He's right, of course. But it makes things damned awkward for Mary."

"Why? She can wait for the Key West packet. You've still time to marry her."

"You can't marry a lady at this hour."

"You can marry a lady at any hour, if she's willing."

"Not *this* soldier, Roy. I've done some thinking since my orders came. Mary's father will be delighted at our match: I've no doubts of that. He may not thank us for marrying without his consent. Perhaps old Merrick has saved me from a blunder, after all."

"Does that mean you're returning her to New York a maiden?"

Andy's scowl deepened; but if he resented Roy's forth-rightness, he gave no other sign. "What else can I do? They're holding my sloop now at the harbor bar. In another ten minutes we'll miss the tide."

"Is Stevens ready?"

"He's already aboard. Ranson's waiting for me in a long-boat."

"I'll dress at once."

"Take your time," said Andy dourly. "You're not going anyplace special today."

"Surely I'm ordered back with you."

"The colonel left that to my discretion—providing you report for duty not later than Monday next. It will take at least that long to provision the boats and lay down a base camp at the falls." Andy had not left off his pacing. Now he turned and clapped a hand on Roy's shoulder. "You've helped me before, my friend. Today you'll be really useful."

Maybe I'm dreaming all this, thought Roy. He stamped into his rough work boots and drew on a pair of dungarees—his usual costume at Dr. Barker's plantation. "What can I do for you here?"

"Look after Mary, of course. Make sure she gets safely aboard the Key West packet. In the meantime, amuse her with your wit and wisdom."

"Dr. Barker will look out for her."

"Dr. Barker can hardly take my place."

"Nor can I."

"You can do your best, Roy. After all, the packet is due here from Augustine tomorrow—or the day after at the latest. Once she's aboard, with a destination, it won't be too tedious for her. I won't have her pining here alone."

"I'd planned to spend the day on Matecumbe."

"An excellent idea. You can take her along—she's wild to see more of the keys."

"Is that a direct order, Captain?"

"A direct order, Dr. Coe. Until that packet leaves, you'll have no excuse for avoiding Mary."

Their eyes met and clashed. Roy's were the first to drop. Looking almost as sulky as Andy, he went to the armoire and took out a white cambric shirt with stock to match. "If I'm to squire a lady," he said, "I can hardly go naked to the waist."

"Go any way you like, my friend. Just meet the girl half-way. She's beginning to believe you dislike her."

She believes nothing of the sort, thought Roy. She knows well enough what my feelings are. "I'm a lone wolf, Andy," he said quietly enough. "Don't try to civilize me too fast."

"Say you'll behave, and I'll leave this room a happy man."

"I'll behave, Andy."

They struck palms on that naturally enough; Andy turned to the doorway as Sergeant Ranson's voice boomed a warning from the lawn below.

"Remember, we've an appointment at the fort on Monday."

"I'll remember, Captain Winter."

"Don't fall in love with her, Roy. I'd have to shoot you for that."

"Is that an order too?"

"The last I'll give you today," said Andy, and went out laughing. Roy found that he could echo that laughter for far different reasons. At least I didn't promise to take her to Matecumbe, he thought. Only to amuse her—and see that she's safely on her way to Key West and home.

He finished his dressing in a rush, without pausing to make conscious plans. The back stairway gave him easy access to the kitchen, where old Queenie, the mammoth cook whom Dr. Barker had bought with the house, still bustled over the sort of breakfast that only the Floridas could furnish, regardless of season. Roy passed over the steaming dish of yams and fresh-shucked shrimp, the cylindrical gems of filleted mullet, chopped okra, and fine-beaten biscuit dough known on this coast as "hush puppies," the nobly sugared ham that sat like a contented sultan on a platter of crisp-fried eggs and hominy. Even Queenie's breakfast seemed unreal today as he devoured a few slices of toast, washed down with black coffee. I'll dine in earnest on Matecumbe, he promised himself. The trick of the moment is to leave this house without being seen.

"Is Miss Grant at breakfast, Queenie?"

"Lord save her, Doctah, I doan' think she even come down yet."

So much the better, he thought as he bolted for the kitchen door. He had a quick glimpse of Dr. Barker through the long lattice of the dining room, seated alone and in state, with a beefsteak before him and a Havana newspaper folded beside his plate. For a moment his stomach rebelled at his instinctive flight. He ignored its rumble and went down to the covered dock on the run.

The boat shed was full of a rich blond light. Beyond the wide-open doors the harbor danced with whitecaps as the wind freshened with the growing day. It was the same wind that had pushed old Ponce past the final outpost of the keys to the Bahama Passage and his rendezvous with history. A fine day for sailing—even for a half-hour's run due north, to the first convenient beach on Matecumbe. Roy checked the catboat that Dr. Barker always used for the journey; there was a grains aboard and enough charcoal to build a fire for his lunch. He had a box of those newfangled lucifers in his pocket and the fat bag of salt that every woodsman carried in the Floridas. For today, at least, he needed no more to supply his wants.

The tide still tugged faintly, even in the covered slip. He cast off the bowline and let the catboat run to open water. The jib caught the wind and held the bowsprit steady. Just in time he remembered to sweep the horizon, making sure that Andy and the Army had cleared the barrier reef. The sloop from the fort was only a dot on the northern horizon now.

Running sweetly toward the channel buoys and the spout of breakers on the reef beyond, he saw the ketch riding at anchor inside the coral barrier, and felt a twinge of conscience as he reminded himself of his duties as a physician. Surely he would have time to examine John. Rachel, wise in the ways of the herbalists, was a more than adequate nurse; he knew that Dr. Barker himself would have been called had a crisis developed. And yet he found that he had put the tiller down by instinct. Gunwales whispered together as he cast his bowline aboard.

Rachel herself greeted him as he vaulted down into the cockpit. The aged Negress was crouched over a brazier, brewing coffee and stirring a thick mush in an adjacent pot. Roy recognized the ever-present hominy bubbling merrily in a thick cream—a palatable diet for a man who had just been snatched back from death.

"How is he, Rachel?"

"He sleep like a baby, Doctah. Head cool as this breeze. Why you come early? The lady, she watch him since daybreak."

Too late, he noted the skiff bobbing at its painter on the far side of the ketch—and a familiar dark head bent over the pallet inside the cockpit door. He nodded curtly to Rachel, as though he had expected to find Mary Grant here all along. Once he had taken the first resolute step forward, it seemed inevitable that they should meet thus, in the first light of day.

"May I ask what you're doing here?"

Mary looked up from the bedside and offered him her best smile. "Spelling Dr. Barker, of course," she said in the barest of whispers. "And waiting for you. Offhand, I couldn't say which is more important."

"When did you come out?"

"At daybreak—as Rachel said. I couldn't sleep, so I came downstairs for coffee. Dr. Barker was already up, preparing to row out. I insisted on coming along. When he found that John was resting quietly, he went back for breakfast."

He forced himself to look at her directly for the first time, and blinked in earnest. She was wearing dungarees much like his own and an Army shirt that had shrunk to a reasonable fit. He dared to glance at her ankles and saw that her legs and feet were as bare as his own. Only the gypsy bandanna in her dark hair advertised her sex at the moment.

"You needn't look shocked," she said. "Dr. Barker said it was a most appropriate costume for a skiff. Or for a day on Matecumbe Key. That's where we're going, isn't it—when you've had a look at your patient?"

"Are you a mind reader too?"

"Andy told me that much when we said good-by across the water." Her eyes, oddly intent despite her airy manner, held him close. "I must say it was rather a shock—having him sail out of my life so abruptly. Almost like being abandoned at the altar."

He felt his heart leap wildly at her matter-of-fact tone. Perhaps she doesn't care for Andy after all, he thought. Perhaps old Merrick has saved my life with his bullheaded order. . . . And then, as he took a step nearer, he saw the glint of tears in her eyes and turned away. Yearning with all his heart to comfort her, he felt the words choke in his throat.

"You may come if you like, of course. I'm afraid you'll find it rather dull. I'm only going to inspect the plantation."

"If I thought it'd be dull, I wouldn't be waiting here."

He turned away from the challenge and went straight to John's bed, blessing the professional manner that covered his feelings. Even before he could take the Negro's pulse he saw that no real examination was necessary. The heartbeat was strong and regular now; John's forehead was cool to the touch. Even the dressing, which Dr. Barker had evidently changed in the night, was normally pink—a sure sign that the sound flesh above the infection was knitting briskly.

"You're a first-rate surgeon, Dr. Coe."

He turned away from the compliment, keeping his voice gruff. "I learned in a hard school. Believe me, this was only a routine job. Sea air will be his best physician now."

"Does that mean it's safe to go—without waiting for Dr. Barker?"

He strode back to the gunwale and stepped down into the catboat, offering his hand without a backward glance. "Whenever you like, Mary."

Mary Grant stepped from ketch to catboat and settled beside him at the tiller, as though she had belonged there always. Setting his course by the tall cluster of palms at the western tip of Matecumbe, he did not dare to notice her presence directly. Even when he heard her warm chuckle and felt the familiar, teasing lash of her windblown hair against his cheek, he kept his eyes resolutely forward.

"Have I said something witty, by any chance?"

"So far, you haven't uttered," said Mary Grant. "I won't offer a penny for your thoughts—they're obviously not for publication. You might tell me why I must be on the water before I have the pleasure of your company."

"I'm sorry if I seem to avoid you," he said shortly. "Can you hold this tiller steady while I break out the jib?"

"Steady she is, sir."

He did not look back as he moved to the bowsprit, but the grip of his toes on the planking told him that Mary Grant was a born sailor too. Once the jib had filled, the prow lifted smartly in the tug of the wind. But their course was arrow-straight when he moved to the stern sheets again and took the tiller from her hand.

"Dead on that clump of palms, Skipper," she said.

"Right you are. Now we'll take the naval station on our starboard tack and enter Matecumbe Bay by the south channel."

He kept his whole mind on his course. The squat buildings on Tea Table Key seemed to rush to meet them. Long before the spout of waves on the reef warned him to put up his helm he could count the masts of the sloops at anchor. The long pier that jutted into the channel bustled with blue-coated marines. He could even pick out the commander of the station—a spare young lieutenant whose epaulets seemed to lift his heels from the planking like an eagle's wings. The stir of bright uniform coats was oddly comforting, though the naval station itself looked as forlorn as ever in that endless wash of sea.

Routine maneuvers, he thought, remembering how the regulars at Fort Everglades had labeled this station the Pelican Patrol. He toyed with the idea of putting in at the dock, introducing Mary to the lieutenant. Perhaps that lonely young martinet would consent to take her aboard his sloop and return her to Flamingo Key. . . . The craven impulse died. For today, at least, he would face her with his defenses down.

"When did you learn to sail, Mary?"

"At my father's estate on the Hudson. Quite unofficially, of course. He wouldn't have approved——"

"But you enjoy it just the same."

"Almost as much as swimming. I learned that one summer too. In the same river, between governesses. They are my only unladylike accomplishments."

"Except acting?"

"I'm not an actress, really. I'll admit I enjoy dressing up and declaiming. Joining the Avon Players was only an excuse to leave home for a while—and find Andy."

"I'm sorry you've lost him so soon."

"Prove it," she said. "Help me to forget I'm still unmarried. Show me how you live when you're—away from everything."

"I'm only crossing to Matecumbe to inspect Dr. Barker's plantation. You'll find it quite similar to those on the other island."

"Don't hold it against me if I want to escape my past," she said, "I'll be returning soon enough."

"You'd like to stay here longer?"

"Forever's the word, Roy."

He let the sigh go unanswered. Fortunately he needed all his skill to keep the little vessel afloat on the last short leg of their run—when the mangrove arms of Matecumbe seemed ready to engulf them and the ever-narrowing estuary, walled by the blue-black jungle, was a tunnel without ending, filled with the sigh of the tide. Then their bowsprit had found open water again. The blue plain of Florida Bay opened before them, dotted with mangrove clusters, flecked with the wings of cruising sea birds. Far to the north, the curve of Cape Sable smudged the sky line, as though some celestian artist, wearied by the haphazard pattern of keys and broken coral, had added a single steady brush stroke before he turned aside from his canvas.

"Is that the mainland?" asked Mary.

"Land's End," he said. "And God's greenest wilderness."

"Is Chekika there too?"

He looked at her in surprise. Somehow, he had not thought she would remember his lecture on the Seminole and his habits. "It's still his legal hunting ground."

"Then I suppose we've come far enough."

"Quite far enough," he said, and put the helm over. They grounded gently, the bowsprit spearing a cluster of sea grape that arched the surge of the tide. He handed Mary ashore gravely, without quite daring to meet her eyes. They stood side by side on the narrow strip of beach. Now that he had reached his journey's end, he felt an odd reluctance to move forward.

"The plantation's in the middle of the island, beyond that jungle screen," he said. "First put our dinner on the stove. Then we'll go exploring."

"Does your Eden seem spoiled now that Eve's invaded it?"

He realized that her hand was still tightly clutched in his and dropped it quickly. In another pulse beat he would have pulled her into his arms. Whʸ did a crazy demon, whispering deep in his brain, insist she would have come there willingly?

"On the contrary," he said. and marveled at the steadiness of his tone. "You ask how I live in the wilderness—I'll show you. But you must do your part if you expect to dine with me. You might begin by gathering driftwood among those mangrove roots. And keep a weather eye for snakes."

"Very good, Skipper," she said. "I'm still taking orders."

He watched her move lightly away among the tide-darkened boles of the mangroves, and ignored the familiar stab of pain at his heart. It was salvation to gather his own armload of wood and carry it to the rough coquina pit he had fashioned on a previous visit. He did not look up when she joined him with both arms loaded.

"Bring me all the Spanish moss you can carry, and soak it in the shallows."

Mary obeyed without words, as though they had built a hundred sand ovens together. Flat stones, spread in a layer across the fire, hissed in the rush of driftwood flame. He accepted the sea-soaked moss from his helper's arms and put it beside the roaring blaze, ready for use. Then, taking a grains from the boat, he beckoned her to his side again.

"Roll those pants legs high—I'll promise not to look. If I'm not mistaken, our dinner is waiting in the coral."

They waded side by side in the shallows, where the tortured arches of the mangrove roots twined with the coral outcrop; he sensed, rather than saw, the flash of her white limbs in the clear water, knew that she was waiting breathlessly for his next move. It came, with no conscious message from his brain, when a shadow stirred in a nest of sea-washed roots. The grains thrust downward, exploding a mighty whorl of sand, and lifted high with a three-pound crayfish speared neatly in the tines.

"Bring that crokersack from the boat, and I'll take him ashore. You can try the next one yourself."

He dared to watch her as he bent above the gunwale to toss his prize aboard. She had rolled both trouser legs well above her thighs. Now her whole body was arched in a breath-taking curve as the tines pinned another crayfish to the bottom. He rushed to help her before the giant crustacean could tear the pole from her hands. Together they fought to extricate him from the tangle of roots that had been his home.

"Eve herself couldn't have learned faster," he said. "He's far bigger than mine."

"Let me try again. I'll manage the next one on my own."

She proved her statement several times over in the next half-hour. Two crokersacks now bulged with quarreling key lobsters; Mary surrendered the spear with reluctance as Roy brought two of the largest crayfish to the fire pit.

"These are more than we can eat. The rest go to Dr. Barker's turtle crawl."

They had timed their return well. The pit was now a mass of glowing coals, and the stones that lined its rim were almost as hot. The moss steamed mightily as he tossed it evenly across the fire. Tight-packed under that protective layer, the two crayfish were weighed down with the red-hot stones, covered with still another layer of moss, and bedded over with a final layer of sand. Roy raked the oven smooth, punctured the sand here and there to let the savory steam gush forth, and stepped back briskly.

"Give our stove an hour and a half—and Madame will be served royally."

"Can we see the nursery now—and can I stay as I am?"

The business of stalking the crayfish had given him an excuse to keep his eyes to himself. Once again he dared to look at her in earnest; in the tight-rolled dungarees, with her hair knotted in a kerchief, she could have passed for a boy—until one noted the fullness of the breasts that strained at the half-buttoned shirt. He knew there was no hint of coquetry in her request. So far they had shared this outing completely. He could hardly ask her to go back to primness now.

"It's quite safe, if you stay close beside me," he said. "The path's wide enough."

They walked through the mangroves together in an oddly contented silence. The plantation was a long rectangle of ground along the spine of the key. Heat brooded here like a visible presence; protected as it was by the dense wall of jungle, the deep, rich soil seemed to burst into spontaneous growth. Even Roy, knowing what loving care the botanist had lavished here, could not believe that this tropic garden was the work of hands and human brain. Among the dusky leaves of the orange trees, the fruit massed like galaxies of suns in miniature. Lemons and limes grew in profusion, as did the tamarind and the broad-leafed sisal. Even the pimentos, tomatoes, and okra in the truck garden might have risen naturally, there in the shadow of the grapes that had, in reality, sprung from cuttings made in Burgundy. . . . Roy found that he was laughing aloud as Mary darted from his side to cup a burst of purple bougainvillaea bloom between her palms.

"Sorry, but there's no fragrance in those blossoms. Even Eden must have a flaw."

"It's too beautiful to take in all at once. Especially in this setting. It's like walking through a plot of rank weeds and stumbling on an orchid. Or, better yet, a rose in full bloom. Will all Florida be like this someday?"

"Not *all* of it, Mary. No soil is rich enough for that. But the Glades can produce all this, and more."

Mary broke off a spray of the bougainvillaea and thrust it in her bosom. "Scentless or not, I'm wearing this awhile. It'll help me to remember you when I'm in the frozen North."

They moved from tree to tree in the groves while Roy described each fruit in detail. Many of the saplings had grown from Mexican seed. The tough-fibered sisal, which Dr. Barker had brought from Yucatan, might someday form the basis of a new industry in the South—the manufacture of hemp. As for the bursts of poinsettia, the silky green of the pepper trees, the flaming hibiscus—these, said Roy, were the doctor's contribution to nature's own flower painting.

"A hundred years from now the poinsettia may be a synonym for Florida," he said.

"Let's hope America remembers the man who brought it here."

"He deserves to be remembered—far more than the man he named it after."

Mary had loaded her arms with specimens of each bloom; Roy's clasp knife had slashed cuttings from all the trees as he pruned expertly here and there. Now, adding a cluster of poinsettia to her burden, he put aside the manner of the guide as he watched her dance happily on. It's this sun she'll remember, he told himself, and this green, sea-washed stillness. Never the hapless fool who brought her here.

"Come back to the beach, Mary. It's time we dined."

"Can't we stay in Eden a little longer?"

"Not another moment. The poinsettia will keep. Our key lobsters won't."

The two crayfish were bright red when he raked aside the last of the brine-soaked Spanish moss. Mouth-watering steam arose from the cracks in their hard armor as he separated a claw from a body, broke it neatly on a wedge of coral rock, and offered the white meat to Mary on an improvised palmetto-leaf platter. "Let it steam awhile, I'll fetch salt and wine from the boat."

In addition to the fragrant lobster meat, there were tomatoes and chopped peppers from Dr. Barker's garden, and a slab of fresh butter melted over the coals. The wine, a fine *rioja alta* from the doctor's cellar, had been cooled for an hour in the sea and tasted none the worse in tin cups washed in the same lazy wave. They ate with their fingers, smiling over the wine like friends. Roy felt his head reel a little when he poured from the second bottle. He would never know if it was her nearness or the medley of sun and wine. Now that the long day seemed to stretch before them forever, he cared less.

"Can't you tell me about it now, Roy?"

"What would you like to know?"

"Why you came here. I can understand why you linger. I'd like to stay with you till judgment day. But you don't belong in this wilderness any more than I."

"That's true enough." He poured more wine and knew his hands were trembling. I must tell her everything, he thought. I can't torture myself any longer. Even if she hates me afterward.

"You know I came to see Andy," she said. "Don't tell me you had no better reason."

"Oddly enough, I *did* follow Andy here. But I was only a shorn sheep at the time—and Andy was my bellwether. Any other pasture would have done as nicely."

"A shorn sheep," she murmured. "Somehow I can't picture you shivering in a blizzard."

"It's true enough. When I first set foot in Florida I was a broken man. What's more, I had no real wish to mend."

"What was her name, Roy?"

"Irene," he said, and his voice was only a hoarse whisper. "Irene Boucher."

"Someone you met in Paris?"

"Someone I met in Paris. When I was finishing my surgery at the Hôtel Dieu. For almost a year we were—everything to each other."

"How did she break you?"

"I'd asked her to marry me," he said. "I wanted to take her back to Boston with me. The next day I came for her answer, and found she'd killed herself. She left a note explaining her action." He had kept his voice hard with a great effort. It broke in earnest as he forced himself to go on. "Just six words: *'I want to spare you that.'* "

"Are you telling me she was—unworthy of marriage?"

"She was a *cocotte*," he said. "D'you know enough French to grasp my meaning?"

"I understand, Roy."

"A *grande cocotte*," he said. "She'd been the mistress of some of the greatest men in Europe. We met at a masked ball. At the Quartz' Arts. We'd been—lovers for some time before I found—just what she'd been before. Her current protector was a colonel on Louis Philippe's staff. He tracked us down and challenged me. I put a bullet through his shoulder and kept her. For one crazy year. The strange thing was, I didn't mind in the slightest—what she'd been. It was enough just to be near her."

"I can understand that too."

How can you understand? he raged silently. How can a girl like you forgive my madness? At least I've told you all I can. The cold facts, leaving the music out. The shared rapture of spring midnights, the joined heartbeats in the dark. And the thirst for life that died with her—until you wakened it again. . . . He said none of this, feeling the kindness in her eyes, the cool touch of her fingers at his wrist. Aloud he said only, "It was nearly seven years ago. I was younger then. Young enough to think that I'd never love again."

"You'll outgrow that in time."

"I've outgrown it now," he said, and his eyes held hers for a long moment.

"She was wiser than you," said Mary at last.

"Far wiser. But she had no right to die for me."

"You can be young just once—and in Paris. She gave you that. *You* gave her something she'd never known. Can't you see now that it was a good bargain?"

"Not with death as a seal."

"Perhaps she'd had too much of life."

"I learned later that her doctors had given her less than a year to live. That knowledge helped a little." He got up from the fire and kicked sand on the dying coals. "At least you've learned why I preferred the Glades to civilization."

"Has it helped you, really?"

"It's helped a great deal. Even if you despise me—I won't mind too much."

"I don't despise you at all. Why should I? You were a student in Paris—and you fell in love with your mistress. What could be more logical? *C'est de votre âge.*" Again she bent forward and touched his wrist lightly. "You see, I speak French too. That's one of my ladylike talents."

"Andy's a lucky man," he said. "I should have mentioned that before."

"Didn't you think I'd sympathize?"

"I had no idea how you'd react. But I felt I must tell you the whole story. Don't ask me why."

"I know why," she said. "We've been friends from the start—no matter how hard you fought against it." And then, as his eyes continued to burn her, Mary colored deeply and rose from the fire to cross the beach and settle on a coral outcrop.

He did not follow her at once. Instead he made a great show of tidying the fire before he carried their utensils back to the boat. When he joined her at last, she was staring into a pool that the tide had hollowed at the very edge of the sea—a natural coral basin where a school of sergeant majors, banded in yellow and black, played like living sunlight.

"Friends, Mary," he said. "Come what may."

"Even if you never see me again after tomorrow?"

"Even so," he said. "I'll remember it was you who brought me back to life. Can you find a better definition for friendship?"

"Shall we be friends together and walk around our island one more time? Or is it too late for that?"

He glanced at the sun, estimating what daylight remained. "I think we can chance it."

She put her hand in his, and he lifted her to her feet. Once again he knew that he could draw her into his arms simply by taking one short step—and once again he put down temptation with a mighty effort. Friendship, he thought, is a poor word to drown the flame that burns between us now. . . . As he dropped her hand at last, he wondered if Mary herself had any real desire to keep the flame in bounds.

xi

They came upon the canoe track without warning when they rounded the last sandspit that curved into the expanse of bay between the two keys. He had been talking fast against his growing malaise, his eyes fixed on the horizon. Mary's quiet voice beside him had seemed oddly remote, as though she, too, had withdrawn prudently to a world of her own. . . . The rough hollow in the sand (so like the track of a wallowing 'gator) shocked him back to awareness of time and place. The fists that closed on Mary's shoulder, forcing her to the cover of a slump of Spanish bayonet, had moved by instinct. So did the hand that clamped across her lips, stifling her gasp of protest.

Then, as his eyes roved on, he saw that the small campfire just beyond was quite cold. The trace that moved into the brush was barely visible. His trained eyes saw that the twigs had been broken hours ago. Like the canoe track itself, the whole scene told its own story—a lone visitor who had spent the night in this snug encampment and departed with the first light of day.

"Of course there may be others."

He realized that he had spoken the thought aloud and let his fist ease its pressure on Mary's shoulder. His voice was dead-calm. He had learned to drive fear deep in his brain, to think with his senses alone.

"Stay where you are. I must check that trace in the underbrush."

"I'm coming with you, Roy."

"Don't be afraid, please. Whoever was here has gone long ago——"

"Are you sure it was an Indian?"

"It's not unlikely. Certainly that's the mark of a dugout canoe. And those sticks were fed into the campfire Indian-fashion. Probably it was a plume hunter on his way north." He forced a confidence he did not feel, and shielded her body with his own as he moved from beach to jungle hammock.

All too vividly he remembered the swish of the ax that had missed his head by inches in the shadow of Dan Evans's warehouse.

There was no sign of life in the hammock proper. The trace ended abruptly in the shade of a tall live oak on the island's spine. Raking the terrain with practiced eyes, he saw that there was no real cover. The sun-shot glade was utterly still; the sigh of the wind in the branches was the only sound. He came back to Mary as her fingers touched his arm.

"Maybe it was a woman camper, Roy. If you can imagine a woman forgetting her mirror."

He turned to follow her gesture and bent to pick up the broken glass from the mat of dead moss beneath the oak. Mary paralleled the gesture, recovering another shard of mirror. He moved into the shadow of the moss-laden boughs, letting his fingers explore the bark of the trunk. For the first time he noted the immense size of the tree—and the small lacerations in the great rising column of the bole.

"Someone was climbing here not too long ago."

Obeying a sudden impulse, he pocketed the broken mirror, set his heel in the precise spot the other climber had used for purchase, and hoisted himself to the first crotch of the oak. From here it was a simple matter to ascend monkey-fashion into the leafy heart of the tree.

"Don't move, Mary! I'll be down directly."

Already he was clear of the screen of vegetation, with the tufted heads of the coco palms far below. One crotch higher, and he could see the whole circle of the horizon, with Flamingo Key nested in the blinding cobalt of the sea a scant half mile to the south. He felt the trunk sway beneath his weight and dared to climb still higher, until he was anchored in the very summit of the oak—the apex of a leafy pyramid streaming its pennons of moss in the fresh sea breeze.

Thanks to that same crystal air, Flamingo Key seemed incredibly near. He could almost read the lettering on Dan's hotel and count the pelicans that squatted like lazy sentinels on each piling of Dan's wharf. Dr. Barker's house, half hidden by its windbreak, gleamed whitely through the wind-tossed fronds of the pines. He saw the flash of an ax as a slave worked over a broken fence in the banyan patch. . . . Crouched like a spy in his green ambush, he let the mirror slide into his hand. Without conscious thought he turned the glass toward the sun until it picked up a ray of light—and splintered it, like an arrow, against a window in the trader's store.

He did not repeat the signal—if signal it was. Instead he descended slowly from his perch and offered Mary a reassuring smile before he joined her on the ground.

"We can go home when you like. We're quite alone on the island."

Watching her narrowly as they retraced their steps, he sensed her reassurance without daring to say more. He was still too puzzled to put his doubts into words. Obviously someone had used the broken mirror to signal across the strip of water that separated Flamingo and Matecumbe keys. But there was no way of knowing if the signaler and his attacker the night before were one. Perhaps it *was* only a stray plume hunter, he thought. Perhaps this signal is routine. It was common knowledge that Dan dealt in every sort of contraband, from stolen egret feathers to slaves. A bit of Indian sign among the palms of Matecumbe was not positive proof that Dan was a traitor as well.

"Was it a woman, Roy?"

Again he came back to Mary with a start, and forced a smile as he handed her into the boat. "This was a male, I'm afraid. Indians use mirrors for ornaments; they've always been a trading staple——"

"What was he doing in the tree?"

"Watching his chance to slip across the water and do business with Dan. I've seen them often in the storeroom—trading their pelts for salt and calico." He forced another smile. "Stray Seminoles aren't too popular with the Navy these days. It's almost impossible to cross that strip of water without being seen from the station."

Mary settled in the stern sheets. The shadows were lengthening over the bay when he spread his sail to catch the last of the afternoon wind. Try as he might, he could feel no real threat in the mangrove wall astern—and no trace of fear in the girl beside him. After all, he told himself firmly, I've stumbled on Indian camps among these keys a dozen times. . . . And yet a sixth sense that he obeyed without question made him cut sharply into his first tack and set a course for the wharf on Tea Table Key.

"You've met the Army, Mary. Would you like to visit the Navy as well, before you go north?"

Mary Grant folded her long salt-wet legs under her and shook her head. "Would I pass inspection in this?"

"Perhaps you wouldn't," he said soberly. "I'd forgotten that we just put Eden behind us. And please forgive the bit of melodrama at the end. I'm afraid I was acting by instinct——"

"I enjoyed the ending most of all," she said. "At least I can tell my New York friends that I've seen an Indian camp on the keys. To say nothing of my escape in the stagecoach."

He noted the change in her tone without comment. In another hour, he thought grimly, you'll be safe at Dr. Barker's. In a week this strange sun-bright day will seem as remote as a dream. An adventure to laugh at over the tea-cups in your father's mansion—along with that brief nightmare in the stagecoach. To say nothing of the swamp rat who was a doctor once—and proved so amusing a companion while you awaited your transport home. . . . He dismissed the last thought as unworthy even of his present mood. Come what may, he thought, I'll never regret opening my heart there on the beach at Matecumbe.

"Stay behind the sail," he said. "I want a word with the officer in charge."

The sloop luffed in the shadow of the Navy pier and rested gently against the stringpiece. Roy looped his painter and climbed to the sun-weathered planks. At first glance the small roadstead seemed as empty as the moon, save for the gun barge moored against the powder shed across the harbor and a pair of beached catboats in the lee of the breakwater. Then he heard the sleepy clatter of boot heels and accepted the salute of the officer of the day—a midshipman with boredom like a tangible weight on his brand-new epaulets.

"Good evening, Mr. West. Why aren't you at sea?"

"Lieutenant Pinckney's orders, Doctor," said the midshipman cheerfully. "He wanted company."

"Don't tell me you two are alone here."

"I'm afraid so. Can we be of service?"

"Where's your flotilla?"

"Gone north since early morning to check a smuggler at Largo." The midshipman stiffened. "You'll understand, Doctor, that such information's off the record."

Remembering the bustle of activity at the pier, Roy stiffened in turn. Apparently that brave show of uniforms had not been a routine maneuver, after all.

"Where are your marines?"

"Half the company's aboard. The rest have gone seining." Again the brave new epaulets snapped to attention, though the ghost of a grin hovered about the young mouth of Mr. West. "We had another report that mullet were running at Lady Key."

So Tea Table Key had been virtually unguarded since noon. Remembering what he had found among the mangroves a mere half mile to the north, Roy damned the Pelican Patrol with all his heart. In the same breath he forgave their apparent laxity. Months of idleness, with no visible enemy in view, had plunged the station into an abyss of laziness, as natural as it was inevitable. He could hardly blame the patrol for seizing upon the first rumor and plunging south under full canvas.

"When will your fishermen return?"

"At sunset, Doctor. You can see 'em now if you'll just step over the sandspit. They went out to Lady Key on foot; they'll wade back, now the tide's rising."

"If you don't mind, I'll talk first to the lieutenant."

"Step right in, Doctor. You're always welcome."

Roy walked into the commandant's quarters with a set jaw, ignoring the irony of Midshipman West's salute. The squat coquina cottage roosted precariously at the water's edge. Within, the snores of Lieutenant James Pinckney (Annapolis 1839) were part of the afternoon heat. So was the bareness of his whitewashed office, the sough of tide in the pilings that counterpointed the lieutenant's ecstatic repose.

Pinckney's immaculate boots hit the floor instantly as his torpid brain detected the strange step on the doorsill. Roy could not suppress a smile when he saw that the lieutenant was as naked as a jay bird save for those resplendent boots. The lieutenant's still unsullied uniform swayed gently on a clotheshorse in the armoire, as though the commandant of Tea Table Key had just been hanged in effigy.

"Sit down, Doctor—and have a drink. It's time for a sundowner." Pinckney was trying hard to seem wide awake, though it was impossible to strut in his present costume. "I hope this is a friendly visit."

"Extremely, Lieutenant. Perhaps it's just as well I'm on your side. D'you realize I could have tomahawked you just now—and no one would be the wiser?"

Pinckney rubbed his eyes with a sudden boyish grin. "Don't tell me that Mr. West is sleeping too?"

"Mr. West could have been surprised just as easily. May I ask just what's become of your squadron?"

"We are tracking down a rumor, Doctor. A persistent report I could hardly ignore. Since we're friends, I might say it's rather serious."

"May I ask the charge?"

"Gunrunning, sir. From Havana and the Bahamas. I'm informed the rendezvous point is Key Largo."

"Who is your informant?"

"A most reliable observer—Dan Evans."

So Dan had hoodwinked this stripling commander for reasons of his own. Roy let another piece fall into place in an incomplete puzzle, and kept his bland mask intact.

"You expect to surprise these smugglers in broad daylight?"

"By no means. With luck, we may uncover their lair. And enough evidence to lodge a protest in both London and Madrid."

"May I ask when your squadron will return?"

Lieutenant Pinckney spread his hands and smiled tolerantly. The age-old smile that commanders reserve for the layman. "Who can say? Perhaps tomorrow, if it's a wild-goose chase. If there is an enemy at Key Largo and he shows fight, this may develop into a major action. That's why I committed the entire naval personnel and most of our marines."

Roy matched the lieutenant's civility with an effort. "You wanted to lead the expedition, I'm sure."

"Unfortunately this is a command post for the district. I was forced to remain and await reports."

"You realize, of course, that this area is undefended at present?"

"I realize nothing of the kind, sir. I've four whole squads of marines and ample ordnance."

"What of Flamingo Key?"

"Flamingo Key is under the wing of the Navy, Doctor. Who'd dare molest it while I am here?"

Roy glanced through the half-open window at the strip of

blue that separated them from Dr. Barker's domain. Lieutenant Pinckney did not miss the unspoken criticism.

"Are you suggesting that Flamingo Key might be invaded?"

"You'll admit it's possible."

"I repeat, sir—no one would dare."

"Chekika might."

"Chekika is pinned down to the Glades. His containment is an Army matter."

"The Navy must do its share at this end. I won't remind you that the Glades are a river flowing into this very bay."

"You needn't instruct me in geography, Doctor."

"I would never so presume. But I am appealing to you to safeguard a colleague—who is also a close friend of our Secretary of War."

"Do you imply that I'm derelict in that—obligation?"

"I imply nothing, sir. But I am suggesting that you patch up at least one of those broken-bottom sloops on your breakwater and send twenty marine muskets to Flamingo Key tonight. Before moonrise."

The slender commander drew himself up to his full height —a scant five feet seven, including boot heels. Thanks to his sweat-glistening nudity, he resembled nothing so much as a bantam rooster whose barnyard reign has just been challenged.

"I don't notice that you wear a naval uniform, Doctor."

"Nor do you, at the moment."

"Your servant, sir! Will you leave the Navy's affairs to the Navy?"

"Gladly, Pinckney. May I wish you luck—and hope you won't need it?"

He strode from the commandant's quarters with the last word, and kept his rage firmly bottled as he went down the pier again and cast off his painter. Mary was already at the tiller. He left her there and settled cross-legged on the foredeck, admiring her skill with the mainsail. The sloop ghosted from channel to bay, nursing what was left of the dying breeze.

"Did you enjoy your visit with the Navy?"

"No more than usual," he said dourly.

Somehow, he could not bring himself to confess his fears even now. Already those fears had begun to seem a trifle ridiculous—with the harbor of Flamingo Key opening under their bowsprit. A dozen small craft rode at moorings before Dan's hotel. In the nearly windless air supper smoke curled above the shacks along the shore. Behind its windbreak of fleecy pines Dr. Barker's white mansion seemed as foursquare as time. . . . After all, he reminded himself, the botanist is Chekika's oldest friend. So (for far different reasons) is that rascal, Dan Evans. Perhaps I deserved that cockerel's dressing-down, after all.

"Something is troubling you, Roy. Are you afraid we said too much on the island today?"

He dropped over the gunwale and settled beside her. Even if we must talk on that topic, he thought, it's less dangerous than the probable whereabouts of Chekika.

"I've told you how grateful I was, Mary. You've been a first-rate listener."

"I'm still listening, Roy."

"When you know everything?"

"Your past is behind you now. What of your future?"

It's quite true, he thought, letting her set the course for the bell buoy. I've broken with my past; the ghost of Irene Boucher is firmly banished. My future is my own, to do with as I like. At the moment, save for the possibility that we may all be dead by morning, it has never looked emptier.

"I've told you about my future," he said. "Dr. Barker wants me here permanently when the war is over. Between us we'll build our Eden. I'll promise you that."

"With or without Eve?"

"Probably without. The good doctor's too old to marry again. As for myself"—Roy spread his hands, a gesture that took in the whole horizon—"I'll be content with what I've found here. It's one thing to live down your first love. It's a bit hard to find another."

"She'll turn up, Roy. Just give her time."

He sat taut at her side, knowing his voice would break if he said another word. Mary put the helm over. The trim little vessel, standing daintily on one ear, ran past the lazy clang of the bell buoy and gained the harbor at last—a dove-gray sweep of water, clear as glass in the dying day. The latticed windows of Dr. Barker's house smiled their own welcome. It's like a home-coming, he thought—the only home-coming we'll ever know.

"When does the Havana packet stop here?"

He spoke without turning, and wondered if she had divined his thoughts. "Tomorrow, if it's on time from Augustine. Surely the day after."

"Suppose it's late? Could we sail again tomorrow?"

"If you like."

"How often must I say this has been the kind of day I've always wanted? Surely you can't blame me for wanting another?"

She had spoken simply, as always. He did not stir when her hand darted across the tiller to press his warmly.

"Andy will bring you back to Biscayne in time," he said. "You'll have your fill of Florida."

"Don't you see? It won't be the same when it's *safe*. When I can sail my own catboat up the Miami, without meeting a single Indian——"

"Or a swamp rat you could mistake for one?"

"You'll have your own paradise by then. And your Eve. I hope you'll find her less capricious than I."

The sloop glided toward her berth, the covered pier that flanked the turtle crawl. He went forward to drop the sail. Like a homing gull, the little vessel slipped into her haven, shuddered faintly as the bowsprit ground against the landing stage, then swung easily as Roy made the last line fast. He stepped to the rough cypress planking, conscious of the quiet half-light that enclosed them, of the protecting walls of the shed, a barrier to prying eyes.

"Up you come, Mary! We're home again."

Mary sat unstirring, her hand still on the idly swinging tiller. "I don't want to come home," she said. "Not today, at any rate. I want today to last."

"Up you come, just the same."

"I want to go sailing forever on that blue water," she said. "I want to spear lobster on Matecumbe Key and watch you hunt for Indian sign. Most of all, I want to forget that I'll be putting on my best gray satin in just two weeks' time and paying calls on my aunts in Washington Square. If that makes me a hussy," she said, and her chin lifted proudly as she spoke, "make the most of it."

"Up you come, Mary!"

Their hands joined with his words. Mary rose from the stern sheets, lifting in a single, fluent motion from sloop to landing stage. With that same easy grace she came into his arms. Much later, when his head had cleared, he would remember that it was she who had claimed his lips in that long, heart-bursting moment.

When she spoke at last, her voice seemed to come from a distance, though she was still crushed in his embrace. "That was for today, Roy. For the most wonderful day I'll ever have."

He lifted her chin in his cupped hand and kissed her, gently but firmly. "That's for tomorrow, Mary. Be happy. You deserve happiness. You deserve all that Andy can give you." He dropped his arms and stepped aside resolutely, letting her precede him to the boathouse door and down the pergola-shaded path that led from dock to veranda. That was goodby as well, he added silently. That was regret for all those tomorrows we'll never share. . . .

Mary paused on the veranda step, in a frame of wisteria leaves. Even now he could observe how much she resembled a boy in those high-rolled dungarees. A rather impish boy who had dared to play truant and enjoyed it thoroughly.

"Where can we sail tomorrow? Could we go south this time?"

"I'm afraid I'll be busy tomorrow," he said, and stepped to the veranda beside her, holding her with his eyes.

"At the plantations? I'd love to help."

"I'm afraid this is work I must do alone."

"You're avoiding me again," she cried.

"Of course I'm avoiding you, Mary. You must know why now."

Her eyes did not waver, and her lips were laughing as she spoke again—this time in a true conspirator's whisper. "Would you like to take back that kiss? *I* wouldn't——"

"Good day, Miss Grant. May I wish you a pleasant journey home?"

He was gone with the words, without quite daring to meet her eyes again. Her laughter pursued him long after he had plunged into the sanctuary of the Shipwreck Bar. He knew that the echo would linger until he ceased to draw breath. Nor did he begrudge her that laughter, when he knew that her own heart was innocent. Hers, after all, had been only a kiss of comradeship.

xii

He had dined on turtle steak and yams with a pair of boat-
men from Havana, arguing the Indian war and pressing rum
on his new-found friends until they boarded their freight
scow and slipped south with the first show of moonlight.
Later he had argued the same subject with Dan Evans himself, until the trader had swept the last beachcomber through
his door and closed his shutters. . . . Now, as he walked into
the bath of moonlight at the corner of Dr. Barker's lime
grove, he admitted that no amount of rum would stop the
throbbing of his brain or yield the oblivion of sleep.

The square white house was shuttered against the moist
night air. A glance at Mary's lattice told him that she was
sleeping soundly. Somehow, he could not go beyond the solid
coral block that served as a step-up to the veranda. His own
bed was waiting on the Bahama balcony that ringed the
upper story; sleep might find him, after all, once the ham-
mering behind his eyes had ceased. But he knew it was safer
here—even though he sat in the shade of that wisteria till
dawn. Far safer to keep an extra door between him and
Mary Grant—even though she slept with a duenna at her
elbow.

He took out the corncob pipe he had smoked at a hundred
campfires, tamped down the shaggy Cuban tobacco, and
struck one of his lucifers. The match seemed to spurt in the
darkness like a volcano in miniature. . . . Perhaps he should
waken Dr. Barker, after all, and report on the discoveries he
had made at Matecumbe. He dismissed the idea at once as
another desperate fumble to avoid his own company in a
sleepless night. He had no right to disturb the botanist's repose with unfounded fears.

From where he sat he could see the whole expanse of harbor and count each anchor buoy in that lake of moonlight.
He was not disturbed to note that the last of the coastal vessels had slipped out during the long evening. Navigating as
they did by rule of thumb (and remembering each reef by instinct) these fisherfolk that plied between Dan's dock and
Key West were accustomed to sailing by moonlight—and
into the cool of the dawn. He did not even stir when a final
sail moved lazily into view from the direction of the trader's

boat shed and he recognized the silhouette of the *Estrella,* the flagship of Dan's coastal fleet.

The vessel, a tall-masted catboat with a special flying jib, glided past the turtle crawl with its nose pointed for open water. He recognized Dan himself at the tiller, and saw that the trader's dusky wife was dragging a mattress from cockpit to foredeck. At another time the sight would have stirred his suspicions. Now, in this state of suspended thought (when he was, in fact, striving not to think at all), he could hardly focus his mind on a fresh doubt. Dan and White Heron will sleep at a buoy tonight, he told himself. He had done the same thing often when it was hot ashore.

When the catboat vanished around the point he knocked out his pipe and strolled down to the turtle crawl. Even the loggerheads seemed restless in the heat; he could hear their shells scraping under his feet as he walked to the end of the covered dock and stepped down to the wide landing stage. Here the water shoaled away to a rich midnight blue. In the prodigal wash of moonlight the open sea beyond seemed as quiet as a lake. He could pick out the masts of the ketch where his patient was spending another night of convalescence in the shelter of the southern reef. It was a good mile from shore, he knew, but a sudden impulse made him strip off his shirt and kick both boots up to the dock above. Thanks to the moonlight on that sandy ocean floor, no sharks would venture inside the reef tonight. . . .The swim will tire me, he told himself firmly. Perhaps I'll find sleep waiting aboard the ketch.

Then, as he stood irresolute in the shadow of the turtle crawl, his whole body stiffened. Bemused as he was, he had not heard the faint sound of footsteps on the veranda he had just quitted. But there was no avoiding the long pencil of light that fell across the water, moved closer as the hand holding the lamp lifted higher, then vanished abruptly as the wick was turned down. Someone had emerged from the house, using the lamp on the hall table as a guide, until the moonlight made artificial light needless. Someone who had already begun to wade into the shallows along the edge of the covered dock.

Without knowing why, he held his breath and made himself small between pilings and stringpiece. Even before she waded into view he knew that this was Mary. Her dark hair,

streaming free almost to her waist, was her only covering;
evidently she had removed the peignoir that hung from one
arm when she moved from beach to water. Seeing that the
sands were deserted and all of Flamingo Key asleep, she had
come here for a last swim—alone.

He tried to call before she could come nearer, but his
throat was too tight for sound. He tried to look away, but his
eyes were riveted to her slender body, white as marble under
that canopy of hair, warm as the moonlight that poured like
rapture about her. She was already at the dock's end, waist-
deep in the harbor. When she tossed her peignoir over the
stringpiece he could have touched her without stirring from
his hiding place. For an instant more she paused there on the
brink of deep water, arms lifted to twist her hair into a knot;
her full, richly pointed breasts lifted with the motion like two
chalices of alabaster.

Roy leaned out from his hiding place; his breath escaped
in a soundless cry. At that moment Mary dived deep, without
a backward glance. Standing where he was on the stringpiece,
with his bare feet still tangled in her peignoir, he could follow the course of her body as she swam ever deeper, until
she coasted gently along the tide-ribbed floor of the harbor.
Thanks to the brilliant moonlight, she floated in an element
purer than air and almost as transparent. . . . Then, with a
sharp upward flailing of slender legs, she darted for the surface. Her head broke into the air in a swirl of phosphorescent
bubbles, and she began to swim seaward with long, firm
strokes.

He cupped his hands to warn her away from the coral at
the harbor mouth; more than once he had watched the great
moray eels sport there by moonlight, to say nothing of a
shark that refused to be frightened by its shadow. But he
knew that he must keep silent even now; Mary could hardly
forgive him if she discovered that he had lurked here like
some Peeping Tom, drinking his fill of her loveliness. Instead
he hoisted himself to the dock and ran at top speed for the
point, pausing to snatch a grains from the first canoe he
passed. Now, at least, he could pretend to be spearing fish by
moonlight—far down the shore line, where the point spindled
away to sand bar and open sea. He would be near enough to
shout a warning (and distant enough for decency) if Mary
dared to swim too near the reef.

Keeping to the shadows of the coco palms (and praying she would turn back in time), he waited for her to pass the point. Mary was a strong swimmer—that much was evident. Already she had passed the last of the harbor buoys; the silver-gold track that marked her progress stretched like a long, dim arrow pointed toward the horizon's rim. She's swimming toward Matecumbe, he thought, and felt a strange stab at his heart. She's gone adventuring alone, this moon-mad night, to find the dream we dared to live together. . . . The fantasy was nonsense, he knew; he could hardly permit Mary Grant to swim much farther alone. Even if he plunged into the harbor now and put forth all his strength, he could not hope to overtake her before she reached the break in the reef.

His heart turned over when he saw those long, clean strokes stop abruptly, as though Mary had turned to stone, far out in the harbor. He heard her scream—faint and incredibly forlorn across that wide moon mirror. He watched her plunge from view, and for a breathless interval thought she would never break surface again. Then her head bobbed into view inside the protective arm of the point. She was swimming in earnest now, as though some monster of the deep were only a stroke behind.

He was neck-deep in sea, with no memory of coming this far, shouting her name as he scrambled to a coral outcrop well offshore and waving his arms wildly. He saw that she had recognized both his voice and his silhouette, though she did not alter her course. "What is it, Mary?"

This time she paused and pointed back toward the open sea, as though unaware that his view was blocked by the long palm-studded claw of the point. "Swim straight for the dock," he shouted. "I'll join you there." Frightened as she was, he could not ask her to waste breath now.

She was still a good hundred yards from the pier's end when he floundered from the water and scrambled up the bank to dry land. As he raced down the planking above the turtle crawl he realized, too late, that his Venus must rise from the deep as naked as the lady of legend. While he waited, he picked up the peignoir and spread it grimly, ready to engulf its owner. His eyes roved the harbor's mouth, but the sea was still as empty as the moon it reflected so brilliantly.

"Swarm over the stringpiece," he directed. "I won't look."

Apparently she was too breathless to speak while she climbed to the dock. Despite his high resolve, he had one brief, heart-stopping glimpse of white limbs and breast before she rushed into his arms, oblivious of the vastness of the wrapper that engulfed her, yearning into the haven of his embrace as though she could never let him go.

"Thank God it was *you,* Roy. It might have been any-one——"

"Tell me what happened—quickly!"

"Indians," she gasped. "Indians by the hundred. The whole sea is black with them——"

"Do you know what you're saying?"

"I know what I saw," she cried, and her voice was near hysteria. "From Matecumbe. From the beach where we saw that canoe track I counted twenty of those same canoes before I turned back. Spread out in a big half-circle—on the oceanside——"

She broke into a wordless sobbing there in his tight embrace. His mind raced forward as the last of the puzzle fell in place. Chekika's scout had come ashore last night on this same beach. The same observer had watched from the live oak on Matecumbe while he signaled to a confederate across the channel. Now that the Navy was hunting a non-existent enemy far to the south, the Seminoles had moved from the mainland in force.

His fists closed on Mary's shoulders, hard enough to shake her free of her sobbing.

"Get to the house and warn Dr. Barker. His slaves sleep with muskets at their bedside. They'll know what to do."

"Come with me, Roy. I'm afraid to move."

"Do as I say," he ordered roughly. "And do it now. There isn't a moment to waste."

As he spoke he dropped his hands from her shoulders and snatched at her wrist. Running with her along the oystershell path that snaked through the clotted shadows of the gardens, he began to plan his next move, feeling the familiar calm that enveloped him at such moments. If Mary Grant had not been there, staggering at his side like a frightened child, he would have shouted aloud for the joy of released nerves.

"Go straight to Dr. Barker," he said, and pushed her up the veranda steps. "Take his orders and keep under cover. I'll be with you soon enough."

"Where are you going now, Roy?"

"To rouse the island. There's a warning bell on Dan's porch—if it hasn't rusted through."

He pressed her hand just once as he left her on the steps. Turning in the shadow of the windbreak, he saw that she had already half run, half stumbled through the doorway.

Years of neglect had not improved the timbre on the big ship's bell that stood before the hotel entrance. The clapper had rusted tight against the bell itself; the metal gave forth no more than an echo of its former resonance when he hammered it with both fists. His thundering knock on the hotel door brought no response. Remembering that Dan and his half-breed wife had gone aboard the catboat, he rushed to the trader's dock to shout a warning. Dan's voice boomed across the water before he could even cup his hands.

"Did you see 'em too?"

"How many, Dan?"

"Thirty canoes, more or less. War bonnets in some. I'm heading for Table Key to warn the Navy."

"The Navy's gone!"

The rattle of a rising gaff drowned Roy's shout. He saw that the catboat, already under full sail, was ghosting for the channel—a crafty maneuver that would carry it behind Dr. Barker's windbreak long before the first of the enemy could round the point. Once more Roy felt his mind stumble over an indignant protest he could not utter. Dan was quite right in putting to sea without waiting for Chekika's arrival. Even with the flotilla still absent from Tea Table Key, he could load enough marines aboard the catboat to strike a telling blow.

"Come back, Dan! You can take the women with you."

But the sailboat, running fast before a sudden gust of air, was out of earshot now. He had a glimpse of White Heron babying the tiller to nurse the last ounce of wind, while Dan broke out an extra jib at the bowsprit. The half-caste looked strangely sinister in the moonlight, more enemy than friend. He shouted again, if only for the record.

"Tell Pinckney to send his whole command!"

Then he was running again, straight down the road that bisected the island. A bellow of drunken protest greeted him as he pounded on the first of the wreckers' shacks—a rage that choked abruptly when the news he was bearing reached the fuddled brain within. . . . *Thirty canoes,* he thought absently, stumbling through the debris in the next yard and shouting his warning through a half-open window. How could Dan be so sure of the number? And how, in God's name, could he count war bonnets across a half mile of moonlit sea?

But Dan Evans and his strange behavior were filed away for later reference. The active portion of his brain—the same instinct that had carried him through an Indian war—was making plans of another sort: deploying the forces at his disposal to meet the first thrust of Chekika's canoes; massing his fire at the harbor mouth to stop the hostiles in their tracks until help came. . . .

People were pouring from their houses in earnest now. They were shaggy fishermen for the most part—Bahama men who had stayed on at Flamingo when the American flag was moved into the Floridas, plus a few frightened Cubans. Most of them were armed with muskets, though a few carried rifles and carbines. All of them moved by common accord toward the square bastion of Dr. Barker's residence and the long, dark line of the turtle crawl. The latter, facing the break in the barrier reef (which was the only ready means of access to the island), made a natural breastwork, even when the tide was high. The house itself, he knew, had served before as a last-ditch fortress. Thanks to the stilted gallery that circled its upper story, it might be held for some time with experienced marksmen at every lattice.

He counted heads as the men streamed by, and grinned, despite himself, as each islander took his place along the turtle crawl without waiting for orders, splashing waist-deep in the harbor and placing guns and ammunition pouches along the sun-dried planks. He would have given his right arm for the comfort of Andy Winter's presence now—or the solid common sense of Sergeant Ranson.

Behind them the house was sparked with light. He saw Mary cross a window, still in her peignoir, her hair streaming, a half dozen guns cradled in both arms. Dr. Barker appeared on the upstairs gallery, swept the horizon in a calm appraisal, and vanished within, tucking a cambric nightshirt into his trousers as he walked. Already, Roy knew, a small arsenal had been assembled just inside those high latticed windows. When the attack came the lamps would wink out instantly. Every workman in the botanist's employ and every slave had been trained to shoot straight in any light long before they set foot on Flamingo Key.

He felt a wild hope rise in his mind. Perhaps they could stop Chekika after all—even if Dan's count was accurate. Thanks to Mary, the element of surprise on which the Seminoles had surely relied was behind them. Had she not sounded her warning, every white soul on the island (with the probable exception of Dan himself) might have been murdered in his bed before dawn.

He had yet to glimpse the enemy. He whispered an encouraging word down the line of heads behind the turtle crawl, then vaulted to the beach beyond and sprinted for the point. Here he worked his way carefully through the screen of coco palms, darting from tree to tree until he reached the water's edge. So far Chekika must believe that he was converging on a sleeping settlement. His intended victims would preserve that illusion to the last.

A patch of guinea grass between two dunes offered an ideal cover; he crept to the lookout and swept the arc of sea to the north. Hardened as he was to the trade of war, he felt his heart plummet at what he saw. At first glance the dugouts seemed everywhere—an endless brown arc moving relentlessly from the shadow of Matecumbe. The arc was changing shape even now, breaking into segments like a living pattern of geometry on that silver plain. A score of war canoes (he could mark their silhouettes plainly and count the war plumes of the polemen) broke free of the formation and swept rhythmically toward the harbor, moving in a tight triangle, almost bow to stern. The rest of the invaders, forming triangles of their own, dropped back and followed the leaders at a slower pace.

Roy had watched Chekika maneuver before on Okeechobee; he knew how carefully the attack had been planned. That first thrust, aimed straight for Dr. Barker's dock, had been deemed sufficient to possess the island. The balance of the canoes would be held in reserve and used as needed. Even at this distance he could guess that not all the dugouts were stripped for war. Some were outriggers and moved across the water like giant beetles; others were more barge than canoe. These slower vessels, Roy assumed, had been brought to transport whatever loot the Seminoles could amass in the raid.

Already the apex of the leading triangle seemed about to thrust through the break in the reef; in another moment it would be within rifleshot of the turtle crawl. Roy had risen on hands and knees, ready to return to his own loophole, when a strange thing happened. First a tuft of white feathers lashed to a pole was lifted high in the bow of the lead canoe. Then, as though that flash of white against the sky had been a signal, each paddle in the triangle backed water vigorously, bringing the dugouts to an instant halt. The lead canoe, detaching itself from the group, shot through the opening in the coral and darted from Roy's view. The tuft of white rode before the prow as it rounded the point.

Roy had already begun to retrace his steps at top speed. If Chekika was sending a white flag into the harbor, a single shot could ruin everything. He let out his breath in a great sigh when he crossed the corner of Dr. Barker's lawn and saw that the botanist had already come out to the veranda.

"You needn't explain, Roy," he said calmly. "I was watching, too, from an upstairs window."

"What do you make of it?"

"I'm not sure yet. But I've lookouts in both upstairs wings. So long as that fleet stays outside the reef, we can let them make the first move."

"What if someone opens fire?"

Dr. Barker smiled; his voice seemed to grow quieter with each word. "There will be no shots. Not until Chekika tells us what he wants. I've given orders."

They fell silent and stared anxiously at the long, gaudily painted dugout. It was well inside the harbor now. Roy could count the braves at the paddles, and guess at the identity of the two turbaned chiefs who sat in the prow, their arms folded, their buckskins insolently white.

"Surely it's a parley, sir. The Seminole doesn't wear white to war."

"It's a war canoe, nonetheless."

"They must want something. Evidently they hope to get it without fighting."

Roy took an impetuous step forward, leaving the botanist in the comparative shadow of the wisteria. Standing in the full moonlight, he made a perfect target—and the canoe was almost within arrow shot now. It was a risk he could not help taking, if only to make Chekika show his hand.

"Let me talk to them," he whispered. "Perhaps we can draw it out awhile. Dan's gone to Tea Table Key for help. If Pinckney's not an utter fool, we can take them from the rear."

"I wouldn't count on Dan," said Dr. Barker. "We watched him take off in that catboat too. He's already aground on the shoals, a quarter mile offshore."

"Accidentally?"

"I wouldn't care to say, Roy. At least he's saved his own hide. The Seminoles will never attack *him*—not if he stays clear of this business. He's kept them alive through too many winters."

"Olé, señor médico!"

He recognized Chekika's voice instantly, enlarged by a long brass speaking trumpet which the Seminole had raised to his lips. Roy took a long step forward, until he stood in full view on the lawn, his hand raised in the immemorial gesture of peace. Chekika rose in the dugout and stared as though he could not believe his eyes. The other chief did not stir, though his hand dropped to the ax at his belt. In that flash Roy recognized the familiar scowl of Chittamicco under that second war turban—and realized, too late, that it was Dr. Barker, not he, whom Chekika had just summoned so imperiously from what the chief must surely have considered a sleeping house.

It was too late to draw back now. Any hesitation, the slightest hint that he was afraid, would be fatal. The Indians were as taut as their own hidden bowstrings; he could sense as much by the way each brave leaned forward on his paddle. Perhaps he could turn his mistake to his own advantage if he acted quickly.

"Olé, Chief of the Seminoles! What brings you here?"

Chekika nodded to his helmsman. The canoe's bow swung toward the beach as the braves sawed at their paddles, then coasted to a stop a scant fifty feet offshore. Chittamicco had risen beside his brother, one fist still knotted on the tomahawk at his waist. Roy waited at the water's edge with folded arms. Let them speak next, he warned himself. Don't let them think you're anxious. Already a plan had begun to shape in his mind—an argument that might still have weight if the Seminoles really meant to parley.

"What brings Salofkachee to the islands?"

"I make my medicine at all hours. Perhaps it is well that I walked abroad tonight."

No one stirred in the dugout. Near as he was, Roy could read each symbol in the painting that adorned each bow—a lifted panther claw (Chekika had inherited the nickname of Wildcat from his predecessor) protecting a deer and a basket of roasting corn. He could see how Chittamicco's knuckles had turned white on the handle of the hatchet, and could feel hate spark between them, a living lightning flash. Yet Chekika's voice was oddly gentle as he spoke again.

"Open your mind, Salofkachee. We are still friends."

"With a war ax at your side?"

"My brother will be my sense-bearer later. But only if this parley fails."

"You say you come as a friend. Prove it by your deeds."

"Open your mind, Salofkachee. You have nothing to fear from me—or from the Seminole nation, while I live."

"And your brother Chittamicco? What is his message?"

"Chittamicco is not yet my sense-bearer. How often must I say this to my white brother?"

"My mind is open, Chekika. Fill it with your wisdom. Tell me how a brother can come in peace with tomahawks behind him."

"How did you know I would come in force?"

"I am abroad at all hours, King of Panthers. I smelled out your council fire at Cape Sable. I counted your dugouts, one by one, before they left Matecumbe."

A low wail rose from the canoe—a primitive exhalation, as though each of the braves had breathed a sigh in unison. Chittamicco muttered an invective in Seminole. With no surprise, Roy watched the Wildcat slap his brother into silence with a careless palm.

"So this is the medicine you make under the moon, Salofkachee?"

"I have done more. Every man on this island is awake and ready. At this very instant a dozen rifles are trained on your belly. Tell me there is no evil there. Empty your own heart of hate—and go in peace."

Another murmur rose from the dugout, and stilled as the Wildcat held up his hand for silence. "We have come in peace, Salofkachee. With empty rifles and loosened bowstrings. We will go in peace if Dr. Barker sits beside me."

"You honor us too highly. This is Dr. Barker's home. Why should he leave it—even in your noble company?" Chekika, he noted, was speaking in purest Seminole now; he matched the other's eloquence as smoothly as he could. "This is his garden. He plants it with his own hands. This is his life and his pride. Would you take a man's pride away?"

"How much of pride has our father in Washington left us? When has the Seminole dared to hold up his head and look into his brother's eyes—unless he is deep in the Grassy Water? It is my purpose to take Dr. Barker to the Glades as hostage—and the daughter who has just arrived to comfort his last years. Perhaps when Poinsett hears this news he will offer us a treaty that cannot be broken."

Again Chekika offered his small, precise bow, and Roy returned the courtesy. Trust that red devil to come to the point, he thought. Now that the threat's on Dr. Barker's doorstep, it seemed odd that no one had thought of it sooner.

Obviously the close friend of Secretary Poinsett might have been snared a score of times, while he checked his plantation on Cape Sable or roamed at will on the fringes of the Glades. This threat in force, now that it had been made so firmly, would carry added weight in Washington, once it became known that a favorite of the administration (which was staggering, as usual, under the other burdens than a profitless Indian war) had been snatched from under the Navy's nose.

He started to put in a word for Mary Grant, and gave up the effort when he noted from the corner of his eye that Mary herself had come out to the veranda and was standing beside Dr. Barker, her arm linked in his. Whoever had informed Chekika of Mary's arrival on the island had bungled the message; there was no possible way to explain her presence now. To Chekika's mind she was part of the prize he would take back to the Glades tomorrow—part of the assurance for the Army's good behavior.

"What if the doctor refuses to come?"

"I will hear Dr. Barker's wisdom from his own lips."

The botanist had produced a corncob from his pocket. He lighted it leisurely now, making the most of the lucifer that still seemed black magic to the Indians. "The great chief honors me too highly. Secretary Poinsett is a friend, I grant you. He is not my blood brother. Nor is this lady my daughter——"

"If Poinsett is no blood brother, why do you make flowers

with his name? If this white princess is not your flesh and blood, why does she come to your house?"

Dr. Barker's eyes sought Roy's and read the wordless message there. His hand closed on Mary's arm as she seemed about to speak.

"So the father of Seminoles hopes to win wars by capturing girls and old men. I had no idea he was desperate."

Chittamicco's arm flailed out from his side, the ax still in his fist. His brother slapped the tomahawk downward with enough force to splinter a gunwale of the dugout.

"We have had enough of wars, *señor médico*," he said, and now he spoke the fluent Cuban Spanish that Chittamicco had always refused to learn. "We would use you and the girl to make a peace that outlasts our lifetime."

"You will never win peace by violence. Believe me, if you set foot on Flamingo Key tonight, you will sign your own death warrant."

Roy spoke quickly into the heavy silence. "I have told Chekika that he stands in a dozen rifle sights. I will say more. Not one of his canoes will reach this land—unless they drift in, bottom-up."

"It is not you who seek to frighten me, Salofkachee," said Chekika. "I cannot let your voice come past my ears."

"No man could frighten the King of Cats. I only appeal to his wisdom. We are well armed here—and we had warning of your arrival. Your braves will be shot down at their paddles before they can touch the beach.

Roy let his eyes stray to the turtle crawl. Twenty rifles and muskets were nested there, ready to fire on the first canoe to move within range. Behind the lattices of the house a half dozen of Dr. Barker's white workmen and eight house slaves would repel boarders till the last. His glimpse of Chekika's flotilla had underlined the pitiful odds against them. At least three hundred braves had joined the kidnaping raid; he knew they would be better armed than the defenders on the island. If Chittamicco's ax became his brother's sense-bearer, the fight would be over in an hour. Especially if the Indians waited to launch their attack in the misty dawnlight, as was their custom.

"The raccoon does not threaten the panther, Salofkachee," said Chekika. His voice was low and a little sad, doling out each word. "All I ask of you is two hostages to the future. Yield them, and you will save both blood and hair."

"You would return to the Glades in peace?"

"We would go back as quietly as we came. If Poinsett meets our terms, we will never leave the Grassy Water."

You've made your challenge, thought Roy; I've just one more word to speak. He lifted his voice, enough for the marksmen along the turtle crawl to hear, as well as the gray-faced Negroes crouched at the windows of the house, the huddle of women in the shuttered hall.

"We will consider your terms, Father of Seminoles. When must you have your answer?"

"No later than dawn."

Roy nodded in sober agreement. He had counted on the Indian's aversion to fighting after dark; it might be their salvation now.

"Rest on your paddles beyond the coral reef. The sea is quiet tonight. You will have our answer with the sunrise."

He had continued to speak in Spanish, which the key dwellers understood well enough. Now he repeated the words in his best Seminole, advancing a step as he did so, to outstare the lynx-eyed Chittamicco. "Send a prayer to your gods, brother of Chekika," he added in a low voice. "Our answer may come wrapped round a bullet." He faced deliberately away from his enemy and lifted his hand to Chekika, palm outward. The King of Wildcats repeated the courtesy as the war canoe swung in a long, soundless arc and streaked for the harbor mouth.

xiii

The jar of bear's grease winking dully in the lamplight on the study table yielded a last handful. Roy slapped the odorous mess into his other palm and went to the mirror to coat an arm that was already gleaming. The pan of lampblack was nearly empty too; he applied a final touch to a sooty forehead and stepped back to study the final effect. The lampblack, mixed with that protective coating, would make his head and shoulders virtually invisible at water level. The grease had proved its worth when he had swum Biscayne Bay a year ago to win one of Andy's wagers. The clock on the mantel hung on the stroke of three: a half-hour till moonset and a scant two hours till dawn. Time enough if he moved fast, encountered no barracuda in mid-channel and kept his temper when he faced Lieutenant Pinckney, United States Navy. He opened the study door and called softly across the hall.

Dr. Barker came in on tiptoe and stared at him in solemn disapproval. Catching his own reflection in the pier glass, Roy could not quite keep down a chuckle. Naked save for his smallclothes, dark as a Madagascar buck from neck to hairline, and gleaming with the redolent grease to his toes, he could hardly have seemed more grotesque.

"I still insist you're mad, Roy." The botanist's voice seemed to come from a great distance. "It would be far simpler if I gave myself up."

"They'd want Mary. We've been over all that."

"Mary is willing too. More than willing——"

"*You* know what it means to be an Indian hostage. Does she?"

Dr. Barker spread his hands in the lamplight. For the first time Roy noticed how old and frail he was—and how indomitable. "Admit we'd be rather special hostages," he said. "At least we'd be guests in the chief's house——"

"How long will Chekika be headman of the nation—with Chittamicco and the others howling for blood?"

"He'd keep us both safe while he lived. How could he do otherwise?"

"I'm not too sure of that. The last time I sat at his council fire I escaped death by a hair."

"At least we'd spare the island if we surrendered tonight."

Roy sighed and glanced at the clock on the mantel. Two hours till dawn; a desperate gamble at best. But they had agreed it was worth the risk. . . . It was quite like Dr. Barker to argue the points one more time.

"You heard his terms, sir. At dawn he'll show another white flag at the harbor mouth and come in to take you aboard the canoe. You and Mary." Roy stared hard at that picture for a moment, then closed his eyes on the aftermath. "If there's the slightest hitch, three hundred braves move in after that lead canoe and occupy Flamingo Key. Three hundred murderers from the Glades itching for scalps and Dan's Cuban rum. Even if you come aboard the chief's

canoe—even if Chekika does turn back for Cape Sable—
d'you think the others will follow?"

"At least they're waiting for the dawn."

"For one reason only. Indians don't like to die after sundown; in their book a man's spirit can lose its way in the
dark. If you ask me, it's the one bit of luck we've had tonight."

Dr. Barker stood aside from the doorway. "Very well,
Roy. It's you who must swim to Table Key, not I. And it's
you who must persuade that chowder-head lieutenant that
he'll win another stripe if he follows you back. I still say it's
the spark that can destroy us all."

"Not if we take them from the north when they least expect it. Not if they believe the whole squadron is behind us."

The botanist sighed and let his hand fall on Roy's
shoulder. "Very well, my boy. I know we've agreed it's worth
the chance. If I argue, it's for the sake of form. Will you say
good-by to Mary now?"

This afternoon, thought Roy, I said good-by to Mary
Grant once and for all. Why should I repeat the ordeal?
Aloud he said mildly enough, "If you don't mind, we'll spare
her that."

"She's waiting now on the side veranda."

"Convey my compliments, please. Say I'll be back with the
daylight to hand her aboard that Havana packet."

They struck palms in the shadow of the doorway. Roy
walked briskly out to the lawn, suppressing an instinctive
tremor as clammy fingers of mist touched his body. The dew
that always settled on the rooftops in these latitudes was
heavy tonight, now that the moon had begun to slip behind
the mangroves on the western keys. Beyond the lawn it made
goblin patterns under the coco palms, blotting out the path to
the beach and the turtle crawl. Roy crossed himself and murmured a silent prayer. He was gambling heavily on that mist
for the first dangerous lap of his journey.

Despite his best resolves, he paused at the side porch to
steal a look within. Mary Grant sat bolt upright in an armchair, with a child's head cradled in her lap. The lamplight
from the room just inside the open lattice haloed her head in
dim gold. He stood for a long time in the misty dark, treasur-
ing the way that nimbus illumined the plane of her cheek, the
sweet curve of her throat. Her eyes were shadowed while she

waited; her lips seemed to murmur faintly. He wondered if they were echoing the prayer he had just uttered and plunged on with that pious hope.

At the entrance to the turtle crawl he paused again to shake the nearest hands along that impromptu barricade. Then, without pausing to weigh the gamble he was taking, he wrenched open the sandcrusted gate that was the only entrance to Dr. Barker's aquarium, and strode boldly into the faint water whispers of that long palmetto tunnel. He had visited the crawl before, in broad daylight, to help select a dinner steak. Now, with the moon well down and no light to guide his passage, he knew he must walk warily. The giant loggerheads, quiescent by day, seemed on the prowl tonight in their narrow quarters. More than once he shied violently, barking a shoulder or a shin against the palmetto pilings to avoid a head-on collision with a barnacled shell or a thrashing flipper. . . . Eyes studied him everywhere—faint yellow orbs that seemed to pick up sparks in the gloom. He knew that these sluggish creatures would do him no harm if he did not impede their swimming. But he could only gasp his relief —and lie for a moment on the ledge just inside the stringpiece at the dock's end—when he fumbled out of the crawl at last.

Here, a good hundred yards from the beach, he could study the open water ahead and weigh his chances in earnest. So far his progress had been screened by the slatted sides of the crawl; from this point on he must swim in open sea, dodging the coral heads as best he could when he reached the break in the reef, and praying that Chekika's braves were dozing on their paddles just beyond. Tea Table Key was a hard mile from the reef. He had swum it before by daylight, with the tide behind him. It would be a different story now, with night like a thick blanket on the sea.

He breathed and plunged, without giving himself time to be afraid. Sounding deep and swimming under water until his lungs were on the point of bursting, he broke surface a good two hundred feet from the stringpiece and began the first leg of his dangerous journey—a long, quiet sprint for the break in the coral. Here, at least, he could orient himself, after a fashion, by the spout of waves at that jagged opening as the outgoing tide soughed through. The naval station, he knew, lay almost due west. Thanks to the shape of Flamingo Key and the curve of the reef itself, it could be viewed clearly only when a vessel had actually passed through to open water. The whole northern face of Flamingo, where Chekika's flotilla was, presumably, riding out these last hours of darkness, was hidden from possible observers at the station itself. By the same token, it seemed likely that a lone swimmer could make the crossing unobserved by the Seminoles—unless Wildcat himself, or a trusted observer, was lurking just outside the reef to forestall a possible dash for help.

Now he could see the tide cream the coral heads at either side of the narrow channel. More by instinct than actual sight, he could feel that he was in deep water, with the last of the coral behind him and Tea Table Key dead ahead. The darkness was almost absolute here; the heavy mist which had begun to brood over the face of the sea was as clammy as death itself on his quietly thrashing arms as he drove on, stroke by cautious stroke. The King of Cats could see in that thick darkness much better than he. . . . At any moment he expected to hear the ghostly stir of a paddle blade, the challenge that would be only another name for death. But there was no sound beyond the diminishing sigh of surf on the reef.

Little by little his eyes were adjusting to the thick gloom. When the mist lifted he could even discern landmarks of a sort. There, riding quietly at its twin anchors just inside the reef, was the doctor's ketch, with John and Rachel still safely aboard; he could be sure that Chekika would not harm the two Negroes, no matter what havoc he might wreak on Flamingo Key. The relation between Seminole and Negro had always been friendly enough.

He could not locate the precise spot where Dan's catboat had gone aground, though he could just discern the tall mast as it rocked against the night sky, beyond the screen of mangroves on the point. Dan, he noted wryly, had left the harbor by another break in the coral. If he had intended to run for Table Key he could hardly have chosen a more circuitous course.

Far from shore now, swimming steadily with the full thrust of the tide behind him, Roy permitted himself a tranquil breath. So far his strategy had gone by the book. Now that he had covered almost half a distance, he felt sure that Chekika's force was massed on the far side of the island, awaiting the dawn. Every waking eye in that flotilla, he knew, was fastened on the harbor mouth; even in this misty time before sunrise the Indians could not have failed to mark the outline of the smallest sailboat had Dr. Barker attempted a last-minute dash for liberty. The head of a lone swimmer, covered with black grease, had escaped their notice after all. . . . Or so it seemed, just before he sounded in earnest as his ear caught the chunk of paddles in the darkness.

He swam as deep as he dared—and deeper still, with blood knocking a warning drum at his temples and eyes straining wide. Phosphorous bubbles marked his passage, and he wondered if they would betray him in this deadly game of hide-and-seek. He did not dare to look above him when he turned at last and rocketed upward toward the life-giving air; if the canoe had marked his presence, it might be directly above him now. . . . It took all his self-control to break surface without a sound, to choke down a shout of exultation as he drew his first straining breath.

He could see the canoe clearly now, though the torsos and heads of the paddlers were deep in the mist that lay like a floating blanket a scant foot above the quiet sea. The dugout (he did not need the daubs at the bow to guess it was Chekika's own) was roaming restlessly at the break in the reef. He guessed that the Seminole leader had been circling thus for some time, watching the harbor with cold-eyed concentration. Even as he waited breathless in the open sea a scant hundred yards away, the canoe circled one more time and moved swiftly toward the second opening in the coral, a half mile down the reef. Chekika, he gathered, had been patrolling these two openings since the parley. It was Roy's good fortune that he had swum from harbor to sea when the dugout was prowling about the second breach in the coral.

He hardly waited for the rhythmic dip of the paddles to grow faint in the night. There was blood on his face from ears and nose after that too deep plunge; if he lingered here it would only be a question of time before the barracuda, singly or in shoals, would scent him out and come swarming for the kill. He could almost prefer capture by the Seminoles to the descent of that voracious horde.

Even now he could not risk a full-armed stroke. It was not until he had swum a good half mile from the encounter with the dugout that he dared put all his strength in the last, long sprint for Tea Table Key. The mist had settled now, smearing the whole horizon with a giant sponge. For a while he was certain that he had missed his bearings and blundered past his destination—with no landfall until the Bahamas, across the remorseless wash of the Gulf Stream. Then, as the first faint wind stirred in the east (a forerunner of the breeze that seldom failed to refresh these latitudes in the hour before sunrise), a corner of the gauzy curtain lifted and he saw the familiar, spider-legged outline of the Navy dock against the starlight.

Thanks to that deep dive, a giant hornet still buzzed behind each of his eardrums, blotting out normal sounds; he could barely discern the hoarse gasp of triumph that escaped his lips. His goal was still distant, but there was no mistaking it now, even when the mist blotted the sea between. He swam doggedly on, setting his course by instinct, feeling the first cold, cramping grip of the open Atlantic settle like a slowly closing vise at calf and chest and shoulders. . . . Four hundred yards: distances by water were always deceptive, but he was sure that the blessed solidity of those planks could be no farther now. He let his mind spin back into the soundless vacuum where he labored. Now that he did not have to fasten his whole energies on the need to survive, he knew that he must plan—and plan with all his senses.

Pinckney had, at most, forty-odd marines under his command at present, unless some units of his squadron had returned during the night. But the two beached sloops were still seaworthy after a few routine repairs; the howitzers aboard that gun barge, packed with grape and scrap iron, could blow Chekika from the sea in a few brisk rounds if the lieutenant could be persuaded to take them aboard, along with his five squads of leathernecks. So Roy had reasoned in Dr. Barker's library while he prepared himself for this swim. Giddy as he was after his long immersion, he could still believe the lieutenant would accept his orders without question. It seemed only natural that not two sloops but four should be putting out from Tea Table Key when he lifted on the next wave and blinked at his destination through salt-caked lids. Even more natural that the last starlight should gleam faintly on the snouts of the four swivel guns mounted on the bow of each sloop, with a gunner ready at the fuse.

He opened his mouth on a soundless bellow and blinked at

the vision again. But it was still there, with all canvas spread, cleaving the morning sea in clean splendor as four smartly dipping bowsprits split the graying night. In that crazy instant when madness and reality merged, he understood the apparition and its import. The four vessels now bearing down upon Flamingo Key were actual enough—an advance unit of the squadron that had gone junketing to Key Largo only yesterday and turned back in time. Pinckney, a young man with a core of common sense, for all his bantam posturing, had taken at least a part of his warning to heart. Today's routine maneuver was a dawn patrol along the south shore of Matecumbe—a tour of duty that would discover Chekika's thirty-odd canoes in a matter of minutes.

A match flared aboard the leading sloop; he saw the gunner tilt his piece on the foredeck, watched the hiss of orange flame rush down the fuse. Though it was too late to warn these fools of their folly, he bellowed a protest there in the trough of his wave. He heard the round shot snore overhead. In the brief flash that followed he picked out a dozen pairs of staring eyeballs in the murk, and realized that the Navy had had a target after all. In that brief red glare Chekika's canoe seemed etched in fire, frozen in flame like a living nightmare. Then the darkness pounced again. The Seminole war whoop, a thin, keening wail of defiance, told them that the shot had missed its mark. The war whoop, running down the coral like an impish echo, seemed to repeat in every quarter of the compass before it died.

When the second cannon spoke Roy saw that Chekika's dugout was already deep inside the harbor—that the harbor itself seemed jammed with canoes. Most of them were empty, save for the poler and a squaw or two. The beach beyond was black with dancing figures. The lawn before Dr. Barker's house, the veranda of Dan Evans's hotel, even the planks of the turtle crawl, were populous with capering red figures, peppered with rifle and musket fire, hideous with screams as red and white flesh joined in combat.

When he looked back on that moment later, he knew that the second cannon flash had revealed only part of that bloody debacle ashore—that the picture seared into his brain as he rose on the crest of a wave had waited to take shape there from the beginning. The first spout of flame from Dr. Barker's gardens, rising like an answer to the Navy's cannonading, was only a footnote to his despair. Now that the savage tide had swept Chekika in its wake, now that the island was, in fact, possessed in a single storming rush, he knew that he had expected no other fate from the moment he had landed at Tea Table Key that afternoon and found the station deserted. The quartet of sloops that towered above him now, barking defiance from brass throats, had come too late.

He shouted in earnest as a bowsprit stabbed the air above his head, and heard his voice explode within his brain as his ears still refused to function. The cutwater missed his head by inches; he felt the stinging impact at one shoulder as he grazed the copper-studded planking and groped for a hand-hold along the flying gunwale. Putting out his failing strength, he lifted head and shoulders overside, letting his body trail inertly in the wake. A bull's-eye lantern, blinking like a giant eye, bathed him in a sudden, baleful glow. He had a glimpse of Lieutenant Pinckney staring down at him in a kind of shocked surprise, and knew that he must resemble some sooty monster dredged at random from the deep.

He tried to shout his name, but no words came from his bursting throat. Before he could speak again, something thudded softly behind one of his still-deaf ears, sending him tumbling down into darkness.

II INDIAN MOUND

i

COLONEL ELIAS MERRICK, ROLLING HIS ARMY UNDERSHIRT above his massive stomach, scratched for a moment of pure content before he swayed back in his chair and fixed his two subordinates with an unequivocal eye. The colonel's apartment at Fort Everglades, cluttered as ever and hot as hell's own furnace in the fag end of afternoon, was ominously calm between thunderbolts. Captain Andrew Winter, still at attention before the commandant's desk, was part of that glacial repose. So, for that matter, was Dr. Royal Coe—still obstinately at ease in a cane-bottomed chair across the room. When the colonel spoke at last, he did not stir. Roy had survived these tongue lashings before; the fact that the present tongue lashing was undeserved made it easier to bear.

"And that's the last thing you remember, Dr. Coe?"

"The very last, sir. Apparently it was Lieutenant Pinckney himself who took me by the scruff. And Ensign West who sandbagged me behind one ear. As I say, I don't blame them. Both of them must have thought I was part of Chekika's skirmish line——"

Colonel Merrick cut in with his heavy-handed humor intact. *"I'd* say you're lucky to be alive, Doctor."

Lucky indeed, thought Roy. And none too happy at my luck. I've still to face my best friend when this ordeal is over and explain why his fiancée is now a Seminole ward. . . . He kept his voice soft and waited for the next interruption.

"You've seen Pinckney's report, Colonel. I've explained to

120

you just how strong a warning I left at the naval station. Can you blame me for crossing the channel with the facts?"

"If I understood that young hellion, he had most of the facts at his disposal. He was on his way to lift the siege when he almost ran you down——"

"Precisely, sir. But we were both too late. Chekika was already inside the barrier reef. He was attacking Flamingo Key in force at the very moment I was dragged aboard Lieutenant Pinckney's sloop. The most we can say for the naval action is this: it did create a diversion. Probably it saved a number of lives on the island. Certainly it drove the enemy to their canoes ahead of time——"

"With their hostages."

"With their hostages. Chekika's invasion of the keys was strictly according to plan. He knew as well as I that we could never yield Dr. Barker as he demanded." Roy cast a despairing glance at Andy Winter and let his eyes drop before his friend's dress-parade stare. "And it was simply out of the question to—surrender Miss Grant. Are we in agreement so far?"

"Perfectly, Doctor. I still insist you should have stood behind your cover and fought it out. Any Army man would have done as much. Am I right, Captain Winter?"

Captain Andrew Winter clicked his heels smartly and kept his eyes straight ahead. "Exception, sir. In my opinion Dr. Coe acted in the best interest of Flamingo Key. It isn't his fault that Jim Pinckney was born a fool. The report admits that he could have put those seven-pounders into action by midnight—if he'd used his head. That would have made all the difference."

Roy chimed in vigorously, feeling a great weight lift with his words. At least Andy had understood his predicament that terrible night. To say nothing of the gamble he had taken on that swim to Tea Table Key. "Believe me, Colonel, our only chance was to find the Navy—and strike from the rear. Once the action was joined on Flamingo——" He spread his hands, closing his eyes on the burning picture that still tormented his dreams. "You have the Navy's own report on its duration."

The colonel picked up a blue-bound manuscript from his desk and weighed it absently. The corners of the foolscap dripped the best Annapolis beeswax; from where he sat Roy could read the flourish of Lieutenant Pinckney's signature across the final line. He turned to grin surreptitiously at Sergeant Ranson, who was scratching busily on a similar report at the side table. All of them knew that the general's own aide was stumping the courtyard at this very moment, waiting to bear the commandant's apologia to St. Augustine.

"Ten scalps were taken," said the colonel. "Dr. Barker lost all of his slaves—save for a sick Negro and his nurse aboard a ketch in the harbor. Dan Evans lost four—to say nothing of a warehouse burned to the ground and another looted of its last sack of corn meal. Every white man dead and skewered—unless he had the good sense to take to the mangroves or hide in a cistern. Dr. Barker and the young lady somewhere in the Glades as hostages—if we're to believe the doctor's own preposterous note." The colonel's saddle-brown face creased in a frown as he picked up a separate sheet of foolscap. "You're sure that it isn't a forgery, Roy?"

"I'd know Dr. Barker's handwriting anywhere, sir." Roy found that he was unlimbering in earnest. The use of his Christian name proved that the colonel was finished with browbeating for the time being.

"Would you say the note was written under duress?"

"It doesn't have that tone."

"Dr. Barker has visited Chekika before, sir," said Andy. "From what Roy has already said, he was resigned to surrender. He'd have gone at once—if it hadn't been for Mary."

Merrick glared briefly at his adjutant. "Sit down, boy, and unbutton. This is a council of war, not a court-martial. Not yet, at any rate."

Andy forced a wan smile and sat at the table where the sergeant was working. "My views are on the record, sir. I won't elaborate them now, unless you insist."

"I'm afraid I do insist. Remember, this discussion goes up to Augustine verbatim. You're ready to step off at a moment's notice?"

"Tonight, if need be," said Andy quietly.

"Including service of supply?"

"Dan Evans will see to that."

"Effectives?"

"Two hundred first-class rifles. Fifty rounds per man, battened under canvas in twenty light-draught canoes. Captain Stevens to be in charge at base camp, which we'll establish just above the Miami falls. Lieutenant Hutchens to serve as my adjutant; Ranson here in general charge of the troop itself. Dr. Coe to act as special scout under my orders."

"Do you endorse this, Roy?"

Merrick offered a black-browed stare with the question, and Roy met the challenge eye to eye. He had come up to Fort Everglades only that morning after two days in the sick bay at Tea Table Key. The hard-driving pace of the inquiry still left him a trifle stunned. And yet he had expected precisely this query for a long time now. Watching Andy train his veterans over the months, he had known that his own part in the expedition was ordained in advance. Just as inevitably, he had known that he must take orders, not give them. . . . He spoke formally for Ranson's flying pen.

"I shall be happy to serve the Army in any capacity Captain Winter desires."

"I think that's about all for the record, Ranson," said the colonel. "Andy strikes into the Glades tomorrow at sunset." He smiled at Roy, as though a sudden weight had lifted from his mind. "We must give our guide's head another day to clear. Besides, Stevens is still busy moving those extra rations upriver." He spoke again for the record. "Two hundred regulars with blood in their eyes and axes that can cut as well as any Seminole's. Liaison to be maintained via Fort Everglades with the general's own force—now moving from Fort King to establish a line along the Caloosahatchee. The general's command to prevent Chekika's moving north of Okeechobee. Captain Winter's command to force an action within the Glades." The colonel stretched mightly, as though he were emerging from a dream. "All straight in the report, Sergeant?"

"All straight, sir."

"Then give the general's aide his copy and get him off the post. I've taken enough of the fellow's insolence; I'm too busy to say good-by."

No one spoke after the door had closed behind the sergeant. The neat exercise in geometry that had just gone down the hall—complete with its glib Q.E.D.—might mollify the commanding general; it might even temper the storm that would soon come roaring down from Washington. All of them knew that it had little real relation to the task before them. When Colonel Merrick rumbled into the speech at last, he seemed to be thinking aloud, with all his guards down.

"As I see it, Andy, we've two items on our side. Point one, the Army is moving in force to the terrain north of Okeechobee. Granted, it may not condescend to get its feet wet—or even muddy—but it's still a lucky chance. Point two, our raiders were ready *before* that holocaust at Flamingo Key. If I read Dr. Barker's note correctly, that's something the Wildcat hasn't counted on so far." Again he lifted the single sheet of foolscap that bore the old botanist's message and stared at it owlishly. "Any other facts in our favor?"

Andy sighed and lifted his booted legs to the table top, a gesture the commandant paralleled. "Can't think of any at the moment, sir."

The Colonel sighed. "All right, Roy. We're off the record now. Say what you really think."

Roy breathed deep and took the plunge. "Have you thought of accepting Chekika's terms?"

"He's singed my whiskers. Don't ask me to give him my head as well."

"The terms seem reasonable enough. Dr. Barker all but endorses them in his note."

"Remember where that note was found, Roy. Pinned to what's left of Dr. Barker's house—with a tomahawk. Chekika might have spared us that bit of bravado."

Roy took the note from the colonel's desk and studied it thoughtfully, although he knew each word by heart now. Penned in the botanist's precise script, the note was short and disarmingly casual. Knowing Dr. Barker's coolness under stress, he still found it hard to believe that this missive was inscribed with death leering over the writer's shoulder:

To Dr. Royal Coe—or Colonel Elias
Merrick of Fort Everglades:

As this is being written, Chekika, King of the Seminoles, has completed his invasion of Flamingo Key. Miss Mary Grant, whom he still insists is my daughter, has gone aboard the chief's own canoe as hostage. I am about to follow her, in the same role.

The King of the Seminoles wishes it clearly understood that both Miss Grant and myself will be Guests of Honor in his House. He wishes, furthermore, to declare a Truce between his nation and the Government at Washington—and pledges that our safety shall be his First Concern, so long as the truce remains unbroken.

His terms for our return to the American Nation are twofold. First, he demanded a Guarantee-in-Fact, from the American Secretary of War, that no reprisals be launched against the Seminole, and that no white man shall set foot in the Present Limits of the Grassy Water (known to white cartographers as the Everglades and the Lake of Okeechobee) now or forever.

Second, he demands, as ransom money, Fifty Thousand Dollars, in Gold. This sum will be accepted by his Emissaries, on the hammock known as Pahokee, in two weeks' time—providing it is brought by Dr. Royal Coe, and none other.

I am permitted to say no more.

Roy tossed the sheet of foolscap back on the colonel's table. "I think we should weigh these words carefully, sir."

"Are you suggesting we meet such a demand?"

"Miss Grant's father is a wealthy man. So, for that matter, is Dr. Barker himself. I'm sure they'd reimburse the government."

"The general would never hear of it. Hell and damnation, Roy, the Army doesn't take orders from an Indian. Wildcat's a criminal, wanted for murder. He must be tracked down and hanged."

"Shouldn't we wait for orders from Washington?"

"Poinsett would give the same order if he sat in my chair today."

"Chekika mentions a truce. Should we be the first to break it?"

"Why not—if we can surprise him?"

"Very good, Colonel. Let's say that Captain Stevens establishes his base above the falls by tomorrow. Let's assume we can move our force to that camp and lay down a supply line without being challenged. Wouldn't it be wiser for me to go on first to Pahokee, as this note suggests, and see what I can do?"

"It wouldn't be healthy for you to go empty-handed," said the colonel dryly.

Roy checked a retort in time. The commandant was right, of course. The King of Wildcats had thrown down his gauge. Surrender to his terms or head-on collision was the only alternative now. If he had suggested the former, it was only for the record. He had known from the beginning that he would join this raid—that he would give his life, if need be, to bring lasting peace to the Floridas by the only means at hand. The fact that the girl he loved was now part of that desperate game had no real bearing on his decision. He had had no other choice, long before he had seen that spout of flame on Flamingo Key.

"Pahokee Hammock is only a day's journey from the falls," he said. "Andy and I might scout it together while the heavy supplies move upstream."

"An excellent suggestion, sir," said Andy. He had spoken but little since the long conference began—and this, in itself, was a sign that the dragoon captain's courage was only a mask for a deeper malaise. "If Roy feels well enough, I'd like to start at once. I'm sure you can both understand my concern——"

Roy nodded a quick agreement; he did not want Andy Winter to put that fear into words. "We can leave the moment the colonel dismisses us. My dugout should be provisioned now. I gave orders the moment I arrived."

The colonel weighed the proposal in ponderous silence. "What if you find Chekika waiting at the hammock?"

"Right now," said Andy, "I'd give my bars to meet that devil face to face."

"It's quite possible that the whole nation is camped at Pahokee," said Roy. "It's a natural stopover for the canoes—and they've barely had time to return from Flamingo Key."

Andy had been pacing the colonel's carpet; he turned eagerly on the points of his brightly polished toes. "D'you think he'd dare?"

"Why not—when he feels sure we can't move against him in force?"

"How can he know?"

"This raiding party of yours is an open secret all over the Floridas. Steven's base is being scouted carefully at this moment. Every canoe you put in the Miami will be clocked long before it can reach the falls. That's why I suggested meeting the ransom terms—even when I knew it was beneath the

Army's honor. It would have saved lives at least. And I'm not counting Dr. Barker now—or Mary."

Andy banged the colonel's desk with both fists. "Leave Mary out of this, please. Have some regard for my feelings!"

"Unfortunately, it's impossible to leave her out any longer. You may induce Chekika to fight somewhere in the Glades. But it won't be at Pahokee, or at any spot you choose. He'll jump you when you least expect. Precisely as Osceola jumped us at the Withlacoochee. The best you can do is make that raiding party a living target—and pray you can outshoot him."

Andy subsided with a weary grin. "You do put things in a pleasant light, Roy."

"If you lead two hundred men into the Glades, you'll be breaking the truce. The Wildcat lost barely a dozen men at Flamingo Key, and he came there with more than thirty canoes. Add all the renegades he left at home and all the runaway slaves he's freed over the years, and you're really outnumbered. We could be wiped out easily, right down to the last man. What's more Colonel Merrick would never find our graves."

"You're not on staff any more, Roy," said Andy. "Why don't you resign?"

"Because I'm in this to my eyes, just as you are." Roy bit off the rest in time. The mention of Mary's name had stirred an anguish he could share with no one—Andy Winter least of all. "When we're in the Glades I'll be your scout, nothing more. You'll give the orders then. With your permission— and the colonel's—I'll give you some advice now. While we're still friends."

Andy threw himself down in a chair beside the colonel's desk and glanced warily at his superior. The colonel's paw was still caressing the iron-hard muscles on his bare torso— and the arrow wound he had brought back from Tampa Bay. "The carpet's yours, Roy," he said gently. "Make the most of it."

"Andy and I will go to Pahokee Hammock, as ordered. My guess is we'll find nothing—but it's worth the try. Then we'll return to base—and disperse the command. If we are being scouted, we'll make it seem that we've abandoned our invasion plan. But we won't go down the falls. Instead, we'll filter into the saw grass in the dark, in small groups, by way of the sloughs——"

"Using what sort of maps?"

"Ranson can take one group, sir. I'll take another. Every trapper who knows Ten-Mile Slough can sign on as militia. I can name a dozen who'll sign willingly if you'll pay the usual bonus for scalps. Once we're in that main Slough, we can't be ambushed, at least. We'll rendezvous and pound north for the lake—two hundred plus, and spoiling for a massacre. We'll time it to camp that night at Indian Mound and dig in for the attack."

Andy jumped to his feet with flashing eyes. "On sacred ground, eh?"

"Sacred since the days of the Caloosas," said Roy. "What's more, we'll light our cook fires on the summit—on the very spot where they made their medicine. Can you think of a better way to break a truce?"

"Or a better way to commit suicide," said the colonel, mildly enough.

"We've been through this thing together, sir. No army that ever fought could go into the Glades and pick its battlefield. We can only make ourselves a target and pray for luck——"

"When you're outnumbered?"

"Precisely. Once the fighting is joined, we must make it a holding action. What I've said so far is only part of the picture. With Andy in command, we should be able to last two days—possibly longer. In that interval you can make personal contact with the troops from Augustine, on the north shore of the lake, and ferry them over to finish the action."

The colonel was on his feet, too, bending over the map with Andy Winter. "You missed your calling, Roy," he grumbled. "Maybe it's just crazy enough to work." He threw down his calipers and put both fists on the map, while he favored Roy with a prolonged scowl. Naked to his belt buckle, and bristling like a gorilla on the prowl, the commandant of Fort Everglades was every inch a man of Mars, rejoicing in his calling. "At least it's worth a try. If I can make the general believe it too. If those regulars are really on their way——"

"They'd better be," shouted Andy, and he was pacing the carpet once again in the exuberance of released nerves. Back at the map, his arm encircled the colonel's shoulder as he traced their route—a gesture of comradeship that went unrebuked. "If they aren't, you needn't look for our bones. Chekika's squaws will have pounded them into amulets——"

"All but our skulls," said Roy. "They'll bury those in the Mound."

He found he was laughing with the others—a bit wildly, it is true, as he sensed their acceptance. A picture rose persistently in the back of his brain to cloud the heady optimism of the moment, and he closed his eyes on the vision of Mary Grant swinging feet-down from the tuft of a cabbage palm. He fought down that image firmly enough. After all, he had other plans for Mary Grant.

He came back to the reality of the hot, shuttered room and the click of Andy Winter's boot heels. The captain had recovered his aplomb, along with his military bearing. Merrick was behind his desk again, with his old scowl in place.

"With the colonel's permission," said Andy, "we'll begin our tour of duty."

"Directly, Captain. I think we should have a word with Dan before you leave. Perhaps he can add something to this discussion."

Roy had already jumped for the door before Merrick could shout for an aide. "If you please, sir—let's keep Dan outside our plans."

"Of course he's outside. This maneuver is a secret among us three. He's still our sutler—and he's traded through that saw grass for years. Shouldn't we ask him a question or two?"

"By all means—if he'll answer truthfully."

"Don't you trust Evans—after all these years?"

"Do *you*, sir?" asked Roy.

"Not at all," said Merrick blandly. "I think he's made a fortune on two-way trades—with every Seminole chief since Osceola and Charley Emathla. His conduct at Flamingo Key was opaque—to use a charitable word. But he'll pick the winning side when he sees we mean business. Perhaps he can even pin down Chekika's village."

"Chekika has many villages. We all know that."

"He's licking his wounds somewhere at this moment. With the best of luck, you won't have too much time to reach Indian Mound. If he's camped to the west, your chances are that much better. To say nothing of my own——"

"With all due respect, sir——" Roy let the spurt of anger die and began anew. "How can Dan pin-point Chekika on this map unless they're in outright alliance?"

"Dan would never be anyone's outright ally, Roy." The colonel's voice was still only mildly reproving. "I don't deny he's a slippery customer; I merely say he can be useful. And if he is in league with Chekika, why did he lose two barns in the raid? And shoot two Seminoles with his own hand, when he finally got ashore?"

"I've said my piece, sir. I won't elaborate." Roy settled uncomfortably in his chair as Merrick bellowed for his aide. It was quite true that Dan had played the role of a minor hero when the Navy had stormed ashore at Flamingo Key. It was also true that his barns and the stolen trade goods were insured in Havana for their full value.

Dan walked into the conference with a bubbling good humor that was in marked contrast to the faces around him and came to attention before the colonel's table, saluting the commandant with slapdash grace. Roy scowled in his corner when Merrick rose and offered the trader his hand. Granted, Dan's service of supply was an important element in their plans. Evans had been an accommodating sutler for this outpost all during the Indian war. There was still something grotesque—and a little sinister—about the way he possessed the room even before he had lighted his cheroot, refused a tot of rum, and settled in the most comfortable armchair.

"No drinks today, Colonel. Too many figures in my head. D'you want the list?"

"Not if you gave Stevens a copy. When will you join him above the falls?"

"Tomorrow at the latest. The moment we unload that last barge from Flamingo. Rather a piece of luck, wasn't it, that it pulled out the night before the raid?"

"An astounding bit of luck, Dan," said Andy dryly. "Did you guess the raid was coming?"

"Lord love you, Captain Winter, it shocked me out of ten years' growth. I won't say I'm ruined, but it was a narrow squeak."

"When did you last see Chekika, Dan?" Roy asked before the colonel could speak.

If the trader resented the question, he gave no sign. "Two months ago, Doctor—more or less. At Pahokee Hammock. When he was still at peace with the Army." Dan's eyes strayed to the map—and the red-penciled line that represented Andy's tentative route of march. "If he was planning to ruin me *then*—he wasn't letting out the secret."

"Did you trade at Pahokee?"

"Salt for otter, Doctor. Nothing more. Wasn't a proper powwow, really. Nothing like the council fire he lit for you a week ago."

Roy smiled thinly; Dan was a fast man on his feet. His remark implied that Roy's own trading journey into the Glades, when Chekika was actually on the warpath, had been highly illegal—a dark contrast to Dan's own conduct. Again he struck back quickly before Merrick could intervene.

"Sure there weren't a few carbines in your trading pack, Evans?"

"You know I'm not a gunrunner, Doctor. So does the colonel." Dan sat up in his chair, a moon-faced monument to virtue. "Give me a little warning next time you call me an Indian lover. I'll bring character witnesses."

"No one's accusing you of anything, Dan," said the colonel. "Roy's been through a hard time—he's entitled to a joke. I'm asking you just one question, then you can be about your business. D'you have any notion where Chekika is camping at this moment?"

Dan blew a cloud of high-grade Havana across the map. "Now that you ask me, sir, you couldn't do better than follow this red line. Who drew it, might I ask—Dr. Coe?"

"*I* drew that line, Dan," said Andy. "And I'm not too sure you should look over our shoulders."

"Suit yourselves, gentlemen." This afternoon Dan's good humor was as monumental as his person. "Dr. Coe needs a map no more than I when he goes into the Glades. We all know it's useless to chart a country that changes its shape with each hurricane—and each high tide. But if you find Chekika anywhere, it'll be west of the Big Slough—as that red line indicates. Camped in a saw-grass sea, on one of a thousand hammocks, with all his squaws and dogs. Frying venison in my corn meal, dreaming dreams over my best rum, and daring the United States Army to smoke him out." Dan leveled his cheroot at Andy. "That's your job, my friend. And I can't say I envy you. The only man I envy less is Dr. Coe. *His* job is to find enough dry land for you to fight on."

The colonel arched his brows. "Is that all you have to say, *Dan?*"

"I'd help you if I could, sir. You must know that."

"Quite so, Dan. And I needn't say I value your opinion highly." But the colonel's brows were beetling, nonetheless. Watching the byplay, Roy could only applaud Dan's oblique attack. If he's really on Chekika's side, thought Roy swiftly, he's using his time perfectly. The implication that the Seminole had outguessed them so far—and would continue to play that same infuriating role—had rankled deeply. The suggestion, made so blandly, that neither he nor Andy could pin Chekika to the map and force an action might have been all the irritant Colonel Merrick needed to throw his entire forces west of Ten-Mile Slough. . . . And then, as he studied Merrick narrowly, he caught the twinkle in the colonel's eyes. Merrick could be bullheaded at times, but he was no fool. Roy got to his feet, certain that Dan would leave this room no wiser than he entered.

"If you'll excuse me, sir, I'll be stowing my gear——"

"Fair enough, Roy," said the colonel. "I won't say goodby now. You'll have your final word at base camp day after tomorrow."

"May I go too, sir?" asked Andy.

"You may not. Stay a moment more and fight with Dan. You can still save the Army money."

Andy went to the door with Roy and punched him in the ribs with one hard fist. "Still a team, Dr. Coe?"

"Still a team, Captain. I'll meet you at the landing stage."

Dan Evans came forward, too, with outstretched hand. "The best of luck, Roy—in case our paths don't cross again."

I'd give a great deal to count on that, thought Roy gloomily as he struck palms with the trader. Dan's handclasp was as firm as any politician's. Dan's magnificent grin, as always, was a perfect mask.

On the terreplein Roy yielded to a sudden impulse and walked down the line of breastworks to the west. From this vantage point he could look down on the landing stage and the mouth of the Miami. A whole company of regulars was busily transferring stores from the last of Dan's barges to the fleet of ungainly freight canoes that lined the bank. His own canoe, he noted, was ready and waiting, its tarpaulin folded back neatly to receive his gear. For the first time today he felt his spirits rise a little. Argument, at least, was behind them now.

He followed his impulse through, walking into an empty sentry box and resting his hands on the palmetto rail while he let his eyes sweep the wilderness to the west. At this hour the Miami gleamed in the sunset like a river of gold—a broad trace dividing the dark earth of the mucklands, a serpentine path that lost itself at the horizon's rim among the crowding jungle hammocks. From this height the saw-grass immensity of the Glades themselves could be sensed rather than seen— an endless, tawny blaze of light that seemed to merge and mingle with the setting sun.

Roy stared into the sunset for a long time, letting the tears mist his eyelids. Somewhere in that tawny desert Mary Grant still lived and breathed. Try as he might, he could not quite believe that he had lost her forever. . . . He turned resolutely away from the sentry box, accepted the salute of a gunner at the ten-pounder that was fired from the terreplein each day at sunset, and walked out of Fort Everglades without seeing it at all. For the time, at least, he was finished with man-made defenses. The only reality was the canoe that waited at the landing stage and the river that snaked west, like a ribbon of murky gold, to the heart of the wilderness.

ii

They had paddled hard since dawn, straining to put the hard-earned miles between them and the base camp. Tending ever westward, skirting the high banks of the river in their search for dead water, they had avoided the seaward tug of the Miami, where the stream rushed into the narrow, jungle-choked ravine that was known as the falls. Now, as that same jungle closed down in earnest on both banks of the river, Roy could feel the backlash of the current slacken with each stroke of his paddle. In another quarter hour he could count on shallow water and the push pole, leaving Andy to supply the motive power at the bow.

He rested for a few strokes to test the strength of the current, and watched the great, corded muscles of his companion's back and shoulders knot to their task. Andy's in his element, too, he thought absently; it was the first conscious reflection he had permitted himself since he had gulped a mug of scalding coffee at Sergeant Ranson's mess table, stripped to a buckskin breechclout in the chill of the morning dew, and taken his place as steersman of the dugout.

Knowing their task so thoroughly, they had had no need of words in the long, grueling hours that had followed that embarkation just above the falls. The sleepy, early-morning sounds of the wakening camp had dropped swiftly behind; the impromptu stockade of freshly felled palmetto logs, the whispered good-by of the last sentry on the bank had seemed strangely misplaced in this tropic stillness. That ageless quiet was part of their blood stream now; after the first stroke of their paddles they had seemed to live with silence forever. . . .

Now, as the ground along the Miami changed from pine-barren to powder-dry savanna, from tropic meadow to swampland ringed with the sullen yellow cypress, it was difficult to tell where land left off and river began. Though it had been days since the last rain, the water was still high around the cypress knees. Here and there, where the dense riot of vegetation thickened, the ghostly trees seemed to arch their arms above the channel, trailing their prodigal fronds of moss like the filaments of a shroud. Though the day was far advanced, the moss still seemed heavy with dew here where the sun could seldom reach. This, too, was part of the barrier that stood between the rich coastal lands and the true land of saw grass. For all its graveyard hush, he felt at home here—driving the canoe forward with full-armed strokes of the push pole, offering Andy an occasional low-voiced warning as a snag or a mudbank showed ahead.

Water birds stalked proudly among the cypress knees or stood immobile on the arch of a mangrove root, waiting for the noonday meal to swim within their ken. When the swamp gave way to the long, humpbacked contour of a hammock, there were water oaks and blue gum, swamp maple and the Spanish ash, knotted in communion by the flying tentacles of the wild grapevine. Orchids gleamed here and there in the green gloom like rainbows. . . . He had promised a girl an orchid for her hair—a white cattleya for choice—back in another world. At the time it had scarcely mattered that she was the promised bride of the man who now sat at the bow of this Indian dugout. He glanced again at his boatmate—near-naked, like himself, and quite as saddle-brown, his eyes slitted to catch the slightest stir of life ahead.

"Is that Lost Creek on the right?"

It was the first word Andy Winter had spoken in an hour. Roy chuckled, forcing a lightness he did not feel.

"Your memory is excellent, Andy. We should fetch the lookout in ten minutes now."

He sawed on the push pole, bringing the canoe to an instant halt. Lily pads, mingled with the first tufts of saw grass he had seen today, all but masked the narrow mouth of the creek, one of several tributary streams that had begun to finger into the Miami. A 'gator dozed in that sick-green ambush—for all the world like a foundered log. Only the little pig eyes, infinitely crafty behind the creature's long, ulcerated snout, reminded them that this was a living thing—waiting, like the mournful waders, for lunch to swim within range of bear-trap jaws. Roy judged that the giant saurian was fully twelve feet from nostrils to tail.

"Cerberus guards the gate," he said. "We'll give him a wide berth. They don't like company at feeding time."

Andy stared incuriously at the brown-black shadow that merged so artfully with the water around it. "What is it—'gator or croc?"

"An alligator, this time. The crocodiles are dying out this close to tidewater."

The 'gator continued to regard them warily as they swung into the creek on the far bank and ghosted respectfully past his lair. They had proceeded less than a dozen yards when a sound like a pistol crack split the quiet of the swamp, sending the waders squawking from their own vantage points and flushing a flame-colored spoonbill from its nest inshore. Roy chuckled again as Andy just missed dropping his paddle in his haste to unlimber a rifle from the forward thwarts.

"You *have* been leading a soft life, Captain Winter. That was our friend sampling his first course."

The water of the creek, he noted, was even clearer than Miami, fed only by the current that flowed outward from the vast shallows of the Glades. Cupped in its bowl of coral limestone, the saw-grass sea discharged its main flow to the south, until it merged with the Gulf above Cape Sable. Here, where the Miami had cut a channel to the east, a hundred tributaries poured their quota from the nearer sloughs— channels that had been scoured long before the First Crusade. Roy counted his strokes, as always, when they had rounded the first bend and entered the hot, green tunnel of grape and live oak that bored through the last of the swamp. A hundred thrusts of the push pole, joined to Andy's muscular paddle, would bring them within sight of the hammock that supported his lookout oak, like a lighthouse in the sea.

Each stroke was shorter now; here and there the push pole grated sharply among the irregular coral masses that showed clearly below—a treacherous bottom when the Glades were really low.

"Can you believe the saw-grass is less than a hundred yards beyond?"

"When I've come this far," said Andy, "I can believe anything. Thank heaven we don't have to fight Chekika here."

The canoe leaped into sunlight as he spoke, shedding the clammy embrace of the swamp like a snake in springtime. With that fluid thrust it entered a channel banked on both sides by tall yuccas, the Spanish bayonet of the Floridas. Here the water was scarcely a foot in depth; Roy was glad that they had decided to travel light today, storing only an iron ration under the tarpaulin along with their guns and maps.

"Heads up, Andy—here's our lookout."

The huge live oak towered over them without warning, rising from the thronging spears of the yuccas like a green tower. The shade of the lower branches enclosed them gratefully. Andy stepped ashore with the painter looped on one arm, pausing to let a dusty-black snake (a cotton mouth moccasin heavy with eggs) glide from bank to stream. Roy followed in a rush, beaching the canoe as he came ashore. The mat of dog fennel underfoot was soft to his moccasined soles as he bent to unload their map case and a spyglass. He broke a sprig of the aromatic green plant and chewed it thoughtfully, letting its rank flavor bring back a score of noonings such as these.

Andy was already in the lower branches of the oak, swinging to the crotch above with all the aplomb of a chimpanzee. "How many men can we bring this way?"

"As many as you like, if that creek gets a good rain. Wait till you've checked your map."

They had spoken in whispers. Now they ascended the tree in silence, taking care to stay well within the shelter of the leaves. Both of them knew that Lookout Oak, as it was called by trapper and Seminole alike, was a favorite observation post for both races. Roy had even weighed the chances of a head-on collision with the enemy midway of that green tower. Now, as he scrambled steadily toward the summit, he realized that his fear had been absurd. Chekika would surely bide his time—with no overtly hostile act—until their rendezvous at Pahokee Hammock.

Behind him he heard Andy Winter give a gasp of surprise as he swung up to the highest crotch of the tree and stood boldly upright on the rough platform that had been clamped there, like a bird's nest open to the sky. Woven of tough green grapevine and strips of lightwood, it resembled the floor of a tree house; once the slight feel of giddiness had passed, there was room for both men to stand, with elbow room to spare. Andy contented himself with a half-crouching posture far from the edge, and stared at the brazier that stood on its tripod, in the precise center of this airy nest.

"Don't tell me you've camped here?"

"More than once," said Roy cheerfully. "It's the coldest bed in the Glades on a summer's night, and that smudge pot keeps it free of mosquitoes." He knelt beside his friend to check the contents of the brazier. "We've enough lightwood knots to build a fire now, if you're willing to risk it."

"Let's have a look to the west before we show our hand."

They took the telescope in turns, sweeping the whole circle of the horizon in a narrow-eyed concentration that excluded words. From this airy vantage point Roy could see that the cypress wall they had just pierced stood a good mile to the east. Solid as the battlement of a fortress, this belt of swamp extended north and south, as far as the glass could reach—empty of life at this height, desolate as the lip of some crater on a forgotten moon. Below them the segment they had just traversed was cut by a dozen streams. Chocolate-dark at land level, these minor waterways flashed silver in the blaze of morning as they linked at the eastern horizon to join the Miami.

But it was to the west that the glass swung, drawn by an invisible magnet. As always, Roy felt his heart miss a beat as the Glades swam into view—a waving sea of grass that swept over the heat-fogged rim of earth without visible limits, a wild, bright plain that was neither earth nor water. This saw-grass empire was colored like ripe wheat in the nearer distance, shading to emerald green and sick chartreuse where the persistent heat mirages mingled grass and sky. Once again he reminded himself that this land was older than time, untouched by human hands. From this height it seemed as motionless as eternity. Yet when you looked again you saw that it throbbed with a heartbeat all its own—visible as the gleam of the sloughs that laced its vastness like mighty veins, real as the flamingos that swept its surface like vermilion dropped from the palette of some artist-god. . . . Watching the birds vanish into the haze, Roy would have accepted a flight of pterodactyls without blinking. Even the birds and beasts of today seemed out of place in the scene below him. This, he told himself, is not the abode of 'gator and heron and soft-eyed otter. This is a bath for dinosaurs.

"Which hammock is Pahokee?" asked Andy.

He came back to reality with a grateful start. It was good to feel his friend's common-sense presence at his side, good to remember that the map spread on the floor of their eyrie was a guide of sorts—even to the grassy maze below.

"Look due south. You can see its outline clearly."

It was always a surprise, after the first breathless shock had subsided, to note that land clumps were everywhere in that green-yellow sea. Humpback islands for the most part (the palm-tufted hammocks that were the last asylum of the Seminole), these spots of earth tended to submerge in the sweep of the saw-grass. Yet under a more careful scrutiny they stood out like oases on a desert waste. Some of them resembled low mounds bristling with violent vegetation, like the backbones of immense porcupines. Others were almost park-like, spaced with magnificent stands of coco-palms and live oaks, magnolias and oleanders. Here and there, for some nameless reason, the trees stood stark and dead—and the bare branches, whitened by years of sun, pocked the green surface like a leper's scars.

"They're talking to us now on Pahokee," said Andy. "Want to answer straight off—or shall we pretend we aren't here?"

Roy lifted his glass and studied the smudge in detail. Lifting like a wavering finger in the motionless noon, the signal fire was pencil-thin against the sky to the south. He saw that it had been lighted in the precise center of Pahokee Hammock, where the Indians had hacked a small clearing from the jungle. Here, in more peaceful times, he had sat over a dozen council fires, or watched Dan Evans and others of his ilk go through the endless ritual of barter with Charley Emathla, Coacoochee, and other chiefs who had preceded Chekika. . . . Now the gray signal smudge, pluming into the blue and arching at its tip like a crude question mark, was forlorn beyond belief in that silent immensity.

His mind told him beyond question that at least one living Indian was nursing that fire a scant two miles away—feeding damp moss above the lightwood coals and watching the leafy mass of Lookout Oak with patient eyes. His mind insisted that Chekika had expected this rendezvous daily, with every confidence that they would come to terms. Another part of his brain, bemused as always, held back from the task of making contact. Once he admitted that the Grassy Water could nourish mankind, white or red, its spell would be broken—along with its overtone of terror.

"Tease him, if you like," said Andy. "I think we should get it over."

Roy snapped the spyglass into its case. His naked eye could just discern the gray smoke plume to the south; he knew that its guardian (whose eyesight was far keener than his own) would observe their answer instantly on this windless morning.

Andy had already lumped the lightwood knots in the brazier; a splinter, heavy with resin, caught the first spurt of the lucifer. The clear thread of flame that hissed through the lightwood gave no smoke as it devoured the fat pine chunks. Roy babied the fire, letting it simmer into coals and adding still more of the resinous wood before he dropped the first moss into the brazier. The dense, greasy smoke, controlled instantly by a strip of wet blanket, rose in a column as perfect as a demonstration of Euclid.

"Does Pahokee answer?"

"It's talking now."

The pencil smudge had wavered and died as they spoke. Now it spurted anew from the frowzy tangle of palm and dog fennel. Three short bursts into the blue, as though some colossus were dozing behind a corncob and ruminating between puffs.

"*Nok-a-tee,*" said Roy.

"I kill them," said Andy. "So far, I don't talk their language."

"He's asking what we want."

"Mary—and Dr. Barker," said Andy. "In that order, if you please."

Roy began sending a hieroglyph of smoke bursts skyward. "One doesn't come to the point so quickly," he said.

"What are you saying now?"

"Im-po-hitch-caw." Roy chopped the blanket into the hissing coals. "In other words—does he hear? He says his ears are open to the words of Salofkachee."

"How can he be sure it's you in Lookout Oak?"

"Even the Seminoles trust us that far, Andy. Now I'm asking the Father of Killers for permission to enter the Grassy Water."

"Don't tell him the Army's coming without it day after tomorrow."

Two puffs answered the query before the last thread of smoke vanished over Pahokee.

"Ask him if he's alone," said Andy.

The question produced another affirmative; there was something oddly proud in the exuberance of those two long bursts of smoke. Alone and confident, the speaker seemed ready to face any threat from the white world beyond his cypress wall. Salofkachee, and he alone, had been granted the privilege of crossing that barrier.

"D'you suppose it's the Wildcat himself?" asked Andy.

Roy shook his head; he did not relish the sudden gleam that had flashed from his friend's eyes. "If Chekika had come in person, he'd expect to see Colonel Merrick. Or you —depending on whom he thinks is the bigger knife. He knows I'm the colonel's sense-bearer, and yours. So he'll send a sense-bearer of his own."

"Say you'll come at once."

Again the smoke signaled across the miles of empty air. "He says he'll hear my voice."

"Fair enough," said Andy. "What are we waiting for?"

The dragoon captain went down the tree trunk in a series of breakneck bounds, beating Roy to the canoe by several strides. "At least he was waiting," he said. "That must mean he's anxious."

"Indians are better at waiting than we," said Roy. "Purely

as a matter of strategy, we should have waited too—until the last day of grace. If it weren't for Mary——" He flushed and began again as quietly as he could. "Naturally, *I* can understand your impatience. I hope Chekika will do likewise. He may mistake this early arrival for fear and double his demands."

Andy was already at his place behind the forward thwart. "Leave that sense-bearer to me. He'll go back to Wildcat with the right impression."

"It's safer if I go to Pahokee alone, Andy."

"I wouldn't hear of it. Suppose they decide they need another hostage?"

"I'm willing to risk that. After all, you aren't invited to this parley."

"It isn't a parley. We're giving Chekika his orders. He's to surrender Mary and Dr. Barker at once, without ransom. If he refuses, he'll get what he deserves. Believe me, I won't mince words."

"I think I should do the talking, Andy."

"You can't go into the Glades alone, Roy. Not any more. We're at war with Chekika, and we're past taking risks. Especially if they're needless."

"Perhaps we're risking more if we stay together."

"Are you sure there's only one brave on Pahokee?"

"Quite sure."

"Then we go together. Since when have we been too stupid to outsmart a single Indian?"

Roy got into the dugout. It was a little late to explain to Captain Winter that they were moving into sacred ground, where his very presence would be an abomination.

"Promise me one thing, Andy," he said at last, when they were in open water again, poling steadily toward Pahokee. "Let me go ashore alone and see what they want."

"We *know* what they want, Roy. Our job today is to convince them that they've bitten off more than they'll ever chew."

"I can say that as well as you——"

"Which means, in fact, that you can say it far better."

Roy, standing high on the transom seat as he plied the sweep, matched Andy's grin. "Take another look," he said. "Wouldn't you mistake me for an Indian at twenty paces?"

"I'm just as brown as you."

"Granted. You could pass for one of Chekika's chiefs as well as I—until we come to that carrot topknot. I've asked you a dozen times to shave your skull before we go campaigning——"

"Don't rub it in, Roy; I knew this is my first real tour of duty in the saw grass."

"You've misunderstood me again. There's no one I'd rather have with me at this moment—providing you'll remember you're a simple scout and not a member of a ruling race."

Andy, who was driving the bow paddle with all his strength, said no more. And yet Roy was certain that the small lecture had found its mark. He tested his belief cautiously.

"Don't you trust me to handle a simple parley?"

"Implicitly. Put that screen of water oaks between us, and Chekika's sense-bearer will never know I left the lookout. But if you *are* walking into a trap, I'll still be covering you."

Roy shrugged, and swung the dugout against the thicket of palmetto and dwarf oak that ruled off the north face of the hammock from the encroaching saw-grass. The water lane was narrow here; he dipped the push pole silently, his senses strained for the first breath of life in the massed vegetation ahead.

"Not even a razorback could break through," said Andy.

"There's a path within ten feet."

They had faced each other as they spoke, letting their lips frame a soundless whisper. Roy backed water and thrust forward sharply. The dugout broke a curtain of grapevine, glided into a hot, green tunnel for half its length, and grounded on a shelving bank. Ahead, a faint trace twisted inland, most instantly in a green mass that roared with sun and silence.

"I still think we should go together," said Andy.

"And I'm asking you to take cover—and keep covered."

"What if I insisted?"

"You won't, Andy. You know I'm right."

Roy went ashore without giving himself time to think. His memory had danced ahead nimbly enough. The clearing was no more than a hundred yards inland; like the trace he was following now, it had been hacked from this hardtack with cane knives. Already the dog fennel was knee-high in spots—mute evidence that this once-peaceful meeting ground had been long in disuse.

"You've come far enough, Andy." Even before he turned, Roy knew that his friend had left the dugout armed to the teeth. The pistols in his belt were primed and ready; so was the carbine nested in the curve of his arm.

"Are you sure he's waiting?"

"You read the smoke signals, didn't you?"

"Did they say he was alone?"

"Alone—and waiting in peace."

Andy took cover reluctantly as the path opened to show the clearing. When Roy turned he noted with approval that his friend had all but vanished in the dog fennel, which grew still higher among the water oaks along the trace. Only the gleam of his eyes in that hot ambush and the flash of his smile betrayed his presence.

"What do I tell the colonel if you're taken?"

"Tell him what you like. He'll understand there was no other way."

"My guess is that it's you Chekika wants—not your hair. Three hostages would be better than two."

Roy stopped dead, feeling his heart turn over. What if Andy were right, after all? In Chekika's book, Salofkachee was still a friend—the last true friend he had in the whole world. Perhaps the signal *had* been a ruse to draw him to the hammock alone. In another moment he might be under guard—on his way to the Seminole village and to Mary. . . . He forced that crazy hope from his mind and met Andy's grin without wavering.

"I'll deliver your terms—and bring back Chekika's. Don't move until I return."

"Be back in five minutes, or I'll follow you."

Roy moved down the path with long-legged strides, letting both arms swing at his sides to show he was unarmed. Five minutes, he thought, will be more than enough to convey my meager message. Now that Andy's warlock mood was behind him, he could feel his mind swing into action along with his free-striding legs. The parley would be futile, of course; he had known that from the beginning. And yet it was highly essential that he meet this sense-bearer face to face—if only to convince Chekika that there could be no drawing back on either side unless the hostages were returned.

Thirty miles to the east, where the Miami dropped down its jungle ravine to meet the sea, the base camp waited only

an order for the dispersal they had planned so carefully at
Fort Everglades. His observations from Lookout Oak had
convinced him more than ever that it would be feasible to
filter the entire force into the Glades, to follow a score of
minor waterways that Chekika could never scout, for the
rendezvous at Ten-Mile Slough. Once they had met at this
great open waterway, less than a half day's hard paddling
from Okeechobee itself, they could throw caution aside and
head straight for Indian Mound—a spot where no white man
save he had dared to set foot, even in the years of peace.

It was more gamble than strategy, of course—and, like all
gambles, it needed imagination and nerve. He could count on
Andy Winter for both, once they were fairly far afield; the
need for an apparent give-and-take at times like these was
something that the dragoon captain refused to grasp.

The sense-bearer would be told that war was the only alternative to surrender; once their demand for the return of
Dr. Barker and Mary Grant had been refused, he would
throw down the gauge of battle. Chekika would sharpen his
knife—and expect them to drive for the very heart of the
Glades in a foredoomed effort to pin him to that watery map.
When he learned instead that they had dug in at Indian
Mound, he would be forced, for once, to attack on the white
man's terms. If he refused to drive the interlopers from that
hallowed ground, the nation would rise against him to the
last man.

It had been easy to plan thus while they bent over the map
at Fort Everglades. Now, as he strode across this island on
the verge of the Grassy Water, he felt his mind cloud with
other conjectures. What if Chekika sensed a trap after they
reached their objective? If his scouts reported the ominous
massing of forces north of Okeechobee, he might refuse to
give battle, even on holy earth. Or he might see the trap
clearly—and strike with all his force before it was sprung.
. . . Roy refused to dwell on that possibility now. The stakes
were on the table; it was too late to withdraw from the game.

For the same reason he could not pause to wonder about
Mary's fate once the war was joined. Hostages were always
of value to the Indians when an issue was in doubt; he was
sure that both she and Dr. Barker would be treated fairly
enough while Chekika controlled the destiny of the nation—
provided, of course, that they were still playable pieces in the

stolid chess game he was waging with Joel Poinsett in Washington. But what if Chekika (or his successor) realized at last that Washington would never yield? What if they reeled out of battle with their power broken forever, and fled to the fastnesses of Big Cypress with two useless whites in their midst?

Knowing the answer too well, and forcing it from his mind, he walked into the full sunlight of the clearing. There was the signal fire in the center of that weed-grown circle; there on a platform between two cabbage palms was the shelter where the signaler had spread his blanket in the darkness while he waited for word from Fort Everglades. A few wisps of smoke still curled skyward in the windless air; a few gnawed turkey bones made a forlorn pattern on the bare ground before the fire, to show where the lone emissary of the nation had eked out his vigil. There was no other sign of life in the clearing. Save for the whir of a hummingbird's wings among the trumpet vines, there was no sound.

Roy had taken his first hesitant step toward the palm-thatch shelter when the war whoop smote his eardrums. A high, keening shout of fury from the pathway he had just taken, followed instantly by the crack of Andy's carbine. Roy, who had flattened by instinct in the dog fennel, raised his head cautiously to test the silence that followed; as his knees bunched, his right hand groped by rote for the knife that wasn't there. Two jack-rabbit leaps carried him to the cover of the first clump of palms at the clearing's edge. Then, still crouching, he ran straight down the path to his friend's aid.

As he turned the first bend he saw that no aid was needed. Andy was striding down the path to meet him, the smoking carbine still in one fist. A stone-dead Seminole was slung across his shoulders as casually as any trophy of the chase. Even from where he stood Roy could see the neat bullet hole between those staring, glassy eyes. With a quick sense of relief he noted that this was not a member of Chekika's council. Evidently Chekika himself had expected little of this meeting, or he would never have sent this weedy young buck to Pahokee.

Andy tossed his burden across the platform between the palms. Naked as some red Adam, and reeking of the fish oil the Seminoles used in the Glades to drive off insects, the tender of the signal fire was no more than twenty; his scalp lock bristled from his skull like a defiant rooster's comb. Roy studied the unknown's face carefully, noting the strong blending of Indian and Negroid features—a blood mixture that grew more complex with the generations as runaway slaves sought asylum within the nation.

"How did it happen?"

The dragoon captain chuckled. "Believe it or not, he tried to ax me there in the dog fennel. You heard the war whoop——"

"And the shot."

"He wasn't too good a stalker," said Andy grimly. "I saw him make his move a good minute before. So I pretended to be watching you—and let him come."

"I hope you're convinced he was alone."

"Quite convinced," said Andy. "Would you be alive now if he weren't?"

"You might have warned him. Let him tell us what he knew."

Andy glanced carelessly at the body sprawled on the rough cypress planking. "Dead or alive, does he look as though he knew anything—ever?"

"Tell me this much, Andy. Did you mean to kill him when you came ashore?"

"Of course."

"When I came here to parley?"

"We came to give Chekika a warning. This will do nicely."

As he spoke Andy lashed the dead Indian's ankles with a length of wild grapevine—that tough green liana of the Florida jungle that outlasted hempen rope. The free end of the lashing looped easily over the tuft of the palm above them. Andy tugged mightily on his improvised derrick, until the body, swinging grotesquely in the empty air, hung dead downward from the very heart of the tree. Roy watched without protest as the dragoon captain opened his long clasp knife and ripped the scalp lock from the dead skull in three casual slashes. The taking of such trophies was highly unofficial —and standard practice among officers and men alike. So was the bounty paid at Fort Everglades.

"So this is why you came, Andy?"

"Tomorrow, or the day after, Chekika will turn up here for his answer. He'll find it, swinging from this cabbage palm. We'll put it in writing, too, just to make sure he understands." Andy opened his bullet pouch and brought forth a folded sheet of foolscap neatly sewn in oilskin. "My last word to the Father of Seminoles," he said. "Would you care to read it before I tie it around this fellow's neck?"

Roy opened the note in silence. The hummingbird, frightened by the shot, had resumed its foraging among the trumpet vines. The whir of its wings seemed to enter his brain while he spelled out Andy's neat block letters and his fluent but inaccurate Spanish:

To the King of Wildcats, Greetings:

When you read these words, I will await the return of Dr. Jonathan Barker, and the lady you have mistaken for his daughter, at the Sandy Bay. My cook fires will light the way to your surrender, from the summit of Indian Mound.

Come back to the wisdom of your father, King of Killers —and resolve to kill no more. Return to the Great White Father himself, who has never wished you harm. Come under his protection, Great Chief, while your own strength is still unbroken—and taste of his abundance and peace.

CAPTAIN ANDREW WINTER
Commander, Glades Rangers

"I wish I'd seen this first, Andy."

"Why? It's part of our strategy."

"Does Colonel Merrick know you've written it?"

"Of course. He endorsed it fully."

Roy frowned and held his tongue as he knotted the challenge into its oilskin container and returned it to Andy. Nor did he offer a protest when the dragoon strapped the message firmly to the body.

"Don't scowl so, Roy," said Andy. "We've got to spell things out for Chekika. You did tell me that he read Spanish well enough."

"D'you think it's wise, advertising our next move in advance?"

"Apparently you've given a great many orders without consulting me."

"Every man in that base camp was chewing out his navel,

waiting for action. I saw no harm in starting our jump-off for
Big Slough." Andy's grin could be disarming on occasion; he
used it to good effect now. "If we move fast, we can still
meet Sergeant Ranson; he's to wait for us at the mouth of
Lost Creek."

"And the others?"

"They'll ghost in on time. Rely on me for that."

Roy subsided with a silent curse. Andy had spoken the
truth, of course: every man in his command, sharpened over
the months into a well-tempered ax of war, was capable of
entering the Glades singlehanded with no more commotion
than a cruising 'gator. Backtracking by a hundred water
mazes, avoiding the main current of the Miami, they could
convince even Chekika that they were breaking camp and returning to the fort. Roy pulled his eyes away from the cabbage palm and the grotesque fruit that swung, pendulum-like,
from its crown.

"If I'm to be your scout," he said, "I must know your
plans in advance."

"You'll have enough worries later. Why shouldn't I spare
you this one?"

"Very well, Andy. Shall we rejoin your command before
Chekika finds us here?"

Andy stumped dutifully in his wake as he followed the
path to the water's edge. "Say it, Roy. We're still friends.
You think I overplayed my hand."

Pray God you haven't, thought Roy. If Chekika sends a
messenger to Pahokee today (and who are we to assume that
this lone brave was left to his own devices?) he can still outdistance us in the race to Indian Mound. With the best of
luck he can jump us there before we've established an adequate defense. And yet he could not damn Andy's boldness
out of hand. Somehow it seemed part of their scheme, down
to the last syllable in the note itself—a concentrated insult
calculated to drive the last wisp of caution from the Seminole
mind.

"I wish I had your sublime confidence that you'll be alive
tomorrow."

"Of course you'll be alive," said Andy. "How can we finish
this war without you?" He got briskly into the canoe and
steadied it against the bank while Roy stepped on the tran-

som. "Take me to Lost Creek by the shortest route—and stop worrying. I'm in command from now on. Worry is my job."

iii

The snores of two hundred sleeping men were all around him as he tossed aside his blanket and rose on cautious tiptoe. Testing each footstep with care to avoid the dog-tired sleepers, Dr. Royal Coe moved across the bivouac to take the pulses of the three who snored in sick bay. The inevitable dengue case, dosed to the ears with quinine and bathed in the sweat that advertised the victory of a healthy young body over the minor scourge that had struck down so many in the Floridas. The equally inevitable victim of skitters, dosed with strong tea and a tongue lashing from Lieutenant Hutchens. Hutchens himself, who had tossed aside his cap for the last grueling mile of today's journey—and had fainted like a schoolgirl just before his canoe skimmed from the mouth of Ten-Mile Slough to gain the open lake . . .

All his patients, he found, would live to fight another day. He moved on, answering the whispered challenge of the sentry at the first barricade, and tossing a leg across that stout palmetto wall to reach their outer line of defense. Here he was challenged again—this time by a rifleman burrowed into a breastwork at the very edge of Okeechobee. . . . Andy may be foolhardy on occasion, he thought. He may be incapable of grasping certain basic facts—including the obvious one that a Seminole may possess a brain. But he's a commander to the manner born. And he's driven the Everglades Rangers to his objective in record time.

Beyond their encampment (just out of rifleshot, to the south) the bulk of Indian Mound thrust up against the sky like an ungainly pyramid. He walked toward it on soundless tiptoe, soothing the running gantlet of challenges. Andy's cook fires still winked on its flank, precisely as he had promised; Andy's lookout (it was none other than Sergeant Ranson) sat boldly on its flat summit, his rifle ready on his knees. Each hour the chain of sentinels would send a new man to that vantage point. Like the insolent ring of cook fires, the sergeant's very bulk was a kind of challenge—like the flag of

Union that would be raised on that same summit with the dawn, if they lived till morning.

Now that they were actually in battle order and awaiting the inevitable assault, Roy was obscurely glad that no attempt would be made to defend the Mound itself. Andy had ruled it out as a *point d'appui*. The spot where they camped tonight was an ideal bastion—a wedge of sand thrust into the lake itself, in the very shadow of that ancient pyramid. An hour's hard work had cleared a fire lane at the neck of this promontory. Long before dusk had fallen they had laid down their pits for the advance line of sharpshooters, backed by a ridge of palmetto logs that rose to a height of six feet, boxing their redoubt perfectly, with a solid line of rifles to hold the box intact.

On the lakeside Andy had hastened to throw up still higher breastworks at every point where Chekika might force a landing. Faced two ways against an enemy onslaught, he had no real need to divide his forces; thanks to the snug dimensions of their fortress, he could shift his fire power at will, as rapidly as his men could reload. And though they were not fighting from Indian Mound, they could deny it to an enemy from both breastworks, whether the Seminoles attacked from land or water.

Their invasion of the Glades had been a minor saga in itself and, like all sagas, had contained more sweat than poetry, more sunbitten frustration than clash of steel. So far they had used no steel at all save for the cane knives that had hacked their path to Big Slough, the axes that had made their bivouac secure. There had been moments when that battle with the saw grass had seemed blind folly—whole hours of panic when his detail of four canoes had clung to mudbanks in a driving rain squall and tried to remember north from south. Compass and map had seemed lying counselors at such times, when the only reality was the endless scream of the gale.

The sun had reassured them with its return, even though it brought agonies of its own. At each morning, when they had sought the cover of a hammock to gnaw their cold rations, Roy had forced a quota of salt down each parched throat to repair the energy drained from sweat-soaked bodies. At the day's end, when they had pitched another cold bivouac (even a smudge pot was ruled out until they made their rendezvous), he had looked in vain for the signs of fatigue that goes beyond bone-weariness, the first whimper that is a prelude to madness in the strongest man. For all their youth, these men were veterans. All of them had lived through years of campaigning in the Florida scrub. And though war in the Glades was a new adventure for them all, they were taking their duty in stride.

Always the pitiless sun between those bursts of rain—always the yellow, steaming silence pressing from all sides as ruthlessly as the razor-sharp saw grass. . . . The sun told them that Big Slough was still to the north and west, with the wider reaches of Ten-Mile Slough and Okeechobee itself well beyond. The yellow-green silence, closing on each heart like a hot and ominous hand, was nature's answer to their feeble effort. The silence had its own voice—warning them to turn back, without words. Assuring them that heat and exhaustion would conquer them before Chekika turned his first bowstring. Yet the four canoes, with Roy's own dugout in the lead, had continued to drive onward—their only reality the next dog-leg bend in the channel they were following, the only enemy the next unlooked-for mud flat, the next saw-grass tuft where clear water should have been.

Sometimes their channel had led them through a 'gator wallow—the air sick-sweet with the exhalation of a hundred underwater lairs, the banks aswarm with the sluggish young. Beady eyes had watched their progress incuriously as they had steered a course in the dead, weed-crusted water—avoiding the twelve-foot bulls that seemed to snooze so peacefully just below surface, knowing that one careless nudge of a paddle, one swinging blow from those powerful tails, could mean death for each man aboard. Once they had blundered to the edge of a shallow lake where canvasbacks were floating by the thousands, blanketing the whole surface in a whir of restless wings. They had given the ducks a still wider berth. Had that vast flight of migrants lifted against the sky in sudden fright, it would have marked their whereabouts more clearly than any cook fire.

Always they had tended north and west, even when the compass had seemed to lie most flagrantly. At times they had heard the mourning of whippoorwills in the saw grass above and below their course and knew that other units of Andy's command (using the agreed-on signal) were fighting their way through the silt—converging, like their own unit, on a common objective. When they had first glimpsed that objective through the skirts of a dying rainstorm, they had refused to believe their eyes. Big Slough, a whole quarter mile in width and blessedly free of such hazards as gumbo and dozing 'gators, had seemed as inviting as heaven and twice as remote from mortal aspiration.

Birdcall had answered birdcall along the eastern bank. Unit by unit the Everglades Rangers had burst from their cover and swung into formation—a long double file of war canoes, each bow heavy with its quota of lead and rifles. At a command from Andy the double file had merged into a narrow triangle, the commandant at the apex with his scouts on either flank, the heavier supply canoes at the base. They had paddled in this formation for six hours, until Big Slough had opened into the baylike reaches of Ten-Mile Slough, until that chocolate estuary had yielded in turn to the flashing aquamarine of Okeechobee. They had swung into Sandy Bay and grounded their dugouts in the shadow of Indian Mound sharp on the stroke of noon.

Andy's training and his genius for command had shown in every detail of that maneuver. It was just as apparent in the hard-driving afternoon, when each minute to darkness counted—and each minute was used. Roy had watched the Rangers deploy on the shore of Biscayne Bay—a practice game that had possessed a beach in a few minutes' time, arched a thick line of rifles into the scrub to cover the first ax strokes, and lifted a stockade (complete with loopholes and sally ports) less than two hours after the first canoe had grounded. Today they had bettered the record and had used the time remaining to bolster that first rough defense.

To the north the vast surface of the lake had danced with whitecaps as an easterly breeze had swept the last rain squall from Atlantic to Gulf. To the south the cypress ring that girdled Okeechobee at this point, separating it from the sawgrass sea beyond, had steamed with miasmic heat. The shadow of Indian Mound had moved crazily in that mirage-like shimmer, then settled like an inky triangle as the cool of evening descended on lake and jungle alike. A file of pelicans on a sandbank well offshore had watched their labors like so many feathered judges; there had been no other sign of life, no stir of war bonnets in the great siesta of nature. If that stony silence had mocked their efforts a little, only Roy had noticed it. . . .

Now, with one foot on the shell-littered flank of the burial mound, he paused to breathe deep of that silence, and measured its import as calmly as he could. He was positive that Chekika was watching and waiting somewhere in that encompassing darkness, measuring his own striking force for the morrow, planning his assault with the fatalistic coolness of his race. Delivered with his full strength, and reckless of losses, that assault could overwhelm them in a matter of minutes; once the Seminoles were over those palmetto breastworks, the very snugness of Andy's fortress could turn it into a death trap. . . . But that, too, had been a calculated risk. The living target was ready, hoping to receive and throw back the first furious impact, relying on its will to live—until help came from the north.

The ring of cook fires still glowed brightly halfway up the slope of the Mound; Andy had ordered his sentries to replenish them each hour. It was part of the bravura gesture that had brought them here; if Chekika had read the message they had left on Pahokee, he would see the threat fulfilled. To these hard-bitten regulars it had seemed only logical to set up their skillets outside of camp. The pine-knot fires had burned as well on this man-made hillside; beans and bacon had tasted none the worse after simmering on a pyramid of skulls.

Roy had dug too often in this particular mound to pause in his ascent tonight. Dr. Barker had agreed with his conclusion that it was one of the most ancient burial middens in the Glades, if not in all Florida. Timucuan and Caloosa skeletons had been laid to rest here centuries before the first white man came. Succeeding tribes had increased the size of the pyramid as generations of chieftains had gone to their reward, surrounded by the bones of their enemies. Many of the later bodies had been laid in open graves to facilitate the ascent of the spirits to happier climes. As the fortunes of war had shifted among the tribes, still newer conquerors had shown their contempt for these former tenants by smashing their skeletons to bits and plowing the remains into the heart of the Mound, to make room for their own heroes.

Today the midden stood all of thirty feet above the shore of the lake—a landmark for a generation of Seminole canoes, an object of worship for the whole nation. The Seminoles themselves had not used this beach as a burial ground, since their own necrology dictated a separate grave for each chieftain. But they had always used the Mound as a focal point for each important powwow, each propitiation of their gods. On many occasions, as Roy knew, it had also been used as a kind of execution hill, when important enemies or doomed members of the nation itself, had been dispatched according to ritual.

Lank grass tangled his legs as he finished the climb; his foot dislodged a skull just under the summit, and he turned to watch it bounce down the side of the midden like a bleached ball. Sergeant Ranson sat cross-legged atop the mound, holding another skull at arm's length. Roy sat down at Ranson's side and pulled out his tobacco pouch. Somehow it seemed quite proper to touch a lucifer to his corncob; to sit here, in clear silhouette, with a grinning skull between them.

" 'Alas, poor Yorick,' " said Roy, and scratched a second lucifer to light the sergeant's own pipe. "We can hardly say we knew him well."

"Judging by his size, sir, he might have been a don. Not that they all had monkey skulls, you understand——"

"I daresay that more than one Spaniard is buried here."

"And more than one honest infantryman, Doctor."

"Would you believe I dug an Inca image out of this Mound a year ago?"

"An Inca image from Peru, sir?"

"Exactly. Take a look if you don't believe me."

Roy opened his shirt with the words and took out the jade figurine. Ever since its discovery he had worn it round his neck on a leather thong. Though he believed himself the least superstitious of mortals, he was comforted to feel that cold stone just over his heart. Its touch reminded him that the world was small—that death could come full circle with no effort.

"Looks like some sort of devil-god, Doctor."

Roy studied the figurine in the glow of the two pipe bowls. The head was large, with pointed ears; beneath it, the body was twisted in an agony that was grotesque and strangely moving. One of the basilisk eyes seemed to wink back at their scrutiny, as though this dim deity held a secret on its tongue tip and was about to whisper it aloud.

"You haven't asked me, sir," said Ranson, "but he's the spitting image of Chittamicco."

Chittamicco. The naked knife that stood between the Seminole and peace. Roy stared at the unwinking gray-green eyes. Ranson was right, of course: the twisted effigy and Chekika's heir were one. There would always be a Chittamicco, ready to fight progress to the bitter end.

"How d'you think he came here, Sergeant?"

"Pick your route, Doctor. He might have washed ashore from the Bahama Passage—or come overland from California on the King's Highway. He's still proof that gunpowder's better than arrows—you can name your century."

"Would you call him a good augury for tomorrow?"

"Wouldn't you, sir?"

Roy grinned behind his pipe and restored the jade figure to its pouch. Ranson, he reflected, was a poet of sorts; like himself, the sergeant had been born with a brain that clamored for answers. Unlike Captain Andy Winter, who was sleeping the sleep of the just at this hour and snored as lustily as any private in the stockade, Ranson had never accepted the status quo blindly—or wasted an hour of worship at outworn altars.

"Be frank, Doctor. D'you think we've an outside chance?"

"Not if the Wildcat hits us with all he has."

"Luck may be with us, sir. At this moment, I wouldn't know."

"Don't you approve of this action?"

"I don't approve or disapprove, Doctor. I take orders—and try to handle 'em the best I can." The sergeant had not spoken humbly; he was smiling as he drew on his corncob. "The Army's no bed of roses—especially now, when we're pinned down in the East and can't make up our mind to take on Mexico." Ranson spat into the dark. "You'll admit it's still a living—when a man can't decide what he wants next."

Roy accepted the veiled rebuke in silence. Ranson was right, as usual: the Army of the United States (that fledgling giant who had yet to flex his muscles or measure his strength) was hardly a career. He permitted himself to wonder why a man like Dr. Royal Coe (with an assured future awaiting him on two continents) should be seated atop a stack of prehistoric skulls tonight with a man like Ranson (a sergeant for the book—and yet a man destined, like himself, for better things).

"I came up here to spell you," Roy said at last. "Go get your rest. You've earned it."

"Offhand, sir, I'd say you'll need rest tomorrow more than I." Ranson weighed the sun-whitened skull in his hand and matched its bizarre grin. "If all goes well, I'll earn a real sleep at the fort next week—or the week after. If things go badly, sleep won't matter."

"Tell me one thing, Sergeant. Have you ever played Hamlet?"

"Never in this world, Doctor. I did see Mr. Booth enact the role more than once. If you ask me, it's an overrated play."

"Why d'you say that?"

"We're a young country, sir. And we're growing up in a young century, with all the winning cards. We're the last best hope of earth—and we'll prove as much if we last another hundred years or so. Why shouldn't a few of us die along the way to make that hope come true?"

"The last best hope of earth." Roy repeated the words in a whisper and blinked at Ranson in the moonlight. "Have you any idea whom you're quoting?"

"Certainly, sir. Thomas Jefferson, our greatest American. *He* wouldn't waste time looking at a skull and wondering why he was born." The sergeant emphasized his words by sending the death's-head spinning into darkness. "Go back to your blanket, Dr. Coe. I'm comfortable here."

"I'm taking your watch, Sergeant. What are your orders?"

"If you insist, sir. Keep an eye on that notch in the cypress where the slough meets the lake. It's the one point they can't see at ground level." Ranson shifted his carbine to Roy's knees so quietly that Roy scarcely felt the pressure of the cold steel on his dungarees. Then he had vanished, as soundlessly as Hamlet's father on the battlements of Elsinore.

Roy shifted his weight on the summit of the Mound, breathing the acrid smoke of the cook fires far below, and fighting down the absurd conviction that he had been drawn here deliberately (by an impulse outside himself) to stop Chekika's first bullet. Try as he might, he could not control the spasmodic motion of his arms and legs as those rebel limbs forced his body down the slope, until he was resting comfortably with his heels anchored in the loose sand, his arms cradled on the summit. Here, at least, he was no longer

a living target. If he could fight off drowsiness until he was relieved, he could keep that notch in the cypress under his rifle
sight—ready to sound an instant warning if Chekika struck
from the land.

The fragment of Inca jade pressed hard against his chest.
More than once he had asked himself if that emblem was a
symbol of life—or of death. Perhaps, like Ranson, he had
clung to the Army's buckskin shirttail to hasten his rendezvous with the grim reaper. Perhaps the figurine (in its way, a
replica of the human soul in its final agony) was only a symbol of that wish. . . .

Come what may, he reminded himself, I've no real reason
to go on living. If tomorrow's action fails, the girl I love will
still be a captive. If it succeeds, she will be a prisoner in an
even more sinister sense—unless Chekika sues for peace on
Andy's terms. Then, of course, she'll return to Andy's arms.
I'll be kissed just once for the part I played in that deliv-
erance; I'll have the choice of turning plantation boss for Dr.
Barker or bully-boy for Sam Houston in the land beyond the
Rio Grande.

Come what may, he thought, I must live out my days
alone—or die tomorrow. If Mary dies, my choice is death as
well. Never this long sterility that is only death in another
form. If she lives, I must put at least one wilderness between
me and her happiness.

iv

He knew that he had dozed awhile before the drums
began. His mind cleared instantly as he awakened, though his
skin was still wet with the aftermath of nightmare. The
drums had been part of that evil dream—and the clouded
image of Mary Grant, pinioned to this same sandy pyramid,
naked and screaming under the torture knife. The scream
continued in his waking brain, muted and far away, along
with the tom-tom of the drums. Both were real enough. The
scream of the catbird had come from the cypress swamp a
scant three hundred yards away. The war drums were talking
softly to each other far out on the lake. The bird call was repeated from a dozen points as though every nest were stirring
in the thick darkness. Only a trained ear would know that
these signals issued from human throats.

So it's coming with the dawn, he thought. Just as we hoped and feared. An attack from land and water, a two-day hurricane that may flatten us under its first wave. Now that the crisis was upon him, he found that he was calm enough. At least they had moved to a prepared position and stood ready to receive the onslaught. . . . He heard a soft click at his elbow and realized that his hand had moved to cock the carbine, with no orders from his brain; in the pits below the Mound a score of rifle hammers were tensed in unison, as though answering a common signal. There was no sound from the stockade itself, but he knew that it was waiting too. Waiting and ready and unafraid.

Beyond, the catbirds continued to quarrel in the night; he had heard those human bird orchestras before and realized once again that the Seminoles on the land side, at least, were tuning their courage to concert pitch while they waited for the light. Out on the lake the drums continued their throbbing—a monotonous rhythm that crept nearer to their defenses, though darkness still cloaked the drummers. With each beat the number increased, though there was no real effect of crescendo, even when the hands whispered in unison on the taut buckskin of the war kettles. The effect, thought Roy, is deliberate; the purr of the panther before its spring. . . . He heard his name whispered in the darkness, the quick rush of footsteps in sand as Andy Winter scrambled up to rest his own elbows on the summit.

"Can you count them, Roy?"

"Fifty, at least."

"I made it fifty-three from the stockade. Does that mean as many canoes?"

"It could."

Andy laughed softly in the night. "Then I've begun my report correctly. I've just written that we were jumped by the whole nation at the crack of dawn." He peered eagerly toward the lake and the faint gray smudge that had begun to cut across the darkness to the east. "Fifty canoes or a hundred, there'll be mostly boys at those paddles. The main smash is coming from the swamp."

Roy nodded and strained his eyes toward the promise of dawn. It was quite like Andy Winter to pen a formal report in advance. He could picture his friend scratching busily at his foolscap ledger in the stockade, his table a drumhead, his only light a hooded bull's-eye. Napoleon himself could not have been more confident on the eve of Austerlitz—or Waterloo.

"They'll still take their signals from the lake."

"And they'll escape that way if the attack fails. We must make them hang on, somehow—until Merrick can move in from the north."

"D'you honestly think we'll outlast today, Andy?"

"I'm sure we can. So sure that I'm only using half my strength to stop their first wave. Ranson and a hundred men are behind that last screen of palmetto. If we hit 'em with all our rifles, they may turn tail and skedaddle. It's happened before."

"So has Dade's massacre—to name just one."

"Are you always this gloomy when you're about to die?"

"Are you always this cheerful?"

"Why not? Killing Seminoles is my trade. I won't deny I enjoy it."

"How do you propose to end the action?"

"When our relief comes, we'll still be holding here. Merrick will spook what's left of 'em—from three sides. I'll march out from my palmettos and accept their surrender. It's as simple as that—if we last till tomorrow."

The gray band had widened along the eastern horizon. Here and there it had begun to be tinged with a kind of tarnished green, a sure harbinger of a brilliant Florida sunrise. Thankful for small mercies, Roy prayed that the day would be clear throughout. Of course there was no escaping the clammy mist—it was really more rain than dew—that would come boiling out of the cypress with the first real flush of dawn. The Seminoles had counted heavily on that dawn mist in other encounters. They would hardly waste its cover today.

"Shouldn't you go back, Andy?"

"By no means," said the dragoon calmly. "I'm directing fire from here."

"They'll pick you off in an instant."

"Not if I keep my head down and dig in. *You'd* best go back at once, Roy. It's coming any minute now—and coming fast."

"Did someone remember to lay out my instruments?"

"Ranson will give you two mates. He's already arranged

everything in your sick bay. When I run a war, I run it properly."

"Who gives orders while you're here?"

"Hutchens, pro tem," said Andy cheerfully. "He's already up and about. I'll rejoin you if things get really hot. Keep that carbine cocked. You may need it before you're over the wall."

"Come back with me, Andy. Don't be a fool."

"Don't slander your superiors, Dr. Coe—you might be court-martialed." Andy's chuckle followed Roy into the darkness, all but drowned by the insistent drums. His voice could not have been calmer had they been chatting on the ramparts of Fort Everglades.

Dawn was a visible streak of silver now along the cypress tops. Here in the palmetto hollow between Indian Mound and the first sand pit of the stockade, the gloom was still absolute. Roy held the carbine high and went down the last slope. At that precise moment the drums ceased their throbbing, as though muted by a single hand; in the swamp to the south the last catbird ended its raucous scolding. They're moving, he thought. Ghosting in with the mist, crawling through the dog fennel and the gumbo like a hundred brown snakes. Only five hundred is a nearer figure. Most of them will be over that breastwork before Hutchens can mount a second volley; they'll save their lead this time and strike with ax and knife and war club.

He could avoid all that in a twinkling, merely by circling the Mound to the right and plunging headlong for the first open slough. Andy had cached a few light-draught canoes in dead water, far behind the camp site. He could move to the Seminole's rear while the attack was at its height, use all his knowledge of Indian sign to reach Chekika's village, while Chekika's main force was devoting itself to wholesale murder. Surely he would never have a better chance to rescue Mary. . . . He fought down the tug of that desire—and the sophistry that had masked his instinct for flight. Moving swiftly to the left, avoiding the clump of yucca that Andy had paced here to mask the farthest rifle pit, he whispered the password into the fast-breaking dawn and dropped into the trench beside the sentry.

"You're just in time, Doc. So help me, I can smell 'em out there in the damp——"

"Keep that hollow covered. They're thick as fleas in the dog fennel, and moving fast."

He went over the stockade on the run and felt Ranson's hand on his arm as he landed on all fours safely within the enclosure. They moved wordlessly down the second line of riflemen to the sick bay—a neat palmetto box at the far corner of the stockade, padded with blanket rolls. His instrument case was open on the improvised table; his two mates (young stalwarts fresh from the plow, with the faces of patient plow mules and nerves to match) waited, with identical grins, to bring the first wounded. He checked his bandages at a glance; Ranson, as usual, had done a thorough job with meager equipment.

"With your permission, Sergeant, I'll watch from this sally port."

He moved to the outthrust angle of the stockade as he spoke and took his stand beside Lieutenant Hutchens, who was glaring into the mist through a telescope, as though the glass had some hidden power to pierce the cotton wool. The silence outside the breastwork was part of that drenching white dew, boiling coldly into the cracks between the logs, touching each brain with its own premonition.

Hutchens was chewing a dead cheroot and cursing round the tobacco in a steady whisper; his saddle-brown profile was creased in a deep scowl as he lifted to the top log of the stockade and rested his elbows there for a better view. Roy was on the point of following him when the first pencil of sunlight, striking above the dew-soaked trees of the swamp, splintered on the brass tube of the lieutenant's spyglass and haloed the lieutenant's young whiskers in a fine golden glow.

Somewhere in the mist a fiddle string twanged a single, strident note, matched instantly by a second twang to the left. Roy felt his hat lift and sail away into the morning, plucked from his head by an invisible hand. He heard the lieutenant cough at his side, saw him tumble, face down, across the breastwork. The ugly tip of the arrow, a sliver of bone like a hag's fang, gleamed red in the burst of sunlight as it quivered at the back of the lieutenant's neck, a good four inches beyond the vertebrae it had bisected so neatly. Outside the stockade, where the breastwork sloped down to meet the bright new day, the telescope banged furiously against the palmetto, then lay still against it, gripped in the lieutenant's lifeless fist.

Scrambling expertly for cover and noting facts as he moved, Roy was already behind the main line of defense. The first flight of arrows, he saw, had been discharged deliberately when the shafts of sunlight picked out a few targets on the breastwork. His own battered Army sombrero, lifted by one of those deadly shafts, had been pinned to a live oak well within the stockade; had he raised his head a fraction more, the barb would have found his eye socket. The Seminoles had used the ancient weapon by preference for the first assault from the mist. Gunfire would have established their positions too precisely.

He glanced down the dawn-bright stockade to count their losses. Corporal Wood, he saw, had been killed instantly in another sally port—his body, lifted an incautious six inches above the last log, had been skewered through the heart. Another dragoon, his face a waxen mask of pain, had just plucked an arrow shaft from his shoulder and was doing his poor best to stop the red pump of blood that followed it. Still another was screaming his life away on the sandy floor of the stockade—the victim of a ricochet that had driven a shaft into his abdomen, haft-deep. The surgeon's mates had already sprung into action. He rushed to join them, ducking by instinct as a second flight of arrows roared into the enclosure, sending a plague of splinters whistling about his ears.

The boy on the sand was dead before he could separate arrow from murdered flesh. The dragoon with the punctured arm, submitting to the steel with a veteran's calm, was soon led back to the sick bay with a ligated artery and a better than even chance to conquer the gangrene that invaded so many wounds of this type. . . . So far, thought Roy, we haven't seen the color of their livers—or their heart's blood. At least they haven't dared to take our line by storm; the mist is on our side as well. He looked up into Ranson's face and read a certain assurance there.

"How's it going, Sergeant?"

"Well enough, sir. The light's improving steadily. They'll have to use lead from now on."

"I hope you realize you're now in command."

"Quite, Doctor. I'm waiting Captain Winter's signal from the Mound."

Once he had circled the wall of the stockade, he saw there were no more wounded. Outside, across the hacked-out fire lanes, the mist was shredding in the sunlight; even in the deeper gloom of the cypress he could pick out landmarks of a sort. To the north the lake still lay deep in cotton wool, sun-shot here and there as the morning burned through to the hammocks and mudbanks offshore. There was no sign of hostilities from this side; Roy could only applaud Andy's instinct as he counted heads along the southern breastwork.

An idiot voice was talking now deep in the swamp. A voice that babbled a music of its own, as nerve-racking as man's first despair. Inured as he was to that battle trumpet, Roy felt the hackles rise along his neck. He had seen the giant conch shell that was used by the Indians to produce that toneless babble and the long reed pipe that rounded off the signal with an endless wail. And yet that despairing cry had always poured cold spring water down his spine.

The war whoops were coming fast now, from the dog fennel, from the saw-grass scrub along the lake shore, from the lake itself, though he could not find the silhouette of a single canoe to the north. Babbled in unison with the wail of the conch shell and the counterpoint of the pipe, those all-too-human voices had begun to take human shape as well—scuttling bodies that seemed to hug the earth as they darted from the last scrap of cover. And then the dozen had translated to fifty, a hundred, a red tide past counting. An avalanche that swept through the fire lanes, up the sandy slope to the rifle pits, to the palmetto ramparts.

Roy found that he had snatched a carbine from the stack behind the breastworks and stationed himself at a loophole; he heard his breath go out in a great sigh as his cheek flattened against the walnut stock and his eye sought a target in that fantastic copper tide. His finger was frozen inside the trigger guard; an instinct that went deeper than self-preservation (a will born of similar encounters) forced him to wait.

Even now he had time to note that the attack had been launched by a master hand. Their position had been scouted carefully. Though the enemy had arrived too late to strike a deathblow while the stockade was building, he had calculated his chances precisely. The assault was massed to carry the southern stockade, where the ground was open and no power on earth could keep part of the attackers from coming to grips with the defenders on their own ground. Or so the King of Panthers had reasoned as he flung his braves against the palmetto in three tight wedges, with axes flashing in every fist.

Roy's finger was still frozen on the trigger guard. Like every man at the breastworks, he knew that those copper wedges were bunched too tightly now that they were almost at point-blank range. Like the other veterans in that line, he waited for the order that would make the first volley count.

"Fire!"

It was Andy, of course, bellowing from the summit of Indian Mound. Andy, who had made himself small in the mist while measuring the tempo of the assault. His order, delivered at the precise moment, laid down a sheet of orange flame between breastwork and Seminole. Feeling the kick of butt on shoulder, watching his man go down like a squirrel under the rifle crack, Roy was sure that nearly every marksman in that line had found his target as well.

"Fire!"

The second volley, delivered with equal fury, all but overlapped the first. Each man at the breastworks, turning with machinelike precision, had lifted and aimed a second loaded rifle stacked under the loopholes. Just as precisely, a hundred powder-blackened fists snatched up a hundred stacked carbines. The third order, thundered above the billowing smoke of battle, seemed to come out of the sky, The short-nosed guns, blasting the red wave as it lapped the breastworks, seemed to wither the enemy in his tracks. Waiting with a clubbed rifle at the ready, one with the defenders of the breastworks, Roy watched the invaders waver, then reel back.

Perhaps a dozen braves succeeded in boarding the stockade. A few well-thrown axes found their marks, spilling blood and brains on the dew-wet sand. A ragged volley, fired tardily from the dog fennel, splintered harmlessly in the thick palmetto logs—an obligato to the crash of Ranson's gun butt on the last live Seminole head within the enclosure. Silence descended on the stockade almost before the acrid cloud of gunpowder lifted in the clean morning air—a quiet broken only by the low moaning of a dragoon bleeding his life away under Roy's scalpel.

For the next half hour his knife moved swiftly. The dragoon, with an English hatchet in his throat, was beyond surgery. So were the nine tumbled bodies at the breastworks, Lieutenant Hutchens among them. As so often happened in these head-on encounters, there were few real wounded. Roy stitched a broken head and tied off another artery in time to save a life; he knelt on the blood-soaked earth beside a sally port to ease the last agony of a boy with an arrow wound just under his heart. . . . Throughout, his hands moved by rote, healing as best they could; his brain was a thing apart, hanging on every sound beyond the enclosure.

The first assault had ended in a matter of minutes; thanks to those deadly, point-blank volleys, he knew there must be nearly a hundred Indian dead in the fire lanes. There was no sign that a second attack was in the making—and no stir of life in the palmettos save for the rustle of the wounded dragging their broken bodies toward the swamp. From time to time he could hear the sharp, nerve-wrenching screech of lifting hair, and guessed that the regulars, braving Ranson's wrath, had slipped outside the stockade to take what scalps they could.

The sun was well above the cypress when he washed the last red stain from hands and forearms and turned to answer the sergeant's summons. Ranson was standing on the fire step to the north, with a cautious head at one of the loopholes facing the lake. "You'll have to see this to believe it, Doctor," he said. "*I* don't, even now."

Roy moved to the next loophole, and felt his breath leave his body in a stifled gasp. At first glance the whole shore line of Okeechobee seemed to sprout canoes—spawned, like giant tadpoles, in the mist that still blocked the horizon. As they watched, the cotton wool rolled back under the bite of the sun to reveal other elements of the Seminole flotilla. At Flamingo Key, Roy had counted thirty-odd canoes. There were nearly sixty here today, facing the stockade in a wide arc and floating prudently out of rifle range.

Despite the dead they had left in the dog fennel, the Indians made a brave show of strength; thanks to the mist-dimmed water, the nation seemed endless and prodigal of its strength. And then, as the mist burned away in earnest, Roy felt his heart resume its normal beat. Seen clearly in the full glare of morning, most of the dugouts were short of both paddles and firearms. Others were manned by old men—or by boys too young for combat. On the tips of the arc Roy counted a dozen canoes that were really mud scows, piled high with camp gear. This was, indeed, the Seminole nation *in toto,* save for the squaws and the dogs. It had descended on Indian Mound, prepared for a first-rate massacre or a prolonged siege. Judging by its disposition at the moment, its leaders had decided on the latter course.

"They've been moving out ever since the attack failed," said Ranson. "If you ask me, sir, there isn't a buck left in the swamp. Not unless he's too dead to drag aboard."

"Will they move in from the waterside?"

"It'd be murder, Doctor. Murder pure and simple. I'd say we convinced 'em of that much an hour ago."

"Surely it's time we called Captain Winter back to the stockade."

"Cast your eye at the pyramid, sir. He has a better view than we."

Roy dared to glance at Indian Mound for the first time since the action began. Bathed in bright sunlight, the man-made hill seemed natural enough at this slight distance; the few loose skulls that had tumbled down its flanks, the white highlights of bone shards that showed here and there in the rank cloak of vegetation that covered it were oddly innocent in the candid day. There was no visible sign of Andy's presence.

"Are you sure he's there, Sergeant?"

"Look again, Doctor."

Roy shaded his eyes against the glare, and saw a glass eye wink back at him from the grass-tufted summit. It was the lens of Andy's telescope, trained on the lake and level with the sandy apex, as though the dragoon had somehow made himself part of the pyramid.

"He's dug in, sir," said Ranson. "Dug in right up to his whiskers, and covered his carrot top with grass. No wonder he didn't draw their fire."

"I still say he should rejoin his command."

"Leave that to Captain Winter, Doctor. He'll pop out of that ambush at the right time, you mark my words."

A sentinel on the lakeside shouted a warning, spinning them back to the water. One of the larger canoes had just detached itself from the waiting arc and moved boldly toward the stockade. Already it was almost within gunshot, but the lone paddler seemed quite unaware of his peril as he drove even closer with long, smooth strokes, his head bowed under a prodigal white turban. There was something compelling about that one-man approach to certain death—something that kept a hundred rifles uncocked, even as a hundred sights were trained on the paddler.

"Feathers at the bow, Sergeant," called the sentinel.

"Hold your fire, Simpson. I see 'em too." Ranson threw a quick grin at Roy. "Egret, not flamingo. That means they've lost enough blood today."

"From here I'd say it's Abraham."

"Abraham it is, sir. The Wildcat's number-one sense-bearer."

The paddler rose proudly in the dugout, his feet spread wide between the thwarts. Save for the turban and the half-moons of silver that all but covered his chest, he was as naked as some ebony statue. The sun caught highlights from a brightly oiled shoulder as he lifted the feather-tufted spear from the bow and sent it winging across the water. The weapon sang through the air in the long arc and drove home in the top log of the stockade. A lusty cheer greeted this gesture of peace, even before Ranson thrust a rifle above the stockade, inviting the sense-bearer to draw nearer.

Abraham, a Negro who had served under every Seminole chief since the long war began, lifted a second pole from the gunwale and began to force the dugout through the reedy shallow. Roy felt the whole stockade unlimber—a subtle easing of tension; when Abraham crossed between the lines, compromise was always the order of the day.

The dugout grounded on a mudbank a scant hundred feet from the shore. Abraham stepped out, with the push pole still in his hand. Walking with all the mincing gravity of a dandy on parade, he climbed to dry land, drove the pole deep in the beach of Sandy Bay, and sat down beside it with folded arms, awaiting the white man's move.

"Speak to him, Sergeant."

"The captain must speak, not I."

"Take the spear. Offer it to Andy. We must do something to bridge the gap before they get restless."

Ranson nodded and tossed a leg over the stockade. No one stirred in either camp as he walked deliberately down the breastworks, plucked the spear from the ground, and laid it across the cradle of his arms. Abraham's mask was unchanged when they met on the beach; the arc of war canoes did not stir as the sergeant took a dozen strides toward the Mound, turned precisely, and spoke in purest Seminole, loud enough for the farthest canoe to hear.

"Do you come in peace, Abraham?"

"In peace, *amigo*,"

"Has the Father of Seminoles bled enough?"

"More than enough for now."

"Will he speak to the captain who commands us?"

"The King of Panthers is far away. He rests in his house and shuts his mind to the sound of white feet in his kingdom."

"Do you speak as his sense-bearer?"

"Today I am the sense-bearer of Chittamicco, the Wild-cat's brother."

So far, thought Roy, it's gone by the book. And yet he was sure that every word was true. It was logical, after all, that Chittamicco should command today's attack. Chekika, the general who fought to the bitter end, was probably with his squaws today, planning his retreat if today's action should fail.

"Speak your meaning in English, Abraham," said Ranson. "The captain who commands us has not the gift of tongues. Only an understanding heart."

"Then why does he profane our earth?"

"No profanation was intended. We have come to your hunting ground for one reason only. Must I give it a name?"

"We know why you have come. You would discuss the question of hostages. Did you bring our ransom money?"

"We did not come to discuss ransom."

"Then you have no right to come at all. You read the message from the King of Panthers?"

"Did he read the message we left at Pahokee?"

"Withdraw from the Indian Mound. Swear that there will be no further violation of our holy ground."

So far, thought Roy, the Negro has matched us for eloquence, down to the last florid metaphor. He found that he had tossed his own voice into the discussion for what it was worth.

"Tell me this, Abraham. If Chekika resents our presence here, why does he send a sprout from his tree to defend his honor?"

He had spoken in Seminole, letting the last words boom

across the lake, in the hope that they would find the right ear.
An ominous rumble from the brown arc of dugouts was his
reward. He forced his advantage quickly.

"If Chittamicco has orders to press the attack, why does
he put off dying? No man is immortal—not even the fledgling of a king."

Abraham spoke quietly in English before the sudden babble died behind him. "I am the King's sense-bearer, Salofkachee. I would speak to your commander—not to you."

He swallowed the rest of his ornate phrase and reared
back on his haunches, for all the world like a statue come
alive. Behind him, in the long half-moon of canoes, a murmur rose and died, mixed with the frantic backlash of three
hundred paddles. The arc of dugouts, moving as one unit,
broke free of the shore, backing pell-mell into the mist that
still clung to deep water. Only Abraham was left, to stare at
the volcano that had just erupted at the summit of Indian
Mound; to lift both his hands, palm outward, as Captain Andrew Winter stormed down the slope of that sacred burial
ground in full regimentals, his shako a dark victory against
the blaze of morning.

"The captain of the Everglades Rangers is at your service,
Abraham," said Andy, and his voice was silken-smooth, the
parade-ground purr he reserved for great occasions only.
"We will speak as friends awhile. Beyond the ears of your
nation and mine." He bowed, with his poise held before him
like a shield; the gesture that offered Abraham the path along
the beach was the epitome of charm. Andy had parleyed before with the Negro on more than one disputed field; he
knew the value of protocol.

Sergeant Ranson offered the tribute of a silent whistle from
the ramparts and dared to rest both elbows on the stockade
as he watched his commanding officer settle in the shade of
an oleander, open his snuffbox, and offer the Negro a pinch.

"What did I say, sir? Could the captain have chosen a better moment to show his face?"

v

High noon brooded over the lake shore now, and the
snuffbox still passed from hand to hand in the shade of the
oleander. On the ramparts the most avid watcher had begun

to doze at his loophole; even Ranson had stepped down inside the stockade to supervise the distribution of rations and the precious midday tot of rum. Only Dr. Royal Coe still waited—and cursed Andy Winter wholeheartedly as the hours drained away. Not that he had any real excuse for damning the dragoon captain. It was quite like Andy to lay down his terms and cling to them stubbornly through a whole day of suggested compromise. . . . Beyond, a safe mile from shore, the flotilla of dugouts bobbed in the glare of noon. Andy, whose eyes had claimed Abraham's from the start, had yet to glance beyond the shore line he dominated.

When Andy lifted a negligent hand at long last and rose from his squatting position with a courteous bow to Abraham, Roy needed all his self-discipline to keep from vaulting the stockade and meeting his friend at a full gallop. Instead, as befitted the medicine man of a nation powerful in war, he made himself stroll casually through the first break in the palmetto wall and paused, with the same air of abstraction, in the shadow of the stockade itself—far enough from Abraham to underline his rank, and near enough for Ranson's ears to pick up any items of value.

Andy strolled to meet him, just as coolly; he paused to pocket his empty snuffbox and thrust an unlighted cheroot into the corner of his mouth. He spoke around the tobacco so quietly that Roy could scarcely hear.

"They'll jump us again before dark unless we meet their terms."

"Is that what you want?"

"I'm not sure we can stand a second attack. You see, they *do* know our strength—to the last man. I was a fool to think I'd hoodwinked them on that point." The captain of dragoons admitted his error with a careless gesture. "That first jump was a trial, nothing more. I might add it was Chittamicco's idea, not Abraham's. *He* wanted to parley before a shot was fired."

"Do you believe Chittamicco is in command?"

"So far, I think Abraham has spoken nothing but the truth."

"For five hours? Wasn't that a bit of a strain for Abraham?"

"On the contrary." Andy grinned around his cigar. "That black diplomat is an old hand at this. So am I."

"What are his terms?"

"They're simple enough. First off, he wants you to return with him to Chekika's village. There seems to be a job waiting there for you. A job no one else can handle——"

"Wasn't he more definite?"

"He promises to be very definite with you. Naturally, I refused to call you until we laid down our own conditions. I think we can make them stick."

"Shouldn't we go back to him now?"

Andy glanced briefly at Abraham, who was still squatting in the shade of the oleander. "Let him wait; he's used to waiting. If Chekika really needs you—and I'm sure he does —we're in an excellent position. I think we can stay right here if we promise no more violations of the Mound. With luck, we can make our truce last until we're relieved. And I think they'll deliver Mary to the stockade if you're willing to go over in her place."

"Are you telling me that Mary's out there on the lake?"

"If I'm to believe Abraham, she's in a canoe behind one of those cypress islands."

"And Dr. Barker?"

"He's with Chekika—ready to help you when you arrive at the village."

Roy breathed deep and pulled his eyes away from the lake —and the envoy who waited so patiently at its shore. Events had moved at a snail's pace through the long hot morning. Now they were moving too fast for comprehension. One part of his mind refused to believe that Mary Grant was actually within hailing distance at this time. Yet her presence was quite logical. Though Chekika himself had held aloof from this conflict (for reasons of his own), the entire nation was involved. It was good strategy to bring a hostage to the battle —as a trump card if all else failed.

"Surely they won't let you stay in the Glades. Not after Chekika's ultimatum."

"I'll promise to withdraw the moment you're returned to me in good condition." Andy was grinning in earnest now. "Perhaps I should ask if you're willing to go. You'll be running a risk, of course. Even if Abraham isn't lying——"

"You know I'll do anything to help Mary."

"Then I think we can join Abraham with a clear conscience."

But it was Roy's turn to hold back now. "What if they do

deliver Mary to the stockade—and you aren't relieved? Chittamicco may break the truce at any time."

"I think we've an even chance to hold out indefinitely."

"You weren't so positive a moment ago."

"I said I'd prefer to suffer no more losses until help comes."

"Why don't you take to your canoes and head north?"

"How can I? Our whole action is based on my position here. I must maintain it until tomorrow or the day after. A truce would suit me perfectly—but I'll fight, too, if need be."

"And risk Mary's life in the fighting?"

"Leave Mary to me. She's my problem, not yours."

Roy bit back his retort in time, though the words still trembled on his tongue. He could not deny that Andy was right. Mary would be safer in this beleaguered stockade under Army guns. He could trust Andy to protect her with all the wiles at his command.

"Suppose you're overwhelmed?"

"Then we die side by side," said Andy, and he was still grinning around his cigar. "We'll be a pair of unsung heroes, and you can plant poinsettias around our graves."

You don't really love her, thought Roy. If you did, you could never dismiss her life so lightly. Soldiering is your trade, and you've every right to accept dying as one of its hazards. It's hardly fair to include a wife-to-be in that desperate game. . . . And yet, he thought swiftly, what choice had Andy today? Committed as he was, he could never draw back on the pretext of saving a woman's life.

Aloud, he said only, "Let's talk to Abraham."

"Fair enough. Just let me make the conditions."

They walked down to the shore line side by side, returning the Negro's salute with military crispness. No one spoke while they squatted in a solemn, three-man circle about the bamboo staff that Abraham had planted at the meeting place of lake and land. The white tuft of egret feathers that was the sense-bearer's badge of peace danced in the breeze. Roy dared to steal a glance beyond Abraham's shoulder and saw the arc of water canoes still waited prudently—a mere dark accent on the horizon's rim.

When he pulled his eyes back to the circle Abraham met his stare as tradition demanded, without flinching. The Negro's face was broad-browed and noble—the open countenance of the scholar, sad-eyed with too much wisdom. A face that belonged to civilization, indomitable and strangely proud. It made a shocking contrast to the bone ornaments in Abraham's ear lobes, the double necklets of shark's teeth that hugged his neck like an old-fashioned choker, the barbaric white turban heavy with egret and ibis plumes. The beaten-silver crescents on his chest tinkled faintly as he bowed at long last, acknowledging Roy's presence as usage demanded.

"We are well met, Doctor."

The Negro's English was as pure as his own. Roy remembered the fantastic legends that had sprung up around the sense-bearer. Veterans at Fort Everglades insisted that Abraham was the natural son of a Deep South statesman—a black firebrand who had plotted an uprising of slaves in his native state and escaped to the Floridas in the nick of time. Others said that he was the offspring of Osceola and an African princess, educated in London to take over the chief's mantle. It was Roy's own guess that the sense-bearer was a freedman who had risen too far above his station and now preferred the benign tyranny of the Seminoles to a white world that would never grant him equality.

Meeting now on that equal plane, he kept his own voice level and did his best to match Andy's dress-parade glare. "Well met, Abraham? When you come with arrows and lead?"

"Chekika defends his domain. As you would do if we crossed your borders."

"You know why we came?"

"The King of Panthers has your message."

"Is this attack his answer?"

"I said that *we* were well met, Doctor. My words were for your ears alone. Not for the Army's." This time Abraham offered Andy Winter his small, ironic bow. "Our attack, as the captain well knows, was a warning. I trust he has taken it to his heart."

Andy entered the discussion with a kind of weary courtesy; his voice was dead calm, as though he were reciting a litany. "My presence here is also a warning. So are the hundred dead that went down before our guns. Does Chekika wish more of that medicine?"

"The Wildcat rests in his lair, Captain. I speak with his

voice today. I order you to leave his hunting ground or die here."

"But Dr. Coe is welcome to remain?"

"Chekika would use the doctor's skill."

"The doctor is my right hand. Why should I give my right hand to my enemy?"

Roy cut in quietly before Andy could speak again. He knew that this train of argument had been repeated ad infinitum as the long morning had passed and Andy sparred expertly for time. If Andy rehearsed it now, it was only for the sake of form.

"What does the Father of Seminoles require?"

"Little Egret is on the point of death, Doctor. You remember her?"

"The chief's wife was great with child when I saw her last. Surely the chief's son is born by now."

"There was no child within her. The swelling came from evil spirits. Only the knife of Salofkachee can let the evil out."

"Does Chekika flatter me this highly?"

"Chekika has always believed in the magic of your knife and the wisdom of your hands. But it is Dr. Barker who advises that we send for you. His own hands would let out the evil, but they are old now and afraid."

Roy kept his mask unbroken, but his mind raced behind it. Dr. Barker had conveyed the picture precisely enough. The chief's favorite squaw was obviously dying of a tumor which might well be inoperable. And yet the old botanist would never have asked for his help had he felt the case to be hopeless. He spoke carefully, with one eye on Andy.

"How can I come now, when I am under Captain Winter's orders?"

"The captain can send you."

Andy let the silence build. When he broke it, his voice was careless enough. "Would you enjoy making this magic, Roy?"

"Why not?"

"Then I release you from my command. But the Father of Seminoles must meet my conditions."

"Name them," said Abraham. "I will prove that I speak with his voice."

"First, I must await Dr. Coe's return in my present camp."

"That is a great deal to ask, Captain. You have entered the

Glades unlawfully—that is bad enough. We cannot permit you to remain on sacred earth."

"Our bivouac is well beyond the Mound."

"Last night you lighted your cook fires on its slope."

"We will profane its slopes no longer if it displeases you. But I will await Dr. Coe in its shadow."

"What if we forbid you?"

"*Forbid* is a strange word to the American Army. We do not understand its meaning."

"You are alive today because we will it, Captain. You will die at our pleasure—unless you leave the Glades."

"Come to me when you wish, Abraham. You will walk on a carpet of your dead."

The sense-bearer shifted his attack abruptly, as though he had tired of ritual insults. "Two hundred men cannot live without food. Dr. Coe may be gone a long time."

"We have ample rations."

"You would stay within Sandy Bay?"

"Word of honor. You may post lookouts if you like."

"I will accept your word," said Abraham. "I will also post lookouts."

"And keep the truce?"

"Unless you break it, yes."

"The truce stands until Dr. Coe's return. And we must have assurance that he will return."

Roy listened, bemused, as the voices dragged on. Try as he might, he could not pin his mind on what Andy was saying. Now that he was sure of Andy's victory, he felt he must summon all his strength to face the ordeal ahead—when Mary walked into his friend's arms again, unharmed and unafraid. He could not believe that they would find her the worse for her brief captivity, or that she had been cowed for one moment by her captors. Somehow, he must surrender her to Andy Winter without a flicker of emotion.

What happened thereafter was hardly important if he knew that she was safe. Perhaps he would never reach the Wildcat's village; with Chittamicco in charge of the flotilla, anything might happen on that journey. The operation he was to perform was certainly risky enough. An ovarian tumor, most likely: a touch-and-go affair in his own clinic. What would his chances be on the platform of Chekika's hut?

If his knife failed, he had no illusions about his future. The nation would order his execution, and Chekika would yield, no matter what his own feelings. He had seen more than one medicine man vanish abruptly when his magic refused to function. Stripped of his last charm, the tribal doctor had been smeared with the blood of wild pigs and lashed to a sapling deep in the mosquito bogs. Usually his body would be drained of life in a single night. Living or dead, he would be hanged at the nearest cabbage palm when morning came—a present for the vultures, and a warning to his colleagues to practice a dangerous calling more carefully. . . .

He fought down that image; he had taken the risk before, in that same stilted wigwam, and brought back his prize to civilization. Otter skins, the pelts of bear and panther, a fortune in egret feathers—these had been the visible signs of Chekika's favor. This time (and he made the promise silently) he would ask only for Mary's freedom. He had no right to ask for Mary's happiness as well. Andy Winter would see to that.

Beyond the tight trap of his nerves he heard the voices go on. He was not surprised when Abraham rose at last and saluted them both with his bamboo peace wand.

"Hilolo will be your assurance. I have spoken. Now I will prove my words."

"And who is Hilolo?" It was a routine question: White Ibis was a name that belonged naturally to Mary Grant. Without knowing why, he found it vastly reassuring that the Seminoles had bestowed a tribal title on her so quickly, though it was true that they renamed all their captives in time.

"The girl whom Dr. Barker says is not his daughter," said Abraham. For an instant it seemed as though the dark, sad face would crease into a smile. "A woman for a man. Somehow, I thought the Army would ask for more."

"I would ask for Dr. Barker, too," said Andy. "But you tell me he is needed."

"You know our price for Dr. Barker, Captain."

"In a week's time I will take him free. And you will be glad to make the surrender."

"My ears are heavy with threats," said Abraham, and stepped into his dugout.

"No more than mine," said Andy. "When will you return?"

"In five minutes' time." The sense-bearer had already picked up his paddle. "Hilolo will be seated in the bow. I will bring four canoes as escort."

"That is agreed."

"Dr. Coe will be waiting here in a canoe of his own. He must have his knife case in plain view for all to see. I need not say he must be unarmed."

"That, too, is agreed. You are still the voice of Chekika."

"You will wade out in Okeechobee to take your lady in your arms. She will speak no word to Dr. Coe as you bring her to shore. Dr. Coe will then proceed as we direct. Is that also understood clearly?"

"Dr. Coe is a friend of Hilolo's. May she wish him luck in his venture?"

"That, too, is forbidden. I, for one, see no harm in a friend's greeting to a friend. But Chittamicco rules otherwise."

Andy glanced at Roy, who shrugged an agreement. Both of them understood this final bit of arrogance well enough. For his part, Roy could almost welcome Chittamicco's ruling. Who could tell what Mary might cry out if she guessed where he was going and why?

"Return with Hilolo," he said. "I will be ready to visit the chief's house."

Abraham bowed to each in turn and spun the dugout toward the open lake. Roy felt Andy's hand at his elbow and smiled ruefully as he permitted his friend to lead him back to the narrow beach. Pure instinct had made him wade knee-deep in the shallows to watch the canoe vanish among the cypress islands to the west. Until he saw Mary Grant with his own eyes, this would still be a wishful dream—one from which he did not dare to waken.

"It's a great deal to ask of any friend," said Andy. "Did I remember to thank you for going?"

"Don't say another word. You'd have done the same."

An awkward silence fell between them, but they remembered to stand grimly at attention. Chittamicco's flotilla was still all but invisible out there in the heat-misted lake, but they both knew that anxious eyes were watching from that cypress screen.

"I'll get your instrument case," said Andy at last.

"Let me go."

"It's better if you stay in plain view. They might think we were backing out of our bargain."

When Andy had gone Roy stood immobile on the beach and fought down another impulse to wade into the shallows for that first longed-for glimpse of Mary. His mind refused to focus on what lay ahead. Somehow, the ordeal awaiting him at Chekika's village was less terrible than his present yearning and the fear he might betray himself to Andy.

He heard a scattering of cheers from the stockade and realized that word of the truce had spread among the ranks. The cheers swelled to a lusty roar as an American flag, broken out on a staff improvised from a pine sapling, whipped bravely in the hot noonday breeze, flaunting its stars above the sere yellow of the swamp. All at once he realized it was he those men were cheering, that the flag had been raised to honor the risk he was taking in their behalf. He forced himself to snap to attention once again and offered the banner a crisp salute.

There was Abraham's dugout, no more than a black speck among the islands, but moving swiftly inshore. There, fanned out on either side, were the four war canoes, bristling with tufted bonnets—with a show of white at each bow to signify that they came in peace. Behind him Roy heard rifle hammers click along the stockade, though Andy was too wise to show a single gun muzzle. Two regulars marched through the palmetto paling with a light canoe on their shoulders; at the water's edge they lowered the dugout into the lake without a splash, laid a paddle across the gunwales, and returned to the stockade as silently as they had come.

Roy was dimly aware of this bustle. He heard Andy's boots in the sand, felt the heavy solidity of his instrument case as his friend tucked it snugly under his right arm. Marching as a man in a dream, he moved to the water's edge, placed the surgical kit on the bow, and settled into the dugout—with the paddle raised high in both hands to show that he was unarmed and ready. His eyes were still riveted on Abraham's canoe and the figure in white muslin poised in the bow. All else had faded before the knowledge that Mary Grant was alive and unharmed—and, so far as he could see, entirely unafraid.

The vision was a reality now. He saw that it was the same sprigged muslin she had worn on their first encounter at Fort Everglades; there was a bandbox on the thwart beside her

and a thick portfolio of drawings. At this distance she looked
as serene as the morning; she might have been returning
from a picnic or a day of sketching. He stared at her dully
and wondered how she had persuaded Chekika to ferry her
baggage from Flamingo Key to this uncharted wilderness. It
was quite like Mary Grant to dress with care for this moment
—and to play her part to the hilt.

Then, as Abraham's dugout entered the shallows, he saw
that she was watching him with wide, staring eyes and that
those eyes were brimming with tears. He choked the wild cry
that had risen in his throat and dug his paddle into the chocolate-dark water. Without looking back he knew that Andy
Winter had kicked off his boots and was wading in his wake.

"Roy!"

Her voice had broken as she cried his name, as though the
cry had been wrenched from her heart. He kept his face like
stone as the two dugouts swam abreast, and braked his own
canoe while Andy came alongside, waist-deep now and careless of the fact that his best dress uniform was drenched
beyond repair.

"Come, Mary."

"Can't Roy even speak?"

"Come, my dear. We've given our word."

Roy kept his eyes dead ahead; he would be lost forever if
he turned. From the corner of his eye he saw her rise and
step into the competent cradle of the dragoon's arms. He saw
Abraham lean forward to hand her the bandbox and the
bulging portfolio—and knew that Andy had staggered just a
little under this extra burden as he began to wade toward the
beach.

"Anda, señor médico!" Abraham had spoken in Spanish
this time for the benefit of the braves who waited on either
flank with their paddles poised. He let his eyes move round
that half circle of intent copper masks and read no message
there. These, after all, were men at war. They had put all
emotion aside for now; the mask of Mars has no place for
hate or love.

He paddled offshore as slowly as he dared, feeling the wall
of copper flesh close in without a sound. Daring to lift his
eyes, he noted that the main flotilla had moved well forward
during the exchange, bunched in a tight arc to receive
him—an arc that closed like a lazy claw as he drew nearer.

. . . Perhaps this is my moment, he thought. There are the braves who take orders from Chittamicco, ready to form a gantlet and hack me to ribbons. There's Chittamicco himself, itching to give the command. But there was no time to be afraid—and no real cause for fear. Chittamicco still took orders from the Wildcat. He was Chekika's hostage now, and he would live on while the King of Panthers had need of him.

"Rise, Salofkachee. You must receive the blindfold."

A dozen fists held the gunwales steady while he stood upright and faced the leader of the flotilla. Chittamicco had spoken quietly enough, but the spark of murder had never glowed more brightly under those hooded eyelids. One of us must kill the other someday, thought Roy. He held up a detaining palm as Abraham stepped into the dugout beside him, refusing the blindfold a moment more.

"I will cover my eyes willingly. Let me look back first."

He knew it was a mistake even before he could find Mary. Andy's arm was around her; they stood at the water's edge, watching the flotilla move northward. Behind them the mass of the stockade already seemed absurdly small as the Seminole's paddles increased their beat. The candy-striped flag, limp on its staff now that the breeze had died, seemed dwarfed against the waste of swamp that hemmed it.

Roy felt his eyes fill with tears and welcomed the bandage that Abraham had just folded over his head, shutting out the last forlorn glimpse of his happiness.

III FAKAHATCHEE HAMMOCK

i

"As you can see, Roy," said Dr. Barker, "she is beyond pain. I can hardly protest the opiate. But it's far too strong to be continued. Her heart won't stand the strain. I think we should operate immediately."

"With the whole village watching?"

"You expected that, didn't you?"

"To be frank, I'm not sure just what I did expect."

"What's to be gained by delay? She'll only grow weaker."

Dr. Royal Coe stepped back from the rope bed where his prospective patient lay. More than ever he could envy the botanist's almost Olympian repose. Dr. Barker could hardly have been calmer had they been consulting in his own study; the fierce noon glare that cut through the palm thatch overhead showed a face that was as serene as his friend's manner. Even the sun-bleached twill trousers and Indian moccasins seemed part of that detachment. Roy knew, of course, that the other doctor's poise was only a necessary shield. Standing where they were, on the platform of Chekika's own house, with a hundred eyes watching from every point of the compass, they must pretend to be white demigods to the last. The low-pitched tone of their conversation was part of that bravura performance.

"How long has she been under an opiate?"

Dr. Barker addressed a few words in Seminole to the aged squaw who sat cross-legged at the foot of the Little Egret's bed, keeping the flies at bay with a brushwood fan. Both of them suppressed a frown at the woman's muttered reply.

"So they've been dosing her for a week now. Hoping the devils would drive themselves out of her body. Why weren't you consulted sooner?"

The botanist shrugged. "Chittamicco, it seems, was in charge of the case. I gather he's added medicine making to his other duties. Certainly it was he who put that image at the bedside. And Little Egret's nurse has strict orders to keep the snake basket here until he returns."

"When were you informed that the girl was ill?"

"At yesterday's council. Just before they set off for Indian Mound."

Roy nodded glumly. It was quite like Chekika's brother to assume this responsibility—and surrender it, in a white surgeon's favor, when he decided the case was hopeless. He stared down at the loosely woven basket where the rattlesnake lay in sluggish coils, its dusty-diamond markings clearly visible through the gaps in the wicker. Blessed by the whole medical council of the nation, the reptile was sometimes used as a last resort. Placed in the patient's bed and teased into sinking its fangs just above the swelling, it was considered a kill-or-cure remedy that never failed.

The doll (it was really a miniature of Little Egret), standing on its pedestal beside the bed, represented a still more ancient therapy. Roy had no need to question the import of the bone bodkin that had been thrust through that mud-and-wax abdomen. Like the snakebite, which was supposed to drive out poison with a still more deadly venom, the needle wounded only to cure.

Obeying a sudden impulse, he lifted the doll between his palms and walked toward the edge of the platform. Beyond the thin shadow of the palm thatch a low murmur rose, expanded swiftly to a full-throated roar of protest. He had known that every squaw in the village and every brave in the escort that had brought him from Indian Mound would be squatted around the ritualistic blaze. He had known it would burn there on the hard-packed mud before the chief's hut, day and night, until the chief's favorite wife should die or rise from her sickbed again. He had known that Chekika himself would be throned in the midst of those patient watchers, with Abraham crouched like a black mastiff at his feet and a medicine man chanting at either elbow. Now, as he faced their gathered wrath, he forced a mocking smile to his lips, drew back his arm, and flung the doll headforemost into the fire.

For that instant, at least, he thought that the platform would be overwhelmed in a concerted red rush. The two medicine men, forgetting protocol for once, flung themselves at the fire in a vain effort to rescue the effigy, and recoiled as Chekika kicked them both aside. The babble of voices died as the Seminole leader walked into the shadow of his own house, paused at the ladder that was its only means of entrance, and bowed twice as usage demanded.

"Do you affront our gods, Salofkachee?"

"That was no god of the Seminole, Chekika. That was a charm of your brother's. He has resigned the case to me; so be it. I begin by casting out his magic."

"And the snake? Would you kill that too?"

"The snake must be returned to Chittamicco's hut. Send the crone to watch the basket, if you like. Dr. Barker and I must be alone together on this platform when we open the body of your wife."

Again the deep-throated murmur rose from the group that ringed the platform. Once more Chekika stopped it with a gesture.

"The platform will be cleared. Salofkachee must make his magic as he sees fit."

Roy accepted the accolade with a bow and returned to Little Egret's bed. He just escaped grinning as he caught the glint of Dr. Barker's eye.

"A bold move, Roy—but a brilliant one."

"This is our show, Doctor. It must be all ours, including the scenery. May I wish you success in your role?"

ii

He retired to the upper end of the platform while the botanist prepared the patient for her ordeal as best he could. This, too, was ritual; as the principal maker of white magic, it behooved Roy to remain aloof until the first scalpel stroke. From where he stood he could look out across the long slime-green slough they had crossed at dawn today on the last lap of that interminable journey from Indian Mound. He could see the tawny sweep of cornfield that boxed the low hump of the hammock where Chekika's village stood. All else was a saw-grass sea sweeping to the horizon's rim, relieved only by the darker mass of vegetation to the south and west. This, he knew, was the Big Cypress Swamp—an endless water maze in itself that opened eventually to the tidal thrust of the Gulf of Mexico far to the south.

Silence brooded over the village and the sluggish tarns that surrounded it. Far to the west he noted the flash of silver light just before Big Cypress began. Intrepid explorer though he was, he had never ventured quite this far. But his sense of smell recalled that flash of silver, though his eyes had been blinded at the time. Even at this distance that clean quicksilver mirror seemed endowed with a life of its own. Surely this was the Big Sulphur—that strange welling spring that burst from its limestone cavern where Glades and Cypress met and merged. His nose remembered the hydrogen sulphide vapor that had hung in the still air of dawn just before his blindfold had been removed. Shortly thereafter they had turned sharp east again, to run ashore at Chekika's village.

Chekika's village. Now that he stood in its very heart, he could scarcely recall the details of his journey. For the most part, he had rested face downward in his nest of buckskin at the bottom of Abraham's canoe and had tried not to think at all. They had driven at full speed across Okeechobee, surrounded by the warring gulls that came here to feed in all seasons. Later they had slipped into a saw-grass maze that whispered under their keels with no apparent ending. Later still, when he was sure that the rasp of grass on cypress would last forever, he had sensed the deep, enveloping miasma of the great swamp itself—and had guessed that his escort had swung far to the westward in its journey to home base.

Even without his blindfold he would have been hard pressed to memorize every landmark on the watery trail they had followed. Now that he was free to seek his first orientation he noted the limits of the sulphur spring to the west and the stagnant curve of the bayou that swept up to Chekika's island. There were no visible landmarks beyond; without them, he could never retrace the route they had followed.

The hammock on which the village stood was all of fifty acres in extent—an oblong island screened off from the long

bayou by a thicket of water oaks, with a snug, sandy beach
for the canoes on the western shore. It was the largest land
mass he had encountered in the Glades. And yet, thanks to
its remoteness, it was a secure hideaway for the nation; there
had been no attempt to mask the hundred-odd palm-thatch
houses that stood high on their stilts among the water oaks. It
was evident that Chekika had chosen this island deliberately, secure in the knowledge that no invasion force could
venture this far without a map—or at least a guide who
could thread a path through that grassy labyrinth. Roy's eyes
swept the full circle of the horizon and came back wearily to
the snug little settlement. Dr. Barker had called it Fakahatchee Hammock. Clearly, it was a self-contained world, capable of sustaining the nation indefinitely. Just as clearly, he
was now a prisoner of geography as well as Chekika.

But there was no time for brooding now. Hearing the
water bubble in Dr. Barker's kettle, feeling the massed hostility of the watchers that ringed the chief's house, he could
welcome the coming ordeal. In an hour he would know Little
Egret's chances of survival—and his own; the stakes in this
game were real and immediate. He could hardly pause to
wonder how Mary was faring at Indian Mound, or nourish
the crazy hope that he could lead Andy Winter back to Fakahatchee for the final blow.

He turned to his patient at last in response to Dr. Barker's
low-voiced summons. Instruments were ready at the bedside,
such as they were; there were even enough sutures to close
his incision if he kept it small. He took the girl's pulse, making an occasion of that simple routine, holding the massed
glare of a hundred eyeballs with his outward calm unshaken.
As he had expected, the beat was thready but sustained
enough to give him hope. The girl's forehead was cool, and
she was still sleeping deeply under the narcotic. He had only
to turn back an eyelid and check the constriction of the pupil
to guess the nature of the potion. Almost certainly it was the
seeds of the coontie plant, the cyclamen whose roots fur-
nished a gruel called *sofkee* and whose seeds were a powerful
narcotic.

"Can we risk an internal examination?"

Dr. Barker shook his head. "Even an Indian midwife
wouldn't dare. We'd be shot down where we stand."

Roy nodded grimly and drew in his breath as he flicked

aside the white doeskin blanket that covered the patient's body, exposing the naked flesh beneath. The watchers sighed in unison, and he heard a musket being cocked behind the crazy dance of the fire. The expected shot did not come as he let his fingers outline the operative area and the probable cause of the swelling that had distended that abdomen like a monstrous drum.

"The tenderness is definitely to the right," said Dr. Barker. "It extends above the umbilicus."

Little Egret flinched under the testing fingers, but there was none of the hardness which would have indicated a solid tumor. Almost certainly this was an ovarian cyst—a pendulous, water-filled sac that had already twisted the Fallopian tube that led from ovary to uterus. Unsuspected by the tribal medicine man (who had assumed the phenomenon to be a by-product of pregnancy), the balloon-shaped swelling had constricted the whole area, shutting off the blood supply to vital organs. Already distended to the breaking point, it might burst at any moment. Even if the sac held firm within the girl's body, the picture could only terminate in gangrene and death.

Few surgeons in his time had dared to open the abdomen. Roy himself had never risked this operation, though he had seen it performed successfully in the clinics of Edinburgh and Paris. There, at least, the armamentarium of the surgeon had been complete, the assistance adequate. There had been no swarm of bluebottles above the patient's body, no quarreling of curs and grunting razorback hogs beneath the operating table, no dusty bedlam outside the arena itself. He looked up one more time at the dervish capers of the medicine men, the intent, murderous masks of the braves who had dared to creep to the very edge of the platform, awaiting only a word from Chekika to cut him down.

He turned his back on that threat and checked his surgeon's kit one more time. Three scalpels, honed razor-sharp Two forceps, their teeth scarred from probing a hundred bullet wounds. Flat metal hooks, used normally to divide flesh from bone during an amputation, ready to double now as retractors. Crude suture needles with their meager quota of whipcord. At least Dr. Barker had been able to assemble an adequate stack of linen dressings, and the bare wooden platform had been scoured free of vermin, save for the flies that hovered overhead as though awaiting the first show of blood.

Roy picked up a scalpel, letting the steel catch the sunlight —a melodramatic gesture, but highly necessary. Every eye in that dust-caked compound had seen the healing knife to which he owed his nickname. He bowed Dr. Barker to his place at the head of the table—if the rope bed on which the patient lay deserved such a name. He would have given a great deal for the white-pine trestle in his surgery at the fort, and still more for the solidity of his mates. But he knew it would have been fatal imprudence to ask for assistants among the Indians. At least the girl's narcosis seemed complete. Dr. Barker would anchor her as best he could when the knife went in.

Roy had already decided to make his entry through the center line, below the navel; although the swelling extended to the right, above this point, the whole abdomen was engaged. About to make the first slashing stroke, he remembered the ritual in time and walked again to the edge of the platform, raising his arm in a salute to Chekika, careful to keep the scalpel in plain view.

"Does the Father of Seminoles give us permission to enter the body of his beloved?"

"Enter at will, Salofkachee. Drive out the devils."

Chekika's voice had been raised in a ringing shout. The village echoed his cry. At the fringes of the crowd Roy saw the crone with the wicker basket, lingering to glimpse the start of the operation. He watched her lift the lid, saw the giant reptile thrust the flat evil triangle of its head above the rim. Even in the din, the whir of its rattles could be heard, mingled with the ceremonial beat of the gourds brandished by the two medicine men. For that instant Roy felt the hypnotic stab of the snake's eyes across the compound. Even when silence clamped down on the watchers, the rattles continued to whir softly.

Back at the table, he remembered to lift the knife high one more time as his free hand spread-eagled across the copper drum of the girl's abdomen. The steel whipped down, opening a three-inch incision precisely where the muscles joined in the mid-line; the watchers sighed as the first bubble of blood escaped from the wound, then leaned closer, their avid interest redoubled. Linen pledgets, pressed down by Dr. Barker's expert fingers, stopped the red flow before it could attract the insect swarm above their heads. The scalpel shifted, ready to make its next slash—the cut that would answer their most pressing question. If this were indeed a cyst, he would recognize its contour instantly when he had opened the wound to the depth of the peritoneum.

The steel moved on, enlarging the incision without daring to lengthen that first bold stroke. Muscle fiber, separating smoothly under the razor-sharp pressure, revealed the sheen of the peritoneum, the thin membrane that lay below the fibrous junction of these tissues. Roy breathed deep and completed the enlargement. If this were indeed an ovarian swelling, a simple water-filled sac that had involved the Fallopian tube, there was a fair chance of success. By puncturing the sac, by releasing the intense pressure within, he could untwist the stalk of the tube, permitting the surrounding organs to resume their normal function. No manipulation might be needed once the pressure was relieved; the sac would be drawn to the edges of the wound, permitting the fluid to gush forth. If no sign of gangrene had developed, the collapsed swelling could then be allowed to heal itself.

The whitish layer of the peritoneum was now revealed down the whole length of the incision; so far, thanks to his dexterity and the constant pressure of Dr. Barker's fingers, there had been no significant bleeding. He could afford to drop the scalpel now and let his fingers explore the depths of the wound. His breath escaped when he felt something press up against the gleaming membrane—something that was tense but not hard, giving under his fingers, and regaining its contour instantly when the downward thrust was removed.

"A cyst is indicated, Doctor."

"Pray it isn't fibroid."

Roy took up a forceps as he spoke and tried to grip a small portion of the thin, tense membrane of the peritoneum. The tissue eluded the bullet-scarred jaws of the instrument; distended as it was by the swelling beneath, the membrane was difficult to manipulate from any angle. Yet it would be unwise to attempt an outright incision. The blade might easily penetrate the wall of the cyst as well, permitting its contents to escape within the abdominal cavity itself.

"Let me have a needle, please."

Dr. Barker handed a suture needle across the copper

mound of flesh, whipping out the thread as he did so. The curved shank fitted easily in Roy's palm. Nesting the half-moon of steel against the bulge of the peritoneum, he worked the point gingerly into the tissue of the membrane until he felt it was firmly anchored. Then, tenting the already dangerously taut abdominal sheath, he took up a second needle. When this was tented in turn, he motioned to Dr. Barker to grip both needles. A single stroke of the knife, moving without danger between the two steel points, opened the peritoneum down the entire length of the wound. Both doctors leaned forward sharply to peer into the depths of the incision, anxious to observe the structure that began to pulse gently into the valley of severed flesh. Here, at last, was the cause of the patient's long coma—the factor that would decide their future.

"A non-fibroid sac, Roy. It certainly doesn't seem hemorrhagic."

"It had better not be," said Roy fervently. "I don't dare deliver it entirely; there aren't enough sutures to close the wound."

The cyst continued to pulse like a living thing—a pale blue and vaguely cabbagelike in shape. Noting its texture with careful finger tips, Roy yielded to his second inspiration of the morning. Stepping away from the table, he moved to the front of the platform and summoned Chekika with an imperious gesture. It was gratifying to note the alacrity with which the King of Panthers obeyed that summons. Gratifying, too, to observe the Indian's instant recoil as he looked up at his wife's body and the protuberance that winked out of the wound like a giant eyeball clasped in red-rimmed lids.

"The devil looks out at you, Father of Seminoles. Stand back and let me drive him forth."

"She will live, then?"

"If God wills it."

Chekika bowed and strode to his place beside the propitiatory fire; the medicine men, who had come howling in his wake, slunk back like frightened dogs. The warriors who had crowded forward so boldly a few moments ago had moved to an even safer distance now. Roy could not suppress a smile as he picked up the knife again and tossed it high in the sunlight. The will to murder, so evident in those hawk-proud faces, had changed before this terror no man could name and none but Salofkachee himself could exorcise.

"We'll put two sutures through the sac before we open it."

"Will you deliver it after it's emptied?"

"I don't think delivery is advisable. It should destroy itself once it's drained."

Roy studied the structure of the cyst while he spoke. Dark blue at first glance, the walls were mottled here and there with light yellow patches where the fluid within threatened to burst forth. He saw that they had exposed the sac just in time; in a matter of hours the distended tissue would have disgorged its contents. Yet there was no sign of infection in the area; the sac itself, for all its mottled surface, seemed healthy enough.

"Here goes the first anchor, Doctor. Pray that it'll hold."

The whipcord streamed freely from his palm as the curved needle thrust home, deep in yellow-blue mass. In and out in one fluent dip, the steel point emerged as easily as it had entered, drawing the horsehair thread in its wake. Before the knot could pull taut, a thin stream of fluid spurted within the wound, controlled instantly as the knotted cord closed the puncture. Roy tied off and repeated the puncture at the other extremity of the wound. Dr. Barker had already grasped the first knot between his fingers; when they lifted in unison, the cabbagelike organ throbbed gently under the two-way tug, then rose dutifully until it had all but escaped from the incision.

"Hemorrhagic or not, we've a chance of finding the pedicle once we've made our puncture."

Dr. Barker nodded and took the second knot from Roy's hand. Moving as solemnly as an acolyte in a high mass, the surgeon marched twice round the table with the knife held high, then stepped to the far side so that the patient's abdomen was in full view of the whole village. The steel moved downward, then paused as the doctors' glances locked.

"Lean forward if this draws blood," said Roy. "I'll nick your carotid artery first, then my own. We have time before they jump us."

Again the botanist gave a solemn, Argus-eyed nod; the hands that held the whipcord knots were as steady as that unwavering stare. If the next stroke of the scalpel failed them, death would be a boon indeed, an escape from greater horror. The knife hesitated a second longer, then swooped down on the copper drum of flesh.

"Behold, Chekika!"

The scalpel entered the cyst point-down, then sliced forward and out in a clean, inch-deep cut. The geyser that lifted from the wound was pale yellow, without a tinge of red. A howl of amazement rose from the watchers around the platform—a deep bass bellow from the braves, mixed with the keening of the clustered squaws. Chekika was on his feet, too, forgetting his dignity for once to howl with his tribesmen. Roy had already tossed the scalpel aside. Spreading his fingers with Dr. Barker's, he began to knead furiously at the flesh of the abdomen, sending recurrent spouts of bright topaz fluid into the sunlight as the cyst spewed forth its contents.

When the two doctors stepped back from the table, the wound was closed with tight purse-string stitches; the patient's abdomen was as flat as a board, and the patient herself, still deep in narcotic slumber, seemed relaxed in a pleasant dream. Both the surgeon and his assistant stepped to the front of the platform with folded arms and bowed in unison to the chief according to custom and again to the medicine men, who were still groveling in the dust without daring to raise their eyes. Then, moving in unison like well-trained marionettes, they returned to Little Egret and settled with folded arms until they were seated cross-legged on either side of her bed. Roy spoke from the corner of his mouth—the first whisper he had permitted himself since the climax of the operation.

"We've made big medicine today, Doctor."

"We have indeed, Roy," said the botanist in the same whisper. "May Hippocrates forgive us our quackery."

They did not stir as Chekika's moccasin creaked on the lowest rung of the ladder that led from compound to platform. Roy found he could breathe in earnest when the chief advanced on tiptoe, as though he were reluctant, even now, to cross the magic circle the two white doctors had drawn round this bed of pain. Roy kept his mask intact as Chekika reached out a tentative hand and patted the normal contour of the girl's body.

"The devil has escaped."

"As you see, Father of Seminoles."

"With a single knife stroke?"

"It was you who named me Salofkachee. Have I deserved the honor today?"

"Your magic passes understanding." Chekika's face clouded, and he seemed about to say more. "Little Egret will live, then?"

"If God wills."

"Tonight we will feast in your honor. You will join our council fire?"

"The time for councils is past. We are at war. Remember how I came here—and why."

Again Chekika seemed about to speak and thought better of the impulse. "Shall I send the woman now?" he asked, and his voice was strangely humble.

"It is our wish that no one save yourself ascend to this platform until your wife rises from her bed."

"Your wish is our law, Salofkachee."

"The King of Seminoles must sleep with his councilors tonight—and for many nights to come. That, too, is understood?"

"The King of Seminoles has other women to console him in his waiting. If Salofkachee desires a wife tonight—or many wives—he has only to ask."

Roy felt his mind darken. It was unlike Chekika to make such offers, even in the emotional release of the moment. Perhaps he was trying to atone for a broken promise elsewhere, now that the threat to Little Egret's life was removed. Perhaps Chittamicco was butchering the last of Andy's command at this very moment in the shadow of Indian Mound. Such a move would not seem inconsistent to the Indian's mind. Hating all whites impartially (save Dr. Barker and Roy), he might deem it logical to surrender Mary to the Army—and to his brother's scalping knife.

"I desire one thing only, King of Panthers," he said quietly. "Permit me to serve as nurse at your Queen's bedside—until I am assured of her recovery."

"Nursing a woman is woman's work."

"Do you doubt my wisdom?"

"No, Salofkachee. I only wish to ease your burden."

"It is a burden I accept gladly."

Chekika raised his arm, palm outward, and vaulted to the dust of the compound. A single imperious gesture sent the whole village scuttling about its business, down to the last lean hunting hound. When the compound was empty, the Wildcat himself strode heavily to its edge and paused in the shadow of a water oak with folded arms.

"I will clear the village if you like. You must work your magic in peace."

"Keep this platform empty. It is all we ask."

"Chittamicco returns from the lake tonight. It is only right that he should view your magic."

So Chekika's brother had left Indian Mound. Did that mean that the attackers had pulled back, too, before they were caught in the pinchers from the north? Or did it mean that Andy's command was now wiped out and that the warriors were returning to their village to lick their wounds?

"Tell me this much, Father of Seminoles. Does Chittamicco speak with your voice when you are present?"

"Never while I have life, Salofkachee."

"Then he has no right to set foot on this platform. You have given your word. I know that you do not break your word to friends. Only to enemies."

Chekika took this bit of off-center philosophy in stride. "Little Egret is his sister by marriage. May he observe her condition from a distance?"

"Yes, if he does not set foot in the chief's house. We must make our magic here alone—or Little Egret may still die."

"That is your last word, Salofkachee?"

"I have spoken."

Chekika's face clouded in earnest, but he did not speak again. After he had stalked out of sight among the clustered palm-thatch huts, Roy did not stir for a long time. Behind him he heard Dr. Barker's low, appreciative whistle.

"That was a near thing too, my boy."

"Chittamicco wanted her to die. We both know that. He still wants it. Enough to hurry back to witness our demise. Can you imagine his feelings when he finds us sitting guard over a convalescing patient?"

"How can we make him keep his distance?"

"Chekika has given his promise. If necessary, we'll ask that a guard be posted. Above all, we must stay at her bedside until she's really on her feet. Spell each other at nursing, if need be."

He had spoken with his eyes on the solemn file of Indian

dwellings. Somehow, the village looked unutterably forlorn
now that its inhabitants had scattered under Chekika's wrath.
Save for the grunt of a lone razorback that had returned to
forage under their platform, he could have believed this an
abode of the dead. Dr. Barker's chuckle reassured him mightily. That ancient philosopher, he knew, could extract a grain
of humor from any situation whatever.

"We're still alive, Roy," said the botanist. "To be frank,
I'm not too sure I enjoy it."

They were smiling together as they turned to their patient
and began the task of policing their operation. Survival, after
all, was enough to occupy them for the present. This was no
time to confide his terrible doubts, thought Roy. The certainty that Chittamicco was returning to Fakahatchee Hammock
with Andy's scalp at his belt. His thoughts stuttered, refusing
to focus on Mary's fate if that dire suspicion should prove a
reality. Tired as it was, his mind could not cope with Mary
today—or with Mary's future. Survival was the role he must
play henceforth, and he would act it with all his senses.

iii

He sat on the platform's edge, with the sketchbook open on
his lap, his eyes on the caperings of a dozen Indian children
in the compound. Once again the village drowsed in the siesta
hush of another endless afternoon; once again its stilted
houses seemed empty of all life save for the wail of a sick in-
fant, the ritualistic strutting of the naked papooses in the dust
at his feet. It was hard to remember that a week had gone by
since his scalpel had turned Little Egret on the road to health
again. Harder still to believe that the mahogany-brown face
that looked back at him from Dr. Barker's shaving mirror
belonged to Dr. Royal Coe.

From this vantage point he could look clear across Fakahatchee Hammock. There was Dr. Barker, poking along a
steaming mud flat in search of nesting spoonbills. It was
strange, in a way, that his colleague should show this interest
in the mating habits of an all but prehistoric bird, said by
some observers to have descended from the waders of the
Nile. Reluctant as ever to turn the pages of the portfolio, he
watched the old doctor's palm-frond hat bob among the tufts
of grass, for all the world like some contented green insect in

search of food. A botanist, he reflected, could pass the time anywhere and show a profit at day's end. Dedicated to the earth rather than to the unpredictable doings of man, he could ignore most things in search of knowledge. He could even live and breathe in a limbo that Roy himself was beginning to find unendurable.

He turned a page of the portfolio and stared down at one of the sketches Mary Grant had left behind—a great white ibis poised for flight on the crest of a mangrove. Hilolo, the graceful bird that was her namesake . . . For all he knew, the hand that had sketched in those firm lines was lifeless now. He closed the sketchbook, wishing once again that he could shut the door of memory with as firm a hand. Roaming the platform of Chekika's house, he paused to look down at the sleeping form of Chekika's squaw. The girl was mending fast —he could at least take satisfaction in that fact. She had taken her first hesitant steps today with a hand on his arm. Tomorrow she would rise from her bed in earnest, and he could remind Chekika of their bargain with a clear conscience.

Spelling Dr. Barker at Little Egret's bedside during that long, tense week, he had refused to consider himself a prisoner, though it was evident from the first that neither doctor would be permitted beyond the narrow confines of the island. Save for his brief visit at his wife's sickbed, Chekika had remained aloof for reasons of his own. Perhaps he had been offended by Roy's refusal to take part in the revel that had followed the casting out of Little Egret's devil. Perhaps he now shared a secret with Chittamicco that made him reluctant to meet his white friend's eyes. It was a question that Roy did not dare to answer now.

Most of the inhabitants of the village had taken their cue from the King of Panthers, and though there was no open hostility, Roy was soon made to realize that his days of easy camaraderie with the Seminole were over. Backs were turned pointedly when he approached a cook fire: laughing voices were stilled when he dared to come within earshot. Miracle man though he was, by Indian standards, he was still a white —and a sworn enemy. At first he had been sure that this universal coldness was Chittamicco's doing. Now he felt that the cause went deeper.

Chekika's brother was everywhere these days, swaggering

like a true hero, drumming his chest in the endless powwows that roared around the council fire where Salofkachee was no longer an honored adviser. Hugging his knees and his loneliness on the chief's platform, watching the swirl of dark dervishes howl and stamp by firelight, Roy had had time to wonder if Chekika or his warlock brother would decide the future of the nation. If there was wailing for the losses at Indian Mound, Roy could not distinguish it now. Normally there would have been a traditional pause for mourning when the bodies were brought home for burial—with or without hair. He had seen no evidence of cadavers when the first canoes crossed Big Sulphur—and no white scalps. Perhaps the Seminole dead had been honored in secret far from his prying eyes. Not even Chittamicco would have been rash enough to advertise the fruits of a second assault at Indian Mound.

One fact was certain—and Roy could curse that certainty even now: the strategy they had planned so hopefully at Fort Everglades had been a failure. He had counted too many braves in those homecoming canoes to hope for an instant that Chittamicco had been trapped by their relief force from the north. Decimated though they were, those red ranks seemed more than ever defiant. Try as he might, Roy could not believe that they had retired from Indian Mound without striking a final blow. Since they had returned to Fakahatchee so promptly, it was evident that they had eluded the regulars from Augustine with time to spare.

Today's powwow was being held at Big Sulphur and, to judge by the distant bellowing, it would continue beyond sunset. Probably this was the ritual bath, thought Roy, as well as a council of war. Dr. Barker had explained that the Seminoles believed the sulphur spring possessed miraculous qualities of its own—that it rejuvenated the aged and gave new power to the young. Like the tail of the bull 'gator or the heart of an enemy legitimately slain in battle, this deep silver spring was said to add steel to a warrior's arm; the deeper one plunged into its wildly bubbling depths, the longer one would live to cut down enemies of the nation. It was a legend that belonged to this forlorn bird-haunted land. Certainly, thought Roy, it explained why the village was deserted today; even the boys and old men who had not stirred from the campfire since the days of Osceola had pushed down the slough in the long war canoes. Only the squaws were left behind—and the children who still paraded in the dust of the compound. For once it had not been necessary to leave a guard, since the beach before the village was empty of canoes.

Roy knew that he should have walked across the hammock long ago to join Dr. Barker in his sketching. He sat on in the doubtful shade of the palm thatch, listening, from long habit, to the pulse of Little Egret's breathing and damning the lethargy that had begun to invade his spirit with the declining day. Dusk, he reflected, is the prisoner's worst hour—if one leaves out the dreams that come at midnight.

He saw the botanist's green-chip hat come bobbing through the rank stand of saw grass along the northern shore of the island. He rose a bit guiltily to go through the routine of checking their patient's pulse and the nourishing meat stew that bubbled in the saucepan at a corner of the platform. Isolation had had its good points, after all; in the past seven days he had not been plagued by so much as an errant flea, thanks to their daily scourings with lye above and below the floor level of Chekika's house. Even the bluebottles, he thought wryly, had given these white interlopers a wide berth.

The palm-frond sombrero sailed gaily through the spent air of afternoon and landed at his feet as he stood irresolute on the chief's platform. Dr. Jonathan Barker vaulted to his side with an ease that belied his years.

"You should have joined me on the mud flat, Roy," he said mildly. "I waited long enough."

"Sorry—I'm afraid I napped at my post."

"A man could be excused for napping on a day like this. Are you still convinced that Chittamicco means to undo our good work here?"

"I'm sure of it—if we give him the chance."

"Then we'll both stand guard tonight. You've had your rest. At my age I can do with two hours' sleep in twenty-four." Dr. Barker went to the gourd and poured water over his face and neck. "You should get out more, Roy, even if it's only to observe the habits of the roseate spoonbill. It's the prisoner's first duty to himself."

"I've been working, after a fashion. In fact, I copied Mary's sketch of that same spoonbill, as you requested."

The botanist settled at their patient's bedside and studied

the sleeping girl carefully. "I've had time to grow weary too, Roy. Believe me, it's a dull business, wondering if you'll be alive this time tomorrow. It can grow so dull you cease to do your work at all. And a man's work is important—no matter who the jailer may be——"

"You're more fortunate than I, sir. Your work is here. Part of it, at any rate. Mine ended the day I put my last stitch in Little Egret."

"Can you deny we've saved her life this past week? Merely by keeping this nest free of vermin—and midwives?"

"I don't deny it for an instant. I only say it's a tiring job for two men to do alone."

The botanist chuckled. "Mary didn't find it in the least tiring here at Fakahatchee. But of course she's only a woman— and she does enjoy sketching. Far more than you, it seems."

"Are you suggesting I follow her example?"

"Certainly. If only to cheat your boredom. I'm glad I could persuade you to come with me yesterday—and the day before. It made you look far more natural today when you sat working on that copy of Mary's drawing."

Dr. Barker's voice had been calm enough, but the bright glance that fixed Roy's own tired eyes blazed with tension. Roy felt his own mind catch fire, though he had not yet grasped the botanist's meaning.

"Don't tell me that Mary's sketch of a spoonbill is part of some—*plot?*"

"You might call it that."

"Why didn't you tell me sooner?"

"I didn't dare. We've been watched every moment. Some-one has always been within earshot. Abraham, for the most part—or another ear that knew a few words of English. They've been careless today—don't ask me why. I suppose it's war fever."

"Never mind their war fever now. What about Mary's drawing?"

"You say you copied it carefully?"

Roy swallowed his impatience and went over to the portfo-lio to extract the sheet of drawing paper he had labored over since noon. Dr. Barker drew out the original and examined the two sketches side by side. As usual, Mary Grant had caught the roseate spoonbill in a characteristic pose—with one leg stiffly extended, the other crooked at its side to preserve its balance as the long shell-pink neck darted downward to snare an unwary fish.

"An excellent copy, Roy. If you'd used water colors one could hardly tell them apart."

"Are you telling me that Mary brought these paints from Flamingo Key?"

"It was part of my rather hasty bargain with Chekika. Mary loves our wilderness too, you see."

"What are you driving at, sir?"

"I'm making my point, Roy—in my own way. Mary did a great deal of sketching when we first entered the Glades. That was my suggestion too. You see, she's only a squaw in Chekika's book. Why should he expect her to have a bump of direction?"

"I still don't follow."

"You will if you study that drawing carefully. We came to Fakahatchee via the big lake—*and* Indian Mound. Even Chekika could never have found his camp without some orientation."

"Are you telling me that this sketch is also a map of Chekika's route?"

"Look at it more carefully—you'll see what I mean. No, never mind Mary's water color. Go to your own sketch. That's a good bit rougher—the composition stands out more clearly. That's why I asked you to make it."

Roy studied his drawing in detail—the long, spatulate bill of the giant wader, the curve of neck like an inverted S, the taut, widespread legs that seemed to buckle under the weight of the fish in the extended mouth.

"Look again at Little Egret," said the botanist. "I'm positive she's sleeping, but we must be doubly sure. And look under the house while you're about it. One of those papooses may be a ward of Abraham's—and understand English perfectly."

"You can see we're alone, sir."

"Fair enough, Roy. I won't tease you any longer. As you may have gathered, I was blindfolded after we left Ten-Mile Slough and entered Okeechobee. Chekika knew that I'd explored this country before—too deep for comfort. It never entered his head to suspect Mary——"

"Are you telling me that this is a map?"

"Precisely. Mary was allowed to sit beside me and sketch

to her heart's content. All the way from Sandy Bay to the Big Cypress."

"Didn't Chekika realize she was drawing a map?"

"Not when it was disguised in that spoonbill's plumage." Dr. Barker turned over the sketch as he spoke and let his finger trace the contours of the long-legged wader's neck. "The Seminole is intelligent, after his fashion, but he's a primitive, after all. He's yet to realize that women possess a brain."

Roy studied the sketch in turn. Even now he could not realize that this was anything more than a giant wader, its neck contorted by the weight of the fish in its bill. And then, as though a film had dropped from his eyes, the beginning of the design came clear. The fish (it had been sketched in roughly) was the terminus of Sandy Bay; the spears of saw grass that surrounded it were the cypress islands where Chittamicco's flotilla had taken shelter. The long curve of neck was the shore line of Okeechobee. Where neck joined body, the pattern of a half-spread wing marked the maze of sloughs that led westward to the Big Cypress Swamp. He had come this far on his own a dozen times. Beyond was the unknown maze of the saw grass—a labyrinth that no white man had explored. He looked inquiringly at the botanist. Dr. Barker smiled, as though he was rather enjoying his bewilderment.

"Your mind is slow today, Roy," he said. "Surely you haven't forgotten that these spoonbills have albino markings among their plumage?"

"Of course I remember. Does that mean the white feather in the wing is the one to follow?"

"Observe it's the fourth feather from the joining of wing and body. Note, too, how it fans back to meet the body again near the tail feathers. That shadow is the blue-gum swamp that blocks the saw grass from the lake itself. But there's another albino feather to take you through and down—to the joining of body and leg."

"A much bigger feather, this time. Does that mean the slough is wider too?"

"Your map reading is improving fast. Those black dots are saw-grass islands. The whitish line down the leg itself is the channel. Don't miss the big bend at the knee joint—you're in the home stretch now."

Roy felt his heart beat faster as he followed the patient

tracing of Dr. Barker's finger. "The five toes of the foot are five smaller sloughs that open toward this hammock a good three miles to the north and west. Even if you'd come this far by luck, you'd never know which one to take. Can you pick the right toe now?"

"Naturally. It's at the extreme left. The one that's stirring a white whirlpool in the sand. That would be Big Sulphur."

"Right again. All five toes cut through jungle to the spring; the left-hand toe is by far the shortest route. Once you've entered it, you can't make a mistake; you simply follow your nose."

Roy closed his eyes on the image. He could see why Dr. Barker had insisted he make an accurate copy of Mary's sketch. Now that the key points had been explained, the whole drawing was burned into his brain. "She brought a whole portfolio of water colors to Indian Mound," he said slowly. "Did she take a copy of this one to Andy?"

"No, Roy. She was positive you'd join them soon. So positive that she left the map with me. Besides, she wanted me to go over it with you in detail. Both of us know this country better than Andy Winter."

Roy nodded, and hoped that Dr. Barker had not noticed the flush that spread under his tan. There was something heartening in Mary's faith that he would survive—that he could not fail to return to Andy's headquarters with the map. Perhaps her reluctance to take the map to Andy at this time went even deeper. Knowing the chance he would run at Little Egret's sickbed, and knowing Andy's blind eagerness to track the King of Panthers to his lair, he felt sure that she had left the map at Fakahatchee Hammock deliberately.

"Now that you've explained the route to me, I think I could follow it in the dark."

"It isn't quite that simple. Mary has memorized certain landmarks along the way. She'll draw them into the diagram when you return. She feels—and I must say that I agree—that no one but you can lead the rescue party to Big Sulphur."

Roy nodded again and kept his eyes on the sketch. The first flush of excitement had died in his heart. He had just reminded himself that Andy's command might be wiped out by now, or reduced to a few survivors too terrified to do more than scramble for safety.

"I'd give a great deal to leave here at once."

"So I anticipated, Roy. That's why I didn't show you this sketch until the last possible moment."

"Do you think I'll be sent back tonight?"

"Tonight—or tomorrow at the latest. Chekika all but promised me that much before he went to the powwow at the spring. If I'm not mistaken, they're returning early, after all. Perhaps he'll send you at once."

They rose together and crossed to the western rim of the platform. The sun was a red magnificence now behind the ragged saw-grass spears; he could see the plumed headdresses of the chief and his sense-bearers gliding, like phantom birds, just above that yellow screen. Chekika and his subchiefs, as behooved their rank, were evidently standing upright in the canoes while a dozen paddlers sweated at each gunwale. He knew that they would return to the village refreshed by their plunge into Big Sulphur and keyed to concert pitch by Chittamicco's rhetoric.

"It's my guess that they're planning another attack along the coast," said Dr. Barker. "Andy must strike soon, or he'll lose them again."

"Surely Chekika doesn't plan to leave this hammock before his corn is harvested?"

"One never knows. It's evident that he feels safe here. But he may still feel it's prudent to move on—especially after another raid. There must be hammocks larger than Fakahatchee beyond Big Cypress."

One never knows. That, thought Roy, summed up the whole fruitless, fumbling business of dealing with the Seminole. Driven by the advancing white man, the Indian had withdrawn deeper into his swamps—and deeper still in his own mysterious heart. Forced to lead the double life of hunter and hunted, protected only by the vastness of the Grassy Water, he would elude the white man's understanding to the end. Forced by that same interloper to live by tooth and claw, he would make no further treaties, ask no further mercy. The carbine smuggled from Cuba, the tomahawk forged in England would be his only sense-bearers. . . . Somehow, thought Roy, I must get back to Andy—or his successor. We must move down on Fakahatchee Hammock in force and stamp out Chekika's power finally and forever.

While his mind hardened on this resolve, the canoes had

swept up to the beach in shoals. Already more than two
hundred braves had surged into the compound, their naked
bodies still glistening from their bath in Big Sulphur, their
mouths rounded in a soundless war whoop. Roy perceived
that there was a pattern to this advance upon the chief's
house, this silent note of defiance. He grasped its import
when Chekika's warriors began to file past the platform one
by one. As they passed the two white men, the Seminoles lifted their fists in a hostile, mocking salute; soundless war
whoops continued to distort those hate-twisted masks long
after the last brave had stalked across the compound and settled in a vast circle around the council fire.

"Evidently they've decided on their next raid," said Dr.
Barker.

"Here comes Chittamicco now—he's our answer."

Chekika's brother had never been more magnificent—or
menacing. Covered from head to foot in a robe of flamingo
feathers, with wide tufts of the same plumage at wrists and
ankles, he marched up from the water's edge like some pagan
emperor and paused before the chief's house with folded
arms. A medicine gourd was clutched in each fist; Roy could
see a dozen strings of amulets beneath the robe and guessed
that his enemy had resumed his function as witch doctor.
Three careful steps behind Chittamicco, a small Negro slave,
naked save for a breechcloth and a pair of white Army ban-
doleers, bore the snake basket high on his palms. The whir of
the diamondback's rattles was the only sound that broke the
stillness as Chittamicco spat deliberately into the dusty earth
—four times, to mark the compass points. Then, raising his
fist as the others had done, he marched solemnly to his place
in the council.

Four of the subchiefs followed, their eyes as hard as stone,
their upraised fists thrust almost into the faces of the two doctors, who continued to stand grimly at the platform's edge,
refusing to flinch under this massed hatred. Last of all was
Chekika, with Abraham a dutiful step in the rear. Though
the King of Panthers walked with bowed head, there was
nothing humble in his bearing. When he raised his chin at
last and motioned to Abraham to come forward he was every
inch a nation's king. An untamed monarch in snow-white
buckskins, he carried his destiny bravely today and seemed
proud of the burden.

The sense-bearer came up to the platform and rested his knuckles boldly on the edge. When he spoke his voice rang across the compound. Since the words he used were Seminole, Roy sensed that Chekika's message was intended for the council's ears as well.

"Is the chief's wife cured of her devils?"

"The chief's wife is well again," said Roy, and he found he was shouting, too, from sheer nervous release, letting his voice defy the whole nation. "Tomorrow she will rise from her bed for good."

"If she is well, Salofkachee, why are her eyes unopened?"

"She sleeps today because we desire it. The bellows from your council fire would weary her. It is better that she rest while your war drums are beating."

"So you still give her white medicine?"

"A pellet that brings deep sleep—no more than that."

"Tomorrow you must give her back to her own doctors."

"Tomorrow she will need no doctors."

"I speak with the voice of Chekika. Do you defy his order?"

"It was Chekika's voice that put me here. While I am here no one but he sets foot on this platform. That was our bargain."

"Little Egret will be well tomorrow. You swear to that?"

"I have sworn to it before. Must I repeat my oath?" There's something behind this mumbo-jumbo, thought Roy. Even now Chittamicco is working hard to plant a doubt in these simple minds. At present they can see with their own eyes that white magic has saved a girl's life. They can't understand why she sleeps in broad daylight; bed rest, under a light opiate, cannot be translated into Seminole. Until she wakens from that last long sleep—until she really walks again—they won't quite believe in her cure.

"Tomorrow you will see how well she walks," he said. "Tomorrow her long sleep will be over."

"We will wait till tomorrow, Salofkachee. If what you say is true, you will leave us with the dawn."

"Will the King of Panthers say he is grateful?"

"The King of Panthers has no word for you now. Only that he remembers his promise. He will speak his mind when his squaw rises to greet him once again."

Abraham raised his hand with the last solemn words; the

first war drum spoke from the council precisely on cue, as though that ebony limb had been a conductor's baton in an orchestra. Another drum answered instantly, matched by a muted chant that ran round the circle like a goblin fire. Three hundred palms had begun to strike the sun-baked earth in unison, pacing the slow, sad beat of the drums. Roy knew that this heartbroken wailing would grow in volume as the night advanced. Sparked by the two rum kegs that had just been broached within the circle, it would reach its frenetic climax at midnight—and die, from sheer exhaustion, with the dawn. He had lived with that chanting for a week now; it was part of his dreams.

He held his place at the platform's edge until Abraham had joined the council; he stared back, unwinking, as Chekika himself crossed the compound with his back deliberately turned, to take the place of honor among his braves. Only then did Roy dare to turn his back, just as insolently, and walk with Dr. Barker to the shaded corner where Little Egret still slept peacefully.

"What does it all mean?"

"I wouldn't dare guess, Roy. But I do think we should both stay awake after dark. Somehow, I'd prefer to meet death face to face. I wouldn't care to have him creep up while I slept."

iv

Despite his best resolves, he admitted that he had dozed more than once since midnight. Now, as he wakened with a start, he knew that Dr. Barker, too, was deep in slumber across the platform. The botanist's gentle snoring was surprisingly loud in the black stillness that blanketed the island. Perhaps it was the quiet that had wakened him; when he had slipped into his dream the drums had still sounded around the council fire and strangely costumed dancers had capered to their steady pounding. Now, it seemed, the last dervish had spun to a dead stop, to sleep beside the ruins of the fire. The council itself had dropped into clotted groups that snored as rhythmically as Dr. Barker. Even the drummers slept, with their hands cradled on the taut buckskin. Only Chekika and Chittamicco were missing from this finale to hours of rum and riot. Still wavering between sleep and waking, Roy marked the empty seats of honor and surmised that the chief and his brother had retired to the latter's house across the compound, to spend what remained of the night with the squaws.

At least he would stay awake till dawn, he thought. Dr. Barker could continue his cat nap at will. Actually, the night had been no more anxious than usual. They had watched the dancers leap and howl for hours on end, bemused by the insistent monotony of the rhythms; they had merely opened their eyes a bit wider when Hamlet leaped like a black grasshopper into the revel, to caper in unison with a white-clad Ophelia, an Othello as gaudy as a Venetian sunset, a Macbeth whose tartan clashed oddly with the copper limbs it covered. These, of course, were the costumes that Chekika had stolen from the Avon Players when Mary Grant was still a member of that strolling troupe; these, too, were part of the white man's magic. Someday they would be worn in battle against that ancient enemy.

The revels were ended now; Lear and Romeo snored cheek by jowl with a naked brave whose fish-oil aroma rose like incense in the still air before dawn. The quiet, thought Roy, was almost suffocating tonight—a part of the unfallen rain that seemed to press down on the palm thatch above him like choking vapor. Outside the eaves of the chief's dwelling the darkness was absolute save for the dim glow of the council fire. Here on the platform the smudge they had lighted in the brazier had simmered down to embers long ago; Roy knew that he should replenish that bed of feeble coals, but the languor of his waking dream still held his limbs captive.

It was enough for now to discover that they had come through the night alive. To insist that his part of the bargain was fulfilled. In another hour, with the first gray light, Chekika would emerge from his brother's house and keep his word. He could trust Chekika that far. . . .

He heard a smothered gasp in the blackness and sat bolt upright. Apparently he had dozed briefly after all, for Dr. Barker was no longer snoring. It was he who had just cried out. It was his eyes, wide open now and glazed with fear, that focused on the narrow opening (it could hardly be called a door) that divided the latticed north face of the chief's dwelling and gave to the ladder that served as a step-up from earth to platform.

A coal burst softly in the brazier, casting a feeble, tantalizing glow across the slatted floor. Roy's eyelids, still weighed with sleep, had refused to pry apart so far. What he saw (and did not see) in the darkness that lay between him and the patient's bed stabbed him into wakefulness even as it threatened to paralyze his brain.

Something was moving from ladder to door—and from door to bed. Something that flowed with an effortless motion across the slatted pine. For a moment his tired brain insisted that this was darkness itself, taking a visible, sinuous form. Then, as the thing entered the pale circle of light around the brazier, he saw the gigantic diamond markings along its back. The creature was neither brown nor black; it seemed to pick up livid highlights as it moved through the fire's glow. In that flash he knew just why Dr. Barker had frozen to the far wall—and why he felt himself chained to his own corner.

This was indeed the king of all rattlesnakes, the *chittamicco* from which Chekika's brother derived his name. This was the same huge reptile that had once slept in the basket at Little Egret's bedside, the same coiled fury that had sounded its defiance at the end of today's powwow. Obeying a logic of its own, it was returning to the chief's house tonight—or, what was still more likely, obeying an order from its owner. He had seen other medicine men control these huge reptiles before, with thought rather than word. More than once he had watched a snake rear to strike at its victim while its master sat removed, directing the fangs as precisely as oriental fakirs are said to guide a cobra.

The idea was fantastic, he knew, and yet the snake was enacting Chittamicco's will before his eyes. Now, as he watched with spine-prickling terror, he grasped the meaning of Abraham's questions that afternoon—and why the sense-bearer had reminded him so forcibly of his bargain with Chekika. Little Egret was still in his charge; the whole nation had observed how deeply she slept. If she died tonight (as she surely would when those fangs found their target) he would be accused as the killer.

Had he slept the night through, the snake might well have struck without sound and returned undetected to its basket. No one would have looked beneath the blanket for the two blue-red pin points where death had entered. The knife of Salofkachee and Salofkachee's medicine would be blamed, and he would pay the penalty. Chittamicco could not have picked a better time; like the diamond-marked horror that advanced to do his bidding, he knew how and when to strike.

The snake lifted along the first segment of its monstrous length; he saw the flat wedge of its head in the fading light of the brazier, a triangle of exquisite overlapping scales. The head was as black as the pit around the slitted eyes, deep-pouched where head and body joined, and as livid as the flesh of a corpse. The flowing-forward motion ceased; for a second the snake seemed confused, its eyes darting to the far corners of the platform, as though it awaited a further order before moving toward the bed. Then the slitted yellow glare fastened on Roy and held firm.

Man and snake poised eye to eye for a breath-taking instant that seemed to extend to eternity. Then the head and neck began to sway gently, and Roy felt his body swaying, too, as though a current ran between them. Sure of its mastery now, the reptile flowed on toward the bed, holding the man against the wall and rearing even higher as it prepared to strike.

Roy felt the sweat burst out along his back and shoulders as he fought to break the communion between himself and those pitiless eyes. Then, without knowing why, he found he had risen to hands and knees, pulled toward the reptile as a steel scrap in the field of a magnet. Perhaps if he moved fast enough he could throw his body between the bed and that rearing black wedge. He felt his brain fog over with the intensity of his effort and shook his head blindly to clear the film from his vision. With that move the invisible current snapped. He was on his feet now, moving down on the snake with cautious deliberation, and it was his eyes that dominated his enemy, holding him motionless to the floor, though the hideous arc of head and neck still hung just above the bed.

To his right he heard Dr. Barker struggle to his feet and pause outside the circle of light from the brazier. Like himself, the botanist knew that a sudden move would be fatal; Roy's only hope was to advance upon the reptile step by step, until he stood between those fangs and their target.

He came into the glow of the firelight with quaking knees. One step more and he, too, would be within range of death. He took that step, and yet another, while his mind raced on, groping frantically for a means of attack, A cane knife, swung in a sudden, biting arc, might have stopped the thrust in time; he had cut down both rattler and cottonmouth with such a weapon. But there was no cane knife on the platform —not even a stick. His eyes picked out his instrument case on a table beside the wall. Not daring to take his eyes from the snake's, he leveled a finger at the box and knew that Dr. Barker had backed away from the brazier, understanding his demand without words.

The knife sailed through the darkness, winked in the fire-light as it landed in his outstretched hand without breaking his concentration on the snake. It was good to feel the bone handle against his palm, even though he realized that the scalpel itself was a pitful weapon indeed. Inch by inch, not daring to breathe, forcing all his energy into the glare that still held the snake poised, he put his body between the couch and the rearing head. His free hand, fumbling in empty air, moved cautiously downward until it touched the blanket that enclosed Little Egret in its warmth. The blanket was as taut as a lashed-down canvas under his groping fingers, and he took time to curse his thoroughness this morning when he had tucked his patient in securely for her all-day slumber. Then he felt an edge lift in his fist, heard the girl stir softly beneath the coverlet as he ripped it free, taking infinite pains to make it a single, flowing motion that would not galvanize the reptile into action.

Man and snake were now a scant two feet apart. He felt his heart turn over as the first warning rattle sounded like doom in the darkness. Coiled as it was, and alarmed at last by the threat of this strange new adversary, the snake was capable of striking any target for a full third of its length. He watched the jaws gape, saw the glitter of the darting tongue deep in the white slaver of the mouth. The fangs gleamed in the firelight, delicate as two curved needles at their tips, bone-white at the base where they joined the poison sacs embedded in the skull. Already they were winking with moisture at their hollow tips as the first drops of venom pulsed from that deadly triangle. The snake's whole body was vibrating now, taut as a fresh-plucked harp string. The pitch of the rattles had risen to an angry whine.

Roy stamped hard on the floor and flung his whole body forward. The snake struck at that easy target just as the doe-skin blanket fell between them. Pouched in that shield, the black lightning stroke blunted, recoiled on itself, lost its impact in a frantic thrashing within the blanket folds. The force of the attack almost jerked the doeskin from Roy's hands. Overbalanced as he was by that first despairing lunge, he stumbled and fell, with the blanket ends still anchored in his fist. The snake, trapped for the moment, struggled to break out of the blind cave that confined it. Roy, struggling in turn to find a foothold, tugged desperately on the blanket ends and shouted his relief when he was sure that the blanket had penned his enemy, down to its madly vibrating rattles.

Remembering that crazy wrestling match later, he knew that it was only the peculiar hinge in the fangs that had saved him. Dropping as they did from the snake's upper jaw, the fangs pointed forward sharply as the reptile struck. Angling downward, they were ready and dripping when they sank home. Tonight the bite of those powerful jaws had lost itself in the doeskin—and snarled there as the needle points thrust deep into the hide.

Scrambling for purchase on the smooth floor, Roy managed to pull the blanket ends into a rough knot. The doeskin, he saw, was stained milky-white—an automatic discharge from the poison sacs in the reptile's skull. Trained as it was to kill on the first strike, the snake had wasted most of its venom on that blind puncture. Now, with its hinged fangs anchored in the blanket, it was firmly trapped. Avoiding those needles by instinct, Roy noted that his enemy was caged, after a fashion. If he could contain those fangs entirely, this attack might still be turned to his advantage.

From a great distance he heard Dr. Barker rush to the edge of the platform and bellow for help. There was no time to look beyond the full-muscled adversary that threatened, even now, to best him. The fangs continued to slash to right and left, dripping with the white exudate that could kill in an instant once it was injected into a victim's blood stream.

Already Roy had confined the head to the tightly gripped knot of the blanket. The scalpel, still nested in his right palm, moved expertly downward. The first stroke missed its mark, slashing the doeskin to expose the gyrations of the scaly neck beneath. The next stroke, timed with its objective in full view, struck downward, where the reptile's spinal column joined the brain. Again and again the steel rose and fell, chopping between the elementary vertebrae until the great nerve trunk beneath was split at a dozen points. Venom pumped from the needled fangs in a whitish flood. And then, subsiding in a series of agonizing twitches from tail to brain-pan, the king of rattlesnakes grew quiet in the blanket folds. Roy brushed the splintered palm thatch from his eyes. Now that the battle was ended, he realized that he had coasted across the platform on his haunches in his effort to confine the giant reptile to its blanket. The rising hubbub out-side reached his brain but dimly. It was enough for now to shake free of the sun-dried vegetation that powdered his neck and shoulders—to realize that he had backed into the north wall of the dwelling, bursting a mighty hole in the woven palm fronds that boxed this side of Chekika's house. Then he was on his feet, with no conscious memory of what had gone before—aware only of the coiled iniquity that still throbbed inside the blanket.

Yearning to throw aside his hideous burden, he continued to hold it at arm's length as he joined the botanist on the edge of the platform. At first glance he thought the entire na-tion had spilled into the compound in response to Dr. Bar-ker's cry and the tardy shouts of the sentries on the beach. Torches were blazing under every platform in the village as family after family responded to the alarm. Then he realized that Chekika's braves, fuddled by rum though they were, had already moved down to the beach to defend the village from attack. Squaws and children, herding by instinct to the center of the island, had moved toward the chief's house as an obvi-ous rallying point. The chief himself had emerged from his brother's hut and was moving toward his own dwelling on the run, with Chittamicco close behind. Roy could see his enemy clearly enough by the light of the torches and ob-served that Chittamicco was stifling a yawn. The elaborate bit of play acting was all Roy needed to convince himself of the other's guilt.

He pocketed his scalpel and waited grimly at Dr. Barker's side, the doeskin bundle knotted in one fist. As Chekika stalked into the compound Roy took time to glance over his shoulder and caught the gleam of triumph in the brother's eyes. He was hardly surprised when Chittamicco moved boldly forward and put one foot on the step-up to the plat-form itself. Matching his enemy's boldness in one long stride, he stood at the head of the ladder and barred his path.

"Stay where you are! The chief's house has been profaned enough tonight."

He had sent the words ringing out over the compound. Now he took a quick step down the ladder and stood in full view of the village. He watched the braves move in to join the squaws as they began to realize that the disturbance had come from the chief's house. He stood firm as Chekika came forward and put his own moccasin on the step-up, jostling his brother aside.

"Was it you who cried out, Salofkachee?"

"It was Dr. Barker who sounded the alarm. As you see, I had other business." Roy lifted the doeskin and its bulging contents. The king of rattlesnakes still twitched spasmodically within the knotted folds. The whole village recoiled, to the last shivering papoose. Even Chittamicco hastened to withdraw to the front rank of the watchers, as though he had already sensed what was inside the blanket. Only Abraham, who had stumbled tardily into the compound with his ceremonial turban askew, ventured to move to the chief's side. Chekika silenced the sense-bearer with a peremptory gesture.

"I will be my own voice tonight. What do you hide in that doeskin, Salofkachee? Is it more of the white man's magic?"

"No, Father of Seminoles. Our white magic is ended. This is the last devil to threaten Little Egret. As you see, I captured him in time."

"Did this devil come to my house tonight?"

"Tonight—while your people slept. All but your faithful servants on this platform."

"Does the devil still live?"

Again Roy lifted his bundle high. "He is dying now before your eyes. He was cut down by the hand of Salofkachee."

"Who sent this enemy to my house?"

"It is not for me to say whence devils come," Roy spaced the words evenly, letting the cadence of the Seminole tongue make its own music behind the melodrama he was acting so tellingly. "I can only give it a name."

"Speak, Salofkachee!"

"Its name is—*chittamicco!*"

He had dropped the blanket as he spoke. Now he seized the snake's tail in both fists and flailed the eight-foot body about his head, like a shot-putter about to toe the mark. With the third whirl he flung the black carcass into the compound, where it fell in a spurt of dust at the feet of its namesake. The whole village wailed in unison as every eye recognized the dead monster—and moved, just as inevitably, to its owner. The whole village began to converge on Chittamicco —a spontaneous movement, as yet more curious than hostile. Chekika, with a foot still on the ladder, stopped it with a shouted word,

"Enough! How does my brother explain this?"

"Salofkachee accused me falsely," shouted Chittamicco. "He stole the snake from its basket while I slept."

"This platform is guarded, as you know. How could Salof-kachee leave it?"

"The guard slept tonight."

A voice from the crowd entered the argument instantly. "Chittamicco lies. It is I, Matlo, who speak. I have watched that ladder since sundown, as Chekika ordered. The white doctors stayed within."

The brave stepped forward with his last shout and shook his fist in Chittamicco's face. Chekika turned his back on the furious discussion that ensued and stood below the ladder with folded arms. On the platform, Roy and Dr. Barker duplicated the gesture—an indignant pose to match that withdrawal from the argument of underlings. Under his careful mask Roy suppressed a grin. For once, he thought, my arch-enemy is speaking gospel. Matlo *did* doze at his post to-night—at the precise moment when Chittamicco released his namesake from the basket.

Chekika raised his hand at last, and the warring voices stilled. "No more of this bickering. The snake escaped—that much we know. Salofkachee killed it in time. For this we are grateful——"

"Who can say it died in time?" Chittamicco dared to come forward with his words. "Little Egret still sleeps. Perhaps she will never waken."

"She has wakened now."

It was Dr. Barker who had spoken from the deep shadows behind the brazier. Even Chekika's eyes opened wide as the girl on the rope bed stirred faintly, stretched her limbs, then sat up abruptly, like any sleeper after a long, refreshing rest. Silence clamped down on the compound when she put both feet to the floor and stood upright, ignoring Dr. Barker's helping hand. If she falls now, thought Roy, if she so much as stumbles, I'm still a dead man. But the girl's walk was steady enough as she crossed the platform and moved into Chekika's waiting arms.

"The King of Panthers honors me too highly," she said, and only Roy caught the ardent whisper. "Have I disturbed his rest?"

Chief and squaw touched foreheads solemnly in a ritual greeting before Chekika released her. They stood hand in hand for an instant, facing the stunned watchers below. Then Chekika lifted his hand again to bring the shout of triumph from every throat. The affirmation of life that has outwitted death one more time—driven home, in this instance, with a blend of mumbo-jumbo and pure luck. Roy backed out of the tableau with bowed head. If he had saved Little Egret's life a week ago, she was returning the compliment now with interest.

"Return to your bed," said Chekika. "You are well—but you must rest again."

"The touch of my lord's hand is the only rest I need."

"It is true, then, that Salofkachee cast out your devils?"

"Twice over, Father of Seminoles. Once with his knife— and again tonight." The girl lifted trusting eyes to Chekika, pulling Roy to her side with a shyly extended hand. "I was only half asleep when *chittamicco* came——"

"Do you accuse my brother as well?"

"I speak of the snake, not of the man. Though I was but half awake, I could feel its presence. And I saw Salofkachee trap it in a blanket from my bed——"

"Do not speak further. I can see it tires you. Rest on your bed awhile. I will sit at your side till dawn."

No one stirred in the compound as Chekika led the girl to the rope bed and folded a blanket tenderly about her. A murmur rose and died as he dismissed the watchers with a single flailing motion of his arm. The Indians returned slowly to their huts with many backward glances, as though they could not quite believe the miracle they had just witnessed. Only Chittamicco remained, his face a wooden mask, though his chin still lifted proudly.

Abraham lingered beside the ladder, awaiting orders. When the chief returned to the platform's edge, he fell on hands and knees, as though it was he, and not Chittamicco, who deserved the lash.

"Return to your house, brother," said Chekika. "We will talk in the morning."

"Salofkachee has accused me without proof. I demand his apology now," said Chittamicco.

Roy spoke up promptly. "I have accused no man tonight. I have killed a snake, nothing more."

"The snake that bore my name. You will eat your words. Or I will cut them from your craw in fair fight."

So the challenge had come at last, now that other means had failed. Roy's memory went back to a hot afternoon weeks ago at the mouth of Ten-Mile Slough, when Chittamicco had trailed him with the same cold murder in his eye. Once again, a dare of this nature could not be refused—especially with Chekika at his elbow. If Chekika endorsed the challenge, he knew that he must walk out of Fakahatchee with his enemy's hair at his belt—or not at all.

With this knowledge to steady him, he spoke the ritual words clearly. "The nation knows I have never refused to fight fairly. If the chief wills it, I will meet you at the first light—with any weapon the chief names."

His eyes met Chekika's and held them firmly. It was the Seminole who turned away and stepped down to the compound. Roy watched, with fast-beating heart, as Chekika strode over to his brother, lifted his left hand, and struck the younger man across the mouth.

"Salofkachee is our honored guest. While I live, you will not threaten him again. *Go to your house!*"

Blood showed in a thin line along Chittamicco's lip. He lifted his hand to wipe it away, stared blankly at the red stain on his palm, then turned and stalked into the darkness without a word.

When Chekika spoke again, his voice had lost its resonance, and his eyes refused to meet Roy's.

"Will you leave us now, Salofkachee? Or will you wait for dawn?"

"I would go at once, Father of Seminoles."

"As you wish. Your own canoe is at the water's edge. Abraham and two paddlers will take you as far as Okeechobee. Once there, can you find your people?"

"Yes, King of Cats."

Little Egret spoke softly from her bed. "Go in peace, Salofkachee. You are the last friend we have."

"I was your friend once," said Roy. "Our friendship ends tonight because Chekika wills it." He paused with one foot on the ladder, wanting to say more and knowing in his heart that he had spoken his last word. If he spoke again regardless, it was only ritual.

"Farewell, Father of Seminoles."

Only you *won't* fare well, he thought sorrowfully. From this night you're doomed and damned. It hardly matters if the blow falls now or later. He picked up his instrument case and the portfolio that might well contain the nation's death warrant. Chekika continued to stare impassively as he went down the ladder. He heard the girl on the rope bed sob just once, and guessed that she had understood that parting well enough.

Dr. Barker followed him at a careful distance, bearing the portmanteau that contained his poncho and the few extra garments he had brought from Indian Mound. "That was a near thing, Roy," he whispered. "He may hold you even now."

"Chekika doesn't break his bargains. I only wish you could go in my place."

"You might have offered him your hand. You parted like enemies."

"We *are* enemies now."

At the water's edge Abraham's gaunt form took shape in the darkness; a low whistle brought a brace of paddlers from the row of canoes that rested in the shallows. Roy's own dugout was brought forward, and Dr. Barker waded knee-deep in the black water to stow his gear away.

"Hand me your instrument case, Roy. And that book of sketches. I'll stow them forward out of harm's way."

"One moment, Doctor," said Abraham. "We must see for ourselves what Salofkachee has taken from the house of Chekika."

"Bring a pine knot from the fire. Who are you to call us thieves?"

"The torch is coming now."

They stood in a tight group around the dugout as a boy ran down the path from the compound with a blazing lightwood knot. Roy let his eyes move from the impassive faces of the two paddlers to Abraham's own level stare. If there was suspicion in these eyes, it was well masked. He settled

casually in the stern of his own canoe and waited, with no
sign of impatience, while the Negro counted the instruments
in his surgeon's kit, then untied the portfolio and studied the
sketches one by one.

"You are a good artist, Salofkachee. Almost as good as Hilolo."

"If you're quite done——"

"Quite. I will store your things under the bow. Rain is
coming fast. We should reach Big Sulphur before it catches
us."

Another canoe had already swum into the orange flare of
the torchlight. Abraham took up the sweep and shouted the
two paddlers to their places. "Tie your painter to our transom, Salofkachee. You will ride easily enough here in the
shallows. I will take you aboard when it is time for the blindfold."

Roy pressed Dr. Barker's hand. Somehow, he had not expected their departure to be so casual. The painter squeaked
in its groove; the light dugout bounded easily in the wake of
the larger craft. When he turned back to look at Fakahatchee
Hammock a few drops of rain had started to ooze from the
leaden sky. Dr. Barker still stood in the water offshore, both
hands raised in farewell; the torch, beginning to sputter in the
growing shower, sparkled on the dark surface of the slough.
Roy turned away and stared into the darkness ahead, trying
to pin down what landmarks he could.

"Lie down, Salofkachee. We are entering a tunnel of
branches."

He obeyed just as the first strand of moss touched his
cheek; Abraham's voice had sounded very near in the gloom.
The water oaks, laced in a tight arch overhead, shut out the
last scrap of light. He wondered if it was true that the Seminole could see in the dark like the panther. At least Abraham
had not disobeyed orders when he left off the blindfold.

The tunnel opened abruptly to the long bayou he had studied a hundred times from the semi-prison of Chekika's house.
Even in the rainy gloom he could sense the iridescence of
that slime-green expanse. This was the lowest point of the
swamp, a backwater in the saw-grass river where no current
ever stirred. A bull 'gator coughed somewhere in the dark,
but it was the only sound he could hear above the steady
chunk of the paddles, the whine of the tugging painter

against his gunwale. Even the denizens of the Glades seemed quiet tonight, oppressed by the stifling threat of rain.

Dawn had begun to show faintly under that moist blanket when they swept up to the mat of jungle that ringed Big Sulphur to the east. Roy leaned forward sharply and noted that this stagnant tangle of palm and water oak was rutted with many small streams where the overflow from the spring spilled into the saw grass. The powerful odor of the water, boiling into the still air of morning, had already begun to invade his senses like some heady drug. As the canoes darted into yet another leafy tunnel he could feel the push of that bubbling giant under the keel and note where the overflow had stained earth and tree trunk in its passing. The silver-white deposit shone like an endless spider web under that canopy of palm fronds. It seemed to glow with a goblin radiance of its own, a fair substitute for the watery light that had just begun to glimmer in from the east.

He heard the rain drum down in earnest on the spring before the canoes could burst out into the great limestone bowl that contained it. The clouds seemed to lift a little with that deluge; he could see that Big Sulphur was a rough ellipse, perhaps a quarter mile across, boxed on four sides by that same dense wall of oak and palm. Even in that wretched light the water beneath his keel seemed crystal-clear; he cupped both hands across the gunwale and drank deep, watching the bubbles roil the surface and feeling the dugouts bounce in the steady upward thrust from the fissure far below. Perhaps this was the fountain of eternal youth that Ponce de Leon had sought so long in vain.

He let the bizarre fancy die as Abraham, his naked shoulders shining with rain, rose to his full height on the transom and scanned the wall of palms to the west. This, as Roy remembered, was the spot where Mary's map began. He let his eyes follow Abraham's and felt his heart leap as he saw the five sloughs that furrowed that jungle rim, marked clearly by the white sulphur tracing of their banks. These were the five toes of the spoonbill—and, if Mary's cartography was true, they would enter the fifth opening to the right on their outward journey.

"Come aboard with us, Salofkachee. It is time for the blindfold."

He submitted resignedly, settling in the bottom of the

larger dugout as the strip of cloth came down over his eyes, and offering no protest when Abraham spread his poncho like a tent above his head, shutting out the growing light of day. There was no need to listen to the sense-bearer's first whispered order to the paddlers; he had managed to sit facing the west and knew that they had swerved sharp right. That was knowledge enough for now. His visit at Fakahatchee Hammock had brought results, after all. Thanks to Mary Grant, he could return to Chekika's village at will.

v

"You may sit up when you like, Salofkachee."

Roy heard the words through a thick haze of drowsiness; he rose on his haunches in his snug nest of buckskins and stared up at the shadow that was Abraham on the transom behind him. Apparently his blindfold had been removed while he slept. Until his head cleared he had the absurd illusion that this was a ship at sea and that he and the sense-bearer were the only passengers. Then he heard the grunt of the paddlers at the forward thwarts, the whisper of gunwales meeting as Abraham tugged hard on the painter to bring the lighter canoe alongside.

"How long did I sleep?"

"Since an hour after sundown. It is well that you rested. You will have a long journey alone."

"Where are we now?"

"That I am not permitted to answer," said the sense-bearer. "You will see for yourself with the morning. Earlier, perhaps, if the storm lifts."

As he spoke the sense-bearer leaned down to steady him; a hand at his elbow was already lifting him across the gunwale to his own canoe. Both dugouts rode uneasily on a long, oily swell. A starless night, heavy with thunderheads on both horizons, pressed down on the water—but Roy sensed that this was Okeechobee. Evidently they had been paddling for hours while he slept, He knew that they were far out in the lake, well beyond sight of land.

All that day they had driven at top speed through the sloughs of the Grassy Water; all that day he had played out the last act of his prisoner's role, content to take shelter under his poncho from the rain squalls that had pursued them from Big Sulphur. Later, when the midday sun had burned the rain away, he had drowsed in that same shelter, lulled by the singsong chant of the paddlers, unwilling to spoil his long, heat-drugged trance with geography. When branches blotted out the sun once more and the familiar stench of rotting vegetation assailed his nostrils, he knew they were in the blue-gum swamp; when saw grass whispered against their gunwales, he surmised that they were driving down the dog-leg waterways that led, in turn, to the cypress ring of Okeechobee. It was a journey that held no special interest for him now that he had the means to retrace the route at will. Guessing that Abraham would abandon him at some distance from Indian Mound, he had forced quiet on both limbs and brain.

Thunder rolled again under the horizon as he settled in his own canoe and fumbled for the bailing can, only to find that the dugout was bone-dry. There was an extra paddle under the gunwale; his questing fingers told him that both his instrument case and the precious portfolio were snug under their buckskin lashings. Abraham had no compunctions about leaving him in an open lake treacherous with sand bars and bogs, where water and gumbo seemed to flow together to the despair of the voyager. At least he had bailed his captive's canoe and supplied him with the means to stay afloat— if the twin storms now quarreling like rival armies at opposite ends of the lake did not join to overwhelm him.

"Go with God, Salofkachee."

It was oddly fitting that Abraham should address him in Spanish now that the two dugouts were drifting apart. He replied in the same language, doing his best to hide the involuntary note of fear in his voice. The ritual farewell had summed up his present situation all too accurately. He was indeed in the hands of his Creator, and the ragged, violet lightning flash that had just split the sky was a potent reminder of his insignificance.

"Be kind to Dr. Barker, Abraham. Kindness will repay you later."

"You have every right to use that word, Salofkachee. Even now, when you are no longer one of us."

Roy smiled sadly in the darkness. Intelligent as he was, Abraham had realized long ago that they must end as enemies. "We are still brothers in the sight of God."

"Not when we were born to kill one another. My prayers go to a different God than yours. You will understand when I pray we never meet again."

Abraham had taken up the sweep as he called the last words across the strip of water that divided them. Now he shouted an order in Seminole to his weary paddlers. Roy lay quietly on his own paddle, watching the larger canoe vanish in the enveloping dark. Twice, as lightning flashes opened the horizon, he glimpsed the dugout on the crest of a swell. Then he was alone with the night and his own rising dread.

Abraham was surely paddling south; had he dared match his strength against the six iron-muscled arms in the other canoe, he might have followed the sense-bearer to the nearest land. He knew that such a race would have been futile even by daylight. Now, in the rainy blackness that all but blotted the bow of his own dugout, he would have lost his sense of direction instantly between the lightning flashes; paddling in a hopeless circle, he would have been exhausted long before morning. Though it would be an eerie vigil, he would have to ride out the coming storm as best he could and pray for a sunny morning. Once he could set a course, it would be a relatively simple matter to fetch the southern shore and follow it to Indian Mound. If he paddled north in error, he might well die of hunger before reaching land.

The storms were moving together overhead—he dared hope no longer for a harmless rain squall, over before it was fairly begun. The lightning was beginning to be a deadly threat now as bolt and thunder crack all but overlapped. Most of the charges were running into the lake itself; more than once he felt the brimstone tingle of a flash that seemed to miss the canoe by a matter of yards. Then came the rain in a great, howling burst, heralded by a ball of green fire that pursued him malevolently across the inky water like a will-o'-the-wisp in Brobdingnag. For a time he felt sure that the deluge would pelt down faster than he could bail. The oily swell had begun to froth with whitecaps now, to break into long, crashing waves that lifted his tiny craft on their crests, held him there for a dizzy moment, then sent him hurtling down the foam-flecked slope. The lake itself was filling the dugout faster than the rain. Three times in the next hour he was forced to roll overside for his life, sloshing enough water across the gunwale to make himself seaworthy, and scrambling aboard again a split second ahead of the next following surge.

Here and there as the lightning that still crackled on the horizon threw the lake into blinding day he saw a sand bar wild with pounding surf and paddled hard to avoid a shipwreck. Once he rammed headlong into an endless mud flat covered with a skin of white water that barely floated the dugout. When a wave rose here, he was helpless to keep the canoe's head to the wind; when he slid into a trough, the whole dugout slammed into the treacherous bottom with a crashing impact that almost deprived him of his senses.

Then, as strangely as he had come, he was in deep water once again as the storm reached its screaming climax. Clinging to his lashed paddles (an improvised outrigger to keep the dugout upright), not daring to pause to bail, he lost all sense of reality but that keening wind. In the next hour life had whittled down to a grim battle for survival, with towering waves for enemies. The rain was a cold whip that drove him on, until he slept from sheer exhaustion, still anchored, by some miracle that passed his understanding, to the forward thwart of the dugout.

He scarcely heard when the wind died at last and the slick, dark surface of Okeechobee shaped into long running swells. When daylight came he was dimly aware of mirror-smooth water all about him and, later, of a scorching sun that seared his eyeballs when it struck highlights from his surface. Later still, when his raging thirst awakened him in earnest, he saw that he was still far from land, closed in the blue waste of waters as completely as though he were a shipwreck in mid-Atlantic. The dugout wallowed in the lake almost to its gunwales.

He plunged his head overside without stirring from his crouch and drank deep, feeling the iron return to his body with each straining swallow. Once he had bailed, he saw that his gear was still undamaged under its lashings. A few scraps of sun-dried venison and the remains of a bowl of *sofkee* were the only food aboard. He wolfed it where he sat, knowing he could trust to his new-found strength to bring him safely to land. Thanks to that blessed sun, which was still low in the east, it was a simple matter to set his course.

After an hour's hard paddling the horizon was obstinately blue. Okeechobee was still an authentic sea in the midst of land, a limitless mirror for the brazen sky. Then, as his flailing arms began to tire in earnest, he picked out a blur to the south that spoiled that perfect round. . . . He paddled doggedly on, refusing to lift his eyes until he had counted a thousand strokes, fearful, even now, that it might be a mirage.

There was no mistaking the landfall when he looked again, and he laughed aloud as his sun-dried lips shaped its name. This was Promontory Point, an immense yellow tongue of saw grass thrust into Okeechobee's milky blue. To the east, beyond the screen of cypress islands that were now beginning to lift over the horizon one by one, was the curve of Sandy Bay, his destination.

From this point on he could have paddled with Abraham's blindfold. Skirting the yellow-green wall with long, sure strokes, he ignored the first blind-pocketed bays, until he picked up the landmark that told him a clear course lay beyond. When he had driven through the neck of Promontory Point and burst into the western curve of Sandy Bay, he knew that he was trembling with a mixture of eagerness and fear, and forced himself to pause in the shadow of the first cypress island. From here he could see the truncated summit of Indian Mound thrust boldly above the screen of the swamp. Even at a distance there was something forbidding about that naked, grass-matted eminence. Indian Mound, he reflected dourly, had presided over this desolation for centuries. Why had he hoped to find the American flag at its summit this morning?

Tired though he was, he knew that he could contain his impatience no longer. Now that he was in the shallows, he unlimbered his push pole and sent the battered craft skimming among the islands. When he had cleared the last cypress knee and gained the open bay, he leaned hard on his pole—positive, for a sickening moment, that he had overshot his mark. Then, as his eyes picked out the wedge-shaped point where the Everglades Rangers had made their stand, he saw that his sense of direction had been all too accurate.

Nine days had gone by now since he had left that encampment in the misty dawn. Viewed in the merciless glare of the sunlight, its blackened remnants seemed to melt into the shore line as though they had never really existed. Viewed head on, it was apparent that a camp of sorts had once stood on the point. Had he approached from either side, he might have missed the fire-gutted shell entirely.

He was near enough to pick out details now. The palmetto breastworks on the lakeside had burned down to sand; a faint green haze of dog fennel had begun to creep between the ashy contours of the logs. Toward the cypress swamp, where the main defenses had stood, the logs had apparently been tumbled into the bog, so that this portion of the camp resembled a stand of palms mowed down by a hurricane. And yet —his heart gave a great bound as both nose and eyes verified the fact—there were no dead among the ruins. Indian bodies had vanished along with white; the very cook fires had been scattered into the encroaching scrub. In another month, he thought, Okeechobee would claim its own. Andy Winter's battleground would be one with time—and the creeping jungle.

But there was still no sign of death when he stepped ashore. He beached his canoe and walked gingerly through the ruins. Thanks to the riot of green life that thrust up from every clod, he was hard put to decide where camp had ended and wilderness began. Yet there were landmarks of a sort. The sally port on the landside, where Hutchens had fallen with an arrow in his spine. The masked exit where Andy had ranked his canoes row to row for a quick evacuation if all else failed . . . He paused here and studied the furrows at the water's edge. One thing, at least, was evident here: Andy had cleared his command from Indian Mound with a minimum of casualties. What had happened thereafter was any man's guess on the evidence available.

Chittamicco had buried his own dead far from this spot; Andy had cleared his wounded, via dugout, for an unknown destination. It seemed evident, too, that the major striking force from the north (moving with such magnificent slowness from the rough log forts along the Kissimmee) had failed to reach the Mound in time. Had Chittamicco been wise enough to let Andy quit the Glades in peace—and had he brought that proof of cowardice back to Chekika's village in lieu of a triumph in battle?

He had expected to find Mary's body swaying from a palm tree, with Andy close beside, twisted in the final agony of death. Yet he was sure that no murder had been done in the shadow of Indian Mound. The sky was clear of vultures; the savage exhalation of the earth, for all its stenches, held no

overtone of human decay. . . . Roy turned his back on the
enigma and returned to his canoe. A measure of calm returned when he knotted his fists around the push pole,
though he could hardly name his next port of call. It was
enough for the present to put that fire-gutted ruin behind—to
thrust boldly for the cypress islands while he pondered his
strategy.

Andy Winter had surrendered his position without a fight.
He could read no other answer from the evidence at hand.
Perhaps he was already safe at Fort Everglades (with the
wife of his choice), preparing for a second raid and trusting
his chief scout to return in time. Perhaps he had only pocketed his pride for the time being and scuttled north to join
Colonel Merrick's relief force from St. Augustine.

However he interpreted that strange withdrawal (so unlike
Andy, on every count), one thing was evident. The Grassy
Water was Chekika's domain once again. The Seminole
could grow fat on this land forever—and loot the Floridas at
will.

He drove on through the tight-bunched islands while he
fought down the anticlimax of his return. Now that the
charred remnants of the camp were behind him, he was not
quite sure what he had expected from this moment. Surely it
was too much to hope that Mary Grant would be waiting
here—ready to cheer his escape from the enemy's stronghold
with the key to victory in his hand. . . .

"Yohohee!"

The Seminole war whoop, bounding from the wild-grape
thicket on his right, had chilled him to the marrow. Another
lilting, high-pitched challenge was lifted instantly from the
wilderness of cypress knees ahead—and yet another from the
hot green wall of water oaks that grazed his port bow. Behind those howling voices he heard the whistle of a dozen
birdcalls that signaled the closing of his ambush, the faint
whisper of moccasins among the leaves. Brooding on the
problems of Andy Winter, he had signed his own death warrant with a careless hand. Had he kept to the open lake, he
might have returned to Fort Everglades unmolested, he had
blundered head on against the very island where Chittamicco
had posted his lookouts nine days ago.

An instinct that rose above panic drove his madly pumping
arms to send the canoe racing down the narrow estuary that

divided his enemies. A whole aviary of catbirds was talking in the underbrush now; behind and before him he could feel the red noose tighten. A capture of this sort was mere child's play to the Seminoles, and they were enjoying it like children —permitting him the illusion of freedom for another moment while they sharpened their knives on every side.

There was the curve in the narrow waterway, rounding the smaller of the two islands, with the lake itself just beyond. A final war whoop seemed to split his eardrums as he dug out of this leafy trap. The first of his enemies burst into view from the nest of green. Another followed, and yet another, until a dozen naked braves stood ranked in the shallows, daubed with marl to the eyes, their bodies slashed with the black and vermilion paint of battle. The sun glinted on the crossed blades of a dozen axes as he backed water frantically and retraced his route in panting haste. Thrown from that distance, a tomahawk could bury itself in his brain; but there was no real attempt to stop his retreat, though a single ax sang past his ear, insolently wide, to quiver in a cypress trunk ahead. He heard the braves splashing lazily behind him, the catbirding of invisible enemies ahead.

At least they've orders to take me alive, he thought. Perhaps Chekika wants two hostages after all. Perhaps he's learned of the map I have aboard and means to stop its delivery.

A narrow waterway opened to his left, and he turned down it blindly, though he had no notion where it led. For a crazy instant he felt sure that he had hoodwinked his pursuers after all. Then he saw that his escape route was really a cul-de-sac, ending almost as soon as it began in a shallow bayou choked with lily pads, arched by the shining leaves of a magnolia. The birdcalls were thicker than ever now, and he knew, as he rose to his full height in the dugout, that the Seminoles had pocketed him here deliberately and were closing in earnest for the capture—or the kill.

"Yohohee!"

The copper faces seemed to ring him now, bursting in clusters from the green gloom—as fearful as so many devil masks, the eyes circled with ocher rings, the tufted black scalp locks bristling. He let the dugout glide into the snarl of lily pads and swung clear on a branch of the magnolia just before it grounded. He saw red fists close on both gunwales, watched a cane knife slash the lacings that covered his gear

—but it was too late now to save the map. He had nearly scrambled into the doubtful haven of the magnolia when a pair of arms enclosed him.

"Anda, señor médico!"

The guttural voice was oddly familiar, but he had no time to turn as he tumbled to earth with his captor spread-eagled above him. He felt the ax pink his scalp at the base of his brain, driving his face deep in spongy muck, and waited for the all but effortless slice of razored steel that would sunder his vertebrae as easily as a steer's in an abattoir. Instead, the torture of the two hard knees lessened against his sides, though his adversary's fist was still knotted in his hair. He heard the other man grunt as he rolled free, and rose to his hands and knees without daring to look back.

"Arriba, muchacho!"

The command lifted him to his feet, with the shadow of his captor looming above him. He marched forward on order, the tomahawk blade still caressing his neck. From the corner of his eye he noted that his canoe had been stripped of its contents and that other willing hands had lifted it bodily from the water as his enemies fell into single file behind him. The path he was following so willingly under the compulsion of the ax snaked into the underbrush to the left, then climbed toward the island's spine.

For the time being the fact that he was still alive dominated his brain, shutting out externals and blunting their impact. It seemed quite natural that a long file of canoes should be drawn up in the sheltered cove they were skirting now, that a whole arsenal of rifles should be stacked neatly under a shelter just beyond. He did not find it strange that the circle of palm-thatch huts on the rise should be spaced out with canvas tents, or that the mingled aroma of beans and bacon on a hundred cook fires, like the whole clean smell of the encampment, was as un-Indian as he.

It was only when Sergeant Ranson rushed from a canvas shelter with both hands held out that his brain spun back to reality, for though the sergeant was dyed as copper-dark as Chekika himself from the waist down, his barrel-shaped body was unmistakably Army, down to the lovebirds tattooed across his chest. So was the fist that dismissed the tomahawk from Roy's neck and the parade-ground bellow that froze his captors to attention.

"So you're back at last, Doctor. If you knew how anxiously we've waited——"

"What does all this mean?"

"The captain will explain that, sir. It's his story, and I wouldn't spoil it for the world."

"Do you mean Captain Winter's *here?*"

"All of us are here, Doctor. Including some regulars who don't know your face. Like Corporal Poore there in the war paint. He's the one who captured you just now——"

"And Miss Grant?"

"Up and about again, sir, after a touch of dengue. She's been a great help with our disguises. But I *am* spoiling the captain's story——"

"You are indeed, Sergeant."

They turned as one man to the pinned-back flap of the shelter. The Seminole brave who stood there was grinning from ear to ear. Only the grin spoiled the illusion that this was his Osceola returned to earth; the dark skin was the same, and the hawk-proud stare, and the last silver crescent on the white doeskin chest. Then, as the chieftain lifted one hand to toss aside his feathered turban, Roy saw the brick-red topknot beneath and Andy Winter's eyes, laughing at him behind deep-dyed cheekbones.

"Come off it, Roy," said Andy. "Must I black my hair to convince you that I'm an Indian?"

IV BIG SULPHUR

i

"OF COURSE I SHOULD HAVE DYED MY TOPKNOT," SAID ANDY. "But Mary wouldn't hear of it. She wants me *au naturel* for the wedding—if I make myself clear. Incidentally, don't you want to pay your respects? She's sleeping late this morning, on my orders. But she'll want to see you when she wakens."

"I want to see Mary. Very much indeed—if she's been down with fever. You're more important right now."

Andy yawned luxuriously and poured a second mug of coffee from the pot that stood between them. Now that the sun was well up, the shade of the headquarters tent was grateful to Roy's tired body. So, for that matter, was the prodigious breakfast he had just put away while he listened to his friend's story—told, as usual, with Andy's flair for the picturesque as well as his total disregard for coherence. The dragoon captain was still grinning broadly when he put down his cup. Thanks to that outlandish headdress and the hightented shade in which he lolled, he was more sultan than Seminole at the moment. A supremely confident sultan who would grace any costume he wore.

"You might stop staring, Roy. I've worn these buckskins for two days now to get the feel of them. Just as I've kept my command in full war paint. You must admit they enjoy their roles."

"Couldn't you have warned that new corporal that I was returning?"

"Don't blame Poore. He had strict orders to jump anyone who approached this encampment, white or red."

"Including your head scout?"

Andy grinned in earnest. "Admit you were good practice. Besides, we didn't give you time to be really frightened."

"I'll even admit it's a magnificent idea to hunt Indians in Indian costume. I'm still asking how it all happened."

"The costumes were our commanding general's inspiration, not mine. I've already thanked him in my report."

"So this regalia was shipped down from Augustine?"

"War paint, axes, and turbans. Most of it was stripped from prisoners' backs at Fort Marion. I don't blame you for thinking I was Osceola himself. This turban came from his head. Back in '38—a week before he died."

"When I went into the saw-grass you were planning to fight the last engagement of the war at Indian Mound. I still don't see the need of masquerade."

"I'm coming to that, Roy. Remember, you've been away nine full days. That's a long time in any war."

"Surely you were relieved on schedule?"

"Precisely. By a single courier. With orders to evacuate my position as untenable."

"At least I understand why you burned the stockade."

"That was insurance, in case Chittamicco was napping at his post. I felt it was important to convince him that we'd run for our lives. That we'd pulled out of the Glades in earnest, exactly as Chekika ordered."

Roy nodded his approval. It was quite like Andy to turn an apparent act of cowardice to his advantage. "Why were you ordered to give up the Mound?"

"Apparently our little plan had misfired. Chekika was aware of our strategy. That's why he attacked at once—before our relief could arrive. And why he pulled back to a safe distance when he thought the relief was about to cross the lake."

This, too, was part of the picture, as Roy had observed it from Fakahatchee Hammock. The return of Chittamicco's flotilla had evidently been planned from the beginning. Chekika had been too clever to linger at the edge of a carefully baited trap.

"So he was informed all along."

"In detail—by our friend Dan Evans. Dan, it seems, has

shown his true colors since we left Fort Everglades. Once
he'd collected his insurance for that barn burning at Flamingo Key, he skedaddled across the straits to Havana. He's already set up there as a gun-runner. English rifles on the barrel head, to the highest bidder." Andy smashed his fist on the
drumhead that served as their table. "I'd give a great deal to
stage a one-man raid in Cuba and bring Dan back to justice.
I'd enjoy hanging him even more than Chekika."

"Never mind Dan now; he's done all the harm he can. I
gather you crossed straight to this island when you learned
that Chittamicco had pulled back to the saw-grass."

"While the stockade was still burning. We moved the entire command between midnight and dawn. The enemy had
left only a few hours ago—his campfires were still warm in
this same clearing." Again Andy frowned down at the drumhead. "It was touch and go until morning, of course; I still
half expected another attack. But there hasn't been a speck of
Indian sign this past week—if you ignore the fleas they left
behind. My guess is that they watched that stockade burning
from a safe distance—and went back to boast of a victory
they'd won hands down."

"That's what I gathered at Fakahatchee. What's more, I
think that Chittamicco really believed he'd frightened you
away."

"We've worked hard to create that impression. Be honest:
isn't that just what *you* thought when you landed at the
Mound?"

Roy found that he was matching the dragoon's grin. Strategy of this sort, with a dash of melodrama added, was Andy's
specialty. Obviously it had been a risk to burn his defenses
and dig for open water. Now that he was safely established
on the island, he had nothing to fear from a surprise attack
—even if Chittamicco were rash enough to appear again on
Okeechobee. That long file of canoes was ready for instant
action—an invasion of the saw grass or flight to the north, as
the situation dictated.

"From what I've seen so far, it hasn't been an idle week."

"We've been busy every moment. It isn't an easy matter to
turn an Everglades Ranger into a Seminole. But I think I've
done a fair job—with an assist from Mary."

"Ranson said she was ill."

"Only for the past few days. I'd planned to send her north

with the next convoy. After she came down with the fever it seemed best to keep her here. It wasn't a serious case, thank heaven——"

"So you've been getting convoys from the Kissimmee?"

"We've been reinforced nightly. Sixty-one regulars came in last night in the teeth of that storm without losing a boat. I've over six hundred men now. Every one of 'em is sharp as a knife and ready to start cutting Indian hide."

Six hundred regulars, thought Roy, was perhaps the largest force in this field since the ill-fated battle of Okeechobee. He had scouted Chekika's village carefully and compared his notes with Dr. Barker. Even counting slaves and the handful of half-breed renegades who still served under him, the King of Panthers could never summon more than half that number to the defense of Fakahatchee. A surprise attack (the only maneuver that would accomplish their purpose) would probably find the enemy outnumbered three to one after the losses he had suffered at Indian Mound.

"You can move tonight if you like," he said calmly. "Give me a few hours' rest. I'll be ready to blaze you in."

Andy's eyes shone with a familiar glee. Roy settled deeper in his place at the drumhead and watched his friend pace the narrow confines of the tent—a hunting dog, superbly trained, who had spoiled too long at leash. At this very moment, he thought sadly, he's killing in his mind—and planning Chekika's hanging part, down to the last grisly detail.

"Are you sure you know the way?"

"Thanks to Mary."

"How on earth could *she* help you—when she was safe with me?"

So Mary had kept the spoonbill drawing a secret until his return. For no reason at all Roy felt his heart contract painfully at that knowledge. He lifted his portfolio to the drumhead, took out Mary's water color and his own matching sketch, and spread them wide. "Believe it or not, that's all the map I'll need."

Andy let out his breath in a low whistle as they traced the route together, point by point. "Why didn't you shout this out the moment you returned?"

"You didn't give me a chance."

"Never mind that. I enjoy my own voice; I'll admit it freely. You could still have made me listen——"

"You're listening now—that's all I care about."

But Andy was not quite done with his pacing. "Mary did this painting at the hammock. Why did she risk leaving it there?"

"Because she happens to know you even better than I. Don't deny you'd have stormed down on Fakahatchee the moment you had the route—long before you were ready."

Andy ducked his head sheepishly outside the tent flap and shouted for Ranson. "We'll go over this with Mary in a moment. And I won't court-martial either of you, now that the map's at headquarters. Just remember to keep no secrets from me in the future."

There's one secret I'll always keep, thought Roy. The fact that I'm in love with Mary Grant—and will remain in love with her when she's Mary Winter. So desperately in love that I'm afraid to speak her name even now. Aloud he said only, "Keep the water color as your guide. I'll take my own sketch when I go in. All you'll need are a few blazes. We'll check the points now———" He broke off as Ranson hurried into the tent and snapped to attention in the entrance. The sergeant's dye job was complete now, and yet even in a beaded breech-clout, with a dozen scalps at his belt, he was still vaguely military.

"Seminoles don't come to attention, Ranson," said Andy. "Look at this work of art and tell me how soon you can memorize it."

The sergeant rested capable knuckles on the drumhead while Roy explained the symbols hidden in the drawing. "If you ask me, gentlemen, art is the right name for it. Miss Grant should get her stripes for this."

"The observation does you credit, Sergeant. In fact, it's too bad she can't accompany Dr. Coe when he leads us in." Andy studied the painting in detail with a faint frown. "Are you sure you can leave blazes, Roy?"

"I could follow those sloughs in the dark."

"I'm afraid that's just what you'll have to do. You'll have to move well ahead of us and bed down in the saw grass by daylight."

Roy nodded a silent agreement. The whole success of their maneuver depended on the accuracy of Mary's map and his skill at interpreting it. A key point, missed in the darkness, might lead the whole troop down a water maze from which they would never emerge alive.

"We'll have five hours of moonlight. That should take me through the blue-gum swamp. Tomorrow the moon will be almost full. If I move out by dusk, I should be at Big Sulphur well before the second dawn."

"You'll have to hole in there and wait for us."

Roy stepped back from the map. Now that Andy's mind was functioning in earnest, he knew that it was useless to interrupt. He waited in silence while captain and sergeant went over the map in detail. Ranson could scout those turnings as well as I, he thought. If Mary's well enough to travel, I could withdraw from this business now and escort her back to safety. . . . He put that enticing temptation behind him and shouldered his way back to the discussion.

"I'll take three axes to make sure I've a sharp blade. You know the entrance from Okeechobee. I'll make the first cut here, where the slough turns in the blue-gum swamp." He let his finger rest for an instant on the map beside Andy's red-stained digit. "I've been that far on my own; there are any number of big trees at the water's edge. A triangular blaze should be simplest—with the point southwest."

"You've scouted for us before, Roy. I'll pick up your markings. So will Ranson."

"Would it be simpler if the sergeant came with me?"

"That's for you to decide. But I'd say go alone—if the idea doesn't spook you. I'll need Ranson to lead our vanguard."

Roy smiled thinly. He had put the question only for the sake of form. Andy would never reach Chekika's village without a veteran swamper in his lead canoe. "Suppose I pick up Indian sign?"

"From what you've just said, we could move right up to that sulphur spring by daylight."

"We probably could—with luck. But I may flush a hunting party en route."

"*You* won't be seen—unless you've lost your skill entirely."

Roy's sad grin was intact. "I won't be seen. You can count on that."

"Then you couldn't have a simpler tour of duty. Cut those blazes and wait for me at Big Sulphur. If you smell red meat, report back to Ranson. Remember, he'll never be more than five miles behind you."

"Why must I wait at the spring? I'd much rather cross the slough and bring Dr. Barker out for company."

"I wish you could, Roy. But that's a risk we just can't take."

"What about the risk he's running? How can he stay alive after you move in on the village?"

Andy struck fist to palm. "I hope to hit Chekika fast. So fast that we'll have his neck in a noose before he can open his eyes. You'll move in with us, of course. Your only job will be to save Dr. Barker——"

"Poinsett will break you if Dr. Barker turns up dead—no matter how many scalps you send him."

The dragoon pondered gloomily, his eyes still on the map. "How could you get into the village without being seen?"

"Easily. I've scouted every foot of that shore line. The main beach, where they keep their canoes, faces west. Even that is masked on both sides by thickets of water oak. You come straight in through a blind tunnel from the bayou. I could hug the saw-grass and swim the whole way from Big Sulphur in a half hour. Even if they've a guard on the beach, I could go round the island and come in through one of the corn patches—"

"And waken every dog in the village."

"I took care to make friends with those dogs in the past week. Dr. Barker is only a nominal prisoner. I know just where to find his hut and how to cut through the palm thatch."

"You'll never smuggle him off the island. He's too old to swim that far."

"True enough. But we can at least get free of the fighting."

Andy considered the idea briefly. "I'd say no if it were anyone but you. D'you think Dr. Coe can get that far, Sergeant—and keep his hair?"

"It's a gamble, sir. I'm sure the doctor realizes it too. But I'd say it was worth taking."

Andy rolled up the map. "Very good, then. We'll work out details at mess. Unless you two gentlemen would like to settle them now." He included Ranson in his gracious gesture as he sat down beside the drumhead one more time. "Actually, there's very little to discuss. Dr. Coe—and my fiancée—have supplied the map; for once Chekika will be forced to fight——"

"If he's at the hammock when we arrive," said Roy. "Remember, he's planned a new raid——"

"There'll be no more raids until Dan ferries up a new supply of ammunition," said Andy.

"That may be sooner than you think."

"Sorry, I refuse to worry over Dan Evans now. I've given you permission to enter Chekika's village on your own. Let's assume you reach Dr. Barker without rousing the guards. What's your next move?"

"We'll take cover and ride out your attack."

"How will we establish the time?"

"I'll set my watch with Ranson's before I leave tonight," said Roy. "You'll follow behind me—*slowly*. Is that agreed on?"

"It was my idea," said Andy testily. "Don't question my judgment."

Roy laughed inwardly. The fact that the dragoon was piqued was all the assurance he needed now. Thanks to a few adroit arguments, he had settled Andy's mind in the precise groove he had selected the moment he had set foot in the encampment. The only groove they could follow if they meant to succeed.

"Ranson will be my link to you if anything goes wrong. He'll follow with the vanguard, not less than five miles in my wake——"

"We settled that too."

"It's still a point worth emphasis. Five miles is a good hour's paddle in those dog-leg sloughs. Let's say that he stays close behind me until we reach the blue-gum swamp, then waits a good hour at every blaze. That should keep us well spaced."

"Fair enough," said Andy. "If the weather turns bad, you'll be the judge. Cut a second triangle above the first—that'll be Ranson's sign to hug the bank."

"No matter what the weather is, I'll be there a good hour ahead of the sergeant. If we're on time. I'll be ready to move into the village while it's still dark. One sunrise from tomorrow, if all goes smoothly. Two, if there's bad weather. Or three, or four——"

"We all know it's the hurricane season, Roy."

"It's a point I can't stress too often. We must move by night—and you must strike by dawn. My job is to be on that hammock a good half-hour before you enter Big Sulphur—and you must wait before you order the attack."

Andy shot a quick glance at Ranson. "D'you agree to all this, Sergeant?"

"Dr. Coe is our chief scout, Captain. If I were you I'd let him do just that."

The dragoon shrugged. "Very well, Roy. I'm just as anxious as you to earn Joel Poinsett's laurels. You may enter Fakahatchee Hammock at will—and do what you can to save Dr. Barker. If you fail, we'll bury what's left of you both—with full military honors. If you succeed, you may launch our attack."

"There'll be no chance for a signal. If I'm caught, you must give them a while to—do what they wish with me. It's still a question of timing. Come into that breach from two sides and strike with the first light. If the doctor and I are alive, we'll keep clear as best we can."

"Naturally, you know the risk you're taking."

"I'm used to taking risks."

Andy got up briskly. "You can visit Mary now. I wouldn't tell her too much of this."

"Perhaps it's best I don't see her at all."

But Andy had already led Roy into the sunlight. "Don't tell me you're *still* avoiding my promised bride. I won't hear of it."

"I've never meant to avoid her."

"When this interview began you said you wanted to see her. As a doctor, of course. Keep it professional, if you insist. In fact, that's an excellent idea. I want you to tell her she's still very ill—that's important."

They walked down the file of tents together and paused where the clearing sloped to the water's edge and the endless file of canoes. Mary's sick bay was on the ridge above—a high-roofed canvas shelter with an added tent of woven cedar boughs to break the sun's impact. Roy smiled inwardly as he found the spot where she was convalescing, with no help from Andy. A sixth sense had told him where to look.

"Naturally you'll keep her here until the attack's over."

"That is my firm intention," said Andy. "We've already had words about it."

"You can hardly blame Mary for wanting to return to the fort."

"She refuses to return to the fort. She wants to come with us to Fakahatchee."

"Surely you've told her that's impossible."

"She still insists we'll need her. Of course I didn't know about the map when she first asked to be included. I suppose she feels you can't find your way without her help."

"Come with me, Andy. We'll soon argue her out of that."

"Somehow, I think you'll make better progress alone."

Roy glanced quickly at his friend. but Andy's eyes were innocent of doubt. You've always trusted me, he thought bitterly. Why shouldn't you rely on me to put your fiancée in her place? He kept his voice cold with an effort. "You should have sent her to the fort long ago."

"I could hardly send a fever case through Ten-Mile Slough. The water's low; they'd have to portage on the upper Miami—and again at the falls."

A sudden suspicion invaded Roy's mind, but he kept it to himself. "When was she first taken ill?"

"Five days ago, to be exact. I'm sure it was dengue. At least she complained of all the symptoms."

Roy nodded soberly; Andy had told him all he needed to know. "I'll see the patient myself now, if you don't mind. And I still think you should come along."

"Why? Are you afraid she'll bring you around?"

"She'll never bring me round. That's one thing you can count on."

He went up the ridge with long, quick strides, hoping that Andy had not caught the hidden meaning behind his words.

ii

At the door of the shelter he paused to breathe deep before he dared lift the canvas flap. Mary was sleeping soundly on a bed of fresh-cut pine boughs. with a light blanket drawn up to her chin. When he folded this covering down he saw that she was wearing the white nankeen trousers that were regulation Army issue in the Floridas and a rough buckskin shirt from the same stores. In the shadowed tent her hair seemed as dark as midnight. It framed a face that seemed innocent of guile and remarkably fresh for a patient who had just weathered a bout of fever. He bent to kiss her cheek softly before he lifted her wrist to test the pulse. Somehow, he felt he had earned that quick caress.

"Will you wake up, Miss Grant, and talk to your doctor?"

He had tried to make his voice light, but it was a woeful effort. Now, as Mary stirred in her aromatic bed, he released her wrist almost guiltily and sat quietly while her eyelids fluttered wide. For a while she lay motionless in the tumbled glory of her hair and stared back at him as though she could hardly believe him real. Then her hands moved upward until the fingers closed about his shoulders. Slowly, as though she still feared to put him to the test, she drew his mouth down on hers for the kiss of welcome he had feared and longed for in equal measure.

"It's really you," she said. "I believe it now."

"You knew I'd come back, Mary."

"I *prayed* you'd come back. Andy's immortal; I couldn't be so sure of you." Her hands still clung warmly to his shoulders; her lips brushed his cheek like drowsy temptation as they drew apart. "Now you're back, don't ever leave us again. I won't allow it."

He knew that she was still only half awake, for all that burst of ardor—that the ardor was only a natural friendliness at his safe return. But he could not stop the thudding of his heart or the blush that seemed to burn his whole body. He blessed the shadows that lay thick between them; she must never know how keenly she was torturing him.

"Sit up, Mary," he said sternly. "You aren't dreaming."

Mary pushed the blanket aside and sat up in her pine-bough couch, hugging her knees. She was smiling in earnest now, and he forced himself to offer her a matching grin he didn't feel. At least he had saved himself from betrayal in her arms; there was no danger of another embrace, now the amenities were over.

"I wish all my dreams were as good as this awakening," she said, and her eyes still explored his face as though she could not get her fill of staring. "All this week I couldn't sleep without seeing that dreadful dugout. And you—like an effigy of yourself in the stern. Trading your life for mine——"

"Believe me, it wasn't quite that dramatic."

"You might have died," she said. "Don't deny it."

"I'd go again, regardless. There was a life to save at Fakahatchee. The fact that you came back to Andy was only incidental."

Mary ignored the rebuke. "Andy explained all that. I still couldn't get you out of my dreams. Or stop wondering what they'd done to you."

"Was this before your illness or after?"

"I wasn't ill for a moment. Roy. That was only a way to remain here with the Rangers. I *had* to be on this island when you returned——"

"I guessed as much," he said, "even before I examined you. It's handsome of you to admit it."

"Promise you won't tell Andy. I've made him angry enough now."

"Never mind Andy. You've more than redeemed yourself with that map."

But Mary had already brushed his praise aside as she leaned forward earnestly and covered his hands with her own. "That's quite enough about me. Tell me everything that happened. Tell me that Dr. Barker's well and safe."

He poured out his whole story then. holding nothing back. When he had finished, Mary's eyes were shining.

"I'd have given a great deal to be there," she said in a whisper.

"And I'd have given much more than I did—to keep you right here."

"You'll admit I helped a little?"

"You've helped enormously. Andy is more than grateful."

Mary continued to hug her knees; her smile was an enigma now. and her eyes were fixed on a distant point he could not see. "He's told you we quarreled. of course."

"He did indeed. You might even say that I'm here as a peacemaker."

"Does that mean I stay with the Rangers?"

"No, Mary. You're to stay at this base camp and welcome the heroes' return."

"Somehow, I didn't think you'd take sides with Andy."

"There's no argument, really. A pitched battle is no place for a woman."

"I can keep out of danger. And I can guide you straight to Chekika. That's what you both want. isn't it?"

"Your map is all the guide we need."

"No one has been through that swamp by daylight without

a blindfold. Not even you. What happens if you lose your way?"

"You can trust me that far, Mary."

"Then Andy doesn't need you at all. Not if it's *that* easy to follow my map. The sergeant could lead him in. Or another of his scouts——"

"I wouldn't put things so simply. Remember, I've been over a good bit of that route before. I know all the important landmarks——"

"It isn't true. This is the first time I've really felt needed in my life—and you tell me to hold back because I'm a woman. Only a man could be so unfair."

"Are we quarreling too?"

"On the contrary." Mary let out her breath in a long sigh. "I'm merely stating my case—as a woman. Naturally, I realize there is no appeal."

"Then you'll promise not to pester Andy any further?"

"Thanks for your choice of verbs," she said. "I've quite done with pestering."

"In that case, I'll pronounce you cured. You may have the freedom of the camp."

"Thanks for that small favor." She got up from the bed as she spoke and held out her hand. "I didn't realize I was confined to quarters."

Roy took her hand and shook it solemnly. Try as he might, he could not bring himself to censure her crazy desire too harshly. Even now he could see that she was acting a romantic role and enjoying her own performance. Somehow, the blood and toil and soul-searing boredom of Indian hunting had escaped her entirely. It was best to keep her illusions intact. To hold her here, secure with the reserve force at the base, until this final tour of duty was ended. Then she could go north to make ready for her marriage to Andy—with a portfolio of tropic memories no less colorful than the sketches she had brought out of the Glades.

"I'll go to Andy in a moment and say I'm sorry," she promised. "Just tell me how you plan the attack. As your map maker, I think I've earned that much confidence."

He stared at her owlishly, remembering Andy's warning, then brushed the memory aside. It was quite true that the whole company was deeply in Mary's debt. Surely she would rest more easily here if she had a clear picture of the impending action, including the risks.

"This must be our secret too," he said slowly. "Andy warned me that you'd want to know too much."

"I want to know everything," she said. "Is that a crime?"

"Perhaps you were born a few centuries too soon, Mary."

"Perhaps we both were," she cried, and he was shocked by the sudden passion in her tone. "You, at least, can see why I want to be a part of the world—even if it is a man's world so far. *He* never will. He wants to put me on a pedestal, with cotton wool in my ears——" She broke off on that and laughed a little at her own vehemence. "Can you see me on a pedestal, Roy?"

"Isn't that where a lady belongs?"

"So you won't admit I can help you at all?"

"You've helped us more than I can say. In fact, you've made this operation possible. Without you, the command would have no choice but to leave the Glades——"

"I don't want compliments," she said dully. Her voice was colorless now, as though her outburst against Andy had drained off her emotion. "I want to be someone's partner. Not just someone's wife. I can't afford to wait another century."

"I'm afraid you must," he said gravely, and turned away so he need not see the sudden tears in her eyes.

"Put me in my place," she said. "I know I deserve it. Just give me some notion of the attack. You might even tell me if you hope to come out alive."

He spoke carefully then, and at length. Striving to give her a true picture of the action, he found that his spirits were rising with his fluent words. Until he had entered Mary's tent he had faced the raid with the dulled fatalism of the veteran, refusing to let his mind go beyond tonight's jump-off, the desperate need for accuracy as he followed the tortuous course to his objective. Now, as he described the attack as a whole, the part he would play came into sudden focus. For the first time he realized how essential he was to Andy's success—until he reached Big Sulphur. From that point, of course, he was quite literally on his own.

"You can't go into that village by yourself," said Mary. "It's too much to ask of any man."

"Someone must get to Dr. Barker before the fighting begins."

"Why must it be you? You've done more than enough."

"We won't argue that. As it happens. no one in Andy's command has ever seen the island—or the village."

"No one but me," said Mary.

"You promised to be good."

"Go on. I'll try not to interrupt again."

"There's nothing more to say. really. If I've made myself sound like a fool, I ask your pardon. But I must lead Andy to his objective—and I must do my rescue work alone. There's no other way."

"Why don't you go on ahead, if you must? The sergeant could do the map work for Andy."

"Possibly. But it's just as important that we keep in touch throughout. I can't reach Dr. Barker too soon; once I'm discovered on that hammock, the game is up for fair." Roy found that he was on his feet, pacing out the one problem that he had not solved in his long conference with Andy and Ranson. "On the other hand, I can't join the general invasion of the island—Dr. Barker wouldn't have a chance."

"Are you thinking aloud—or asking my opinion?"

He pulled up short and managed a grin of sorts. "Both, I suppose. Tell me I'm a fool, if you must; I probably deserve it."

"You probably are," she said. "On more than one count."

"What do you mean by that?"

"If you don't know, it's no good my explaining," said Mary demurely. "I won't even pity you if you'd rather not. But you are quite likely to die for your pains—if you go alone."

"I've gone most of my life alone." he said doggedly. "Perhaps it's only fitting to die as one has lived."

"Suppose I went to Andy now and suggested that you escort me back to Fort Everglades—at once? Would he let us go?"

"Are you implying that I'm a coward as well as a fool?"

"No one who knows you would dare to say that. But a man can overdo even bravery."

"I don't want to boast," he said slowly. "But this raid can hardly succeed without me." A strange grayness settled on his spirit as he put this last temptation aside. After all, it was quite possible that Andy Winter, eager to claim all the credit for the Wildcat's capture, would prefer to continue without his help; he might even welcome his fiancée's suggestion that she return to Fort Everglades with a competent guide. . . . But Roy knew that he would stay with Andy until this business ended. He had met Mary Grant in the shadow of an Indian war; he would speak his last farewell while that shadow still lingered.

"Have it your way, Roy," said Mary. "If you must be a hero, how can a mere woman prevent you?"

He did not stir as she crossed the tent and linked arms with him before she rose on tiptoe to kiss his cheek lightly. Keeping his eyes straight ahead, he spoke through clenched teeth, cursing the effort it cost him to keep his voice light.

"What was that—the hero's reward?"

"What else? Now take me to my betrothed. I'm quite prepared to kneel and ask his pardon."

"He's quite prepared to grant it," said Roy, and bowed her through the tent flap. For a moment he stood in that doubtful shelter, wondering if she had seen the glint of moisture at his eyes when her lips brushed his cheek. Then he squared his shoulders and marched stolidly after her.

iii

Far out, where the lake shaded into the mauve curtain of night along the horizon, a dying blade of sunlight cut the water with a glint of silver. Darkness had moved in on the island long ago, muffling the bow of Roy's dugout and swallowing the shore line to the south like a tangible curtain. The sixty-odd canoes, drawn up in a long file along the beach, were no longer visible; save for the quiet breathing of six hundred Rangers, the occasional flirt of a paddle in the shallows, he would have sworn he was alone in the fast-dropping twilight. Alone and forlorn and ready to thrust forth into the inky beyond. . . .

Then he heard Andy's bare legs stir the lake behind him, and waited taut at his paddle as the dragoon waded out for a final word. Rehearsal time is over, he thought petulantly. We've no more to say to one another now. Yet he leaned forward briskly from long habit when Andy cupped both palms about his lips and bent close, for all the world as though they were about to pounce on Chekika's stronghold in the next quarter hour.

"You'll lead us through Promontory Point and into the saw-grass. Don't forget to save your strength till we turn south."

"Oui, mon capitaine."

Andy chuckled quietly in the dark. "We'll spread behind you until an hour before dawn. Then you're to go on ahead and make your first blaze. We'll hole in all day at the swamp and wait for the moon. Then we'll move on—an hour in your wake."

"We've been over this, Andy."

"So we have. Tell me what happens if a storm comes in from the Gulf."

"I'm to hole in myself—at the first key point. When it's safe to move, I'm to cut a warning above my original marker and go on to the next turn. Ranson's to stop dead at the warning and flag you back into the saw-grass—or wherever there's a safe handhold. The moment he can see far enough to paddle, he's to follow me—and take his cue at the next blaze."

"You'll remember not to move too fast, Roy. That's very important. You're our barometer in bad weather—and bad weather's the one thing we can count on. We may need four days for our strike—or six, or eight. It doesn't matter, now we're moving. A rain squall will pin Chekika down too——"

"I'm aware of that." Roy had not meant to speak testily, but he could feel the mounting impatience of the men in the shadows behind him. It was quite like Andy to repeat his lesson to the end.

"All right, Roy," said Andy. "I know you can handle this. Move out when you like."

"Say good-by to Mary," he muttered. and wondered if the gruffness in his tone was cover enough for the deep ache beneath. In a way, he could understand why Mary had held aloof from their last hurried preparations. After all, they had said their real good-by in her tent hours ago. . . . He could not quite down his resentment at her absence now. If only for the sake of form, she should be at the water's edge, speeding the Rangers on their way.

"Mary asked to be excused," said Andy. "She hoped you'd understand."

Roy lifted his paddle. "Fair enough, Captain Winter. I won't wish *you* luck. You've made your own luck from the start."

"So have you, Doctor. Shove off and we'll follow."

The whisper was really a command, enforced by the hard push that Andy gave the dugout. Roy let himself coast into the dusk-dimmed lake and dug his paddle for the first stroke when his momentum died. He heard a whispered order run down the beach behind him and felt a score of canoes slide into his wake without lifting his eyes from the course ahead.

That would be Ranson and his vanguard. Andy and the main body of Rangers would swim after them in a moment, a tight triangle of destruction, ready to spread for cover at the slightest warning from the group ahead.

Now that the strike was really under way, he could not believe that it had taken to the water so smoothly. He dared to glance back just once and studied the black profile of the island they were quitting, etched like a primitive woodcut against the star-rich night. Even if she had been too hurt to say good-by, he was glad that Mary had been too proud to stage a final scene at the water's edge. He tried to picture her at this moment, curled in a hard cocoon of rage in her canvas shelter atop the ridge, and wondered if she could be lonely as he. Then he set an arrow-straight course across Sandy Bay and dug for the long saw-grass point with all his strength.

During these first hours he had been sure his heart would pump madly at every sound; he had expected a patter of gunshots from the tight-packed canoes behind him or, at the very best, a panic rush when they had cut through the neck of Promontory Point and entered the first long leg of the Grassy Water. Actually, it was a sweat-stained night with no apparent ending, a gruelling battle to build up mileage, with the eternal barrier of the saw grass and the menace of the next mud flat the only visible enemies.

Thanks to the sense of direction that rode at his finger tips and the long familiarity with this initial stretch of water maze, he was able to drive on with no real pause. When the slough they were following with such blind confidence made an abrupt turning, he raised his paddle, grinding the file of dugouts to a halt while his lungs fought for air. Later, when the gibbous moon swam into view at last above the river of grass and blue-black silence, he pulled the whole flotilla hard against the bank. For the next three hours they sought deep water by instinct. When the last scrap of moonlight faded, they rested again on their paddles until the first glimmer from the east began to pick out landmarks in the velvet cave ahead.

For the first time since they had quitted their base he permitted himself the luxury of a small sigh. If his memory and Mary's map were both correct, this would be the ending of the blue-gum swamp—an excellent shelter for the flotilla. The long, wide-open slough that was now barely visible there to the south was the beginning of the unknown—the leg of the spoonbill on Mary's sketch. This, of course, was the critical stretch of the journey; he would need all his skill to mark the Rangers' route.

Even in this bad light he could see that the stream flowed gently south in a well-defined channel. Knowing the Grassy Water as he did, he could not hope for the same clear-cut distinction between land and slough for the whole distance. Inevitably there would be spots where he would find no apparent path in that legion of yellow-green spears; others where a dozen parallel waterways would invite entrance. He was already paddling fast, without pausing to check on the canoes behind him. Ranson would stop in his wake now that dawn was coming. Though it involved a certain risk, he was determined to push on five miles more and camp beside his first blaze.

The light came slowly this morning, and for once he could bless the heavy blanket of clouds that seemed to graze the saw-grass spears, though there was no feel of rain in the gray promise of dawn. Little by little he could pick out landmarks that would help Ranson to find his channel—a brace of islands flanking the current like dozing whales, a long palm-fringed mud flat that merged with the green-grass sea and turned the lazy stream in a gentle arc to the west. The slough was mirror-smooth under the humid morning, shining with a bizarre opal light. Curiously enough, he could mark his course perfectly by that water gleam, though the facing banks were deep in shadows. The bow of his canoe, riding low under its buckskin lashings, seemed to resist every stroke of the paddle, as though it were reluctant to move farther in that turgid, goblin-hued liquid. He knew that he was tiring fast; the dugout, heavily laden though it was with Army gear, had been manageable enough in the swamp.

Thanks to the pressure of that unfallen rain, there was no real sunrise. A glance at his watch told Roy that he had paddled for slightly more than an hour; a check of the bank warned him that he would soon be a visible target. Try as he might, he could not believe that Chekika's braves were within miles; in fact, it seemed absurd to imagine that any craft but his own had profaned this virgin repose. Yet a training that went beyond thought drove him instantly to the shelter of the bank. His eyes, roving the channel ahead, picked out a den of live oaks, bearded deep in moss; here, at least, was a spot of real earth that had outlasted hurricanes.

He beached the canoe in a kind of cove that curved inward from the bank between high tufts of saw grass. It was a made-to-order haven, he noted, boxed in a solid wall of green, with no 'gator sign and eight clear feet of water under his keel. The boles of the oaks were between him and the slough, and even here, thanks to the inroads of the strangler fig, there was no real break in that cover of green. He staggered a little as he stepped out on the deep mat of moss beneath the canopy of leaves, but it was less from weariness than from the blessed relief of cramped legs and shoulders aching from twelve solid hours of paddling.

Pushing through the twisted branches of the fig trees, he stepped out to the bank of the stream and checked his position by rote. The islet on which he stood was no more than a pocket handkerchief of earth, held firm against the tug of the southward-flowing water by its myriad tree roots; he guessed that it was all that remained of a larger land mass, silted away by years of storm, encroached on by the violent sawgrass growth. He lifted the moon-shaped fighting-ax at his belt and notched the place, high up on the trunk of the largest oak, where he would cut his blaze—a triangular assurance that Sergeant Ranson was firm on course.

A glance downstream, where the current had already begun to meander crazily into several channels, told him that his task would be harder from this point on. He could only pray that the storm would blow itself out by moonrise. If this leaden pall of clouds hung on above the Glades, Ranson would never venture beyond the rim of the swamp—and he, in turn, would be forced to sit out the night in this snug haven of leaves.

A swim in the cove, he decided, would sharpen his appetite for the cold rations under the dugout's bow. He grinned faintly as he stared down at his hard-hit body, then stepped out of the breechclout that was his only garment. Ranson had shaved his blue-black hair into the ritual scalp lock, but it had not been necessary to apply the pokeberry dye the other Rangers had used so lavishly. Burned as it was by years in the sun, when he had worn no other garb but this, his skin was darker than any Seminole's.

Under the morning light this water would soon have turned as tepid as a bath. Today, thanks to the canopy of clouds, it was deliciously cool against his parched body. He swam twice round the little cove before returning to the canoe, rejoicing in the flowing freedom of his limbs after that endless journey from Okeechobee—then sounded deep and came up, porpoise-like, beside the stern. . . . Something about the position of the dugout opened his eyes wide while he was still coasting along the bottom; his head just missed collision with the copper-shod keel as he broke surface and anchored a fist on one gunwale. Shaken by a slight but visible motion, the canoe had dislodged itself from the bank while he swam. Bit by bit it had backed into the cove, as though pushed from the bank by an invisible hand.

He saw the source of trouble instantly, and damned his folly. Weaponless and naked in the midst of the cove, he looked warily over the gunwale at the lashing of buckskin that covered the whole forward half of the dugout. Something was stirring under that sunfaded lashing. He heard a faint sound, as though a hand or foot had groped along the thongs that held the matched buckskins in place. It was this gentle, rocking motion that had dislodged the keel from the bank and warned him, in time, that an enemy had taken refuge in the canoe.

Roy lifed an arm and shoulder over the stern and trod water quietly. His heart gave a leap when he saw the rifle tucked neatly under a tarpaulin on the bottom of the dugout, and remembered that Andy had asked him to stow this extra weapon aboard along with the rounds of ammunition. A single flick of his wrist dislodged the barrel and laid the long muzzle firm against the midship thwart. As he made this

move he saw the shape of a fist, unmistakable now and
bunched hard against the restraining buckskin. The knife
blade flashed, probing until it found the knot, and slashing it
in a single downward stroke. The lashings parted without a
sound, and Mary Grant sat up calmly in the bow of the dugout, her shoulders still hidden by the buckskin, her lips parted in a pleading smile.

"Don't shoot, please," she said. "I'm still your friend."

"How did you get here?" He heard his tongue frame the
inane question while relief and rage fought to possess his
brain. But Mary only continued to offer that maddening
smile as she tossed the buckskin aside and, womanlike, began
to arrange her hair. He saw that she was still wearing those
nankeen Army trousers, though she had replaced the shirt
with a thin band of doeskin that accented rather than concealed the swelling of her bosom. Her face and the generous-
ly revealed portions of her body that met his eyes seemed
quite as dark as his own. Her hair was plaited in two long
braids, Indian-fashion, and bound in a twist of doeskin stud-
ded with bits of mirror and heraldic thunderbirds. He took in
these details while he groped for an attitude—even as his feet
trod water helplessly in the deep center of the cove.

"Don't think me immodest, please," she said at last. "I've a
respectable Mother Hubbard I'll put on presently. But it was
hot as hinges under that cover. Thank heaven I managed to
sleep after a fashion———"

"How did you get here?"

"Isn't that rather obvious? Someone obligingly pointed out
your canoe to me when you and Andy were still arguing over
my map. Once I'd made sure it was properly loaded, I
stowed away. As you've just observed, I even managed to
lash myself in—and left the knot handy———"

"You had no right," he said hoarsely.

"I had every right. I'm part of this expedition, even if you
don't choose to admit it."

"You promised to stay behind———"

"No, Roy. I only promised to stop annoying Andy. *He* still
thinks I'm back on the island, so he won't be troubled in the
least."

Roy pushed the dugout firmly against the bank and started
to climb aboard, but remembered, just in time, that he had

left his meager clothing ashore. "Andy's going to be very troubled in another hour. I'm taking you back to him."

"But you can't, Roy. You're under orders to stay here until dark. Then you must go straight on. And I'm going with you."

He spoke eye to eye with her, moving down the gunwale to make his point. "Even in your present mood, you must see that's impossible."

"Why? I'm just where I belong—as I told you yesterday. From here to Big Sulphur you can use me a hundred times over."

He scowled in earnest, even as he admitted in his heart that Mary was right. Trained though he was in the vagaries of the Grassy Water, he had felt his heart sink when he had looked southward down the slough and seen how it shredded away in the saw grass. Mary had come down that same sluggish river by daylight. Granted a moon, she might save him hours of costly blundering in the race to Big Sulphur.

"Has it occurred to you that we may both stop a bullet at any moment?"

"Would you be here at all, Roy, if it weren't worth that risk? Can you deny I'll save you a few of those risks? What's more, I can handle a bow paddle as well as most men. Andy himself admits that. He let me practice with the Rangers every day—before I was taken sick——"

"Before you *pretended* to be sick," he said acidly.

"Admit it was worth the pretense. We're together, and I'll pull my weight. You'll see, Roy——"

"Stay where you are," he said firmly. "And turn the other way. I'm coming ashore for my clothes. Then I'm taking you back, orders or no orders."

"You wouldn't dare," she said calmly. "Have you any idea how furious he'll be if he finds I've passed a whole night in your canoe?"

"He'll know who's to blame for that."

"Don't be too sure, Roy. He's jealous enough of you now." Mary laughed aloud at his openmouthed stare. "He's thought for some time that you were in love with me. Naturally, I've told him it was nonsense. But how would we convince him now?"

"It's hardly my fault that you're here."

"Hardly. But you'll never explain that to Andy."

"It'll make matters far worse if I take you to the spring. That means another night in the sloughs. at least——" He bit the sentence short as the full import of his words sank home. But Mary was still laughing as she turned her back and sat with folded arms in the bow.

"Come ashore, Salofkachee," she ordered. "Make yourself as decent as possible. I won't look. And we won't argue this any further. Not till we've breakfasted. at least."

Roy stormed from water to land and scrambled into his clothing in record time. He did not pursue the discussion while he dressed. As Mary had said, this was not the time for argument, when she held most of the visible cards.

Breakfast was cold beans and corn pone, with a generous slab of bacon and two ounces of Jamaica rum to wash those iron rations down. He poured a tot for Mary from his own canteen and handed it into the canoe without comment. Even in his anger he was a bit shocked to observe how casually she tossed the fiery liquor down.

"It's quite all right, Roy. Andy has allowed me my two ounces for over a week. He says it'll keep most fevers in control."

"Including the fever you're suffering from at this time?"

Mary tossed her head. "I don't know what you mean."

"The age-old desire of man to blunder beyond his depth."

"Believe me, Roy, you'll eat those words before we reach Big Sulphur."

"Who says we're going that far together?"

"Be honest. Admit we've already gone too far to turn back."

He looked deep into her eyes, searching for the hidden meaning behind her words, and found only an offer of comradeship there. A frank reaching out on Mary's part to bridge the strained silence that divided them. He spoke sternly, refusing to meet the offer halfway.

"Andy is no more than five miles behind us. As I said before, we can reach him in an hour—and no harm done. The chances are one in fifty that Chekika has patrols out this far from Fakahatchee."

"How can you say there'd be no harm done? This raid is running like clockwork so far. It'll be just as smooth when we reach the spring—if no one forgets his job. Just think what the men will say if you paddle back to that swamp with a woman in your dugout."

"You might have considered that before you came aboard."

"I did, carefully. And I decided you'd be too sensible to turn back—if I could stay under that buckskin for the first twelve hours."

He scowled at her logic and made no effort to answer. In one stroke she had appealed to his need for her (a need more poignant than she would ever know), his *esprit de corps*— and man's urge to take the easiest way. An urge no less universal than that other tendency to blunder into a situation without an exit. Rising to dispose of the remnants of their breakfast, he crossed the islet in three long strides, knowing in advance that she would dog his footsteps. They stood for a long time without speaking in the riotous tangle of fig leaves that chocked the edge of the dark-flowing channel. Taut as he was, he could not help admiring her ease as she swept the vista before them. No woman under heaven, he reflected, could be more positive of her eternal rightness.

If I take you back, he thought, Andy's command will be thrown into an uproar—to put things mildly. There'll be no detail to spare for an escort to base—even if the escort could find its way to Okeechobee again without my help or Ranson's. Perhaps she'd be safer in the group than here—but that, too, is an arguable point, especially when the raid is launched. . . . He paused briefly to damn his sophistry, then plunged on with his silent argument. Obviously, a lone female would be safer with six hundred men than with one— unless that six hundred blundered into ambush. Just as obviously, the note of tension she had brought into his dugout would be magnified six hundred times. What right had he to pass on that burden to the Everglades Rangers, when Mary Grant had crept into his canoe of her own free will?

"Have you won your battle with your conscience?" she asked softly. "Or is self-interest a better word?"

"Never mind the reason. You may stay where you are—if you'll put your weight on that bow paddle."

"Tell me why, Roy—it's important."

"It's simpler," he said shortly. "Simpler and cleaner. Women are supposed to be bad luck in a boat. I'm praying you're the exception." He turned quickly to the canoe and began an entirely needless rearrangement of the gear, avoiding her eyes.

"So you won't even admit I'll be useful?"

"You'll be damned useful," he said. "And I'll never forgive myself if you're hurt. Will that satisfy you for now?"

"That will do nicely," said Mary Grant. "In fact, I'll forgive you a great deal if those words come from the heart."

"I'm glad you're with me, Mary," he said. "Glad and sorry —if that's clear."

Mary put one bare foot in the crotch of a water oak and pulled herself up into the nest of leaves. From this vantage point she commanded a good view of the slough and the tributary maze that engulfed it to the south. "You're forgiven, Roy," she said. "Go get your rest—you've earned it."

"What are you doing in that tree?"

"Earning my keep, and standing the first watch."

"Come down at once. You'll do no such thing."

"It's my turn. Remember, I've just had a long sleep—of a sort."

He hesitated, beating down an urge to seize those long nankeen-draped legs in a sudden hammer lock and drag her earthward. He had planned to sleep through the daylight hours in this haven, risking a surprise visit from Chekika in favor of the rest he so badly needed. Certainly there was less risk involved with a watcher on the bank. Yet he was reluctant to leave Mary here, even though the canoe was only a few feet away.

"How can I be sure you'll stay awake?"

"Surely you can trust me that far, Roy."

I'll trust you, he thought. I've no other choice. "If you insist," he said coldly. "Just be sure to waken me at noon."

"Give me your watch so I'll know the time."

He opened the oilskin bag at his throat and took out the huntingcase timepiece. Handing it up into the leaves without a word, he was about to move toward the canoe when Mary leaned down and caught his hand in both her own.

"Shake hands on our bargain," she ordered. "I promise you'll have no regrets."

"I wish I could believe that," he said, even as he found himself returning the warm pressure of her fingers. Then he strode across their tiny domain and forced his mind to the task of making a bed inside the dugout. His pulses still hammered a furious obbligato to his desire, but it was easier now that Mary Grant was lost among the leaves. So long as he turned his back on temptation, he could even pretend that this was an impossible dream.

The buckskin lashings, spread wide above the forward end of the canoe, made a tent of sorts. Once he had moved the powder boxes, there was space to spread his blanket roll. This time he was careful to draw the canoe to high ground before he settled in that snug bed. Perhaps I'll waken in the dusk and find her gone, he told himself piously. Though it's more likely that I'll toss here with wide-open eyes and curse my weakness to the end of time.

Lying on his back in his nest of blankets, he found that he could just discern her faint white shadow in the water oak, and wondered if this, too, was part of a dream that would desert him utterly if he dared to close his lids.

God keep her safe, he whispered, to no one in particular, unless it was his conscience. God forgive her for what she's doing to me now in her innocence. . . . He turned on his side to shut out that tormenting half glimpse among the oak leaves, and felt sure that sleep would never come. But he was dead to the world and all its lures before his next conscious breath.

iv

White light exploded in his brain, lifting him instantly to one elbow. For all his training, he needed a good ten seconds to remember where he was. Rain drummed a devil's tattoo on the buckskin tent above him; the sky outside his shelter was as black as midnight, though the wind-tortured tree limbs looked green, even in that eerie darkness. The thunderbolt that had followed almost instantly on that blaze of lightning still roared against his ear drums; a second flash, dead-white like the first, bathed the islet in garish day. His eyes moved instantly to the water oak where Mary had taken up her vigil. The lookout was empty now, so he knew he had dreamed Mary there, after all. . . . And then, as the thunder crashed, he came awake in earnest and found that he was not alone in his shelter.

"Did I waken you, Roy? I'm sorry, but I'm a coward, after all."

He had no way of knowing how long she had been stretched full length at his side—the only position, in those cramped quarters, that would have given her real protection from the storm. At this confused moment of wakening he knew only that she was as real as sin and just as dangerous. There was no time to move or to collect his wits when the next thunderbolt crashed—seemingly a few feet from the rain-lashed bow of their canoe. No time to do more than set his teeth against the mad leap of his heart when Mary Grant flung both arms about him and clung to him desperately, as though she could not bear to let him go.

"It's the lightning," she whispered. and her voice, though shaken. was calmer than her manner. "The one thing I couldn't ever face alone. I didn't startle you—really?"

"You should have wakened me sooner." He forced iron into his tone with a great effort. "I'd have wanted you out of that storm——" Again the thunder crashed, and she buried her face against his shoulder.

"You don't mind if I stay—like this? Now you're awake, I'm not afraid."

"Perhaps I should stand guard."

"Don't leave me—please!"

He moved closer with what he hoped was a soothing murmur. "I'll stay as long as you like. The lightning will pass over in a moment. It always does."

"You don't think I'm a coward?"

"Of course I don't."

"I saw it coming from that tree. By noon the sky had almost cleared. Then those thunderheads came marching up from the south—like black giants ——" A spurt of violet fire licked at the tent door, and her whole body molded to his own in a throbbing arc. "Giants rumbling at a joke of their own—with snakes in their fists." She laughed a little at her wild conceit. Her laughter changed to a muted scream as a thunderbolt crashed into the saw grass just across the slough, joining earth and sky in a flaming white charge Roy felt the electrical tingle at toes and fingers as though the elements themselves had conspired against them His arms had gone firmly round Mary now—an instinctive gesture of protection that had nothing to do with the desire that threatened to consume him.

"You're afraid too," she whispered. "I can feel your heart beating."

"Of course I'm afraid. Who wouldn't be?" He did not pause to explain that his terror had little to do with the squall raging outside. "Lie quietly, Mary. It'll be over soon." But even as he spoke another mighty crash belied his words. This time the bolt was two-pronged- -a forked discharge that hissed into the spongy earth downstream. One of the prongs, he noted, had lost itself harmlessly in the slough. The other, splitting a cabbage palm as cleanly as some monster ax, sent a spout of fire roaring skyward lost almost instantly in the cloudburst that was blotting both earth and heaven.

"When it rains like this, it means the lightning is moving on."

"Don't take your arm away—please."

"Look to the south," he said hoarsely. "See how that next flash ran into a hammock a good mile away?"

"You're leaving me, Roy. Don't leave me, ever."

He had risen from their shared couch within the dugout, on the pretense of arranging the tent, as the downpour threatened to fill the bow of the canoe The clouds still pressed down above the saw grass, making a deep darkness at noon. Here in the shelter of the buckskin lashings the gloom was even deeper. He could just see the dim outline of Mary's form, the lift of two pleading hands. Her heart was still thudding as he yielded to that mute appeal and put one gentle arm about her.

"Rest easily, my dear. The danger's over." The endearment had come easily to his lips, and he did not mention the other, more personal, danger that threatened to engulf them both now that the threat of nature had passed overhead. That heartbeat against his own had told its own story; the fear that the lightning had aroused in Mary Grant had yielded to quite a different emotion. *Whether she knows it or not,* he thought darkly, *whether she'd even dare give it a name, there's a passion in her veins at this moment that is ready and willing to match mine. It needs only a touch to bring it alive.*

"Hold me close a moment more," she said, and her voice was a whisper now. A murmur that needed no words to make its meaning plain. A current that passed from flesh to flesh, as real as the great thrust of fire from the skies, as primitive as woman's first helpless cry to man. *This isn't*

Mary Grant, he thought. This is a thousand generations of loneliness—calling in the darkness for its mate. Then he heard her chuckle softly and knew that she had come back from that lonely place to be herself again, though she had not stirred from the prison of his arms.

"I was a hussy to creep into your tent like this," she said. "Rain or no rain, you should have me court-martialed."

"I'm glad you came—really. I was a little frightened too."

Mary laughed again in the gloom; her hair teased his cheek as she leaned back in his arms and tried to study his face in the ghostly light. This time there was a hint of coquetry in her laughter. "Now you're being polite," she said. "It doesn't sit well on you. Not in *this* theater."

Roy sought his own desperate refuge in banter. "Tell me my role. I'll improvise the lines."

"You're the first Adam, of course. And you should resent the intrusion of Eve."

"If I'm to believe the book of Genesis, he welcomed her."

"To his sorrow, of course."

"You're here," he said gravely. "That's what really matters. Now that you've come, it seems inevitable that you should be —just where you are."

"You're being polite now, Roy."

"No, my dear." This time he spoke the words deliberately and felt her stir within his arms.

"If I say I'm glad it's raining, would that make me a hussy twice over?"

"So you did invade my quarters deliberately. All you wanted was an excuse."

"Don't take your arm away. This is a chance I haven't had before. I intend to make the most of it."

"Take care I don't misunderstand," he said, and tried hard to force a note of gaiety he didn't feel. "Perhaps I *am* the first Adam, after all."

"If you are," she said, "you're civilizing too fast for comfort."

"I don't know what you mean."

"Never mind that now. At long last I've pushed you into a position where you can't avoid me. Not unless you want to drown in rain water. You'll simply have to answer my questions. Truthfully, I hope."

"Try me," he said, and his voice was still light enough, though it was costing him a real effort.

"Why have you always avoided me, Roy?"

"But I haven't——"

"Evasion number one," she said. "I'll admit our meeting at Fort Everglades was a bit unusual. I didn't blame you for sulking in your quarters that night when Andy invited you to dine with us. But you had plenty of time to find out who I really was before we reached Flamingo Key—and you avoided me there like the plague. If I hadn't smuggled aboard your boat for that day at Matecumbe I wouldn't have laid eyes on you. Even when you risked your life on that swim you refused to say two words to me——"

"You had enough on your mind that night. So had I."

"Evasion number two," said Mary cheerfully, and her voice seemed to grow gayer with each word, as though she were enjoying this catalogue. "Your next move was to arrange with Chekika that he trade hostages. Me for you—and if that's bad grammar, I don't care. You wouldn't even *look* at me that dreadful morning at Indian Mound when they brought me ashore and took you away——"

"That was part of our bargain."

"Evasion number three. Couldn't you even look up when I called your name?"

"Sorry—it wasn't allowed."

"Very well, Roy. Here's one question you can't evade. Why do you dislike me?"

"But I don't——"

"Is it because I'm taking Andy out of your life? Or are you still angry because I made you talk about your past?"

"I'm not in the least angry. And I think Andy is a very lucky man."

"Then it's because I've forced myself into this raid—just as I'm forcing myself into your arms."

"Now you're getting warm," he said grimly, and pointed his remark by tightening his embrace. Mary did not shrink from the implication behind his flat statement. On the contrary, she seemed to melt into his arms, as though she had belonged there from the beginning.

"Of course I can always sit in the rain," she whispered. "Would that be what you're hinting?"

"It's I who should sit in the rain," he said. "Don't you know why, even now?"

"Tell me, Roy."

He told her, quite without words—bending above her slowly, giving her every chance to draw back, then kissing her, long and hard. It was the sort of kiss he had been saving for Mary's lips from the moment of their first wild wrestle in the Miami. A kiss that burned his weeks of yearning away in its joyous flame as though they had never been.

"Does that answer your question, Mary?" he asked.

"Adequately," said Mary Grant, and smiled as she lay unstirring in his arms. The rain still roared down on the tent above them, but a little pale sun had begun to burn through the clouds, bathing her in aqueous light. He had the curious sensation of floating—drowned, as it were, in the deep wave of his desire, too tranced by her acceptance to draw breath.

"Admit I worked hard to cover up," he said at last. "Admit you never knew till now."

"Why be ashamed of wanting me?"

"You're Andy's promised bride, for one thing. For another, I'm a poor catch for any woman. Especially the daughter of a New York nabob——"

"Don't say another word, Roy. Just kiss me like that again. I don't mind being wanted. Not in the least."

"No, Mary. It isn't fair—to either of us."

"Why not? Has it ever occurred to you that I might want you?"

He stared down at her as though he could not credit the evidence of his ears. "Have you any idea what you're saying?"

"Of course I have. Why do you think I pursued you—right up to the edge of Chekika's village? Why did I wait nine days on that island—and pray every moment that you'd come back safe?"

"Don't, Mary!"

"But it's true, I'm not ashamed to tell you, now *you've* confessed." Now it was she who drew his lips down on hers, and her kiss matched his own in abandon. Just in time he broke free and half leaped, half reeled from the fragrant temptation of her embrace. Once he felt the clean wash of the rain, he was his own master.

"I'll go stand guard awhile," he said gravely. "Stay where

you are and try to rest. You'll need all your strength to-night."

"Come back, Roy," she said. "You needn't even say you love me. Just come back——"

"Do you know what would happen if I did?"

"Of course I know. I've always suspected I was a hussy at heart. Now I'm sure of it——"

"And what of Andy?"

"Andy's a thousand miles away. We're Adam and Eve, and this is the dawn of time. I won't reproach you later. And you needn't say you love me, really."

"But I do love you," he said. "That's why I couldn't hurt you now."

Much later, when he tried to recall his panic flight, he knew that she had cried out just once from the buckskin tent that had almost enclosed his surrender. Then he was safe on the bank of the slough, with the storm a solid curtain be-tween them. There was no sound but the hiss of the rain and the monotonous, half-whispered chanting of his own voice as he cursed Dr. Royal Coe and all his works.

Three times in the next hour he all but turned back to the cove, but each victory of mind over flesh was firmer than the last.

v

The rain had died just before dusk; the whole eastern sky, opening like a flower around the moonrise, promised a flaw-less night. Dr. Royal Coe shook the last hint of the storm from his shoulders and rose from the doubtful shelter of the yucca clump, where he had stood watch through that endless afternoon. It was time to proceed to Chekika's village—and time to face Mary Grant. As he moved gingerly across the islet he had no idea which was the greater ordeal.

When he stepped into the cove he thought at first that she was gone. The canoe stood empty, its buckskin lashings in place again, bailed bone-dry after the long downpour. Pad-dles and push pole were ready; even the rifle lay across the gunwales, with a charge rammed home. But there was no sign of Mary; his heart turned over at the obvious supposi-tion. Shaken by his savage withdrawal (or overcome by re-morse at the depth of her own revelations), she might well have fled into the saw-grass rather than face him again. She might even have done herself physical harm while he held obstinately aloof. . . . He cupped his hands to shout her name just as Mary herself spoke from the screen of fig leaves.

"It's quite all right, Roy. I've done my tempting for today." She came into the growing moonlight as she spoke, and he saw that she was plastered with mud from head to foot. "But I won't say I'm sorry—so please return the compliment."

He felt his tension ease a little while he trimmed the canoe. "Very well. I won't say a single word."

"Don't, please. For the next few hours we can't afford to be people. Too much depends on us."

"Apparently we can never be people, Mary. Not when we're together——"

"Careful. In another second you *will* say you're sorry—and that I won't permit."

"Get into the bow," he ordered gruffly. "I'll do the steering." He was plastering himself with mud while he spoke. "Who told you to blacken your face when you went raiding?"

"Don't forget I watched the Rangers at their maneuvers." Her voice was quiet now and entirely impersonal. We might be strangers, he thought, making small talk while we prepare to share a journey. He glanced at his watch and frowned when he discovered that he could see the hands by the moonlight. Ranson had already left the blue-gum swamp, if his timing was accurate. It would never do for the sergeant to overtake them tonight.

"Remember two things before we start," he said. "If I tell you to lie flat, obey instantly—it'll probably save your life. And if we are boarded, try not to scream. It's just possible you'll be mistaken for a boy—and I'll demand to be taken straight to Chekika. We can always pretend we're messengers from Washington."

"Will it come to that, Roy?"

"I hope not," he said gravely. "But we must be ready for the worst. Above all, we must keep our heads and try not to spook ourselves."

"I'll keep my head," she murmured, and he noted with a sad thrill of pride that her voice was quite as steady as his own.

"Off we go, then," he said. "Try to feather your paddle quietly."

The dugout glided from cove to slough and swung in a wide arc above the islet they had just quitted. Roy saw with approval that the triangular blaze he had just hacked on the trunk of the largest oak showed clearly in the growing white ardor of the moonlight. Ranson would have no difficulty picking up their sign when he passed this way in the next hour. He let the canoe ride gently with the current and watched the rhythmic pump of Mary's arms and shoulders as she bent at her task at the forward thwart. For the moment, at least, it was blessedly easy to pretend that his slender helper was indeed a boy, trained to take orders without question.

"Sharp left," she whispered without looking back. "Between that point and the magnolia clump."

"The main current flows to the right."

"So it seems. But you'll lose yourself in a bog a hundred yards. I remember those magnolias distinctly."

"Heaven help us if you're wrong," he said, and skirted the bank to chip a wide, triangular blaze on the largest tree. A dozen paddle strokes proved Mary's memory was excellent; the narrow passageway widened with dramatic suddenness in the tight-packed jungle, then opened to a long, ruler-straight slough that seemed to glimmer away to infinity there on the moon-misted horizon.

"The leg of the spoonbill," she said. "Will you admit the hussy can draw?"

"I've always admitted that," he said. "Even Andy could follow this channel."

"Don't be too sure. There are islands below, and a few crazy bends. You may need another blaze or two. I'll show you the spots as we move on."

"Careful," he said. "A few more timesavers, and I'll think you're indispensable."

"Just be sure Andy mentions me in his final report. That's all I ask."

He found that he had flinched at her casual mention of Andy Winter—and rejoiced that she had not turned back as she spoke. If we come out of this alive, he thought, there are several items we can never mention to Andy—or admit officially, even to ourselves. But there was no time for regrets over the madness they had shared in the buckskin heaven.

Still less to rejoice (a bit dourly, to be sure) that there could be no possible aftermath.

"He'll mention you with honor."

"Don't be so gloomy, please. Neither of us is dead, so far."

I'd be better dead, he thought. How can I go on living now that I've opened my heart to you? But he did not speak his agony aloud. "Keep your head low," he said. "I'm going to skirt the east bank awhile. That grass will cut your flesh to ribbons."

"What about yours?"

"I'm used to that sort of wound," he said, and smiled, despite his mood, when Mary dropped under the forward thwart just before their gunwale grazed the thronging spears of saw-grass. Here, along the eastern bank of the slough, the shadows were thick enough to cover their steady progress, in the remote event they were observed. He did not speak for a long time as they drove southward. Nor did he flinch at the occasional lash of a saw-grass blade. He had chosen the channel deliberately for this stage of the journey, hoping to save Mary's strength for the last grueling miles.

"Swing out to midstream, Roy. The channel turns just ahead. You can see the landmark against the moon. Three dead cypresses, like witches in Macbeth."

"Didn't I order you to keep your head down?"

"I have. I can still follow your course. This bow is peppered with old bullet holes."

He cursed under his breath as he felt the dugout coast on mud, and backed water vigorously until they were afloat again. The three cypresses, thrust boldly against the moon on a small island in midstream, were a perfect landmark. He swung back penitently until he found deep water again and paused in the dead shadow to notch a blaze for Ranson. Mary laughed softly as she took up her paddle again.

"Imagine the confusion if six hundred men had piled on that mudbank."

"Don't rub salt in my wounds, please," he said dourly. "I was only thinking of you."

"Think of yourself next time. We'll reach Big Sulphur sooner."

Roy found he could endorse her advice a dozen times in the next few hours as they forged steadily southward under that high round moon. More than once long experience in these waterways made him protest her directions, only to prove that her memory was better than his instinct. Twice, when he had overruled her insistence on a certain landmark (only to backtrack down an apparently endless slough that had suddenly ended in a wall of jungle), he could have sworn he heard the chunk of Ranson's paddles in the north. Then, with another blaze notched, he would follow Mary's choice of routes and burst once again into open water, with another precious five miles behind him and the threat of Big Sulphur all but visible on the horizon.

The last turning was the most difficult—a right-angled bend, represented on the sketch by the knee joint of the bird. Here their route was choked in dog fennel, pocked with 'gator wallows, hideous with the bellowing of courting bulls. The channel threaded intricately through the green maze; Mary herself was forced to stand in the bow and con their passage, and it was she who swung the war ax now, marking a whole series of blazes on both banks to speed Ranson on his way. When the dugout had nosed into open water once again, she settled in her place with a contented sigh.

"You may take us in, Skipper. The pilot rests on her laurels."

Roy rose in turn to bow his thanks, and took up the push pole. Here, with the din of the wooing saurians behind them, the slough was as spacious as a bay in the moonlight—and so shallow in spots that the canoe staggered under the thrust of the pole before it eased free. But there was no mistaking that dense semicircle of vegetation to the south and east—or the hypnotic odor that grew stronger with each forward spurt. There, milky-white in the dark water ahead, was the first stain of Big Sulphur—the overflow from a continually bubbling spring that spilled from its limestone basin at every point of the compass. Where the slough oozed away into spongy muck were the five channels that snaked through that last quarter mile of jungle to join with the Grassy Water to the west.

"The left toe of the spoonbill," said Roy, almost humbly. "I remember."

"Should we check the time before we go in?"

He braked the dugout sharply in the shadow of the bank and drew out his watch. The hands still showed clearly in the moonlight: three o'clock, less a quarter hour. Thanks to Mary, he had reached his objective with time to spare,

"We'll go up to the lip of the spring and scout the bank," he said. "Chekika may have a guard at his back door. I'll have to swim, in any case, from there on."

"We'll swim together, Roy."

"Let's argue that point later," he said, and sent the canoe bounding toward the spring, already a visible presence in that dense screen of leaves. At that precise moment he heard the first throb of the drum from the village beyond, joined almost instantly by the familiar victory chant that had robbed him of sleep during his imprisonment.

"What does it mean, Roy?"

"War talk. The same war they've been discussing since I was a guest."

"Will they move out tonight?"

"I don't think it's likely." Roy braked the canoe again and listened carefully. "The Seminole nation is like any other—it talks war a long time before it fires the first shot."

The tempo of the drums had increased in frenzy while they moved toward Big Sulphur. That, too, was a familiar phenomenon—after Chekika had broached his second keg of rum. Poling toward the spring with all his strength, Roy prayed that the drumbeat would build in this last hour before dawn. A fuddled village was precisely what Andy would have ordered as he drove his Rangers to their target.

"Are they half as drunk as they sound?" asked Mary.

"Keep your fingers crossed. We'll soon know."

He beached the dugout where the slough opened to the gin-clear bubbling of the spring, drawing it deep in a mangrove thicket and marking his last blaze by rote on the trunk of a towering blue gum at the very edge of Big Sulphur. His hand closed on Mary's wrist with no words needed. They moved into the gnarled maze of the mangrove roots and climbed to clear ground beyond—a kind of natural bluff that stood above the limestone basin of the spring itself. Here, thanks to the path of moonlight that still marked the route to Chekika's village, he could form an accurate picture of the task ahead. A gesture brought Mary to hands and knees beside him. Together they inched forward until they knelt at the edge of Big Sulphur, with a view of the eastern bank and the green tunnels that led to Fakahatchee Hammock.

"You were right," said Mary. "He *did* post a guard."

Ever since moonrise he had observed the enemy in a hundred masquerades—as a clump of yuccas at the bank, as a palmetto fan changed in a flicker to a war bonnet. These silent enemies had melted into their natural shapes, thanks to the clarity of the moonlight—a sly magician who began by giving everyday objects an extra dimension, only to trim them to size at the last moment. But the wavering profile of the Seminole on the beach below them remained an Indian, no matter how carefully he was scouted. Roy could only rub his eyes and look again—positive, even now, that this was a mirage born of his own inner fears.

"I don't think it's a guard. Or if he *is* a sentry, he's too fuddled to see this far."

"How can you be sure?"

"Look how he's swaying. They're talking war around the council fire. Offhand, I'd say this was one of the younger braves about to purify himself at the spring—and renew his courage."

Mary nodded solemnly at his side. "We saw that happen often enough when I was here with Dr. Barker. They'd come over by the dozens to kneel on that bank and ask for help from above. Why aren't there more tonight—if they are really talking war?"

"Judging by the drums, most of them are too far gone in rum."

"Then we couldn't ask a better chance to reach Dr. Barker."

"Once we've disposed of our friend below."

"Must you kill him, Roy?"

"Only in case of a tie. Stay where you are."

Roy had already inched forward behind the protecting arch of mangroves. The Seminole was directly below him now—a young stalwart much the worse for alcohol, naked as a jay bird in the moonlight, and apparently unarmed. As Mary had surmised, he was strengthening his spirit by deep draughts from the spring—kneeling on the sandy beach and scooping the sulphur water between his hands. Drinking and laving his body in turn, he chanted a ritual prayer with each lift of his arms. Glancing across the spring as he moved down to the beach, Roy saw a small canoe drawn up on the far bank. He guessed that the Indian had plunged into the water on his arrival from the village, swum to this bank as an initial act of this solemn ceremony, and would return to the council fire when his head had cleared.

The ax was in his fist now, though he never remembered lifting it from his belt; he whispered softly to bring his target upright. As the Seminole shifted to hands and knees, the blunt side of the tomahawk swooped in a stinging arc, connecting neatly with the right temple. The Indian collapsed without a sound. Roy flipped the unconscious body face up on the beach just as the Seminole was about to slide into the moon-shot depths.

"All right, Mary. Come down here for orders." He looked up from his handiwork and frowned when he saw that the girl was already at his side. Apparently she had ghosted through the mangroves as quietly as he.

"That's his canoe," she said. "On the far side. Shall we swim to it together?"

"Stay where you are. Ranson will be here in a half-hour at the most."

"I'm coming with you, Roy."

"You can't swim in your clothes."

"Look again—you'll see I'm quite ready."

Coated as she was with mud, Mary had seemed part of the darkness while she stood among the mangrove roots. Now, as she moved into the moonlight, he saw that she had stepped out of her Army trousers. The breechclout she wore beneath them was a replica of his own; the doeskin band that confined her breasts might have been part of her skin.

"Will you go first, or shall I?"

He swallowed a curse as she dived cleanly from the bank without waiting for his answer. The strong upward thrust of the spring caught her body instantly, bouncing it like a silver chip in the moonlight as the last of her muddy masquerade was washed away. He followed in a long, flat dive, putting out all his strength to outdistance her in the race for the far shore.

Thanks to the clear water and the strange upward thrust beneath his body, he had the illusion of floating on air. The heady sulphur vapors, rising like a mist around him, spun his brain backward in time as he sprinted even with Mary and reached out to touch her hand. For this brief moment, at least, Eden was theirs alone; he resisted a crazy impulse to revel here till daylight, letting Ranson and Andy manage the raid between them.

"Let me go in first. There may be others on the bank."

She nodded her agreement and swam close behind him until mossladen branches began to arch overhead. He swarmed ashore without stopping to weigh his chances, flattened behind the first tree trunk, and checked the moonlit woods that sloped down from the lip of the spring to join the swamp. There was no sign of life on this side of the spring— no sound but the insistent cacophony of drum and rumfogged voices a good half mile to the east. The small Indian dugout on the bank might have been a log, forgotten since the last storm. He motioned Mary ashore as he eased the canoe into the water, averting his eyes carefully from the white glow of her limbs.

"Apparently he left his clothes aboard."

Mary had already lifted the spangled garment against the moonlight; her breath escaped in a gasp of pure rage. "It's mine, Roy. The robe I wore in the last act of *Romeo and Juliet*. For two pins I'd go back and scalp that red devil now."

Despite the tension of the moment, Roy found he could laugh aloud. "Put it on then, since it's yours. You might as well be decent."

"*You* must wear it for now," she said. "Especially if you intend to use this canoe."

"I'm afraid I don't follow."

"It's simple enough. A drunken brave paddles out to Big Sulphur dressed as Juliet. He must paddle back as he came."

Roy swallowed hard and offered no protest when she draped the white winding sheet about his shoulders. It was a fair fit, even when he flexed his arms.

"Are you suggesting I paddle straight up to Chekika's beach?"

"Why not? You look the part."

"And you?"

"I'm where I belong," she said, and made herself small in the bow of the canoe. "Cover me with his blanket, if you must, though I'd say it was a poor time for modesty."

"I'd much prefer to leave you here."

Curled like a white kitten in the dugout, Mary offered him

her most brazen smile. "If I'm shocking you at this moment, think what I'd do to Andy."

"You saw how I handled that Indian," he said. "Would you like the same treatment?"

"You wouldn't touch me in my present state. You're too much a gentleman."

"This is no time for levity, Mary!" He rose in the dugout, with the paddle held high, but Mary's low-voiced laughter was as serene as ever.

"Say what you like of me later. Roy—I've been good company tonight. And what's a small joke between friends— if it keeps our minds off the next half hour?"

He bowed his head to the inevitable and dug furiously down the first leafy tunnel that led from spring to swamp. For the last time he was forced to admit Mary's essential rightness. Now that he had brought her this far, he had no choice but to take her all the way. He could hardly ask her to wait alone at Big Sulphur—all but naked in the moonlight. Other warriors from the village might appear at any moment to drink the healing waters. And there was an excellent chance she might stop a bullet when the Rangers swooped down on the spring.

If I keep her close, he told himself, I can give her back to Andy somehow. And clinging firmly to that resolve, he kept his eyes fixed on the next turning in the slough, above and beyond the white moon-mystery of the girl's body tucked away so neatly in the dugout's bow.

Here was the long, stagnant bayou that swept up to the final screen of water oaks that masked Fakahatchee Hammock to the south and west. He drove through it boldly, keeping well to midstream and letting his paddle strokes crash down full-armed. Now that he was a Seminole in masquerade, there was no point in caution.

Here was the green, aromatic tunnel that bored through the thick wall of leaves. He braked down on his paddle one last time to whisper a warning to Mary spreading both hands wide to keep her head below the gunwale.

"I'm going straight into the beach it's the only way. Pull that blanket over your head—and don't budge until I come back for you."

The council fire was burning high tonight, despite the late-ness of the hour; at first glance the entire nation seemed to be keening in the compound before the chief's hut. His eyes found Chekika at once, throned on the platform of his house tonight, like a sleepy satyr presiding over his own revels. There was Chittamicco, leading the mad prance around the fire—a natural-born dervish with a live snake in each fist, his eyes blazing with the true fanatic fire. The drums throbbed in the darkness, lifting a hundred bare copper feet in unison, stirring the dust of the compound into choking clouds.

Some of the braves were stark-naked and smeared with the hieroglyphs of battle. Others were in full ceremonial robes. The Shakespearean costumes were in evidence on all sides, mingled with odd bits of Army uniform. Squaw and warrior alike seemed reeling-drunk—as much from the shared passions of the dance as from the rum kegs. When he looked more closely Roy saw that the dance revolved around a tall cypress tripod that stood to the left of the fire—a serpentine circle that pulsed inward, seeming to touch this bizarre axis with every drumbeat. Now and again knives flashed in the dust, as though a hundred red butchers were carving a steer on that wooden frame and danced while they worked.

He felt his mind cloud with dread as he steadied at the bow of the dugout, and pressed a reassuring hand on the quiet form beneath the blanket. Then, knowing that hesitation would be fatal, and remembering to stagger with the others, he raised his own voice in a war whoop and made himself one with the capering circle. There was no time to draw back now or to wonder how secure Mary's hiding place really was. Already he had identified the red horror that swung head down on that crude gibbet, though the puffs of dust still hid the face from view—or rather, what the squaw's knives had left of the face at this late hour.

He felt sure his knees would buckle when it was his turn to dance round the gibbeted corpse, howl his defiance into empty eye sockets, and gut the shredded flesh with one more stroke of a war ax. And then, as his tomahawk feigned a stroke, he let out his breath in a shout with real meaning. The man in that cypress tripod was familiar, right enough, though he had already lost ears and nose, along with his hair. It was not Dr. Barker who swayed so drunkenly there in the firelit dawn—but the body of trader Dan Evans.

vi

Five minutes after he had left the butchers' circle he had reeled across the door of the botanist's hut, a safe remove from the fire and curious eyes. As he had hoped, there was no guard tonight—a volcanic snore from the darkness and a prodigious reek of rum told him that Dr. Barker's watchman had succumbed to temptation long ago. It surprised him not at all to pick out the doctor's gaunt frame just inside the doorway. The old botanist sat cross-legged on a pile of bearskins, watching the revel with all the animation of any scientist on a holiday. The cheroot that glowed between his lips was part of his deep serenity. So were the uplifted palm and the mild benediction in Seminole as Roy pretended to stumble and fall in the dust outside the hut.

"Go in peace, brave one."

"Can I talk freely, sir?"

If Dr. Barker was startled by the whisper, he gave no sign; the cigar continued to wink serenely as he blew out a long plume of smoke, then rose and took a step toward Roy sprawled like a gaudy sack in the dust of his doorway.

"Who dares to speak English in the chief's house?" he asked in whispered Seminole.

"Who but Salofkachee?" said Roy in the same language.

"Rise and show your face."

"Is it safe?"

"Quite. Even Chekika has been drunk since midnight. Drunk with blood."

Roy rose cautiously to hands and knees and settled in the comparative darkness of the doctor's palm-thatch wall. Even if he was observed from the council fire, he would now be mistaken for one of Dr. Barker's loud-snoring guards.

"When did they murder Evans?"

"I'm not quite sure. Sometime today at the council fire." Dr. Barker drew deep on his cheroot. "Incidentally, this is one of Dan's best cigars. I'm probably quite callous, smoking it with such obvious enjoyment. I suppose a prisoner takes what pleasure he can find—and doesn't question the source."

"He's been here for some time?"

"So far as I can gather, his freight canoes came in from the Gulf at dawn yesterday." Dr. Barker continued to smoke tranquilly, though his eyes had not left Roy. "The cigars were lagniappe, of course. Like the rum and the calico you'll see flaunted around that fire. The King of Panthers sent me a box this evening for my very own. I took it as proof that he wants me to live a while longer."

Calmness can be overdone, thought Roy. *At this precise instant six hundred Rangers are closing on us from four quadrants of the compass. Mary is lying in a canoe just two hundred yards away, with only a blanket between her and death. And I, like a loof, am sitting in my own disguise—a nightgown from some forgotten actor's portmanteau—praying that the masquerade will see me through.* . . . But he kept his voice to an easy whisper as he told Dr. Jonathan Barker of these facts. He sat unstirring in the shadow of the palm-thatch wall as the drumbeat rose to new frenzy in the compound and the butchered remains of Dan Evans, harried, even now, by incessant knife and hatchet blows, danced redly in the spout of firelight.

"Dan brought them arms and powder," said Dr. Barker, and his voice had a mournful sound, as though he were adding a necessary footnote to Roy's account. "They're planning to step off tomorrow for a new bit of looting."

"Has Chekika distributed the guns?"

"Not yet. They're still stacked like cordwood in his house. So far as I can gather, the quarrel took place under that same roof. And spread to the council fire. Dan was a blood brother of the tribe, it seems. He made his only mistake in coming here alone—and demanding more than half the loot. Even then he couldn't be dispatched without a majority vote of the council." Dr. Barker sighed deeply and drew on the stump of his cigar. "As you've observed, things got rather out of hand after the execution——"

Roy slapped the earth with his palm—an impatient gesture that broke the botanist's sentence in the middle. "Andy will strike in ten minutes now. We must get Mary out of that canoe——and find cover for you both. Why does it matter how a scoundrel lived or died?"

"You'll admit that those guns matter, Roy. My guess is they're the best-type English carbine." The old botanist's voice was still deceptively mild but his eyes were flashing in the gloom. "Think what they'd do to Andy at point-blank range if Chekika had time to arm the village."

"Andy won't give him time."

"Don't be too sure of that. Right now, of course, he thinks himself monarch of all he surveys. And why not? Chittamicco has just reported that the last white interloper has skedaddled out of the Glades. From where he's sitting on that platform, the King of Panthers is the only cat with claws for miles around. In fact, he's so sure of himself that he probably doesn't plan to distribute those guns before tomorrow. But he'll change his mind fast enough when Andy comes howling out of the saw-grass."

"What d'you suggest?"

"If what you say is true, our friend, the dragoon, can put six hundred regulars on this hammock in ten minutes' time. I don't think we could pick a better moment to create a diversion from within."

"What about Mary?"

"Mary must stay in her present hiding place—unless you're willing to risk another masquerade." Dr. Barker took a careful step toward the council fire and turned back with his placid smile intact. "I located that cache of costumes only yesterday—when the nation was giving itself courage at Big Sulphur. In fact, I can transform myself into King Lear at a moment's notice. We could turn Mary into Desdemona or Ophelia just as easily—if you think it's worth the risk."

"Anything's better than leaving her alone."

Dr. Barker nodded and whisked into his hut without another word. True to his boast, he was back in a few seconds, his limbs encased in the brocaded robe of Lear, the mad king's crown above his brow.

"A little war paint to disguise my skin, and I'll be quite ready."

Three minutes later they were reeling toward the council fire together—and skirting the compound as they moved, to reach the line of dugouts along the shore. Two drunken Seminoles, so far as the naked eye could discern in that lurid half-light, they pulled up sharp in the shadow of a hut well beyond the mounting frenzy of the war dance as a third figure swooped to join them. A slender girl in white, daubed to the eyes in marl, with her black hair wild against the spout of the flames. Inured as he was to shock tonight, Roy could only stare blankly when Mary Grant's voice emerged from that clay mask—and recoil a step when King Lear swooped forward to fold her in his embrace.

"Welcome to Fakahatchee, Ophelia." he said quietly. "I see you remembered where to find the costumes."

"Don't stare, Roy," said Mary. "I've only taken what's mine."

Roy took back his authority as best he could and realized that his voice was creaking. "I told you to stay in that canoe——"

"Don't be alarmed, please. I kept the blanket around me until I was decent again."

"Where have you been?"

"In the storage shed, of course. Behind the chief's house. Apparently I know this village better than you."

"Suppose you'd been caught?"

"There's small danger of that tonight. Come into this hut, both of you—it's quite empty. Ophelia's robe isn't all I took."

Roy cursed aloud and followed her into the pallid light of the palm-thatch shelter. The council fire seemed to follow them even here—indeed, the tinder-dry walls of the hut were translucent enough to admit much of its lambent glare. Mary opened her cloak and brought forth a strung bow and a tar-tipped fire feather.

"I thought we might use this as a signal to Andy. He couldn't attack at a better time."

"Andy will be ashore in a few minutes, in any case. We must move fast if we're to get under cover."

"We could fire the chief's house with this, Roy. With luck, we might blow it sky-high."

Dr. Barker embraced the girl a second time; thanks to the raddled velvet robes that encased him and the tin crown tip-tilted over one eye, he resembled nothing more than a conspirator in a melodrama. Like Mary, he seemed to be enjoying his role completely.

"Apparently you've used your time here to advantage, my dear."

"I saw those stacks of rifles on the chief's platform—if that's what you mean. And I counted at least six powder kegs. We might win Andy's war among ourselves."

"And let Chekika know we're here?"

"Chekika has joined the dance. Look through that door; you'll see he's gone mad with the others."

Roy's hand fastened firmly on her arm as he drew her into the darkness; Dr. Barker sighed and followed them without protest. Skirting the compound, they moved out of the firelight's orbit in a few strides. Roy permitted himself one backward glance as they gained the shelter of the water oaks along the beach and saw that Chekika was now capering among his braves, with a cane knife raised high in both fists. The blade swooped above the gibbet that still held Dan Evans's body, slashing the last cord that held him there, and sending the mutilated corpse headfirst into the heart of the fire. The howl of triumph that followed seemed to rock the very earth of the hammock. . . . Roy spoke quickly, his lips against Mary's ear.

"We've done our part, Mary. We've found Dr. Barker. Don't crowd our luck——"

"Where are you taking us now?"

"If you know this hammock so intimately, you'll remember there's a kind of sinkhole where this beach ends. I'm burying both you and the doctor until the fighting's over. Neck-deep. There should be more than enough mud there to stop bullets."

"Do you agree to this, Dr. Barker?"

"Roy's in charge," said the botanist mildly. "We must take orders."

"But I still want to help——"

"You can help most by staying alive," said Roy shortly. "Follow me down the bank, both of you."

King Lear obeyed without protest, coasting from grass to mud in a long, silent wallow. For an instant the white shadow of Ophelia hovered against the glow of the firelight; and Roy, with a fist knotted hard in the hem of her robe, prepared to draw her down by force. Then she yielded with a shrug and dropped beside him where the high, root-scarred bank of the hammock tapered into the viscous mud that bordered this portion of the slough.

Once their feet were engaged in the bog, it held them fast, sucking them deeper in its black embrace. Anchored as they were to the roots along the bank, it was easy to let themselves sink shoulder-deep. With the protection of the muddy wall above them, they were secure from stray bullets on the land side; there was no safer spot on Fakahatchee Hammock now that they could all but feel the breath of the attackers in the night.

"*This* time," he said, "try to stay where I've put you. I'll come back the moment it's safe."

"Don't leave us, Roy."

"I'm afraid I must. If you'll give me that bow and the fire arrow, I'll try to make use of them."

"Do you call this fair, Dr. Barker?"

"No one can handle a bow with more skill than Roy," said the botanist.

Roy took the short arc of cedarwood from Mary's unresisting hands. "Promise you'll hug this cover until we call you?"

"I did want to go on helping till the end."

"This is just the help I need. Keep her safe for Andy, Doctor."

Dr. Barker's whisper was as tranquil as ever. "Promise you'll stay with me, Mary?"

"I promise. But I hate you both."

Roy hurried toward the council fire without daring to look back. If I stop to think this out, he told himself, I'll never take the risk. . . . It was absurdly easy to caper into that wildly whirling circle one more time; to shoulder close enough to the fire to snatch out a lightwood knot. Easier still to back away into the darkness and drop the flaming chunk of pine resin in the sand. No one had marked his presence so far; not even Chittamicco had noticed when he quitted the war dance for the last time.

Far off in the swamp, but moving nearer as he listened, a cry of the whippoorwill stirred in the first faint promise of the dawn. He heard the cry repeated to the north and west; Andy's dugouts were moving in on schedule, a precise half-hour behind his own exit from Big Sulphur. It's now or never, he thought solemnly, and as his lips framed a prayer he fitted the fire arrow to the bowstring and teetered on his heels to measure the trajectory.

From where he stood it was perhaps fifty yards to the rooftree of Chekika's house; a boy of ten could have sent an arrow winging to the midst of that bone-dry covering. He measured the arc a second time, then dipped the tar-soaked point of his missile deep into the flaming lightwood knot. The fire arrow ignited instantly, even before he could lift the bow.

The blazing shaft, arching above the mad medley of the dancers, might have been a comet in miniature—headed the wrong way, for once, and lost briefly among the paling stars. Then it shot earthward in a hissing rush, lost itself in the laminated palm thatch of the chief's roof, and flowered into sudden fearful life as the whole covering seemed to burst into flame with a single breath.

Once it was fairly alight, the burning house of Chekika dwarfed the council fire as though it had never been. The thump of the drums, the dusty padding of the dancing feet slapped down to silence as the fuddled braves realized, too late, what had happened while their backs were turned. The fire had already run down the side wall in that brief pause, twining a dozen red serpentines around the palmetto posts that lifted the roof above the lightwood platform. Thanks to the intense glare, Roy could count the stacked rifles that stood on that same platform, the squat powder kegs nested in their midst. Even as he watched, the first tongue of flame began to lick inexorably toward the ammunition store.

Abraham was the first to detach himself from the crowd and rush forward. A scattering of warriors followed at his heels; most of the Seminoles, too startled to move, seemed to freeze in groups, as though they could not credit this sudden threat. Even Chekika—caught at the far side of the council fire—seemed mesmerized while that roaring blaze closed hungrily on both sides of the powder cache. Only Chittamicco reacted instantly to the threat, and Roy was not surprised to observe his quick scuttle for the shelter of the nearest hut.

The blast came when Abraham was only halfway up the platform ladder. The Indians who had swarmed after him were caught in the full fury of the explosion, which seemed to tear the chief's house asunder, as though a hidden volcano had erupted in the bowels of the swamp. The orange burst, white as daylight at the heart, flattened every Seminole in the compound. It lifted Abraham as casually as a giant might heft a meal sack, and sent his broken body hurtling into the night. The braves just behind him fared almost as badly, though they scrambled back in time to avoid death in the sudden collapse of the palm-thatch house. A great plume of fire geysered skyward as the rest of the powder, detonating in the ruins, rocked the earth of Fakahatchee Hammock.

Then, as suddenly as it had burst forth, the black mass settled in a whorl of smoke and crackling pinewood. The dawn, moving gayly across the island, picked out the gap in the circle of dwellings where Chekika's house had stood so proudly. There was no sound but the high wailing of the squaws—and the insistent calling of the whippoorwills from the thickets that flanked the village on the north and west. No stir of life but the rush of Roy's feet as he ran for his life down the beach and plunged for the first clump of saw grass.

vii

The attack came with a rush almost before he could lodge in his hiding place offshore. It came like a brown wave from the heart of the morning, powered by the flashing paddles of half a hundred canoes rammed head-on against the beaches of Fakahatchee Hammock. It swarmed through the corn patches to the north and west. It flowed over the thickets to the east and south. No war whoops sounded in this quiet tide; there were no shots until the last canoe was beached. Andy's strategy was simple, and he had deployed his force to perfection. Before a rifle was cocked the village was invested on four sides. When the first volley came, it roared out of a steel circle that tightened inexorably with each low-voiced command.

The Rangers were shooting with the dawn behind them and the pyre of Chekika's house as their focal point. Roy saw instantly that Andy had understood and appreciated that skyrocketing explosion even before he closed in for the kill. Thanks to its merciless light—and the instant of hesitation that had frozen most of the braves in the compound—the enemy was a massed target for the finest marksmen in the Floridas. The first volley, precise as a dress-parade maneuver, cut down a third of the Seminoles in their tracks. The second, lashing the palm thatch of a score of huts as the enemy scrambled wildly for cover, was almost as punishing.

Roy found that he was on his feet, his throat wide to echo the cheering that rose from the hammock. Already, with the attack only minutes old, Chekika's last chance for organized resistance had gone glimmering. Surprised and bewildered, unable to tell friend from enemy in the murky light, the Seminoles could only fight back as an individual—and scuttle desperately for the first escape that offered. Roy knew that he could go ashore again at will now that he was on the right side of that ring of steel.

He crept on hands and knees into the dog fennel along the bank just as the first rays of sunlight cut into the mist overhead. A dozen huts were burning around the compound now, though the ruins of Chekika's dwelling had collapsed into ashes. The wolf flurries of combat that swirled on all sides, paced by the crash of war axes, the bark of derringers and carbines, told him how quickly the attack had broken into hand-to-hand combat. Even at close quarters he was hard put to pick out American from Seminole—until he remembered to look for the white arm band that each Ranger wore. Like the thunderbolt abruptness of his raid, Andy's well-planned disguises had already begun to pay a handsome dividend in scalps.

Roy all but stumbled across Abraham's shattered body as he ran across the compound. Seminole dead were bunched thickly around the council fire; others sprawled at the doors of their huts, shot through the back at the moment of escape. Still others had fought off the raiders in tight circle, only to perish to the last man. . . . He reeled on, shouting Andy's name into the fading din of battle. Even now there was no doubt as to the outcome. Outnumbered from the start, and numbed by the explosion that had paced the onslaught, the Seminoles were dying almost too fast to surrender.

There, at last, was Chekika—though the Wildcat's brother had prudently vanished from the field. Ranked by his subchiefs, refusing to take cover in his last moments, the King of Panthers faced a score of leveled carbines unafraid, his back to the Grassy Water that had sheltered him so long. Pocketed where there was no chance of escape, he stood defiantly waiting. There was no formal demand for surrender, no question of yielding. Roy turned aside just before the volley roared out. He was near enough to hear the bullets chunk home and the final panther scream as Chekika took his hatred for all things white into the beyond.

The death of their leader signaled the end of the action, though Seminoles were still giving up in isolated units when Roy found Sergeant Ranson. The sergeant was crouched in the shelter of a kind of storage shed on the island's spine with four surgeon's mates busy all around him. Roy saw at a glance that his own instrument case was open and ready on an improvised board table; the fact that the sergeant could afford to supervise such matters now set the seal of victory on the battle.

"Twenty-one minutes, sir, by the captain's clock," said Ranson. "The shortest action I ever fought—except Tippecanoe."

"Did we bag the lot?"

"Not quite, Doctor. Seventy to a hundred broke through. But they'll never fight us again. Not really. Florida's safe for settlers from this day forward."

"Where's Captain Winter?"

"Inside the shed, sir. This wasn't *his* lucky day, I'm afraid. He stopped a knife the minute we stormed ashore."

Andy lay in the firelit shadow of the storage hut, his back propped on a wooden trestle. Corporal Poore knelt at his side with a pad pressed hard against the captain's chest. Wounded though he was, Andy continued to direct the finale of the action; he was barking an order to a runner when Roy came through the doorway. He managed a grin of sorts as he waved the runner on, though his skin was waxen-pale under the dye that still mottled it.

"How's this for planning, Roy? Could it have gone better in a classroom at the Point?"

"All my congratulations, Captain." Roy had already taken Poore's place at the trestle. He made his voice formal as he took a first quick check of the wound. "Were your casualties heavy?"

"Not more than twenty dead. They were too stunned to fight back. This is the only serious wound." Andy stared down at the pad against his chest, as though the gash beneath had no real relation to his own buoyant spirit. "Ranson's mates will handle the others—if you'll take care of me."

"Don't worry, Captain. You'll live to wear your medals." There was little need, Roy observed, for an extended examination; his hearing had already identified the nature of the injury. Only a chest wound gave out the rhythmic soughing in tune with the victim's breath. To judge by the brightness of the red stain beneath, the intercostal artery had been severed.

He lifted the pad briefly and frowned down at the instant pulse of blood that arched from wound to floor. It was no easy matter to recover and tie off a severed vessel in a deep puncture of this sort. Yet Andy would die in a matter of minutes if the bleeder could not be found and ligated.

"Did you pull Dr. Barker out of this shambles?"

Roy drew back from his diagnosis and nodded mutely. As always, he was concentrated absolutely on the problem before him. There was no time to explain that he had hidden Mary and the botanist in the same bog.

"Was it his idea to fire that hut?"

"Partly."

"Nothing could have helped us more. Is it true that Dan Evans is roasting in their council fire?"

"Quite true. Don't talk any more. You're tiring fast."

"The whole kit and caboodle," said Andy. "Ranson was sure it was Dan—I wouldn't believe it. Maybe I should die, after all, to even the account."

"Just lie quietly. I'll have to hurt you a bit, but we won't let you die."

Roy whispered his instructions to the corporal as he felt Andy slip into a coma under his hands. He would need resin for the job ahead, but the sergeant had a goodly quantity of that curative pine sap bubbling over a fire outside. He had counted the stacks of well-leached bandages, the ready suture needles. Ranson had seen him save too many lives with such standard equipment to neglect his preparations today.

"We'll work right here, Corporal. It'll save time. When you've assembled the things I've asked for, tell the sergeant to bring my instrument case and stand by."

The distant murmur of death in the making, the shrill wailing of the captive squaws faded from his mind as he went over his operative picture one more time. The challenge beneath that bright red pad was terribly real. The intercostals were fairly large arteries that followed the lower side of each rib—just outside the pleura, the membrane of the chest cavity that enclosed the lungs. When cut, these vessels had a perverse habit of withdrawing from the actual wound, so the surgeon could never be sure just how deep to probe. Too often there was the added danger of a concealed hemorrhage—draining life away into the chest cavity itself with no possibility of detection until the victim's collapse.

Watching the mates set up the needed equipment in the shed, feeling the clean light of morning grow at each chink in the palm thatch, Roy welcomed this opportunity to withdraw from the carnage outside. The cyclonic success of the attack, sweeping him into its wake, had brought no sense of victory —no real relief that the war was, at long last, a part of Florida history. He would face these realities soon enough. If Andy lived—but of course there must be no question of Andy Winter's dying. The conqueror of Fakahatchee belonged to history too—no less surely than he belonged to Mary Grant.

"Did you bring the resin, Sergeant?"

"Waiting just outside the door, sir. A whole frying pan— medium hot. D'you mean to seal off the wound?"

"As soon as I can deliver the artery." The scalpel had already come into his hand. He began to explore cautiously; the ticklish part of the ordeal, for Andy, would come when Roy laid bare that whole gash and dug for the bleeder. During that period Andy must breathe as best he could, with his chest wall open on one side. The inrush of air, crippling the lungs with its pressure, might choke off their normal function entirely. There would be nothing to ease the primary agony of the wound itself, the probing needle, the cruel bite of the suture. Once again Roy rejoiced that Andy had fainted. With time of the essence, he could not even pause for an opiate.

"Steady, all. I'm going in."

He loosened the dressing, ignoring the instant spurt of red that geysered upward with each straining heartbeat. Now that the enemy's knife stroke was exposed down its whole length, he saw that only Andy's ribs had saved his life. The blade had skittered across that bony box, opening skin and muscle but missing the heart beneath. Only at the very base of the wound, where the knife had curved to parallel the rib itself, had the point thrust home, penetrating the chest cavity and slicing the intercostal artery as it plunged.

Air sighed in and out of this gaping puncture, controlled partially by the pressure of his thumb; the wheezy tune he was playing sounded ominous enough. He thrust the pad hard against the artery, stopping the blood for the moment. Ranson handed a suture needle across Andy's feebly writhing body. At least the wound is small, Roy thought as he moved the pad aside and prepared to enter the damaged area. It was really no more than a puncture—with no threat of aftermath if he could find and control the bleeder.

Slipping his left index finger into the depths of the wound, with the curve of the needle nested firmly against it, he felt along the rib until he could roll the artery against his finger. Andy's lips, he noted, were ash-blue now as his breathing was cut down to a murmur by the fearful air pressure from without. He hooked finger and needle sharply upward, compressing artery against bone until the red spurting died down to a trickle. At the same time the pressure of his knuckle against the puncture of the pleura, cutting the stream of air from without, permitted Andy's straining lungs to expand again.

"Can you hold it, Doctor?"

He met the sergeant's anxious eyes and nodded slowly. "I think so. At least I'm ready to suture."

The needle point was part of his finger now, probing deep in the tissues of the wound, distinguishing their texture by the degree of resistance it encountered. It had already thrust into the softer muscle fiber and recoiled carefully from the surface of the rib. Now it moved about the barrel of the artery itself, thrusting upward until the point, the curved shank, and the eye end issued from the depths of the wound.

Still controlling the bleeding with the pressure of his finger, Roy clamped the needle in a forceps, lifted it neatly from the gash with the whipcord suture streaming in its wake. The knot came smoothly home as his free fingers tightened; when his left hand emerged from the wound, the whistle of entering air began instantly, but there was no show of blood.

"The bleeding is in control, Sergeant. Now we must stop that intake."

Other strands of whipcord came into his hand, streaming free of the suture needles. Sewing with all the busy concentration of a housewife, he drew the first muscle flap across the puncture, anchoring it with quick pursestring stitches, and matching it with a similar flap from the opposite side of the wound. When the tough filament had crossed the muscles in the form of a rough X, he stepped back to observe the results. As he had hoped, the overlap of muscle fiber now formed an effective dam, closing off nearly all the outside pressure. As Andy's lungs belled out, a little air was forced through the opening from the puncture itself. As they contracted, the living valve of muscle, closing upon itself, prevented further intake, an improvised but trustworthy valve with one-way action.

Sergeant Ranson passed the frying pan across Andy's inert

body, and Roy scooped out a thick portion of resin with the handle of his scalpel. The pine sap was still warm enough to be malleable. He spread it evenly around the edges of the wound and across the muscle barrier itself, until the entire surface was covered with the adhesive layer. A linen square was now smoothed down above this primary dressing and anchored with a second layer of resin; a layer of cloth, fluffed above the wound, was bound into place with a harness bandage looped across Andy's shoulder. Roy tied the final knot and stepped back from his patient, yielding his place to the sergeant.

"Ten minutes by the captain's clock," said Ranson. "You never worked faster, Doctor."

"I had to work fast, or lose him."

Sergeant and doctor looked down at the patient and grinned in unison. The cyanosis that had blued Andy's lips when the operation began had almost vanished now as the lungs beneath that bandage resumed their vital function. Pulse and skin tone advertised the rude health of a hero born to survive most wounds. Roy found that he had spoken the thought aloud.

"At least I've kept him safe for Mary."

"Beg pardon, sir?"

"He's leaving the service to marry Miss Grant. We all know that. We could hardly let him die after his last battle."

Andy sighed, out of his coma. You'll be up in a week, thought Roy. In a fortnight you'll be out of uniform, ready to carve the next step in your career. He turned away and walked to the door of the hut, oppressed by a sadness he could not name. It was time to call Mary and Dr. Barker from their hideaway. The war was over—and his own surrender was complete.

"You're in command now, Sergeant. Can you build a litter in one of the canoes?"

"Several stretchers are ready now, Doctor. I'll take him in my own dugout."

"See that he stays on his back for a week, at least."

Ranson grinned again. "I'll do my best, sir. Won't you be there to help?"

"I think not, Sergeant. *My* tour of duty's over too, you know. If Dr. Barker's up to the effort, I thought we might return to Flamingo Key by way of Cape Sable."

"You'll find he's well enough, Doctor. He got a knock a moment ago. But he's coming out of it nicely——"

Roy whirled as Ranson's words cut into his weary brain. "You say you—*found* Dr. Barker?"

"In that sinkhole, sir. Down beyond the canoe berth. Poore reported it just now while you were tying up the captain. You were too busy to notice——"

But Roy was already gone, with Ranson at his heels. Across the compound he had a brief, nightmare glimpse of a dozen red bodies swinging from the cabbage palms along the slough. The wailing of the squaws seemed part of his heartbeat as he skirted the last of the burning huts and plunged into the thicket to the west.

He saw what had happened before he could reach Dr. Barker. The mudbank above was a welter of footprints now; the underbrush, hacked by a score of cane knives, marked the escape route of the Seminoles clearly enough. The Indians, breaking through Andy's deadly circle at the last moment, had stormed round the bog, reached the slough at the very tip of the island, and paddled west for their lives. He could even see the grooves in the mudbank where the dugouts had wallowed into open water.

Rangers in canoes and afoot were still probing the thickets for survivors. Poore knelt beside Dr. Barker, with the old man's head on his knee.

"He isn't hurt, Doctor. Only stunned."

Roy bent quickly to confirm the corporal's report. There was a small egg-shaped swelling at Dr. Barker's temple and a great stain of mud in his white hair to show how he had tumbled under the blow. But there was no sign of concussion. It was evident that the botanist had been stunned by an expert hand—and left here deliberately.

"Miss Grant—is there no sign of her?" Roy forced the words by rote; the answer was already before his eyes.

"*Miss Grant*, Doctor?"

"She was here too, Corporal—but of course you wouldn't know."

Dr. Barker opened his eyes and spoke quietly, as though he had heard the interchange. "Big Sulphur, Roy. They went that way."

"Are you all right, sir?"

"Quite all right. Stunned by a paddle blow." The old doc-

tor made an effort to rise from the corporal's arms and
thought better of the effort. "Chittamicco wanted you to—
follow. That's why he left me here."

"Chittamicco?"

"He's waiting for you at the spring. Waiting to settle the
score. He—said he was sure you'd come this time." Dr. Barker rose in earnest, disdaining Corporal Simpson's helping
hand. "Look at that cypress on the bank. Don't you understand?"

The morning sun, spreading its patina to every corner of
the island, picked out the flash of white above their heads.
Roy moved toward the cypress bole like a man in a dream.
Ophelia's mud-stained robe, pinned to the bark with a grains,
continued to dance in the breeze like a living thing.

viii

The dugouts lay snugly against the west bank of the spring,
well out of rifleshot; the flawless morning, shining like a benediction above the crystal water, gave the whole scene an element of unreality. Even now, crouched in the bow of Ranson's canoe like a pointer on the scent, Roy could not escape
the conviction that he was dreaming. He had collided with
death before—often enough to know his face. Death had no
right to wait so quietly among those clustered canoes—to
make itself part of this smiling day.

Knowing that a hundred eyes were watching intently, he
lifted his shoulders and raised his right hand, palm outward.
Ranson braked the canoe instantly; behind them, where the
green-tunneled estuary opened to Big Sulphur, he heard the
other dugouts sigh to a stop. This is my moment, he thought;
this is the final sacrifice. God grant that I make it with dignity. Not that dignity (or life itself) would matter unless Mary
was still unharmed. Surely the mud-stained robe still clutched
in his fist could have no other meaning.

He bent his hand, palm downward—and Ranson, detaching the canoe from the green embrace of the bank, brought
them into full view of the Seminoles across the water. Letting
the dugout glide to a stop, the sergeant raised both arms to
show he was unarmed—a gesture Roy duplicated, with the
grains in one hand and Ophelia's robe fluttering at the tip like
a soiled white pennon. For a long, taut moment there was no

sign from the clustered dugouts across the water. Then one of the canoes detached itself from the mass and burst into the sunlight. A white plume of feathers lifted in the prow. Even at that distance Roy could recognize Chittamicco at the paddle.

The two canoes swooped toward one another like a pair of hostile crocodiles, all but grazing as they met in the precise middle of the spring. Chittamicco lifted a grains identical with the one that Roy brandished and jabbed viciously at the bow of their canoe. Roy repeated the thrust with the same ritual insistence. A low murmur rose from the bank as the waiting Seminoles saw the challenge of their new leader accepted.

Chittamicco held up a hand for silence, and when he spoke at last. his voice was strangely calm.

"You will fight, Salofkachee?"

"For the girl, yes. Does she still live?"

"She is alive and unharmed. Would you win her back?"

"Prove your words."

"I will prove them before we go overside. First, your paddler must leave us."

Ranson spoke into the silence. "We can jump him between us, Doctor. Just say the word."

"That won't help Mary Grant."

"If you ask me, he's the last real warlock in the lot. They'll give her up fast enough, once we've brained him."

"How do we even know she's alive? I'm taking his dare. There's no other way."

"Let me fight in your place. I've used a grains before—and we're more of a size."

"It's my heart he wants, Sergeant—not yours. Go back, as he asks. I'll hold him off until you've cleared." Roy reached back and pressed Ranson's hand warmly. "Not that I don't appreciate the offer. Fortunately I can use a grains too."

"It's still another name for murder."

"And the only way to make sure that Captain Winter marries on schedule. Over you go: I'll take that paddle."

The sergeant snorted just once and rolled out of the canoe. Chittamicco raised the spear. and Roy saw the old, familiar light glow behind his eyes. as though a furnace door had opened far back in the Seminole's brain. He lifted his grains in turn as a solemn warning. Ranson swam insolently close to the Indian canoe, shook his fist just once in Chittamicco's face, then dug for the eastern bank with all the grace of a homing manatee.

"You have said that the girl is unhurt, Father of Seminoles," said Roy. "Will you eat those words now?"

Chittamicco accepted his new title with a small bow. "The girl lies between my thwarts, Salofkachee. Her hands and feet are tied; her mouth is closed to shut out speech. But she is untouched. You will take my word when you see her."

Roy choked down his protest and met the enemy's glare. Taunts of this sort, as he knew, were part of the preliminary to any accepted challenge. Chittamicco was quite capable of teasing him for hours with word pictures no more definite than this.

"I have agreed to fight on your terms. Show me that the girl is here."

He had bellowed the words for the ears on the western bank, quite as Chittamicco had bellowed. Now he dared to rise in his dugout and risked a spill overside in an effort to see if Mary's body was, in reality, trussed up just under the enemy's gunwale. Chittamicco backed water instantly, pulling his canoe a good ten feet to the west.

"Do you doubt my word, Salofkachee?"

Roy shrugged and marked up the first score. "By no means. I ask only that you come overside with me. I have picked up your challenge—so." He scooped a handful of water in his palm and tossed it into Chittamicco's eyes. "Will you answer?"

"Gladly, Salofkachee." Chekika's heir wiped the drops from his eyes, ignoring the babble from the shore. "I have said that your lady lies bound in this dugout. Do you believe me?"

Roy saw his mistake too late, and lashed out again before the Seminole could add to that picture. "Show me her face before we begin. Or is your promise as empty as your words?"

The new leader of the Seminoles rose to his full height in the canoe, with both feet braced firmly. Rocking in the upsurging rush of the spring, he flexed his muscles proudly, as though daring his opponent to match that copper brawn. He's risked everything to fight me on his terms, thought Roy. The spring is part of his plan, and the watchers on both sides. If he can spear me in Big Sulphur, he'll prove that his medicine is stronger. Once I'm dead, the nation's last link with the white world is severed—and his authority will be unquestioned. He'll lead that remnant, pitiful though it is at the moment, to the Big Cypress. He'll regroup his ranks, teach his braves to fight again. . . . He froze on his paddle as Chittamicco boomed into speech.

"You will fight if I give you back the girl?"

"Yes, coward. Will you hide behind her forever?"

Chittamicco bent into the dugout and came up with Mary Grant struggling in his arms. As he had said, she was bound hand and foot and competently gagged. At first glance she seemed naked in the white glare of sunlight, but when Roy focused his eyes upward he saw that Mary was still clad in the strips of buckskin she had worn for their descent on Fakahatchee.

A great howl of joy rose from the Indian canoes as Chittamicco, with a mighty heft of his shoulders, lifted the girl on one extended palm—his fingers spread at the small of Mary's back, his whole body tensed like some primitive acrobat's. This, too, is part of his madness, thought Roy. He had guessed his enemy's purpose even before Chittamicco could speak again.

"She is yours, Salofkachee. But you must enter Big Sulphur to claim her."

The girl's body had already left the canoe, tossed in a short arc and plummeting, head down, into the crystal depths beneath his keel. He had a glimpse of Mary's pleading eyes, obscured instantly in a whorl of bubbles as she fought to free her arms and legs. A second thundering splash told him that Chittamicco was already overside and plunging like a copper eel. He followed, without giving himself time for thought.

He overtook Mary in the heart of the spring, groped for a handhold, and anchored at last in her trailing dark braids. The tines of the grains made a poor knife, but he had freed her arms somehow before Chittamicco could turn in the depths and rise for his first thrust. He could feel her gasp in his embrace as she saw the peril rising to meet them, and knew in that instant that she was striving to keep her body between him and the Seminole's trident. Then, in a furious explosion of bubbles, he was treading water that seemed clearer than air, poised for the thrust of that needle-pointed steel, with Mary rolling toward the surface.

The first thrust was met and parried: his feet, gathered like clubs at the end of a coiled spring, caught his enemy full in the midriff and spurned his clutching hands as he shot upward for air. He had a glimpse of Mary struggling to free her legs; he heard her shout as they broke surface together, and knew that she had torn the gag away at last.

"Roy! Are you hurt?"

"Not yet. Get aboard my canoe. He's coming back."

Thanks to the speed of his first dive—and still more to Chittamicco's own deep plunge—he had at least saved Mary from the death by drowning that the Seminole had planned so carefully. Their enemy had hardly expected his victim to swim as well as any man. Sounding to the very depths of Big Sulphur, he had waited to enjoy her agony before he rose to dispatch Roy at leisure. Now, with Mary safely aboard the canoe, he could only wallow to the surface at a safe distance while he fought to regain the breath Roy had just knocked from his body.

"Come aboard, Roy!"

He spoke quickly, without daring to turn from the threat of that trident a scant two yards away. "Paddle for the east bank, Mary. He can't stop you now——"

The trident thrust forward before he could finish that order; he parried for his life, rolling with the counterthrust and swimming fast in order to give Mary a chance to clear. Chittamicco followed his attack with bull-like strength, and it was Roy's turn to tread water now while he fought to keep those steel points from his heart. He was dimly aware of a shadow hovering just above him: as his enemy pressed the attack, he felt his shoulder bruise against bark and realized that this was his own canoe. He sounded quickly and came up on the far side, only to discover that the dugout was empty. Mary called again from a slight distance: he dared to turn and saw that it was the Seminole canoe she had boarded.

"Get back, for the love of heaven!"

If Mary heard, she gave no sign as she continued to circle the two warring figures in the center of the spring. He had no time to question her presence now—and no breath to waste on further orders as Chittamicco came churning in for the *coup de grâce*.

The steel trident, driven forward with all the Seminole's bone and muscle behind it, missed his throat by inches. It had taken courage to await that thrust, pretending to drop his guard as it came, dodging with a split second between him and defeat. He gave an exultant shout as the grains struck deep in the pulpy cypress of the dugout and snapped short under the fury of the enemy's lunge. It was his turn to lunge now, before Chittamicco could recover—and his turn to gasp out his rage when the trident only grazed his adversary's copper hide and snapped, just as casually, against the tough flank of the canoe.

Again he sounded and swam in a long arc, feeling the Seminole's clutching fingers just miss his ankle as he turned at last and rocketed upward again. Chittamicco overtook him before he could break surface. The arms that closed about his body were as powerful as steel coils, choking the last of his breath away; the fingers that raked ever upward, seeking his throat and eyes, were synonyms for death itself. Then, just as nothingness claimed him, he heard the rifle crack explode inside his brain and felt the steel coils loosen.

He knew that he was sinking with Chittamicco to the heart of Big Sulphur, bound to his ancient enemy even now, though the Seminole's grip was lifeless. But he knew just as surely that another hand had fastened in his hair, drawing him back to the air again. He let out his breath in a great shout as the blaze of that flawless Florida morning splintered on his eyeballs. Then darkness invaded his brain in earnest— just before Mary Grant's arm enclosed him in the bubbling brightness of Big Sulphur.

ix

The bare whitewashed wall seemed familiar enough. So did the figure that bent above him, spooning a bitter liquid between his lips and urging him to swallow more. Voice and man still refused to come into focus. He knew only that he had died and lived again, thanks to Mary Grant—that it was Mary, not he, who had struck the final blow to save him. Somehow—and the magic carpet that had transported him hardly mattered—he was back in his quarters at Fort Everglades. The whitewashed wall had become part of a room at long last. He smiled gratefully as Dr. Jonathan Barker be-

came part of the picture too. It was appropriate that the botanist should be at his bedside when he made his triumphant
return from the shadows.

"Why the quinine? I'm well enough."

"You are, my boy. The fever's left you overnight. But it
was a severe attack while it lasted."

"I was drowned," said Roy. "Or the next thing to drowning."

"True enough. For a while we thought we'd lost you. Even
though Ranson did roll most of the water out of your system.
The fever struck before you could regain your senses. You
might say it's been waiting a long time to pounce."

He remembered details now and lay back on his pillows,
letting the fragments fall into place. A litter piled high with
blankets in a canoe—and the endless sun-and-shadow pattern
of branches overhead. Bone-shaking chills, when he cried out
for still more blankets—and fever that threatened to dissolve
his flesh while the canoe swam gently onward. He had only
the vaguest memory of the hands that had lifted him at the
journey's end—or how he had reached his quarters in the
fort. For now it was enough to lie back and let the old doctor's voice enfold him.

"Ten days in all. You've been under a light opiate since we
arrived here. You see, I didn't want you to rise from that bed
before you were rested. As it is, we've had our hands full
with Andy."

So Andy was well again, and bellowing with health. That,
too, had been his doing—and he faced the accomplishment
with no elation. "Never mind Andy now. Tell me about
Mary."

"I'm afraid you'll have to face up to Andy in a little while.
He's been clamoring to see you ever since we let *him* out of
bed."

"Tell me about Mary, please."

"From what I can see, she was never better. Andy doesn't
agree, but——" The botanist just escaped laughing at a joke all
his own. "Don't thank her for saving your life—remember
that. It's something she still can't talk about."

Roy closed his eyes on the memory and found it was crystal-clear. Copper arms enclosing his body like twin snakes,
crushing the last air from his straining lungs. The rifleshot
just above that had seemed to detonate within his skull . . .

Now, at last, he knew how that unequal contest at Big Sulphur had been decided.

"Where did she find the gun?"

"It was a British carbine. In Chittamicco's canoe. Apparently Mary knew all along that it was there. Our former enemy had brought it for insurance; he was taking no chances on finishing you at his terms——"

"Only Mary used it instead?"

"Exactly. When you sounded that last time, she was waiting just above. Waiting for you to break surface or come near enough for a shot that couldn't miss."

"You might say she ended the war singlehanded."

"You might indeed. More than fifty Indians came in to surrender when they saw that Chittamicco was really dead. Offhand I'd say we've cleared the Glades of enemies. There'll always be strays in the Cypress. But they'll mind their business—so long as we mind ours."

"In that case, what's disturbing Andy?"

"You'd better let him tell you that."

"Give me some idea, can't you? His hanging party accomplished its objective, down to the last subchief. It was probably the most brilliant campaign in the war. Certainly Washington will give him every credit——"

"A Congressional Medal is in the offing, I believe."

"Is he disturbed because Mary——" A sudden fear cut across Roy's mind. "Did Chittamicco harm her, after all?"

"He hadn't time," said Dr. Barker grimly. "The fact is, Roy, Andy is gunning for *you* at the moment."

"Surely he knows I didn't smuggle Mary into my canoe."

"Mary made a full confession," said the botanist. His eyes dropped as he spoke, but Roy was sure that his lips had twisted in a smile of pure mischief.

"Mary had nothing to confess. Only a crazy impulse that made her join the raid. An impulse, I might add, that was well worth the risk——" He broke off under Dr. Barker's unequivocal eye. "What are you accusing me of, Doctor?"

"Nothing, my boy. Nothing at all—except an acute attack of integrity. After all, it's natural for a gentleman to shield a lady. Even when the lady doesn't seem to want protection."

"Have you any idea what you're saying?"

"An excellent idea. But it's Andy's quarrel, not mine. Only

this morning he was yearning to horsewhip you—if you were well enough."

"Send him here at once."

"If I'm not mistaken, he's in the hall."

Roy was positive the old doctor was laughing as he went through the door. And there was no mistaking Andy's swagger as he bowed to the botanist and came storming through that same portal. An actor awaiting his cue in the wings could not have come on stage more promptly—or spoke his first line with more aplomb.

"I gather you're conscious, Roy?"

"Quite—though I can't believe my ears."

"I won't challenge you now. You're still too weak. But I will ask an explanation—if you have one."

"For *Mary?*"

"D'you deny you shared a blanket with her in the Glades?"

Roy felt an insane urge to laugh, even as anger rose in his throat. "Surely your fiancée didn't tell you that?"

"She was brazen enough to admit it, in so many words."

"Isn't it better discussed with her?"

"Then you admit it too?"

"I'm admitting nothing, Andy."

"Will you promise to make her honest the moment you rise from this bed? Or must I escort you to the altar at pistol point?"

"She's your bride-to-be—not mine."

"Our engagement is terminated at my request. D'you think I'd marry her—after what she told me?"

Weak as he was, Roy found the strength to snatch the water carafe from his bedside table. Andy backed to the door and dodged the missile just in time. "Besides, she won't have me," he said as he whisked into the hall and held the door a prudent crack ajar. "From what I gather, she likes the sample." He closed the door firmly as a medicine tray clattered against the lintel.

Roy lay back against the pillows, panting with anger and that same insane desire to burst out laughing. He was still fighting the urge when a light knock sounded, and Mary herself put her head through the doorway in response to his roared permission.

"If you're sure it's safe?"

"Quite," he said. "At least for now. When I'm well it

seems we're to be the principals in a shot gun wedding. Does the idea attract you?"

Mary came over and sat down demurely at the foot of the bed. "Speak for yourself, Roy."

"Andy's my spokesman. He'll be behind the shot gun."

"Do you always obey Captain Winter?"

"Not when the war's over," he snapped, and found he was laughing, after all, as he began to see a pattern emerging. "Tell me one thing first. Did you put him up to this?"

"Naturally. It wasn't difficult."

He stared at her in slowly melting fury, as though he could not get his fill of staring. When he spoke at last, he found he was forcing every word. "You told him we—shared a bed?"

"It was quite true."

"Only in a sense. You might have kept it secret."

"And spent my life with a uniform on dress parade?"

"You didn't love him, then?"

"Not when you pulled me into the Miami after you," said Mary. "Not when *you* said you loved me that day in the saw-grass. Of course we were both facing death at the time. Now that the threat's behind us, you may want to withdraw the observation——"

But he had already silenced her teasing by time-honored means. When their lips parted at last, Mary laughed softly and laid her cheek against his. "Then we won't need Andy's shotgun, after all?"

"Why should we—now you know everything?"

"You see, my dear? Even without shot guns it pays to be honest."